Seasons Change

by
Natalie Gould

This book is dedicated to Uncle Jimmy, the most intellectual person I have ever known. Your words of encouragement mean more to me than you could have ever imagined. It's taken me a long time to fulfill my dream- *but I did it*. If you were here, you would be the first person I would share this with. But I know you are smiling down at me from heaven.

Ecclesiastes 3:1-11 NIV

There is a time for everything and a season for every activity under the heavens: a time to be born and a time to die, a time to plant and a time to uproot, a time to kill and a time to heal, a time to tear down and a time to build, a time to weep and a time to laugh, a time to mourn and a time to dance, a time to scatter stones and a time to gather them, a time to embrace and a time to refrain from embracing, a time to search and a time to give up, a time to keep and a time to throw away, a time to tear down and time to mend, a time to be silent and a time to speak, a time to love and a time to hate, a time for war and a time for peace...

Table of Contents

Preface 1

Prologue: I Had a Life Before Jamey Russo 12

Part I. Ninth Grade 17

    Chapter One: The Get-together 18

    Chapter Two: The Confrontation 29

    Chapter Three: Partners 36

    Chapter Four: Friendsgiving 48

    Chapter Five: The Interrogation 60

    Chapter Six: Consequences 79

    Chapter Seven: The Infamous School Dance 95

    Chapter Eight: Defense 112

    Chapter Nine: Spring, Summer, Italy, and the Barbecue 121

Part II. Tenth Grade 130

    Chapter Ten: The Substitute 131

    Chapter Eleven: Little Red Riding Hood 143

    Chapter Twelve: The Kissing Closet 148

    Chapter Thirteen: Equilibrium 158

Part III. Eleventh Grade 163

    Chapter Fourteen: The Back of the Bus 164

    Chapter Fifteen: Uptight and Conceited 177

    Chapter Sixteen: Tailbones, Threats, and Ice 187

    Chapter Seventeen: Kevin LaFontaine 203

    Chapter Eighteen: The Vow 217

    Chapter Nineteen: Alpha Males 233

 Chapter Nineteen: Alpha Males (Part Two) 244

 Chapter Twenty: Pretty and Sad 250

 Chapter Twenty-one: LaVonn Brooks and Kayla O'Neil 257

 Chapter Twenty-two: Prom 265

 Chapter Twenty-three: Desperation 273

 Chapter Twenty-four: Mickey's Secret and College Visits 284

Part IV. Twelfth Grade **296**

 Chapter Twenty-five: Daydreams 297

 Chapter Twenty-six: Kara 300

 Chapter Twenty-seven: Rope Climbing, Volleyball, and Jamey's Hot Tub 307

 Chapter Twenty-eight: Sleeping and Sports 318

 Chapter Twenty-nine: The Point of No Return 325

 Chapter Thirty: Texts and Emails 335

 Chapter Thirty-one: Unknown Caller 339

 Chapter Thirty-two: An Unexpected Visitor 343

 Chapter Thirty-three: Coffee Corner 350

 Chapter Thirty-four: A Lightbulb 360

 Chapter Thirty-five: Purgatory 365

 Chapter Thirty-six: Cold as Ice 372

Part V. College **381**

 Chapter Thirty-seven: A Time to Grieve 382

 Chapter Thirty-eight: A Time to Heal 386

 Chapter Thirty-nine: The Reunion 390

 Chapter Forty: "Contentedly" Ever After 398

Epilogue **402**

Gratitude 403
About the Author 404

Preface

Courtney Grant-
I was Jessica Calabresi's preschool teacher at St. Mary's. I got to know her family very well the year she was in my class. Jessica was the oldest of Anna and Anthony Calabresi's three daughters. Therefore, she was the first one to start school. The Calabresi family lived in a reasonably new development in Jamestown. They were an affluent and influential couple. Most of the well-to-do Catholic families in Rosevalley chose to send their children to St. Mary's because it was a prestigious school known for its high academic standards and promotion of values and morals that weren't necessarily present in the public schools. It was an expensive private school, and students had to pass a test in order to attend. Naturally, Jessica passed with flying colors. She was highly intelligent, even at four years old.

The students at St. Mary's not only had to keep up their grades, but they were also expected to maintain impeccable behavior. That was the main reason families with the caliber of the Calabresis sent their children to St. Mary's.

Anna and Anthony Calabresi were respected in Jamestown and the school. They contributed a lot of money to St. Mary's and were very involved in all aspects of the academic community. Anthony served on the school board, and Anna was a member of the Parent Teacher Association. She ran the book fairs, food drives, holiday parties, field trips, and basically all important activities. She was the room mother who volunteered to help with any and all events that required assistance.

Although she was well-liked and admired, some women were envious of Anna. She was "old money," which was apparent in her mannerisms and overall persona. Yet it was hard for most of us to feel animosity towards her; it wasn't justified. The negative attitudes held by some said less about Anna than they did about the people who held them.

Anna was the product of Hollywood royalty. She came from a long line of beautiful and sophisticated women. She was truly the epitome of class and beauty. Nonetheless, she was always friendly and personable. The thing I liked most about Anna was how genuine she was.

Anthony Calabresi was also very attractive. He was tall, well-built, and had the most arresting green eyes. He was a courteous and good-mannered gentleman. However, he could be extremely intimidating. He was the personification of cool, calm, and collected. He never raised his voice but was always granted attention and respect. Fortunately, he and I always had a jovial relationship. I was the type of teacher who did her best to accommodate parents.

Not all teachers could say the same. On a couple of occasions, he had teachers in tears. I can't remember why, but I know the situations involved his younger daughters, not Jessica. He certainly wasn't afraid to speak his mind if he disagreed about something happening at the school. He was also known to be authoritarian with all three of his girls, especially the younger ones, Sara and Megan, because they weren't as academically driven and well-behaved as Jessica. He expected his girls to get all A's. They had high standards to live up to. He was the disciplinarian in the family. Anna was more like a friend to her daughters.

I not only taught preschool to Jessica and her sisters but also ran the Student Council for the kids in middle school. St. Mary's went from nursery school to grade eight. Thus, I had the privilege of working with Jessica when she was in junior high. She was a representative for the Student Council in sixth grade and became vice president in seventh grade. She and Josh Kowalski tied for president their senior year at St. Mary's.

Over time, I got to know Jessica intimately because she confided in me. I'd always known how studious and driven she was, but it wasn't until I worked with her on Student Council that I realized how high-strung she could be. I once had to take her to the bathroom and console her because she'd gotten an A- on a math test.

Jessica put studying above everything else and was also the "go-to" person for teachers or administrators needing help. She was usually the teacher's pet because she was reliable and competent. Not only was she academically gifted, but she was also enthusiastic about sports and other recreational activities.

I remember thinking that she needed to relax a bit. I encouraged her to put less pressure on herself. She giggled about it; she did have a good sense of humor- she could laugh at herself. She had a fun-loving side that she only revealed to those who knew her well.

Overall, I was rather intrigued by the Calabresi family. All the teachers had a bit of a crush on Mr. Calabresi and were in awe of Mrs. Calabresi. They were a classy family- wealthy, beautiful, and successful. They were the type of family everyone wanted or thought they wanted to be.

Allie Robinson-
I started school at St. Mary's when I was in first grade. Jessica had already been there for two years and was known for being helpful and responsible, so our teacher paired us up. She helped educate me about the school. I still remember telling my mother that Jessica Calabresi was my helper. It was obvious that she was impressed with the Calabresi family. My family was upper middle class, but we certainly weren't as rich as Jessica's family. I could tell my mother admired Mrs. Calabresi because she'd interrogate me whenever Jessica's mom volunteered in the classroom. She wanted to know how her hair was styled or what she was wearing. I thought Mrs. Calabresi and Jessica had similar personalities. They were friendly and charitable. They didn't seem to have a mean bone in their bodies, but they were cliquey. They didn't let many people into their inner circle.

Jessica, her cousin, Nikki, and her best friend, Jenna, were joined at the hip. It was actually kind of a joke. Some people were snarky about it. All three girls were the same age, their fathers were partners in the same law firm, and they lived on the same street. It seemed too convenient and picture-perfect.

My mother desperately wanted to be Anna Calabresi's friend, and it was clear that she tried too hard. She was fascinated by the fact that Anna's relatives were famous movie stars. My mother once mentioned this to Anna. She said it was the only time Anna was standoffish with her. She immediately changed the subject. My mother felt self-conscious about it and never mentioned it again.

Jessica and Josh Kowalski were the smartest kids in school. I always thought they would end up dating because they were both intellectual and ambitious. I couldn't tell if the hostility they seemed to have for one another was genuine. Mrs. Grant ran Student Council and had them serve as co-presidents because she couldn't decide between them. This seemed to annoy Jessica because she thought she'd worked harder than Josh to achieve that goal.

Josh and Jessica had the same friends, but there was animosity between them. Jessica competed with Josh because he was naturally intelligent and didn't have to put as much effort into his schoolwork as she did. Jessica's cousin, Nikki, was the same way. She had potential and did well, but not as well as Jessica because she wasn't as motivated. Jessica ended up beating them both for Valedictorian. I overheard a couple of teachers gossiping one day in the office when they thought no one was around. I can't remember their exact words, but I do recall the assumption they were making. They felt that although Nikki and Josh were smarter than Jessica, it was impossible to match her drive.

Even in first grade, there was rivalry between Jessica and Josh. Josh bragged about getting perfect scores on spelling tests without studying. That irked Jessica, and their competitiveness lasted throughout their years at St. Mary's. Josh knew how to press Jessica's buttons. There was a lot of eye-rolling when they were in the same room together. They sometimes even talked over one another in class. Jessica would get irritated- especially if they disagreed about something opinion-based, like how to interpret the theme of a story in literature. Josh gave the impression that he was amused when they bickered. He would smirk, and there would be a twinkle in his eyes. I always wondered if Jessica secretly had a crush on Josh or if she was one of the only girls in school who was immune to his wit and good looks.

Josh's best friend, Evan Moreau, was the opposite of Josh. Evan was soft-spoken, sweet, and an overall sincere person. Everyone knew he and Nikki had always been crazy about each other. They started officially dating when they were in the fifth grade. Nikki's relationship with Evan was most likely the reason for her lack of motivation regarding her schoolwork.

Cliques exist everywhere; they certainly did at St. Mary's. The faculty unknowingly encouraged it- even Mrs. Grant, who was the most compassionate and well-liked teacher. She was the one who made decisions about who served on the Student Council. It seemed convenient that the most popular kids in school, who were inseparable, turned out to be the officers.

Josh and Jessica were co-presidents, Nikki was vice-president, Evan was treasurer, and Jenna was the historian. There were other talented, promising candidates, but they never really stood a chance. As it was, no one, not the student body, parents, teachers, or administrators, questioned it. It was just the way things were.

I would have liked to get to know Jessica better. She was always nice to me, and we were friends, but she was with Nikki and Jenna all the time- they had such a strong bond; even when they were socializing with other people, they appeared to be more present to each other than anyone else.

Devon Wright-

I fell in love with Jessica Calabresi when we were in preschool. She had the most beautiful almond-shaped chocolate brown eyes with lashes that were so long they curled up and met her eyebrows. I was captivated by her heart-shaped lips and perfectly symmetrical features. I loved looking at her- even at four years old. I stayed in love with her throughout our years at St. Mary's.

Jessica never showed interest in boys, although we all thought she was spectacular-looking. She was beautiful in a different way than her best friend, Jenna Sullivan. Jenna was striking with porcelain skin and an unusual shade of violet eyes. Jessica was more like the "girl next door." When Jenna and Jessica were together, which they always were, Jenna would be the one you'd notice first. But Jessica was the one you'd want to continue staring at. Her face never got boring. It was like apple pie or football- comforting and special.

Jessica was obsessed with her schoolwork and extracurricular activities. She was very athletic- she was a cheerleader. Some guys don't think cheerleading is a sport, but at St. Mary's, it was treated that way. The girls on the team had crazy hard tryouts. I remember several girls sobbing because they didn't make the squad. It was just as competitive as football and basketball tryouts. Even the physical education teachers respected the cheerleaders. They had to be gymnasts, dancers, and singers. We had mixed gym classes, both boys and girls. Although Jessica was petite, I remember thinking she was quicker and had more stamina than many of the boys.

Josh Kowalski was one of the most popular boys in our class. He was athletic and smart, and he looked like a Ken doll. All the girls swooned over him except for Jessica. She found him irritating because he was a showoff. The other girls found him charming. Even Jenna Sullivan, the hottest girl in school, had a thing for Josh. They were mainly friends but did "date" in sixth or seventh grade. Of course, dating in middle school is a joke and doesn't mean anything.

It was interesting to me that Jessica never followed in the footsteps of her two best friends. They started to show interest in boys early on. Josh was Jenna's first boyfriend but not her last. Nikki and Evan Moreau were one of those annoying couples who were together forever. On the other hand, Jessica was only interested in academics, Student Council, and cheerleading.

I never told anyone this, but I got up the nerve to ask her to be my girlfriend in seventh grade. I wrote her a text expressing how I'd always liked her and wanted to take her to an upcoming dance. She turned me down. I was terrified that she'd gossip about it, and I'd be made fun of- but there was no sign she'd ever told anyone else. I appreciated the fact that she kept it to herself. She had always been nice to me, but after that text, she went out of her way to be kind. I genuinely think she was a good person—a nice girl. I never had any hostility towards her, even though she rejected me.

Ed Donohue-

My kids went to school with the Calabresi girls at St. Mary's. My daughter was in Jessica's class, and my son, who was two years younger, was a classmate of the middle Calabresi girl, Sara. Eddie, my son, got to know Sara pretty well. They even secretly dated. Of course, Anthony never knew. From what I understood, he wouldn't let his girls date until high school. It was kid stuff, though, texting and shit. They weren't really "dating." My son learned quite a bit about Anthony's relationship with his daughters. According to Sara, Jessica was a kiss-ass and idolized her father. Sara, on the other hand, couldn't stand him. She thought he was ridiculously strict. I don't remember much more about Sara and Eddie's relationship. Inevitably, it didn't last, but I think they stayed friends throughout high school.

My daughter was friendly with Jessica, but they weren't really friends. There was never any animosity between them- they just didn't have much in common. Jessica was into Student Council and cheerleading, while my daughter was involved with the marching band and chess club.

My wife and I were acquaintances with Anthony and Anna Calabresi when our kids were in school together. We'd known them for years because our kids went from St. Mary's to Lomonoco Creek together. While, most kids who went to Lomonco Creek for high school had attended one of the public schools beforehand.

I always liked Anthony. He was friendly, a very charismatic guy. He was the type of person who didn't go on and on about himself. In fact, I don't think he shared much about himself or his family. When I ran into him, he always made a point to ask about me and my wife and kids. I appreciated that. My wife was also fond of Anna. She said she was surprised by how down-to-earth Anna was considering her looks and background.

One thing about the Calebresis that some people resented was that they had their hands in everything. Anthony went from being the kingpin at St. Mary's to the top dog at Lomonoco Creek. He was always on the school board and president of both athletic committees. Even though he never ran for anything, he was vocal and active in local politics.

Anna was a stay-at-home mom, but she was always volunteering, not just for school activities. She was also the president of the Mom's Club in town, she led the Women's Guild at church, and she ran both the soup kitchen and food pantry in Rosevalley.

I guess you could say they were a pretty busy family. They had their priorities, and even though my wife and I weren't nearly as motivated or involved as they were, we thought they were okay.

June Wallace-
My daughters went to Jamestown Academy, the public middle school in Jamestown, so I didn't meet the Calabresi family until my oldest daughter was in ninth grade. She was a cheerleader with Jessica, and they were friends. Ginny liked Jessica; she thought she was friendly and fun to be with.

I have to admit some of us were reluctant to accept Anna and Anthony Calabresi at first. Although they were both pleasant on the surface, we were suspicious that they might try to change the way things had always been. We knew they were prominent within the community; they were very involved and liked to be in control.

The Calabresis were polite and pleasant, but some of us thought they were passive-aggressive. Although neither ever raised their voice, even during debates about essential school matters, I can't recall a time when things failed to turn out in their favor. They were persuasive in a quiet way.

My original hesitancy to accept the Calabresi family quickly changed, but I'll admit bias. I became very fond of Anna and grateful to her when my mother unexpectedly passed away. She arranged for sympathy cards and flowers to be delivered to my house. She also singlehandedly set up a system with the other PTA and cheer moms for food to be provided for two months. She insisted I allow her and the other moms to take me to lunch after my mother's death once a week. I thought that was very telling. Although Anna was gorgeous, wealthy, and always seemed to get her way, she was genuinely a caring and kind person.

I concluded that Anna and Anthony just wanted to be a part of their daughter's education, and they had just as much of a right to as the parents of the kids who'd attended public school. I decided they weren't trying to take over; they just wanted to contribute. They eventually won most of us over.

Marissa Hill-

I met Jessica when she tried out for cheerleading practice the summer before our freshmen year in high school. I noticed her on the first day of tryouts because she was outstanding. She was probably the second-best cheerleader on the squad. Kelly Bachmann was the best. I'd known Kelly for years because we went all through school together. Kelly was a very sweet, bubbly person; everyone liked her. She and Erin Johansson had been best friends since kindergarten because they were both as "girly-girly" as you could get. Their moms ran the local Girl Scout troop. They took dance, gymnastics, and even junior cheer together before they started preschool. Kelly's mom was a college professor and, aside from Girl Scouts, wasn't as interested in all the activities Kelly was involved in. Her parents divorced when she was young, but it was an amicable separation. They took turns taking Kelly to school and all the numerous activities she participated in. Erin's mother was a stay-at-home mom. Her father traveled a lot for business. Erin took after her very feminine mother. They were more like best friends than mother and daughter. Mrs. Johansson was actually one of the cheerleading coaches we had over the years.

In school, Erin and Kelly were always the most popular girls. They were both not only vivacious but also stunning. They put a lot of effort into grooming. They regularly had their hair and nails done, and the way they applied makeup was nothing short of perfection. Although they were both cliquey, they weren't mean-spirited or snobby.

When cheerleading practices started, it became evident that a new clique was developing even within the yet-to-be-formed cheerleading squad. Kelly and Erin were impressed with Jessica's athletic ability, so they were drawn to her. Jessica and Erin were equally talented, and Kelly was the best, so Jessica also admired them. And Jessica didn't come alone. She wasn't really an individual-she came with a squad. Jessica, Nikki, and Jenna were a package deal. So, that summer, the five girls immediately became close and were always together.

Everyone knew that Jamey Russo fell in what he considered "love" when he laid eyes on Jessica. He flirted with her at practice all the time. She acted as if she wanted nothing to do with him. They were complete opposites. Jamey was only interested in partying and goofing off. He loved football and was a great player, but other than that, he didn't take anything seriously. He also was known for having a bad temper, and he could be cruel. He picked on kids, and some people thought of him and his best friend, Bobby McAllister, as bullies. Bobby and Jamey were tough and strong, so they could get away with picking on weaker kids.

I didn't think anything would ever develop between Jessica and Jamey. She was sweet and studious, and he was just the opposite. But whatever began that summer grew, and although no one understood or could describe the relationship between Jamey and Jessica, there was a connection that only grew stronger over time.

Mason Holmes-

I played football with Jamey Russo and Bobby McAllister from the time we were all in elementary school. I never became great friends with either of them, but they were friendly with the other football players and me. I was never an essential player like they were, but I always made the team. Josh Kowalski started playing football with us the summer before ninth grade. He was a natural-he became the quarterback. Because of their admiration for his athletic skills, Jamey and Bobby let him into their inner circle. Evan became part of their crowd by default. He wasn't a great football player but was Josh's best friend. Before the Catholic school kids started high school with us, Mickey Patera- the class clown, Jamey, and Bobby had been like the three Musketeers.

We practiced on the same field as the cheerleaders that summer. Even before school started, we could all see that the "clique" was developing- a combination of public school kids and former Catholic school kids. They were the popular crowd all through high school. Everyone looked up to them. Interestingly, the "popular" kids don't always have the most friends because they're exclusive. They stick together and don't socialize outside their group, but it doesn't matter because everyone else idolizes them.

Jamey's football group and Jessica Calabresi's cheerleading group formed the in-crowd at Lomonoco Creek. Who knows how it happened exactly; they were all good-looking, but so were many other kids who never reached their level of high school fame. They were also wealthy, but so was everyone who lived in Jamestown. I think it was the attraction between Jamey and Jessica. Everyone was fascinated with them. There was something there- they belonged to each other, although they never were officially dating. Jessica acted as if she could have cared less about Jamey, but I knew differently because I had a major crush on her. I obsessively watched her without ever telling a soul out of fear that Jamey would kill me if he found out. He claimed her the moment he saw her. We were across the field from the girls, and he noticed Jessica. He announced to everyone within earshot that he thought she was hot.

"Wow," he declared, "Look at that sizzling brunette with the short ponytail! She's gorgeous."

Bobby shrugged nonchalantly, "She's attractive," he agreed unenthusiastically.

"She's beautiful, and look at her butt. She's got the cutest butt I've ever seen." Jamey whistled, although she was too far away to hear him.

I agreed. Jessica was perfection. Those huge brown eyes with unusually long lashes, her kissable lips, and that adorable little nose. I can't tell you how often I fantasized about her. I had her face memorized. Of course, I never admitted this to anyone because Jamey would have kicked my butt. He was also infatuated with her, but he was the type who would pursue her relentlessly until she caved. He was aggressive and bold, and he had no shame. He knew he was good-looking and would do whatever it took to win her over.

It wasn't just her looks but her good girl persona- she was a challenge. He liked that.

I don't know how Jessica initially felt about Jamey. When he addressed her, she would roll her eyes, pretend he didn't exist, or order him to leave her alone.

But I knew the truth.

Eventually, he piqued her interest.

I knew because I had fallen for her and watched her all the time.

I was probably the only person on that field who noticed her subtle glances at Jamey, followed by a sparkle in her eyes when she thought no one else was looking.

Prologue:
I Had a Life Before Jamey Russo

For the longest time, I overlooked the fact that I had a life before Jamey Russo. He became such an integral part of my world for so many years that I forgot what life was like before he existed...at least before he existed for *me*. I'd managed to survive pre-Jamey for thirteen years. When that thought initially occurred to me, I was astonished. It was equivalent to an unexpected slap across the face. It was startling because I let myself overlook this reality for an incredibly long and, in my opinion, inexcusable amount of time.

I met Jamey the summer before we both entered ninth grade. He was a running back for the junior varsity football team, and I had just made the cheerleading squad. The cheerleaders practiced across from the expansive, rectangular football field. Lomonco Creek took football very seriously. The stadium was larger than most and could hold up to 30,000 fans. A huge gold banner soared over the underpass that led from the gymnasium to the field with the team's logo spread across it: a black stallion with ivory paws and ears and a solid gold tail. The bleachers were painted royal blue with the words "Rosevalley Stallions" in gilded print.

My father was on the board of the athletic department because he was obsessed with high school sports. When I decided where to go to high school, he'd encouraged me to choose Lomonoco Creek because of its emphasis on sports. Although my father didn't have sons, he was always involved in the male-dominated sports programs at the schools I attended. He had played football from the time he was a young kid until he graduated from college. Although I clearly couldn't play football like my dad, my parents urged me to become a cheerleader. It soon became my passion, and even though he never verbalized it, I could tell my father was proud of how adept and dedicated I became.

Before I knew who he was, I overheard my father mention Jamey Russo's name. He frequently talked to his friend and law partner, Gerry Sullivan, about sports- especially football. After observing a practice, they discussed the promising players. They were invested in the team because their law firm was one of the sponsors who contributed money to the "Rosevalley Stallions." I recall hearing the names Jamey Russo and Bobby McAllister during the course of their conversation. Apparently, they were both extremely talented in playing offense.

They also discussed Josh Kowalski that day. He had been a classmate of mine from St. Mary's. My father had always been impressed with Josh. He had followed Josh's career from when he was in youth football, and he'd predicted that Josh would make junior first-string quarterback the summer before high school. He was right. His admiration of Josh had always irked me because I considered him a "frenemy." Still, I kept my feelings to myself because I didn't want to elicit my dad's disapproval. I was afraid he'd think I was being petty.

I can't recall the specific details of the conversation because although I loved cheerleading, I was never all that interested in the game's intricacies. I liked to cheer for the players but wasn't interested in what was going on as long as we were winning.

During the first few days of cheerleading practice, I wasn't even sure I had made the right choice about attending public high school. I'd made the decision based on my father's influence and the fact that my cousin, Nikki, and closest friend, Jenna, were attending Lomonco Creek. I'd hemmed and hawed about which school I wanted to attend, but my dad, cousin, and best friend selected one for me.

Nikki chose the public school because that was where her boyfriend, Evan, was going. Jenna wanted more freedom; she had always been rebellious and knew she'd easily get away with mischief in a public school. There were other private schools I considered, but the truth is, I couldn't fathom being separated from Jenna and Nikki. Furthermore, although my parents said I could go anywhere I wanted because I was an excellent student, my father made it evident in a "subtle" way that he wanted me to go to Lomonoco Creek, and I couldn't bear to disappoint him.

I didn't notice Jamey or any football players for weeks; my attention was focused entirely on proving myself to the cheerleading coaches. I was very anxious while we were practicing, doing run-throughs, and especially when we were auditioning- and at Lomonoco Creek, they literally did call cheerleading tryouts "auditions." I knew it wasn't easy to make the Lomonoco Creek cheerleading squad. Even though I'd been cheerleading at St. Mary's for years and had always been athletic, flexible, and vociferous, I was still panicked. Strangely, I wasn't afraid I'd be turned away. I knew I was good enough to make the team. In actuality, I was uneasy about being able to demonstrate how skilled I was in such a short period of time.

My confidence increased when the coaches complimented my cheerleading moves, especially my back handspring and cone-motion approach. It was evident that Kelly Bachmann, who became the cheerleading captain, was the best cheerleader on the squad. I wasn't as talented as her, but I was tied for second place with Erin Johansson. I could live with that. Kelly and Erin were best friends and had been since they were in elementary school. Their interest in me also helped to boost my self-esteem. Kelly constantly praised how I performed during stunts, which is the most challenging job in cheerleading. Erin, Kelly, and I were frequently asked to demonstrate how to execute different techniques properly.

I quickly became close friends with Kelly. She was one of the sweetest people I'd ever met. Not only was Kelly talented and kind, but she was also personable and fun-loving. Our alliance started a camaraderie between our respective friends that lasted throughout high school. Kelly and Erin immediately bonded with Nikki, Jenna, and me. We started hanging around together all the time that summer. We became inseparable.

I'll never forget the day that Jamey first noticed me. He made his attraction obvious to not only me but everyone…and I mean *everyone*. It was an unusually warm, humid day. The sun was blinding as I tried over and over again to master a jump. I felt eyes boring into me, coming from the football field. I turned around and noticed a really good-looking football player staring shamelessly at me. He had his hands on his hips and a huge grin on his face. When our eyes met, he started clapping and whistling. He soon attracted the attention of all his teammates. He pointed at me and started animatedly telling everyone within earshot how impressed he was with my jump.

"Do it again!" he demanded, "Come on, pretty girl. Do that sexy, and I mean SEEEXXXYYY jump again."

I flushed with shame and quickly pivoted. The other players were laughing and making indecipherable comments about me. It was humiliating.

I immediately realized that this football player, who I soon learned was named Jamey Russo, had no shame. And that he was the type of guy who could get away with it. He made a spectacle of himself and *me*. All the football players thought it was funny. The feelings among the cheerleaders were mixed. Some were jealous; others thought it was cute or romantic, and some thought it was immature and juvenile. Jamey's initial reaction to me and subsequent constant attention embarrassed me to the point of mortification. For weeks, I dreaded seeing him. At first, I would have full-blown panic attacks, and Jenna and Nikki would have to privately console me because I didn't want to make my unease noticeable to everyone else. I wasn't comfortable showing weakness to people other than Nikki and Jenna, who were like sisters to me. I was closer to them than I was to my actual sisters. After a while, I started to get used to it, and over time, I became less anxious. His attention developed into what felt like normalcy- and my displeased reaction became a daily occurrence. It was like passing by the same photograph or painting every day- no one noticed it after a while.

I never admitted it to anyone before, but once I began feeling less embarrassed and more relaxed with Jamey's attention, I only pretended to be irritated. I secretly started to take pleasure in it. It wasn't because I craved compliments. When it came to my appearance, I had always been secure enough not to need admiration or praise. It was not the attention- it was *Jamey's* attention that I began to yearn for and enjoy.

I didn't realize how I felt until I had a dream about him one night- approximately three weeks after he'd noticed me. In my dream, we were kissing passionately, and I woke up feeling aroused. At first, I was shocked. I hadn't realized until then that I was sexually attracted to Jamey.

The dream occurred in early August, and I never told anyone - not even Nikki or Jenna about it. Over time, my enticement only grew stronger. He was so good-looking. I fantasized about his hooded chestnut eyes and chiseled chest. I soon realized that *everything* about his appearance made my heart flutter. His bronze skin, full lips, camel-colored hair streaked with champagne highlights…

And after that dream, after my subconscious mind informed me that Jamey Russo indeed magnetized me, my life changed. That was when the pre-Jamey Jessica ceased to exist. And it wasn't until many years later that I remembered I did have a life before Jamey Russo.

Part I.
Ninth Grade

Chapter One: The Get-together

At the beginning of September, right after school started, Connie Russo, Jamey's mother, decided to have a get-together for some football players, cheerleaders, and their families. Rumor had it that she only invited families she wanted to impress or families she was impressed with. She jokingly told my mother that it wouldn't be possible for her to invite *everyone*. According to Ms. Russo, even their "English Manor" (her words) couldn't accommodate that many people.

Even though she sent out a Facebook Invite two weeks ahead of the event, she still felt the need to call our landline to personally invite my family. I was in the kitchen when the phone rang, so I overheard my mother's side of the conversation. Initially, I had no idea who was on the phone, but I could tell it was someone she wasn't fond of, considering her voice had a saccharine-sweet quality to it.

When she said, "Ohhhh...Hi. Yes, I'm well, and how are you?" She gave me a wary look and rolled her eyes. During the entire conversation, which lasted less than five minutes, she kept sighing, pacing, and trying to prevent interruption. She quickly made an excuse to disconnect.

My mother finally cleared her throat and assertively stated, "Well, I'm heading out the door now. I'll talk to you later. And yes, we will check our schedule to ensure we're free that night." Ms. Russo continued to yak - I couldn't decipher what she was saying, but I heard her muffled voice.

"Oh no, we would never expect you to change the date for us. Please don't consider doing that. I'll let you know if that works for us as soon as possible. Okay, Connie. Yes. I've really got to go. Bye."

My mother hung up the phone and exhaled noisily. "That was Connie Russo," she told me in a critical yet slightly amused tone.

I raised my eyebrows and widened my eyes, "What did she want?"

"I guess she's having a party for some of the families of the football players and cheerleaders. She made it a point to tell me not everyone is invited as if I should be honored that she invited us." My mother snickered, which didn't surprise me because I'd heard her, my Aunt Gina, and Jenna's mother, Rachel, make reproachful comments about Ms. Russo. It had even been suggested that she was slightly flirtatious with my father.

    The night after a formal dinner for contributors to the athletic department, my Aunt Gina came over to pick my mom up for a yoga class. My father was finishing breakfast with my sisters and me. When she heard my aunt's car pull up the driveway, my mother threw her pocketbook over her shoulder and strode down the steps. She was about to walk out the door when it swung open. My aunt pushed past her and marched up the stairs to pester my father. My father and Nikki's mother were devoted twins but complete opposites. My father was always composed and rarely showed emotion, while my aunt was perpetually restless, outspoken, and passionate about everything.

    Aunt Gina had her hands on her hips as she stared at my father with an entertained yet slightly accusatory look.

    "What is it, Gina?" My father asked with false annoyance. This was characteristic of their relationship.

    "Did you enjoy the attention last night?" she asked snidely. "You know, the *attention* from Connie. Connie Russo."

    I wasn't surprised by my Aunt Gina's allegation because I'd heard her make similar comments, but my sisters gasped. Megan, my youngest sister, who was only nine years old, was flabbergasted. Sara, who was twelve at the time and eternally irritated with our father, was mortified.

    My father took a sip of his coffee and shook his head, "Gina..." he started, but my aunt cut him off.

    "She couldn't keep her hands off you. She kept touching any part of your body that wasn't off limits." She made air quotes with her fingers when she said "off limits."

    My mother giggled, without an ounce of jealousy, as my aunt continued, "And she laughed way too hard at your corny jokes. Sorry, Anthony, but you're just not all that funny."

    My sisters and I remained speechless, unsure how to react. It was strange to think of another woman flirting with your father.

    "Gina, don't be ridiculous," my father chided, "You're exaggerating as usual, and you're making the girls uncomfortable. Go to yoga!" he ordered.

As they headed out the door, my mother and aunt continued to chuckle like teenagers.

When they left, my father calmly took a sip of his orange juice, "You know how your aunt is," he said evenly. My sisters and I exchanged glances and were silent. We knew my father well enough to recognize his comment as the only explanation we would get and an indirect order not to speak of Aunt Gina's accusations.

If truth be told, I had noticed that Ms. Russo paid special attention to my dad at sporting events- the ones she actually came to. She certainly didn't come to all athletic activities like my parents. She attended a few scrimmages, and when the local television stations came by one day to do interviews, she was there, dressed to the nines and showered in perfume. She hung on Jamey like a proud mother hen during his interview. It was evident that he was annoyed. During her rare appearances, I did notice how coquettish she was around my father. Needless to say, it pained me to acknowledge this.

When I found out about Ms. Russo's invitation, I was simultaneously nervous and excited. I wasn't sure if I wanted to go or not. I had no idea what to expect. I still secretly fantasized about Jamey and enjoyed the attention he bestowed on me. Yet, the idea of being at a party together with our friends and family not only intimidated me but also scared me.

My mother and I were both inquisitive about who else would receive an invitation. I was certain my mother wouldn't commit to going until she found out if my aunt's and/or the Sullivan family would be there.

After hanging up with Ms. Russo, my mother immediately called my Aunt Gina. They gossiped about what an opportunist and shameless seductress Ms. Russo was for a while. When she got off the phone with Aunt Gina, she called Jenna's mother, Rachel, and they chatted about how the Russo family was ashamed of Connie and would have disowned her if it weren't for Jamey. They didn't have the heart to abandon their grandson.

My father wasn't one to engage in gossip, but later that night, when my mother mentioned the invitation, he did casually remark that although Connie Russo was very wealthy, it was better to be held in high esteem than to be prosperous. "Unfortunately, for her, she has quite a, I guess you could say, questionable reputation."

My mom, aunt, and Jenna's mother eventually decided to go to the party because, according to them, it would be rude to decline.

The following day, they sat around our kitchen table, drinking tea and debating about what to do.

"Well, it is the kind thing to do," my mother said as if it pained her, "Even though it will probably turn out to be a disaster."

Rachel agreed, "We certainly wouldn't want to hurt her feelings."

Aunt Gina took a sip of her tea and nodded. "Yes, we *should* go. Even though I'd rather not. And, you have to admit, it will make for good gossip." She cackled wickedly as she admitted what all three were thinking.

Everyone in Rosevalley knew about the Russo clan. They were probably the wealthiest family in town. They owned a bunch of Italian restaurants not only in Connecticut but all over the country. The family was admired- even revered, but Connie Russo was not. She had a reputation. A reputation that preceded itself- the type of reputation that everyone knew about, but no one could remember exactly when or from whom they'd first heard about it. In essence, she was considered a hot mess. She was a pill popper and a sloppy drunk. The identity of Jamey's father was a mystery because Ms. Russo had slept with several men shortly before her pregnancy. She frequented bars in nearby cities and hooked up with random guys. Rumor had it that it would be impossible for her to single out Jamey's biological father.

Nevertheless, her family stood by her when she became pregnant with Jamey and never publicly discussed the scandal surrounding the situation. There was plenty of gossip about Ms. Russo, but she was treated with respect because of her money and family background. The Russos helped raise Jamey, and I found out later that he had become semi-famous in our small town when he joined Pop Warner football. He had talent and strength and was one of the best offensive players Rosevalley had ever seen. When I first met him on the football field at Lomonoco Creek, he was already considered a football star.

The morning of the party, I woke up with butterflies in my stomach. My chest felt like my heart was doing somersaults. I couldn't eat all day, and I kept pacing around my bedroom with the door shut because I didn't want anyone in my family to know how anxious I was. I was so grateful that Nikki and Jenna were going to be there because they were my security blankets.

They were the only ones who knew how edgy I was about the party. I wasn't sure how the dynamics would play out with Jamey, my friends, and our families. It felt like my worlds were colliding. I also couldn't anticipate how Jamey would behave toward me in front of my parents. I knew he wouldn't be stupid enough to flirt with me in front of my father, but I didn't know how he'd act because I didn't know how I would conduct myself.

Ms. Russo insisted that everyone travel via party bus to the get-together. She wanted the adults to be able to drink without apprehension. She maintained that she would pay for the limo, and everyone agreed after much coercion. However, they were adamant about taking Ubers home and paying for them out of their own pockets. It was strange riding to a party in a fancy bus. It all felt surreal to me. I was still feeling a mixture of exhilaration and unease. These paradoxical emotions were new to me. I'd never experienced anything like the sensations Jamey seemed to stir in me.

My family was sitting in the middle of the bus when we pulled up to Jamey's house. There was an unspoken agreement that we all sit with our respective families rather than mingle before the party. This was a unique occurrence for all of us, and we were unsure how to behave. Even my mother, who was the personification of grace under pressure, felt uncomfortable.

I'd heard that Jamey had an enormous house, but I wasn't prepared for just how massive it was. I gasped when we approached his stone and brick mansion. I don't think I'd ever seen such an impressive home before. It had a brick walkway that led to an outdoor front patio with candle lanterns, a birdbath, and sectional white couches. There were decorative pillars on either side of the house. It had slate roofs, lighted windows, and an ornate wrought iron front door. It reminded me of an old-fashioned British castle with a modern flair.

"Well, isn't this…colossal," my father whispered as we were driven up the long, steep driveway.

"If you ask me, it's gaudy," my mother murmured, unimpressed.

My father nodded, "I agree. It's a little much."

My sisters and I stared in disbelief at what looked like a home that belonged to the Royals. It was as fancy as some of the extravagant hotels we'd stayed in on our yearly vacations.

As we walked inside, I noticed a sun gazebo with sliding glass doors and a stone hot tub located to the right of the house. To the left, there was a fire pit and outdoor fireplace. There was so much to observe; it was all breathtaking.

Before we could examine our surroundings thoroughly, Ms. Russo greeted us at the door,

"Hello, all!" she shouted with too much enthusiasm, "We are SO glad you could come!"

As we were escorted into the foyer, I immediately detected that Ms. Russo's taste was much different from my mother's. The furniture and adornments were contemporary and up-to-date. All the appliances were steel or chrome with only neutral colors; there were no patterns or embellishments. There was a lot of simulated light. The rooms were peppered with various trimmings but lacked character and warmth.

I wondered how Jamey felt living in a house like this. It seemed fabricated- like not much love was put into it. My mother put her heart and soul into decorating our home. Our house had a personality. Jamey's didn't. It was magnificent yet dull. My mother told my aunt the next day that it looked too millennial. She suggested that maybe Ms. Russo had hired a twenty-year-old as an interior decorator.

I was expecting Ms. Russo to take us on a tour, but instead, she led us straight to the kitchen. My mother later said it would have been pretentious to show us around. Because Connie Russo was accustomed to wealth, she didn't feel the need to brag about it.

The beginning of the night went by in a blur. I felt disassociated like I was dreaming. Everyone was cordial, making dull, small talk about trivial, unimportant things. Jamey didn't even look in my direction, although he had a lengthy conversation with my father- probably about football. The dinner was catered, and I was beginning to think the best part of the evening was the delicious food provided by one of the restaurants Jamey's family owned. It wasn't until after dinner that everyone started to loosen up and have fun. The abundance of wine certainly helped the adults to feel at ease.

After dinner, a couple of maids started clearing the dishes. This was everyone's signal to go to the next "appropriate station" designated by Ms. Russo. She seemed to have a prearranged agenda for the evening. I counted five household helpers in all. Two were clearing the table, one was stacking utensils in the dishwasher, and the other two were leading the adults away from the table. The moms congregated in the kitchen, where I assumed they planned to gossip and continue to drink wine. The dads were escorted to the living room, where they were encouraged to switch to bourbon and would inevitably end up discussing sports. There was no household help to lead the kids to their next destination. Ms. Russo must have known the children and teenagers would find a way to entertain themselves, or quite possibly, she didn't care about impressing us kids.

Truthfully, that was when everyone- the moms, dads, youngsters, and adolescents started to enjoy themselves. Fortunately for us, we were forgotten about. The little kids, including my sisters, my cousins- Phil Jr. and Anthony, and Jenna's little sister- Ashlynn, decided to play hide and seek and catch lightning bugs in the backyard. Jamey convinced the rest of us to come to his rec room.

Jamey's rec room was like nothing I'd ever seen before. We had a space similar to this, but Jamey's was double the size and had triple the accommodations. There was a stone bar with a marble counter, a stainless steel refrigerator, a pool table, and a television with the most gigantic screen I'd ever seen outside a movie theater. There were also large, comfy, solid black couches and bean bag chairs. Everything was brand new and designer-made.

I stood next to Nikki and Jenna, feeling apprehensive. I was unsure how Jamey would behave toward me now that our parents weren't around. Kelly and Erin were relaxed; they were obviously in familiar territory. Mickey and Bobby immediately made themselves at home; they came in and crashed on the sofa- as if they lived there.

Evan stood near Nikki, as always, waiting to take her cue on what to do next. He was that kind of boyfriend. Jenna impatiently shuffled her feet as she waited to hear the plan. Jenna never felt insecure. She was always outspoken and comfortable in her own skin. No one intimidated her. Over the years, I had allowed Nikki and Jenna's protectiveness to make me somewhat dependent on them.

The other kids invited seemed intrigued about what mischievous scheme Jamey had up his sleeve.

He instantly took a bottle of Jack Daniels from the bar and suggested we play "Never Have I Ever." I felt my chest tighten, and a knot formed in my stomach because I knew if everyone agreed, I'd soon be asked to reveal personal information about myself.

There was a murmur throughout the crowd- signifying acquiescence to this idea. Not everyone sounded thrilled, but no one protested.

"Does everyone know how to play?" Jamey asked deviously, looking directly at me.

Mickey and Bobby snickered.

"You know Kelly, and I do," Erin replied unflappably.

"Yeah, of course, I know you girls do," Jamey said brusquely as he tilted his head towards Kelly and Erin, "We've played before. I wasn't sure about the Catholic school kids."

Josh had a somewhat offended look on his face as he retorted, "You'd be surprised at what Catholic school kids have done," he looked pointedly at Jenna, and his voice trailed off.

Jenna rolled her eyes as Jamey pronounced, "I didn't mean any disrespect."

"None taken," Josh replied dryly, glaring at Jamey with what I interpreted as provocation. He was insinuating that he was offended by Jamey creating a distinction between us- the Catholic school kids versus them- the public school kids.

Jamey widened his eyes and nodded, acknowledging Josh's unspoken words and silently agreeing to bring an end to his snide comments. A look can say so much if you're paying attention.

Evan giggled nervously, "We know how to play." He put his arm around Nikki and pulled her in for a side hug.

Jenna cleared her throat and sighed irritably, "*Everyone* knows how to play."

Bobby looked at me and raised his eyebrows, "Even Jessica? Does Jessica know how to play?" his voice had a nasty tone.

Josh, who never missed a chance to ridicule me, parroted Bobby, "Yeah, Jess, that's a good question. Do you know how to play?"

I nodded and looked down, feeling shy and embarrassed.

"Are you sure it doesn't scare you?" Bobby inquired, feigning concern.

"Yes," I muttered.

Josh grinned, "Maybe you're not scared, but are you *mature* enough to play?"

Jenna shoved Josh and told him to shut up. Although they were friends (with benefits), she was accustomed to our rivalry.

Bobby continued to taunt me, "Jessica doesn't seem grown up enough to play a game like this."

Jenna glared at Bobby, "What about *you*, Bobby McAllister? Are you grown up enough to play? Have *you* played before?" She was mocking him in my defense.

"Touché," Bobby said lightheartedly, "I didn't mean anything by it."

"Bull," Jenna retorted.

"Hey, hey…let's just play then," Jamey said, playing peacemaker, "I'll pour us all a glass of Jack."

Jamey started pouring whiskey into plastic cups from under the bar. I was willing to play yet reluctant because it meant I was agreeing to reveal delicate information; everyone knew that that's what this game was all about. Drinking whiskey also scared me, only because I was afraid my father would find out I'd been drinking alcohol, and I wasn't sure how he'd react.

Nikki must have read my mind because she said, "Our parents are drinking. We're all taking Ubers home, so they won't notice if we smell like alcohol."

"Yeah," I muttered, exhaling as Jamey started pouring the drinks. Once he was done, he passed them out. "Cheers," he said. We all clumsily clunked glasses and took a sip of the whiskey. Bobby made some caustic comment when I took a swig about how surprised he was that "prim and proper Jessica" was drinking.

Josh smirked, "I know; I never thought I'd see the angelic, straight-laced Miss Calabresi let any alcohol pass her perfect little lips."

Jenna once again came to my defense. "Josh, Bobby- both of you, leave it alone. It's getting old."

They both shrugged and turned towards Jamey as he began to speak.

"I'll start," Jamey said slyly, "Remember, you have to drink if you HAVE done what the person says."

"We know!" Jenna and Josh shouted impatiently.

Jamey laughed sheepishly, "Okay. Here goes. Never have I ever kissed a boy." He said, gawking in my direction. I was the only girl who didn't drink, which was humiliating. I started to turn red. Bobby smirked. Jamey raised his eyebrows seductively. I knew I couldn't lie because Josh would call me out or question me. Everyone at St. Mary's knew I'd never had a boyfriend.

In order to assuage my embarrassment, Jenna grabbed the bottle and said, "Never Have I Ever gone to second base." There were a few nervous giggles as some girls, including Nikki, Jenna, and Erin, took a sip of their whiskey. Kelly and I exchanged a grin because we were unsure how to feel about the fact that we hadn't ever gone that far.

The next one was harmless, and I hoped the rest of the game would take off in this direction. "Never Have I Ever sprained or broken a bone," Kelly said good-naturedly.

We all drank to that because we were all sporty. It was almost impossible to be athletic and never damage part of your body.

Unfortunately, my wish was not granted. The questions became not only more personal but also quite specific. If someone playing was interested in probing for information, the whiskey soon alleviated any reluctance to ask.

Considering I never drank alcohol, the whiskey went right to my head and desensitized my distress. I only allowed Jamey to refill my glass once. I was not going to get sick enough to vomit in the Uber on the way home. Besides, I didn't have to drink most of the time because I wasn't all that experienced.

We continued to play for a couple of hours. We found out a lot about each other that night. For instance, Bobby was the only one who'd gone all the way. Jamey and Josh had made it to third base. Evan and Nikki were waiting until they were sixteen to have intercourse. Jenna read smut. The boys found that to be very sexy, especially Mickey. He developed a serious, unrequited crush on her that night. Bobby had the desire to murder someone- we all knew it was his stepfather because there were rumors that he was abusive. Bobby and Jamey had tried pot and LSD. And Josh and I were the only ones who had never cheated on a test.

The next morning, I woke up smiling because I did have fun, although I couldn't figure out what Bobby's problem was- he had always been hostile to me for some reason. Jenna said he had a crappy life, so he took it out on innocents and saw me as an easy target. I didn't know why he seemed to hate me so much- why was he targeting me? Was it because his best friend had a crush on me? I only pondered his reasoning for a few minutes before shrugging it off. I realized that I really didn't care what Bobby McAllister thought. Although the night had been entertaining, I had a pounding headache all morning. Luckily, my parents didn't notice because they were also hung over.

    My mother commented during a late breakfast that, no matter her faults, Ms. Russo definitely knew how to throw a party. Apparently, the parents also had a fun night.

Chapter Two:
The Confrontation

I had fantasies about Jamey all weekend after the party at his house. I imagined being wrapped in his muscular arms with his mouth pressed against mine. Just the thought of his full, luscious lips sent shivers up my spine. He was the first boy I'd ever desired, which made my feelings even more powerful because they were new and unexpected. I couldn't help feeling intensely attracted to him, but my emotions were perplexing. I knew he was majorly flawed. Whenever I reminded myself that he was a sexist bully, the over-used adage "no one is perfect" would come to mind. My mother constantly reminded my sisters and me of this whenever we complained about a friend, family member, or each other. My mind was playing ping pong. I was caught in a cyclical web of "Oh, maybe he's not that bad" and "Well, he is a chauvinist who has a reputation for tormenting weak classmates."

In reality, it was pretty simple. *I had a major crush on him,* and even then, I knew people had no control over who they were drawn to.

My girlfriends all inquired about my feelings for Jamey. I was discreet, even with Nikki and Jenna, because I didn't know how to explain my paradoxical frame of mind to myself, let alone other people. Whenever I pictured his chiseled jaw, dimpled chin, and those gorgeous, sleepy brown eyes, my stomach fluttered with excitement.

The Monday morning after Jamey's get-together, Nikki, Jenna, and I were walking down the narrow corridor connecting the freshman homerooms to our first-period classes. Lomonoco Creek had recently been remodeled. Over the summer, all the walls had been re-painted with navy blue and gold to represent the school colors. Travertine tile floors had been installed throughout the building, and they'd added an abundance of glass walls and doors.

The bell for first period was about to ring. We were discussing what color pedicures we planned to get after cheerleading practice. Once a month, our moms took our sisters and us to the salon to get mani/pedis. My mom and I always got a French manicure because it matched everything, but I always alternated the color on my toes.

"Look, there's Jamey and Bobby," Jenna said indifferently as she tilted her head in their direction. I noticed Jamey and Bobby guffawing as many of their friends looked on. Bobby was the center of attention, being demonstrative about something that was most likely inappropriate. They were all standing by Jamey's locker. Jamey was leaning against the wall. He immediately noticed me and raised his eyebrows as he smiled suggestively. Bobby subtly followed Jamey's gaze. When he spotted me, his face took on a look of disgust. Once again, I wondered why he had a problem with me.

"Why does Bobby hate me?" I whispered, more to myself than to my friends.

Nikki shrugged, "He's messed up. Everyone knows his stepfather is a loser who beats him and mooches off his mother."

"Yeah, the word is that the stepfather only married Bobby's mother because she's a pharmacist and can get him pills." Jenna chimed in. "I hear it's Oxy."

I still felt confused as I took in their words, "But why does he dislike me so much? What did I do to him?"

"Who cares?" Nikki remarked, throwing her hands in the air as if it didn't matter.

"He probably decided to target you because Jamey's his best friend, and he has a thing for you. Maybe he's jealous." Jenna suggested.

Nikki snorted, "Well, he's not gay."

We all nodded. Everyone knew that Bobby had more sexual experience with girls than any other freshman.

"Oh well," I said, shrugging, pretending not to be bothered by his aversion to me.

"See you at lunch," Jenna commented as the bell rang. Nikki and I nodded as we hurried off to our respective classes.

Unfortunately, Bobby and I happened to be in the same health class during first period. I sat in the first row, the third seat down. His chair was located a few rows over in the very last seat. He sauntered in a few minutes after I did. It seemed as if everyone acknowledged Bobby McAllister. The girls flirted by waving, blushing, purring a greeting, or fluttering their eyelashes. The boys fist-bumped, nodded, or somehow showed a sign of respect, friendship, or, in some cases, fear.

Considering his desk was not even close to mine, he did not have to walk past me to get to his seat. However, that morning, he decided to stroll needlessly down the aisle where I was sitting. It was evident that he did it intentionally because as he walked past me, he rolled his eyes and smirked antagonistically. I felt as if steam was exhaling from my nostrils as I sat up straighter in my chair and held his gaze; his unfair, hostile treatment of me was becoming annoying.

Towards the end of class, we were told to work silently on a useless project- an idiotic drawing of ourselves with positive adjectives written in the bubbles surrounding it. It was a waste of time, like most health class assignments. I finished quickly and asked to go to the restroom. There were only five minutes left before the bell was going to ring. I didn't have to go to the bathroom, but like most girls my age, I frequented the lavatory to check my makeup. I carried a cosmetics case with me and reapplied two or three times during the day. That morning, I put on another coat of clear lip gloss and ran my fingers through my bangs to smooth them out.

As I walked out of the lavatory, I jumped in surprise when I discovered Bobby standing directly across the hall from me. He was nonchalantly leaning against the wall to the right of the boys' bathroom with a composed, hostile expression.

I apprehensively scanned the hallway as I plodded out the door. When I noticed we were alone, I swallowed soundly, feeling slightly out of breath. My first instinct was to hang my head and walk past him, pretending not to notice him. I was not fond of confrontation and tried to avoid it. It wasn't out of fear; it was more the embarrassment conflict triggered in me. My father had always taught us to avoid making spectacles of ourselves. He thought it was tasteless to squabble publicly. At that moment, I desperately wished Jenna or Nikki were with me. Their presence always provided me with confidence.

Despite this, I abruptly had what was similar to a fight or flight response, and I chose not to flee. I was sick of avoiding an altercation with Bobby McAllister. I realized his harassment would continue if I didn't address it. I didn't run away- instead, I decided I would fight. Sometimes anxiety and degradation can turn to fury, and anger can be a compelling emotion- mainly because I wasn't the type to express wrath. At times like this, I felt slightly dissociated- as if I was watching myself interact rather than being a part of the interaction.

I folded my arms and slammed my books on the ground as Bobby lumbered towards me with a haughty look in his amber eyes. I glared at him, defiantly squinting my eyes, daring him to address me.

"I'm surprised Little Miss Goody Two Shoes would leave class early," he sneered.

"What is your problem?" I questioned assertively, refusing to avert my eyes from his.

"I'm just so sick of girls like you...all high and mighty; you think you're better than everybody else."

At that moment, I was consumed with fury. I took a step towards him and pointed my finger very close to his face, "Who the hell do you think you are, Bobby McAllister? How dare you judge me. You know NOTHING about me- you arrogant jerk! *You* walk around school like you own the place, and you're only a freshman." I paused and took a deep breath.

"If you ask me, you're the one who acts all high and mighty," I continued, "and everyone knows football players like you get special treatment around here...just because, in your case, you're as much a bully on the field as you are off of it. That's really the only reason you're a good running back: because you like hurting people. You're sadistic; you enjoy beating up on players who are weaker than you."

Bobby stood silently watching me. I couldn't decipher his countenance or how he would eventually react. He appeared to be confused.

I cleared my throat and continued, wagging my finger in his direction once again, "And you know what?" I began with false sympathy, "I'm sorry that you have a crappy home life. That stinks. It really does. I feel sorry for you. But mainly, I pity someone like you because to boost your self-esteem, you need to ridicule and harass others. That's just pathetic!"

We stood staring at one another in silence for quite a long time. He had a quizzical look; he was digesting what I'd said. I wasn't sure how he was going to respond or if he would respond at all. Finally, after what must have been a full minute, the bell rang, and everyone started pouring out of the classrooms. I continued to glare at Bobby, daring him to retort. I was still irate enough not to feel self-conscious about whatever he chose to do or say in retaliation.

I kept my eyes focused on Bobby and sighed with disgust. Out of my peripheral vision, I noticed teachers and students roaming the hallway. Bobby remained stagnant. He was silent and as motionless as a statue. I bent to retrieve my books, intending to go to my next class. I was done with this nonsense.

I felt a gentle touch on my arm as I started to march away. "Hey, wait..." Bobby murmured in a conciliatory voice.

I froze and looked at him intently. I wanted to walk away. I was supposed to walk away. My intellect advised me to sprint, but his uncharacteristically peaceful tone and tender stroke compelled me to stay put.

"Wow," Bobby began with what appeared to be admiration. He smiled- an actual, genuine, amiable grin, "I had you pegged wrong. Didn't I? I didn't think you had it in you. I would never have thought you were brave enough to talk to me like that." He laughed good-naturedly. "*No one* in school has ever talked to me like that. Jamey was right about you." He paused, "I mean, I'm NOT hitting on you. Jamey claimed you. He's my best friend, and I'm loyal to him. I would never...."

"Claimed me?" I screeched, "*Claimed* me? I am not- let me repeat, I am not a *thing*. I am NOT a possession. Stop objectifying me—both of you. I don't know if it's misogyny or just plain chauvinistic. You are both barbaric and ignorant. Neither of you knows how to treat girls with respect- especially when conversing and..."

Before I could finish my sentence, Jamey appeared. "Hey, what's going on?" he asked boisterously as he jumped on Bobby's back. "I hope you aren't picking on my girl, B," he continued, winking at me.

Bobby shook his head, "Nope," he insisted, "I'm not picking on her; in fact..."

"Well, you *were!*" I interjected.

Bobby nodded, "She's right. I was, but then she...she told me off, man," he started chuckling with good humor and what sounded almost like reverence.

"Oh yeah?" Jamey asked suggestively, "I knew she had spunk!"

"She sure does have spunk!" Bobby agreed. "You were right, by the way," Bobby said without taking his eyes off me.

Jamey didn't look surprised. He nodded, "I knew you'd come around."

Bobby instantly came out of his trance and cleared his throat as he turned towards Jamey, "I mean, I would never. I would never! Jame, you know…you know, I'm not, NOT going to pursue her…I totally get that you…put your stamp on her first." He was stuttering, but there was genuine conviction in his voice.

Jamey jumped off Bobby's back, waved his hand, and snickered affably, "No worries, B. You're my brother, man; I trust you. I know you're loyal. I'm just glad you can see why I like this girl."

I was initially silent because the appropriate words escaped me. I just stared at them, feeling dumbfounded. As I contemplated their words, I rubbed my forehead with frustration. I was almost too astonished to be angry. Bobby and Jamey continued gazing at me as if I was a trophy or a medal.

I finally stamped my foot and exhaled loudly, "I am not a piece of meat!"

They both adamantly shook their heads. They started talking simultaneously, desperately competing to assure me they absolutely, positively knew I was a *good* girl.

"No! No way! We would never suggest that." Jamey said assertively, "You're pure, innocent. You are so freaking refreshing. Not like these other…sluts…" he stopped himself.

I glared at him, "What gives you the right to criticize these other girls?"

Jamey shrugged and raised his eyebrows, "I'm not judging. I just think you're higher class than any other girl at this school."

"She's like I said 'perfect' in a bad way before, but now I mean 'perfect' in a good way. She's like wholesome- but also spicy and sassy." Bobby added.

Jamey smiled as if he was proud of himself for being the first of them to discover this.

I puckered my lips and sighed. The bell rang, but I didn't rush to class. I knew I had three minutes, so I had time to tell them what I thought of them.

"I. Can't. Stand. Either. Of. You!" I said through gritted teeth, "Don't you dare talk about me in the third person!"

Bobby looked confused, "What does that mean?" he asked.

Jamey shrugged.

"Another thing," I yelled, pointing at both of them, "Don't you dare objectify me."

"What does *that* mean?" Jamey asked.

Bobby shrugged.

"You're both just...." I tilted my head, trying to think of the right words, "You're both simpletons. Archaic. This is not 1950!"

Jamey smiled, that devious smile of his, "Honey- we have no idea what you're saying, but I, for one, like it!"

Bobby smiled and nodded, "We better get to class," he said as they started to walk off. Bobby winked at me- in a friendly way, and Jamey waved. "See you later, beautiful." He purred.

"Preferably not!" I shouted.

As they walked away, I heard Jamey say, "She's so freaking smart too. I never thought a girl's brain could be such a turn-on."

I grumbled loudly and stomped off. They were incorrigible. I was insulted and offended. I was not an object, and they had no right to talk about me as if I wasn't standing right in front of them like I was invisible! They were undoubtedly sexist- typical macho alpha males who thought they had the right to critique their female classmates and *claim* any girl they desired. I huffed and puffed as I strode angrily down the hall.

What I couldn't admit even to myself was that I was flattered. I knew that it was wrong. I recognized that it was an inappropriate emotion under the circumstances. They had put me on a pedestal but treated me like I was a prize- a thing rather than a person. Cerebrally, I grasped the fact that I shouldn't feel flattered by their chauvinistic behavior.

So, I shoved those thoughts aside. I ignored them. I lied to myself and everyone else. I was able to push those feelings so far back into my subconscious that they ceased to exist. And- POOF, just like that, they evaporated into thin air. I subliminally decided to pretend because pretending is much easier than facing reality, especially when you're young and more naïve and inexperienced than you realize. When you're a fourteen-year-old girl, you think you have everything under control and feel optimistic that you can handle anything because ignorance is blissful.

Yes, ignorance is bliss when you're fourteen years old and a virgin, literally and in countless other ways.

Chapter Three: Partners

During my first trimester as a freshman, I had health every morning, right after homeroom. It was the worst way to start the day, especially on a Monday. I dreaded it. Health was my least favorite subject because it was utterly useless. I preferred difficult classes, like advanced biology, over Miss Bayer's version of "health." It was apparent to everyone that she had no idea how to put together a curriculum for what was supposed to be a science-related course. She only taught part of the time. She gave us personal assignments that were more psychological in nature- but not deep enough to be interesting or unique. The physical education teachers were the ones who instructed us when it came to anything that was associated with "health," while Miss Bayer sat and twiddled her thumbs, nodding her head in agreement every so often.

About a week after my confrontation with Bobby, I was sitting in health, internally gripping about how utterly bored I felt. As Miss Bayer lectured us about achieving our goals and aspirations, I sighed and rolled my eyes. Every day, I looked around her zany classroom with a disgusted scowl. It was dreadful. The walls were painted the ugliest orange I'd ever seen. If I were writing a description for a catalog or something, I would describe the color as carrot vomit. She told us on the first day of class that she'd requested this color to brighten the room. She had the oddest collection of glass figurines spread out everywhere. They were all statues of cats. She talked incessantly about her four calico feline friends. She even admitted to having birthday parties for them. She didn't notice the sarcastic snickers from my peers, or maybe she didn't realize she was being mocked. She had pictures of herself on display with each of her cats and one of her with all of them surrounding a Christmas tree. Our first assignment was to write about how animal companions were significant parts of our lives. I had no pets, so I didn't know where to begin. My whole essay was bologna! Miss Bayer loved cliched adages. Therefore, several corny motivational posters hung throughout the classroom- like "There is no I in Teamwork" and "You can make your dreams come true." Her ridiculous poster of a kitten looking in the mirror at itself and seeing a reflection of a lion was the ultimate eye roll.

Miss Bayer was what you would call socially awkward and unaware, which made me feel somewhat sorry for her. Consequently, she gave the impression of being insensitive. She certainly wasn't politically correct. She had no sense of subtlety. She meant well, but her ignorance stood in the way of her coming across as anything but abrupt and rude. With that being said, I was not surprised that she introduced a group project the way she did.

"You will be paired up for our next group project!" She enthusiastically announced, "I will choose the partners, as usual." Everyone moaned because we, of course, wanted to pick our friends to partner up with.

"And," Miss Bayer said, coughing as if she was about to say something delicate, "I have already formed partners. You might be surprised by who you're matched with, so I should explain.

Because this is a class of mixed abilities, I paired higher lever students with…" she cleared her throat, trying to think of the right words. "With, well, students who aren't as academically gifted."

Although Miss Bayer's comments weren't alarming because we were already accustomed to her tactlessness, they did elicit a few mumbled complaints.

She then proceeded to read off who each of us was matched with. When she got to my name, she smiled and looked at me almost apologetically, "Jessica, dear, you will be working with Bobby McAllister."

I couldn't believe it! There were so many kids I could have been teamed up with- so many other students in that class who didn't get good grades, and it had to be Bobby, of all people.

I turned to face him, and he grinned back at me.

Later that evening, my family sat around our cedar log dinner table, which my mother had specifically chosen to complement the rustic theme she'd created in our recently refashioned dining room. I was still reeling from the news that I'd be working with Bobby. I complained to my family that Bobby would have to come over this weekend. I told them that Miss Bayer had chosen him to be my partner on a project.

"I can't believe Miss Bayer paired me up with him, ugh!" I complained as I jumped off my spindle chair.

My father took a sip of his red wine and cleared his throat. "Why do you have a problem with this decision?"

I scrunched my eyes in confusion as I strode over to the farmhouse sink to refill my glass of water. "You know who he is, right?"

"Yes, he's one of the best running backs I've ever seen."

I snickered, "He is a good football player, but he's also a bully and…"

My father cut me off, "He has a tough home life. Everyone knows about that loser stepfather of his. What would you expect the poor kid to act like with a mother who lets a man beat up her kid and supplies her husband with contraband prescription drugs?"

I shrugged, not sure how to respond. It would be tough to have such a horrible home life.

"It will be nice for you to be partners. You're both integral members of the football and cheerleading teams, and you might be able to bring out a different side of him. I have spoken to him," my father continued, "and I think there's goodness there. And you, Jessica, would certainly be the one to bring that out in someone."

I nodded, feeling pleased like I always did when I received my father's approval. I did notice my sister Sara covertly roll her eyes. She complained incessantly that I was our father's favorite, although she was careful not to say too much in front of him. My father never indulged Sara; instead of reassuring her, he would scold her when she said such things. He tended to compliment and trust me more than my sisters, but there was a reason for that. I was the only one of the three who never broke the rules.

The next day, before class started, I invited Bobby to my house to work on the project. He said he could come on Sunday afternoon. We had to interview each other about our future aspirations. We were supposed to make up the questions beforehand and then meet to record one another's answers. We both agreed that the project was idiotic.

"What's the deal with Miss Bayer?" Bobby asked.

I laughed without humor, "My mom told me that she was originally an incompetent English teacher. She wasn't fired because she has friends in high places. I guess her cousin is Dr. Shelley Bayer."

Bobby nodded knowingly, "Ohhhh...she's related to the superintendent."

"Yup," I continued, "Apparently, according to what my mom heard, there were so many complaints made against her when she taught language arts that her cousin had no choice but to remove her from her job as an English teacher. Then, this job was created for her."

"It has nothing to do with health!" Bobby exclaimed.

I smirked, "Remember, she told us it's health-related because it has to do with mental health."

Bobby snorted, "Oh yeah," he muttered as we walked into class.

On Sunday, Bobby surprised me by showing up on time, at noon on the dot. He also brought a bottle of soda and a bag of chips with French onion dip.

"That's very impressive," my mother commented as he walked in the door, "Jessica's other friends don't usually bring refreshments when they visit." She winked at me as she ushered Bobby up the stairs.

My mom and I had prepared snacks. We made a cream cheese dip encircled with various fruits. We'd also concocted a veggie, nut, and cheese platter with avocado hummus. My mom planned to serve her famous punch without alcohol. Still, we silently agreed that it would be insensitive to bring out that fancy stuff when Bobby had been polite enough to bring the chips and soda. We didn't want to offend him.

"Would you two like me to order a pizza for lunch?" my mom asked as we walked down the stairs that led to our family room.

I looked at Bobby for confirmation. He smiled and shrugged.

"Sure, thanks, Mom," I said, "We can work in the family room," I told Bobby as I led him down the hall. Although my mother could have been an interior decorator, my house was not nearly as impressive as Jamey's. Yet, Bobby was very complimentary as he followed me around our colonial home.

"Did your mom hire someone to decorate?" he asked as we walked through our living room, where kids were not allowed to loiter. It had a Victorian theme. My mother spent months redoing it the year before. There were Tiffany lamps placed on side tables with tapered legs and an opal-colored settee surrounded by mocha love seats. This was where my mother placed solid gold frames with pictures of our family at Christmas and on a vacation we took to Hawaii the summer before.

"No, she loves decorating. She designed everything herself."

"Wow," Bobby said, whistling, "Your house is so...I don't know how to describe it. It looks like, I don't know, different from Jamey's. Jamey's seems fake, and yours is just so, I don't know- genuine." He replied with a question, unsure if that was the word he was looking for.

Our family room was much less extravagant than the living room, although my mother renovated our house every few years.

"Here we are," I said, jokingly holding my hands out.

Bobby immediately sat on the red and brown checkered country-style couch, grabbed a coffee-colored pillow, and placed it on his stomach. He put his backpack on the floor, leaned forward, and took out the questions he'd come up with for our interview.

"Wow, the walls are so cool," Bobby said as he pointed to the colorful stone murals my mother had designed and sent to be made into wall paintings by her favorite decorator. "I don't know; it's just so cozy in here. I always wanted a fireplace." He glanced at the unlit brick hearth beside an oak television stand with glass doors.

"It's nice that there are pictures of all of you," he waved his hand in the air as he examined the pictures of my sisters and me doing the things we loved. I, of course, posed with my cheerleading uniform. My sister, Sara, was walking on a beam during a gymnastics competition, and Megan wore her favorite clothes- her horseback riding gear.

I couldn't think of anything to say. I felt sad for Bobby. Didn't every family have pictures of their children displayed? "Thanks," I whispered as I opened the bag of chips and dip he'd brought. I put the chips and dip in bowls my mother had casually provided when we made our way to the family room and then poured the soda into glass goblets she'd also handed me.

I sat on the floor next to him after I gave him his food and drink.

I was surprised when he took out his already-made questions. I hadn't expected him to have completed his part of the project.

"Okay, should I go first?" he asked.

"Sure," I chirped, "I hope there's nothing too personal." I was trying to be polite, considering I had to work with him, and I was trying to put our confrontation behind us.

Bobby's questions were simple and straightforward. What did I want to do when I graduated? What occupation was I interested in? Did I plan to get married and have children someday? I tried to answer as best I could, but I had no idea what I wanted in the future. My answers were stunted and rather dodgy. I apologized for not giving him more information.

The most surprising part of the afternoon was Bobby's responses about his future aspirations. He had his whole life and future planned out. I would never have imagined that someone like Bobby had such motivation- goals, and plans for success. He knew what college he wanted to go to, and he planned to play college football, but he didn't think he was good enough to make it further than that. He planned to become a physical education teacher, marry a nice girl someday, and have children. He said he would never be a deadbeat dad like his father and never put his hands on his kids. He didn't elaborate, and I didn't ask him to. He also said that he would always put his kids first and marry someone he knew would be a nurturing and positive role model.

For a second, I wasn't sure if he was trying to impress me with his responses because they were far from what I'd imagined. Yet, I could tell he was sincere. After his interview, I gained a new respect for Bobby McAllister. I realized that people aren't always what they seem.

When we were done eating our pizza, Bobby brought up Jamey. "You know, he really likes you, Jessica. He'd be good to you if you went out with him."

I laughed, "Well, that's not going to happen," I assured him.

"Would you ever give him a chance?"

"Possibly, later on. I don't think my father would even allow me to date now."

"I don't blame him. I would make my daughter wait until she was sixteen before I'd let her date."

I nodded, straight-faced, pretending not to notice the hypocrisy.

"What about in a couple of years?"

I tilted my head, "Who knows? I might consider it if he changed."

"Changed how?" Bobby asked curiously.

"Like became a better person, nicer- not a bully."

Bobby nodded, "I think he'd do that for *you*," he said firmly.

I looked at him with raised eyebrows, a doubtful expression.

Bobby laughed and shook his head, "Jessica, I'm serious. He really likes you. And you're the type of girl a guy would change for. You're a class act."

"Then why did you hate me so much before?"

Bobby pondered the question for a while, "I didn't hate you," he finally admitted, "I just resented you, and to be honest, you were, or at least I thought you were an easy target."

I looked at him and sighed with disapproval.

He nodded, "I know. I know. I'm an asshole sometimes. But I like you now. And Jamey likes you. Even though we can be jerks, we'd never be like that to you."

"Well, that's comforting," I stated semi-sarcastically.

Despite the unspoken words that floated in the air like the proverbial elephant in the room, we let the subject go.

My father paid us a visit while we were working on our project, which didn't surprise me. My dad was obviously very impressed with Jamey Russo and Bobby McAllister. I didn't know if it was because they were such good football players, and he saw the potential for their future. I was sure it also had something to do with the fact that they kissed his butt because he was a member of the athletic department. Even when Bobby was harassing me, I watched him schmooze my dad when he visited football practice.

"It looks like you two are working hard," my father said amiably as he strolled in.

Bobby stood up and shook my dad's hand. "Hi, Mr. Calabresi," he said, "It's nice to see you. Thank you for having me over."

"Anytime," my father said cheerfully as he grabbed a piece of pizza and poured himself a soda. "It was very generous of you to bring soda and chips, Bobby. Most kids your age wouldn't think to do that. My wife is impressed."

He then asked Bobby about football and what he thought would happen in the upcoming game. They chatted about the game for about twenty minutes while I silently zoned out, politely pretending to be interested.

I came to attention when my father asked Bobby about a bruise he noticed on his face. I hadn't seen it before my father mentioned it, and I realized Bobby had been trying to hide it all afternoon by touching his cheek, tilting his head to the side, and pulling his hoodie up. I was surprised my father would bring something like that up, considering it was a sensitive subject. It probably wasn't a football injury. Typically, my father was very appropriate and diplomatic. I also knew he was pragmatic and didn't say or do things accidentally or impulsively.

Bobby tensed up. His face took on a defeated look I'd never seen on him before. He appeared slightly embarrassed. "I...I walked into my stupid door. I guess I can be clumsy sometimes," he stammered.

"You don't seem clumsy on the field," my father said soberly.

Bobby let out a tense laugh, "Yeah, it was a dumb thing to do."

"How's your stepfather doing, by the way?" my father asked unapologetically.

Bobby's mouth formed an O shape, and he looked down with an ashamed expression. I was shocked that my father was humiliating him like this. I was uncertain about what he was trying to accomplish. "Fine, I guess," Bobby mumbled, "I just try to stay out of his way."

"His parole officer is Mike Hendricks, right?"

Bobby nodded, "Yeah, I think that's his name."

"Strangely enough," my father started, "He happens to be a good friend of mine. He owes me a few favors. I've defended more than a few of the men on his caseload. I've helped him out, I guess you could say, on many occasions."

Bobby looked intently at my father- not sure where this was going.

My dad cleared his throat, "Man to man- no offense, Jessica- I have to tell you, Bobby, I have always admired athletes like you. I can relate to you because I played football, and I can see the same passion in you that I had.

One thing Mike Hendricks and I have in common is a dislike of drug addicts- failures with anger issues. Men who abuse the little power they have because they're losers."

Bobby nodded.

"It would be a shame if your stepfather had to go back to jail," my father said with mock concern, "But maybe he won't have to if you stop walking into doors."

"Um, you don't have to," Bobby stuttered, trying to find the right words, "I mean, you don't have to do anything like that." His voice tapered off.

"Of course, I don't have to. I don't *have to* do anything. I *want* to," my father said. He abruptly stood up and threw his empty soda cup into the recycling bin. "Well, I'll leave you two to get back to work." He sounded nonchalant, as if they hadn't just had a very illicit conversation. "It was nice to see you, Bobby. Good luck next game," he said as he walked out the door.

When my father left, there was an uncomfortable silence between Bobby and me- which seemed to last longer than it probably did.

I finally cleared my throat and changed the subject. "So- you really think Jamey would change for me?" I knew this would pique Bobby's interest. His loyalty towards Jamey was unmistakable, and I knew he'd do anything to help him.

Bobby snapped out of his trance, "Yes," he began, "I do. I really do."

I cleared my throat and asked Bobby a question I'd been wondering about since my dad walked in. "Can I ask you something?" I said cautiously.

Bobby looked nervous, "I guess," he replied with uncertainty.

"Why did you pick on me when you knew who my father was? Weren't you afraid I might tell him, and he'd try to retaliate?"

Bobby shook his head, "No. You might be surprised by this, but I'm a pretty good judge of character. I could tell your father wasn't the type to tolerate tattletaling, and it was obvious you looked up to him and wouldn't want to disappoint him. And I could tell you weren't one of those girls who'd run home and cry to daddy. Your father isn't the type of parent who tolerates weakness, right?"

I nodded and sighed, "Yeah, that's true."

"Anyway, let's go back to talking about Jamey," Bobby said. "I know he will ask me about this visit tonight."

I giggled, despite myself, "Truthfully, I don't have anything else to say about Jamey! Let's get back to finishing the interview."

Bobby shrugged and took another slice of pizza. We went back to discussing the project, and the uneasiness my father's visit had created soon dissipated.

We got our grades back about a week later. I got a 100%, and I assumed Bobby did, too, since we worked together. As we were leaving class, I stopped him to ask what grade he had received.

"I got what I usually get in this class. A 75%," Bobby replied casually.

"What?" I asked incredulously, "A 75%; why would you get a grade so low? Did I give a bad interview? Was it my fault?"

Jamey laughed without humor, "Jessica, it's not your fault. Miss Bayer grades without even looking at our papers. Everyone always gets the same grade."

I was confused, "Really?"

Bobby smiled good-naturedly, "You wouldn't know because you get A's in all subjects, and you deserve to, but she gives the football players C's because she thinks we're stupid. She doesn't fail us because the coaches and administration pressure her to ensure we pass so we can stay on the team. Believe it or not, I usually get B's in classes where the teachers grade fairly."

"I can't believe that. It's so biased!"

Bobby laughed, "Well, you got an A, right?"

I nodded.

He gently squeezed my arm, "Don't worry about it; it doesn't matter- as long as I can stay on the team."

He smiled at me as he walked down the hall.

I was livid about Bobby getting a C for two reasons. For one thing, I knew he'd put as much effort into the ridiculous interview as I did. It was downright unfair. Plus, I felt that we were all essentially victimized because the whole class spent hours completing an assignment that had already been pre-graded. I couldn't wait to hear what my father thought about the situation. I was dying to find out his reaction.

He didn't come home from work that night until 6:00. I knew he liked to unwind with a bourbon alone in his den before dinner, so I had to wait before bombarding him with the news.

We were all sitting around the table as my mother placed the last of the dinner dishes, her famous green bean casserole, on a trivet.

I took a sip of iced water and waited for my mom to ask everyone about their day. That was how dinners always started at our house. She typically proceeded in age order, beginning with my youngest sister and ending with me because I was the oldest. When we were done, my father would unravel all the details he cared to share about work. When he was finished, he'd ask my mother if anything interesting had happened that day. Usually, my mother had juicy gossip to dole out.

Megan always shared trivial details that she found curious or exciting. She was nine years old at the time and still rather childish. "Sister Agnes told us that most people go to purgatory when they die," she began as if this was the most fascinating news in the world. "Some kids decided they would try to live like saints so they could go right to Heaven. I'm not sure I believe her. I mean, don't you think kids go to Heaven? We don't do any real serious sins or anything."

Sara, my other sister, who was twelve then, scoffed and rolled her eyes. "I am so sick of the nuns," she said distastefully, "They're just so old-fashioned. They're ridiculous. All they talk about is suffering and sacrifice and purgatory!"

My father wasn't paying much attention to my sisters. He usually zoned out when they discussed mundane things.

"You can't listen to all the things the Sisters say. They mean well, but they're old-fashioned," my mother said, dismissing the topic. She turned toward Sara. "How was your day, honey?"

As usual, Sara grumbled and brought up all the negative things that had happened to her during the day. She was definitely a glass-half-empty type of person. She droned on and on- you'd think everyone was against her, which was ridiculous. She was probably the most popular girl in class, but I think she was a classic "mean girl." She didn't realize it. She had a chip on her shoulder.

My mother just nodded as Sara continued. The rest of us tuned her out, as usual.

When Sara was finally done, my mom asked about my day. I was desperate to reveal the news. I looked at my father as I explained what had happened to Bobby.

"I can't believe Miss Bayer!" I exclaimed. "How could she do that? And I cannot believe she PRE-GRADES; that's not acceptable!"

Neither of my parents seemed surprised or overtly angry by what had happened. My mother didn't seem that interested.

"It doesn't shock me," Megan said, "I bet lots of teachers do that. I don't like teachers. Except for Mrs. Grant. She's the only one who's nice and fun."

"Yeah, she is the only normal one," Sara added, "And why should you care, Jessica- of course, you got an A."

"Watch your tone, Sara," my father admonished, sternly glancing in Sara's direction.

Sara looked down at her dinner plate and fell silent.

"Jessica, you're a good friend," my father said, sounding pleased. "I'm not surprised that you would care about a fellow classmate. It shows your integrity."

I smiled, pleased by my father's compliment but less than thrilled knowing Sara was internally rolling her eyes and gagging.

My father took a bite of his scalloped potatoes, "These are delicious, Anna," he said approvingly. "Your mother is an amazing cook." His eyes swept over my sisters and me; we all nodded in synchronized agreement.

"Thank you, Anthony," my mother replied modestly.

"Anyway, Jessica- don't fret about it. We'll see what we can do," My father gave me a meaningful look and then changed the subject. He started telling my mother about a case he was working on. My sisters and I silently listened as my mother attentively nodded and asked questions pertaining to the case.

Two days later, Bobby came to me in the hall, holding his health project. "Hey, Jessica, do you happen to know anything about this?" he asked, showing me a "C" crossed out with a red marker and an "A" circled next to it. Miss Bayer had written, "Sorry for the confusion. I made an error while grading this paper." She added a big smiley face for emphasis.

"No," I fibbed, "How would I know anything about it?" I raised my eyebrows, feigning surprise, and then grinned at him mischievously. "I have to get to class. See you later," I said as I marched off, not looking back in his direction.

Chapter Four: Friendsgiving

Jamey's mother decided to invite our families over again the week before Thanksgiving for what she referred to as "Friendsgiving." When my mother opened the Facebook invitation and read that term, she nearly choked on her coffee. My Aunt Gina called our house phone at precisely the same time my mother got the invite. They obviously had a good laugh about Ms. Russo's play on words.

They continued the conversation at Sunday brunch, four days before the main event. "Could she possibly get any cornier?" my aunt asked incredulously.

My mother rolled her eyes and chuckled, "Well, it certainly isn't out of character."

"What does Anthony say about it?" Aunt Gina asked with curiosity. As usual, the males and females had separated and were sitting at opposite ends of the carriage house nook that had become our brunch table. We didn't even have to make reservations. The manager of the Jamestown Country Club made sure he saved this table for us. It was a weekly tradition for us to meet the Moretti and Sullivan families for breakfast after church on Sundays. The waiters expected us and always had our table of thirteen ready.

My mother glanced down the table at my father, who was surrounded by Nikki and Jenna's dads and my twin cousins. They all seemed to be deep in conversation, probably discussing football. Although Nikki's brothers were only in third grade, they were already as obsessed with sports as my dad. I guess it ran in the family.

My mother shrugged, "He thinks she's a hot mess, but he's very fond of Jamey," she said, looking knowingly in my direction.

Jenna and Nikki instantly fixed their eyes on me. Clearly, they were inquisitive about my response. I took a long sip of my ice water and pretended not to react.

Immediately following Ms. Russo's initial get-together, two clans became one. My crew from St. Mary's (Jenna, Nikki, Evan, Josh, and I) had become basically joined at the hip with Jamey's gang

(Jamey, Bobby, Mickey, Kelly, and Erin.) We were essentially thrown together- partially because of Jamey's interest in me, Evan's relationship with Nikki, and Mickey's fascination with Jenna.

Josh and Evan became close with Bobby, Jamey, and Mickey, and although Josh got on my nerves, he was Evan's best friend. And Evan was Nikki's love interest. Besides, Jenna and Josh had also always had a "friends with benefits" (according to Jenna, they'd gone to second base, which meant groping over the clothes) type of relationship.

Consequently, we became one of the many cliques at school. It just fell into place- as if it was meant to happen that way. Our circles had started in middle school before we merged. Jenna, Nikki, Josh, Evan, and I had all been close at St. Mary's because of our mutual interests. And Bobby, Jamey, Mickey, Kelly, and Erin had what I assumed was a strong friendship in middle school because of their popularity and sports. Although our family situations were different, we all lived in Jamestown, and for the first time in my life, I started to realize that where you lived made an enormous difference- it almost became part of your identity. And when something is part of your identity, it links you to other people. Therefore, we were all connected for two reasons- we were cheerleaders and football players, and we all lived in a charmed, sheltered, and relatively wealthy community.

This party started out in an identical fashion as the gathering Ms. Russo had thrown over the summer. We arrived via party buses so everyone could drink without fear of driving while intoxicated. My mom and aunt weren't reluctant to go to the party this time- they were actually looking forward to it. They knew they would have plenty to gossip about afterward, and Ms. Russo's first party had proven to be a success in terms of entertainment.

The night started with hors d'oeuvres served by waiters dressed in black and white uniforms. The women had their hair tied back in severe ponytails, and the men were all clean-shaven. After about an hour of small talk and appetizers, we were all made to sit in Jamey's trendy yet elegant dining room.

We were treated to a delicious pre-Thanksgiving homemade meal of turkey, mashed potatoes, jellied sauce, and roasted carrots- ALL of it was made at home, but not by Ms. Russo. There was a polite conversation among the adults during dinner. Ms. Russo already had too much wine and was talking an octave higher than necessary. She had a date this time- a man who looked to be about ten years her junior. He didn't talk much, but when he did, his thick Swedish accent made it almost impossible for him to be understood. Whenever either Hans or Ms. Russo spoke, I noticed Jamey shake his head or roll his eyes with disdain.

Bobby's stepfather had not come to Ms. Russo's summer get-together, but he made an appearance at this festivity. He was dressed a little too casually with a plaid shirt, dockers, and a badly needed haircut. Mrs. Smith, Bobby's mother, seemed like a meek woman; she was quiet most of the night and clung to her husband, Wyatt as if she was fearful he might say or do something inappropriate. Wyatt didn't drink, but it was clear by his red, dilated pupils that he was high. I probably wouldn't have noticed if I didn't know his history.

Before we sat down to dinner, Wyatt took Bobby by the arm. He led him over to where my father was standing with Jenna's father, Gerry Sullivan. They were laughing about something conspiratorially. They'd been best friends for years and law partners. They were inseparable, the same way Jenna and I were.

"Hey there, Anthony," Wyatt said in a booming voice, "I hear you are following my stepson's football career."

My father nodded, looking Wyatt directly in the eyes with contempt, "Yes, he's quite talented."

Wyatt massaged Bobby's shoulders in a chummy way, "Yes, yes, he is. I'm proud of him." Bobby looked even more uncomfortable than he did when my dad brought the situation up while we were working on our health project. He had his hands in his pockets; he kept shuffling his feet and was looking directly at the floor.

My father glared at Wyatt. He slanted his eyes as if he was considering his words and debating how to respond. Finally, he said, "You should be," with what could only be construed as a veiled threat.

"Always good to see you, Bobby," my father said in a considerably different tone than he used with Bobby's stepfather. He clapped him on the shoulder, "Great job in Friday night's game."

"Thank you, Mr. Calabresi," Bobby said, stuttering.

About a second later, Jamey came over and linked arms with Bobby. He frowned at Wyatt, and after exchanging pleasantries with my dad and Gerry, he led Bobby away with what was obviously an excuse to separate him from his stepfather.

When Bobby and Jamey left, my father turned his back to Wyatt Smith and continued his conversation with Gerry.

After dinner, we were again ushered to different parts of Ms. Russo's McMansion. The teenagers inevitably ended up in Jamey's elaborate, fully equipped rec room. I had butterflies in my stomach as I anticipated how the evening would unfold. I was positive that Jamey would suggest some form of waywardness.

Once we were all settled and sitting comfortably around Jamey's sectional couch, we debated what we should do. The boys contemplated playing video games, and the girls suggested watching a movie. But Jamey, of course, had a different idea.

"How about Spin the Bottle?" he asked deviously, looking in my direction. I sighed and turned away with disdain. I was really hoping someone else would decline. I didn't want to be the only one to refuse, although I desperately did not want to play a kissing game.

"Sure!" Erin and Kelly chirped in unison.

"Sounds fun," Josh declared.

Nikki and Evan exchanged glances. They both shrugged good-naturedly.

Bobby nodded and waved his palm in the air as if to say he was game.

Jenna looked at me out of the corner of her eye; she had an enquiring expression on her face. Before she responded, she wanted to ensure I was okay with this.

"Jessica? Jenna?" Jamey asked impatiently, considering we were the only two in the rec room who hadn't answered.

I swallowed soundly and tilted my head in a slight nod. "Okay, I'll play," I murmured.

Jamey raised his eyebrows and puckered his lips. He looked from me to Jenna.

"Whatever," Jenna said, sounding weary.

Jamey took out a small glass bottle from under the bar. It looked like it could easily be manipulated, which didn't surprise me.

"So, how about the boys do the spinning," Jamey suggested.

No one opposed, so Jamey continued, "Alright...battttter up!" He scanned the crowd, looking for a contender.

"I'll go first," Mickey announced as he took the bottle from Jamey's hands.

Jamey shrugged, "Well, I'm going last," he kept his eyes on me as he spoke.

Mickey attempted to smile seductively at Jenna, but he completely missed the mark. She sighed audibly and gave him a massive eye roll. He made a show of swirling the bottle around in the air as if it were a lasso before putting it on the wooden floor and spinning it. He watched it intently and beamed when it settled on Jenna. She groaned and slumped her shoulders. "You did that on purpose!" she exclaimed, "That's cheating."

"Prove it," Mickey said with a chuckle in his voice.

"Just get it over with!" Jenna grumbled irritably. Mickey had made it clear that he harbored a crush on Jenna for months, so it was apparent he purposely spun the bottle in her direction.

"I get to kiss the hottest girl in the room," Mickey sang as he sauntered toward Jenna, swinging his hips, "No offense, ladies- you are all hot, but Jenna's my personal favorite."

Mickey nudged his face towards Jenna; she allowed him a quick peck and then forcibly pushed him away when he went in for more.

Evan bashfully raised his arm in the air as if he were offering to answer a question in class. "I'll go next," he said in a timid tone. He maneuvered the bottle so it would land on Nikki, and they shared a sweet kiss while everyone giggled either enthusiastically (the girls) or sarcastically (the boys).

"I guess it's my turn," Josh announced in his typical cocky fashion. He pushed his fingers through his sandy blonde crew cut before spinning the bottle. It landed directly in between Erin and Kelly. Both girls' eyes widened eagerly.

"Does he have to pick?" Erin inquired as she twirled her fingers through her long buttery blonde hair.

Josh mockingly put his hands on his cheeks and shook his head, "There's no way I can pick between these two hotties. Can't I just kiss them both?"

"Fine," Jamey bellowed as Josh teasingly bobbed his head back and forth between Erin and Kelly.

Josh then played a seductive game of "eeny meeny miny moe" before choosing whom to kiss first. When he said, "Moe," his finger was pointed in Erin's direction, so he moseyed over to her, put his arms around her shoulders, and drew her in for a sensual kiss.

After that, he turned towards Kelly, who was batting her long eyelashes and smiling coquettishly. Josh put his finger on her oval-shaped chin and then theatrically dipped her as he moved in for an extended and much-reciprocated kiss.

Bobby went next. At first, I wasn't sure who he was aiming for. I saw him glance at Erin, who happened to be standing right next to me before he spun the bottle. Erin raised her eyebrows as she chewed on her bottom lip. It was apparent by the way they erotically scanned one another that they had kissed before.

Except…he accidentally rotated the bottle in such a way that it rested on me. Everyone was mute for what felt like an eternity. I could literally hear myself breathing. Our collective thoughts seemed audible. "Don't panic," we were all silently screaming.

Finally, Jamey flapped his hands and shouted, "Well, it's only a game." He thrust Bobby towards me, giving him permission to kiss me.

Bobby smiled awkwardly and strode towards me. He chuckled and placed his lips on my cheek when he reached me. We all laughed with amusement and relief. Jamey pushed Bobby good-naturedly as he held his hand out, waiting for Bobby to release the glass container. He winked at me and grinned as he placed it on the ground and turned it…literally- TURNED it in my direction.

Jenna was the only one who had the nerve to mutter a complaint. "This is the lamest game of Spin the Bottle ever."

I felt my heartbeat quicken as Jamey fixed his gaze on me. He sauntered in my direction as if he were striding down a runway. He reminded me of a ravenous tiger about to devour an innocent bunny rabbit. I had known this was going to happen, but I still felt highly anxious, and the room seemed to spin as he came closer.

When he was standing right in front of me, he whispered, "I get to be your first kiss."

Then he pressed his warm, full lips on mine and gently kissed me. Our lips connected for at least five seconds. He didn't try to lunge his tongue down my throat or aggressively swap saliva. For an instant, I actually got lost in the aesthetic sensation. It would have been nice and sweet if we didn't have an audience.

I was immediately brought back to reality when Jamey pulled away from me. He threw his arms in the air and cheered like he'd just scored a touchdown, and everyone applauded along with him, except me. I put on my best game face, smiled weakly, and pretended not to feel humiliated.

After we played Spin the Bottle, Jamey predictably asked if we wanted to drink shots of liquor, although he decided to mix it up; this time, he offered us vodka. I wasn't interested in drinking, but I didn't want to be the only one to say no. Although I was generally a strong, confident person, I sometimes felt compelled to give in to peer pressure. I decided I'd only have one slug. Like before, I was sure my parents wouldn't notice because they were drinking, and we had a limo to drive us home.

A few minutes after I gulped down a swig of vodka, I had to admit, I felt looser. Nonetheless, I wasn't going to do a second one because I didn't want to get sick. When Jamey passed the bottle back around, I pretended I had to use the restroom.

When I came back, everyone had decided we were going outside for a game of touch football. Ironically, although I'd spent years cheering at football games, I didn't quite understand the game's complexities. I was reluctant to play because I was competitive and didn't want to engage in an activity that I wasn't good at. Despite that, I once again concurred because everyone else did. I stood by passively as Jamey and Josh chose teams and positions for everyone.

"Jessica's quick; she should be quarterback," Josh suggested.

Jamey looked at me to see if I was in agreement. "Sure," I mumbled.

Jenna, Kelly, Mickey, and I were put on Jamey's team. The other team consisted of Josh, Bobby, Erin, Nikki, and Evan.

Jenna played center and hiked me the ball. I easily caught it and sprinted past Erin and Nikki. The only player on defense I really had to worry about was Bobby. Yet, I was able to maneuver my way around him, most likely because he cheated on my behalf. I tripped and slipped on the wet grass just as I was about to enter what we'd deemed as the end zone. I don't remember exactly what happened after that. I was a little in shock. I'd twisted my ankle when I fell, and my head hit the ground.

When I looked up, everyone was surrounding me. The pain I'd initially felt as my ankle rotated dissipated and was replaced with tremendous embarrassment. I forgot I'd hurt myself for a few minutes as I tried to get my bearings. My friends were all simultaneously asking if I was okay. Jamey's face was so close to mine that I had to shift backward. I was so startled that I couldn't speak.

"I'll help you up," Jamey insisted. He took my arm and tried to get me to my feet. I allowed him to guide me but gasped when I put pressure on my inflamed ankle.

Jamey noticed my pained reaction and attempted to pick me up. "I'll carry you," he said as he put his arms around my waist. He started to lift me, but I protested.

"I'm fine," I asserted, ignoring the fact that my ankle was so tender I had to fight back tears.

Everyone continued to gawk at me with concern. "I am fine!" I said, a little too defensively.

"Are you dizzy?" Jamey inquired.

I shook my head.

"What about your ankle?"

"It's nothing," I lied.

"Are you sure, Jessica?" Josh asked sarcastically, "Remember in seventh grade when you sprained your wrist playing kickball, and you insisted you were okay."

"I am fine!" I demanded, angry but also afraid. I would rather suffer a broken ankle or concussion than go to the doctor. I had a severe phobia of doctors from the time I was a young child.

"Just make sure she doesn't have a concussion," Bobby said.

"Let me look at your eyes," Jamey insisted.

I reluctantly gazed at him. "Are you dizzy? Do you feel nauseous? Is your vision blurry?"

"No, no, and no!" I insisted, "Just leave me alone and keep playing. I said I was fine three times!"

Jenna and Nikki took Jamey's arm and led him away from me. They continued playing the game until our parents told us it was time to leave.

Although my ankle was beyond sore, I refused to limp as we walked to the limo.

"Are you sure you're okay?" Jamey asked, taking my arm and pulling me aside.

"YES!" I said through gritted teeth.

Jamey threw his hands up in surrender. He winked at me, "See you soon, beautiful. I hope you enjoyed our kiss."

I rolled my eyes and proceeded to walk as normally as I possibly could to the awaiting limo.

I woke up the next day in extreme discomfort. I struggled for breath when I looked at my ankle; it was purple and three times its normal size. I panicked, not only because of the pain but mainly because of my fear of doctors. There was no way I could hide this injury from my parents, and my dad would definitely force me to see a physician. My mother was more sympathetic about my phobia than my father. As Bobby had said, my father wasn't very tolerant of weakness.

My fear of doctors started when I was in fourth grade. I fell off the monkey bars at school. The pain was instantaneous and severe. I lay on the wood chips, crying hysterically. I wasn't even embarrassed as kids and teachers encircled me, curious and concerned about my well-being. Two teachers on recess duty had to carry me to the nurse. When my mom came to pick me up, the nurse advised her to immediately take me to the hospital. I couldn't think straight as we drove to the nearest hospital and hurried into the emergency room.

Because of my uncontrollable sobbing and the warped position my arm had taken after the fall, I was quickly ushered into an examination room. A nurse gave me pain medication, which initially did help. A middle-aged female physician's assistant examined me, and X-rays were taken. It felt like hours before a young male doctor who looked like a teenager finally entered the room. I actually felt a sense of relief when he said my arm was broken and he was going to wrap it up to make it more comfortable. Unfortunately, the hospital staff was bustling that day, and he was an inexperienced intern, fresh out of medical school.

He was out of his element, and I was in excruciating pain because he mishandled my arm. My mother actually pushed him away from me. She insisted he get another doctor because I was crying uncontrollably and screaming.

Although a veteran doctor swathed my arm correctly, it still hurt tremendously for days because of the trauma caused by the first physician. I took medicine that didn't touch the sharp, continuous pain. My father threatened to sue the hospital, but they were extremely apologetic, and the unseasoned doctor was severely reprimanded. My mother talked my father out of a lawsuit. Needless to say, it was a traumatic experience, and I developed an intense fear of doctors after that.

Anyway, there was no way for me to avoid telling my parents that I'd injured myself. They were sitting around our kitchen island on leg stools the next day when I came hobbling in.

"What's wrong, honey?" my mother asked with alarm.

"I don't think it's that big of a deal. We were playing flag football yesterday, and I fell. It didn't hurt at the time, but I woke up with a swollen ankle ." I explained offhandedly.

"Let's see," my father said as my mother led me to a stool to take the weight off.

My mother gasped when she saw my ankle, "Oh my goodness, Jessica!" she exclaimed, "That looks awful."

My father frowned, "Jessica, how could you have let this go? You must have known you injured yourself. You could have a broken ankle."

I shrugged, "No, no. I think it's just a little sprain."

"No, it is not," my father insisted, "You need to get over this fear of doctors. It's foolish."

His words stung; I hated the rare times my father criticized me.

"You're going to the doctor," he demanded, shaking his head with disappointment, "You should have told us about this last night."

"But, it really didn't hurt that…"

"Stop talking," my father ordered, "I know why you didn't tell us; you were avoiding getting it looked at. That was irresponsible of you."

I felt my eyes well up with tears, "I'm sorry," I whispered.

"Anthony…" my mother said pleadingly, "She's already hurt. You don't have to scold her."

My father nodded once, acknowledging my mother's words with a grave look.

"I'll take her to the walk-in clinic." My mother stated, diffusing the tension with her gentle tone.

I felt my heart drop. I immediately panicked, but I kept my mouth shut, not wanting to further agitate my father.

The situation didn't turn out to be as bad as I'd anticipated. I did fracture my ankle, but no one hurt me during the examination. The only distressing part of the incident was the panic attack I suffered while waiting to see the doctor. And although he got it over with quickly, I couldn't help but feel ashamed that I'd disappointed my father.

At least once a month, the females in my family had a girls' night out with the women in Nikki and Jenna's families. This usually involved pedicures, dinner, shopping, and gossip. There were seven of us in all. My mom, my sisters, Aunt Gina, Nikki, Jenna, her mom- Rachel, and her little sister- Ashlynn.

A few days after I'd fractured my ankle, we had all planned to have a weeknight out. There was a new movie playing that we were all dying to see. Although it was a school night, our moms wanted us to preview the film the night it premiered. My dad never complained about our girls' nights. He would order out and spend some much-needed alone time. He would laughingly say that it was nice to spend time with himself because he was usually surrounded by girls.

Although I was yearning to see the adaptation of a popular young adult book that had just been made into a movie, I decided to bow out. I had a huge test in calculus the next day, and I didn't feel completely confident that I'd be able to ace it. Nikki was in my class, but she was naturally brighter than me in mathematics. She didn't have to study as much as I did. Also, Nikki wasn't as driven as I was. Plus, her parents didn't require her to get straight A's like my dad.

My friends tried to pressure me into going out, but I was determined to pass the test with flying colors, and I really wanted to get a better grade than Josh. He and I had always been competitive. He was very smug when he scored even one point higher than me.

My mom dropped me off at home after ensuring I wanted to miss the girls' evening to study.

"Of course she does," Sara mumbled with disdain. She wouldn't have commented if my father had been there, but she knew my mother always ignored our sibling rivalry.

When I walked into the house, I heard voices coming from my father's study. I thought it was odd because he'd insisted he was looking forward to some alone time while "his girls" went out. I curiously walked towards the study; the door was slightly ajar, so it wasn't like I was snooping. As I got closer to the door, I recognized the voices of the younger boys my father was talking to. They were Jamey and Bobby's.

"Hi," I replied, approaching the door.

All three males looked startled. They were standing up, and my father had his car keys in hand. Jamey and Bobby had their coats on. "I thought you were going to see a movie," my father said, in a "trying to sound casual" tone of voice.

"I have to study. I have a big test in math tomorrow." My father already knew that math was my least favorite and weakest subject.

"Oh…well, I was just going to drive the boys home. We were talking about the game this Friday night." My father explained.

"Yeah," Jamey said, "Since your dad is such a huge contributor to the athletic department, and...."

"Well, he knows so much about football. We wanted to run some things by him." Bobby added.

I nodded.

"See you tomorrow at school," Jamey said, smiling at me as he rushed out the door.

"Yep, see you," Bobby chimed in.

My father kissed me on my forehead as he followed the boys out of his study, "We'll order Chinese when I get back, honey," he replied, "I'll be less than a half hour."

"Okay," I said in a quiet voice. The whole situation was quite strange. I was eager to ask my father about it, but I didn't want him to get the impression I was questioning him.

As I watched the three of them leave, I decided not to inquire more about their suspicious meeting. It would only irritate my father, and I'd never get the actual truth out of Bobby and Jamey. I was sure their loyalty would be to my father in a situation like this.

I didn't actually put it together at the time, but after that night, Jamey and Bobby's conduct became unusual. They started to act over-protective of me. It was as if they felt they had the right to be inquisitive about things that were none of their business. I always chalked it up to the fact that Jamey had a crush on me and acted as if he'd *claimed* me. And I thought Bobby's solicitousness resulted from his loyalty towards Jamey.

When I think back, I realize there was definitely more to it. They were possibly asked or given permission to safeguard me. At first, it was awkward and uncomfortable, especially when I wanted to start dating. Eventually, like everything else involving Jamey Russo, their possessive behavior became natural and commonplace.

Chapter Five: The Interrogation

When I started high school, I was definitely very inexperienced with boys. And for a few months, I saw no reason to change that. Aside from Jamey, other guys had shown interest in me, but I didn't find any of them appealing. My friends were all much more captivated with flirting and dating than I was. I felt as if the freshmen girls were like "fresh meat" in a cage filled with tigers. The seniors were the only boys who didn't pay much attention to us younger girls. It was looked down upon for a seventeen or eighteen-year-old boy to stoop to the level of asking out a "little girl." But we were up for grabs when it came to other freshmen, sophomores, and juniors.

My four closest girlfriends and I were all considered attractive, but Jenna was definitely the one who stood out in the crowd. Most boys found her pouty lips, platinum blonde hair, and deep-set violet eyes very alluring. She was the only one of us who'd gone out with a couple of upperclassmen. Nothing had lasted, and that wasn't because Jenna had been used or dumped- the breakups (if you could call them that) were mutual. And she made it known that she was only interested in older boys. None of the boys Jenna dated gossiped about her. She was astute about whom she went out with- she hated the kiss-and-tell types and made it known that she frowned upon that kind of immature behavior.

On the other hand, Erin immediately gained a reputation for being promiscuous. She was the type of girl who didn't get emotionally attached when she dated and wasn't afraid to experiment with any guy she found enticing. She had probably already had five "boyfriends" by the second trimester.

The ten of us who had formed our friend group early on and always sat together at lunch. One day, while Erin was flirting with a group of sophomores before making her way over to our usual table in the back of the lunchroom, Josh made a snide comment about her. "It's only December, and she's been through half the guys in school."

Mickey, Bobby, and Jamey chuckled good-naturedly. The rest of us sat quietly, ignoring Josh's rude, unnecessary comment.

"To each his...or *her* own," Bobby remarked.

Jamey nodded, "She's hot- she developed early."

Mickey raised his eyebrows and nodded, "She's a natural flirt," he added. "Super sexy, but not as steamy as my girl." He looked at Jenna as he took a bite of a French fry. She was sitting across from him.

"I am NOT and never will be your girl," Jenna promised him.

Interestingly, Erin was the one who always ended relationships. Because she was pretty- she resembled a Barbie doll, and popular, no one ever spread nasty rumors about her. However, I still thought many guys objectified her.

Nikki and Evan were an item, and they were constantly together, so she was never approached by the opposite sex.

Kelly was shy yet coquettish. Many boys were drawn to her cornflower blue eyes and auburn hair, which hung loosely around her shoulders in waves. I know she and Josh flirted; from what Kelly told us, they'd done some over-the-clothes stuff.

I still secretly harbored a major crush on Jamey, although I wouldn't admit it. I wasn't ready. He continued to shamelessly flirt with me. I told him I wanted to be friends, and he'd said with a wink, "That's okay for the time being."

Before the incident in my dad's den, I'd been approached by a few boys and had politely turned them down. I was a little taken aback when Craig Houser, a boy in my literature class, told me he would love to ask me on a date, but he knew I was already taken by Jamey Russo. I assured him that was not the case, but he didn't believe me.

After I saw Jamey and Bobby talking to my dad that November night, they immediately started acting semi-possessive. There were two occasions when they overstepped their bounds, and I wasn't afraid to call them out on it, but it didn't make a difference. They were not scared away by my demands for them to leave me alone.

About a week after seeing Jamey and Bobby leaving my father's study, I was engaged in an innocuous conversation with a boy from my chemistry class, Justin Bussey. We were discussing an upcoming assignment.

"Do you want to study together?" Justin asked as he walked with me to my locker, "I mean, we have the same study hall in the seventh period."

"Sure," I said, smiling. I was one of the only freshmen in chemistry and could certainly use a study partner.

"Alright, sounds good," Justin replied as he helped me lift a book out of my locker, "I'll see you then."

He almost knocked into Jamey and Bobby as he started walking to his next class. Justin laughed, acting as if it was a coincidence, "Sorry," he said, sliding past them.

"Who is that?" Jamey asked inquisitively as he put his arm on top of my locker. Bobby stood next to Jamey with a quizzical look on his face.

"I've never seen him before," Bobby replied nonchalantly.

"Who is he?" Jamey demanded to know.

"Do you want to know who he is?" I asked.

Jamey did not detect the sarcasm in my voice, "Yeah!"

"He is NONE OF YOUR BUSINESS, that's who!" I exclaimed, pushing past them, "Leave me alone!"

No matter what I said or did, Jamey and Bobby didn't seem to care that I was annoyed by their over-protectiveness. They refused to cease their inquisitions.

Jamey even went so far as to make a rude comment to the president of the freshmen Student Council. Jake Farrow was a very intelligent, handsome, ambitious, talented soccer player who was the Student Council president our freshmen year. Kelly was vice president, I was secretary, Josh was treasurer, and Madeline Irene was the historian. We had all run solid campaigns and beat out other freshmen. Like St. Mary's, teachers and administrators were the deciding votes for the Student Council because the school administrators didn't want it to be a popularity contest, like homecoming or Prom court.

Anyway, Kelly had been teasing me since September about Jake's interest in me. I thought he was nice, but I wasn't romantically interested in him like I, unfortunately, was with Jamey.

One day, we were discussing an upcoming holiday party in the auditorium before an assembly. Jamey and Bobby walked up to us and interrupted our conversation. The rest of our friends were sitting in the bleachers, where we usually sat during assemblies, towards the top of the designated underclassmen area.

"Ready?" Jamey asked.

"I'll be there in a second," I replied through gritted teeth.

"We'll wait," Jamey said, eyeing Jake in an unfriendly way.

I didn't want to make a scene, and I was flustered. Jake laughed while Jamey and Bobby crossed their arms and stood on either side of me. "We can talk after," he said somewhat nervously.

"Yeah, *after*," Jamey said in a snotty tone.

When Jake walked away, Bobby asked if anything was happening between Jake and me.

"No," I said, sighing heavily, "But you two really need to mind your own business."

"Not going to happen," Jamey said in all seriousness as we started walking up the bleachers to meet our friends.

I shook my head and rolled my eyes. I knew I had to do something to stop their domineering behavior; I just wasn't sure what it was I should do.

It wasn't until Liam Flannery, a junior who was the second-string varsity quarterback, showed interest in me that I actually felt attracted to someone other than Jamey. Jenna became acquainted with Liam because she was friendly with a lot of his peers. The male upperclassmen were fond of Jenna- not so much the females. Apparently, Liam asked Jenna if Jamey and I were an item. Jenna told him that although Jamey was obsessed with me, his feelings were not reciprocated.

I knew Liam would be approaching me because Jenna had given me advance notice. I was indecisive about the possibility of going out with Liam. I did find him very attractive. He had sharp, defined features- an aquiline nose, square jawline, and deep-set cheekbones. He was handsome in a sophisticated way. The thing that really stood out about him was his striking blue eyes- they were the color of the sky on a cloudless day. I felt my stomach flutter when Jenna told me he'd expressed interest in me. Yet, I was still nervous about boys in general at that point. I was inexperienced and, to be frank, *terrified*.

The first thing Jenna mentioned when she informed me that Liam wanted to ask me out was Jamey's probable reaction. She laughed surreptitiously as she wiped a piece of hair from her eyes. "Jamey will be pissed," she announced as if I didn't already know that, "But there's absolutely *nothing* he can do about it."

"I know," I agreed, "If I went out with him, Jamey would be powerless to stop me."

"He sure as hell would be. Liam has a lot of friends, and they're older and stronger than Jamey." Jenna went on, "He wouldn't be able to bully someone like Liam."

I smiled at the thought after all the harassment I'd recently endured from Jamey and Bobby.

I didn't have to wait long before Liam approached me. The day after my conversation with Jenna, the two of us were standing at my locker discussing our weekend plans when Liam came casually strolling over.

"Hi, I'm Liam," he said confidently as he held out his hand.

"I'm Jessica," I answered shyly. I offered my hand to him, and instead of shaking it, he embraced it with both of his.

Jenna winked at Liam as he drawled, "Yeah, I know who you are."

"Well, I will see you guys later," Jenna purred as she slithered away.

"Listen, I know we both have to get to class, so I'll cut to the chase," Liam began, "I was wondering if you would like to go out with me sometime."

I surprised myself by nodding, "I think I would like that," I replied, forcing myself to look into his sapphire eyes.

"Jenna gave me your digits. Can I call or text you?"

I nodded, biting my lip.

"Talk to you soon," he crooned as he backed away, facing me with a mischievous smirk.

I laughed nervously and giggled. I felt a grin twitching at my lips until I noticed Jamey standing across the hall, his hands crisscrossed across his chest. He glared at Liam's back and then turned to me, shaking his head in disapproval.

I threw my hands in the air and mouthed, "Mind your own business."

Jamey pursed his lips and shook his head, "No," he mouthed back as he slammed his locker shut.

Later that night, my family was sitting around our dining room table eating dinner. My mother had finished asking all of us about our day. It was a typical supper conversation, nothing out of the ordinary. My dad didn't have much going on at work, my mom didn't have any interesting gossip, and my sisters had already shared their typical nonsense. There was finally a lull in the conversation, so I decided now was the time to ask the "dating" question.

"Um, I was wondering," I began half-heartedly, "If I'm allowed to um...you know, date?"

Everyone's heads immediately turned toward me. My parents and sisters were all looking at me intently, waiting for me to continue.

Finally, Megan wrinkled up her nose and innocently proclaimed, "I thought you were dating Jamey."

Sara nodded with a serious expression on her face. "Me too."

My mom and dad continued to stare at me as if they anticipated that I would agree with my sisters.

"Do you want permission to officially 'date' Jamey?" My dad asked affably.

I shook my head vigorously, "No. No, not Jamey." I stated, "Someone else asked me out."

"Well, what's going on with Jamey?" My mom quizzically probed, widening her eyes.

"We're just friends."

My sisters went back to shoveling food in their mouths, obviously becoming bored with the conversation while my parents swapped curious looks.

"Who?" My dad asked before putting a forkful of steak in his mouth.

"Liam Flannery," I said, "You know, the..."

"I know who he is," My father interrupted, "Second string quarterback..." he didn't sound impressed.

"What year is he? How do you know him? Did he actually ask you out?" my mother shot questions at me.

"He's a junior," I began, "He knows Jenna. He told her he liked me."

"No," My father stated definitively, "You can't date him. What do you think a junior who will likely be the quarterback next year would ultimately be interested in? I don't think he's looking for a relationship with a nice girl."

"Anthony, not now." My mother warned; she glanced at my sisters and continued, "I will talk with Jessica about this later, okay?"

My mother rarely used that tone with my father or anybody, for that matter. Still, when she did, anyone who knew her understood that she meant business. Although my mother never raised her voice, she had a passive-aggressive way of getting what she wanted.

My father nodded as he took a sip of red wine, "Yes, I think that's a good idea."

We were all quiet for another few seconds as I tried to digest the meaning behind my father's words. Was he saying Liam would only be interested in using me? Was he implying that Liam didn't think I was a nice girl?

My mom saw the wheels turning, so she placed her hand over mine, "Not to worry, Jessica. I'll explain later." She winked at me conspiratorially.

My father sighed and took another slow gulp of wine, holding his glass out as my mom got up to refill it. "I just really don't understand the whole Jamey situation; he's a nice boy. If you wanted to date someone your own age, I'd consider it."

"Let's drop the subject," My mother said, sounding slightly exasperated. She looked at my father pointedly, "I already said I would talk to Jessica about all this later, *privately.*"

My sisters were staring at my parents with widened eyes; they weren't sure what was going on. My parents rarely fought; things were usually incredibly civil between them. This was unusual.

My father very quickly acquiesced, "Yes, honey. You're right. Let's change topics." His tone was lighter and pleasant.

"Did you girls realize the next episode of 'The Talent' starts tonight?" My mother asked enthusiastically, referring to a reality show she and my sisters watched without fail.

My mom and sisters began talking animatedly about the show as my father and I exchanged an awkward glance.

Later that night, around 8:30, I was sitting at the desk in my bedroom reading <u>The Scarlet Letter</u> for English class. I became so engrossed in the book that I had forgotten about my mom's pledge to continue our conversation in private. I was a bit startled when she came to my door, which was half open, and peeked in.

"Can I talk to you, honey?" she asked gently.

I placed my floral printed bookmark in the novel. "Sure," I replied. Her presence stirred within me a mixture of inconvenience at being interrupted and relief because I realized I'd been subconsciously disturbed by my father's earlier words, and I was hoping she would clarify his insinuation.

"Great," she cooed pleasantly as she took a seat on the edge of my violet swivel chair. I turned around in my seat and crossed my legs. My mom pursed her lips and scanned the room before saying anything. She rested her eyes on the poster I had of Audrey Hepburn from <u>Breakfast at Tiffany's</u>. "You know she was a good friend of Nonna Jessica? Did I ever tell you that?"

I looked back at the poster from my favorite movie and shook my head. My mother's grandmother and great-grandmother were both celebrated actresses. My mom rarely discussed her famous family members with outsiders. When she talked about them with us, she acted indifferent. Her parents had also been well-known. My grandmother, Sophia Ryder, was a famous designer. My grandfather, Troy Taylor, had been the CEO of a production company. Although my mother had a wonderful and functional childhood, she shied away from fame. She changed the subject when her legendary relatives were mentioned. She communicated with her family members often, and we visited at least two or three times a year, but my mother made sure we were incognito whenever we took a trip to Los Angeles or New York City.

My mother sighed and put her fingers through the fairy lights hanging from my lavender wall. My whole room was adorned in shades of purple. Even though my mother designed most of the house, she allowed my sisters and me to be the interior decorators of our bedrooms.

"Honey, um...I hope you don't think I'm being intrusive or nosy. I just thought it might be a nice time to continue our ongoing conversation about boys and such."

My mother had always been very open with my sisters and me about sexuality. She believed the information, dispersed at the proper time, was necessary. She always said clichéd things like, "You know, girls, knowledge is power."

I chewed on my cheek and nodded. "Okay," I said uncertainly.

I wasn't sure what there was to talk about. I already knew about sex.

"I don't want to sound like I'm an expert..." she began, sounding modest.

"But you are," I said, cutting her off in a jovial way. Everyone knew my mother had an amazing understanding of men and relationships. It had become a joke amongst her close friends. However, she rarely acknowledged that all her female kinfolk were intelligent regarding men. She'd inherited their wisdom and worldliness.

My mother laughed, breaking the moderate amount of tension in the room.

"I know we've discussed your coming of age and all the particulars about intercourse, et cetera." Her words drifted off. I waited because I was uncertain about where this was going.

"I am just going to come out with it, and I really hope you aren't upset with me...but is it okay with you if I just tell you what I know?"

I nodded; my mother was safe. I wasn't as attached to her as my sisters, especially Sara- everyone claimed I was a "daddy's girl." But I knew my mother was incapable of humiliating or hurting me. She had a way of discussing the most sensitive topics in a patient, gentle way.

"I know that you are attracted to Jamey Russo." She paused, waiting for me to object. When I remained silent, she continued, "With that being said, I also recognize something is holding you back from becoming involved with him. Your dad likes Jamey, but you are already aware of that. That's not because he's fooled by him. We both know Jamey has that alpha male, aggressive side to his personality. It's just that it's obvious he has really fallen for you." She placed her hands on her temples and cleared her throat, "I can tell these things," she alleged absently.

She abruptly stopped talking and looked around my room, possibly thinking about what to say next. She stood up and smiled as she traced her fingers along the numerous cheerleading pictures and trophies displayed on my mantle.

"Anyway," she continued, "When it comes to Jamey, I want you to follow your intuition. You'll know when and if it's right. Okay?"

I nodded.

"As for this Liam boy," my mother said, sounding a bit grim, "The truth is that boys his age, athletes who, well, I'm assuming he's good-looking, or you wouldn't be interested."

I widened my eyes and tipped my head to the side, concurring that this was accurate.

"Well, boys like that, when it comes to young girls in high school, they are only after one thing. They crave another notch on their belt. They don't settle down. Boys are immature and unemotional when they're that age. They don't think with their heads. If this junior asks out a freshman, the truth is he is almost certainly interested in a short-term *physical* relationship. "

I took in what my mother said and frowned. I knew she was right. Liam could have his pick of any girl in school; he could probably date most of the junior or the senior young ladies. It wasn't like he would be interested in a monogamous relationship with a freshman. What was the sense of dating someone who most likely wanted to use you just so he could brag about it? When I thought about the situation realistically, I felt appalled.

"Yeah, you're right. I see what you mean," I said. "I don't know. I thought he was cute, but I really don't care about going out with him. I'll just tell him I'm not allowed to date yet. I mean, I would never, *never*, NEVER let someone use me. I don't want to have anything to do with a boy unless I'm in a relationship. I will never let a boy make a fool out of me. I won't let anyone touch me- nothing beyond kissing until I'm in a steady relationship with a boy who respects me."

My mother raised her eyebrows and looked at me with a mixture of curiosity and amusement.

I realized I'd been droning on, but I was being sincere. "I'm being honest, you know?"

My mother walked over and patted me on the head, "I know you are, honey. And I'm glad you have that kind of respect for yourself. I only hope your sisters feel the same as they get older."

She went to open the door but turned back before leaving, "Just let me know if you ever need to talk; promise me that?"

I smiled widely. "Of course," I replied.

I met my mom's eyes, and we shared a look of understanding before she said, "Goodnight," and left me alone with Hester Prynne.

Liam texted me that night, but I didn't respond. I was reluctant to put anything in writing. I was afraid Liam would show people, and they might mock me for not being allowed to do what most other girls my age took for granted. I decided it would be better to tell him in person so I could phrase it in a way that wouldn't sound immature or offensive.

The next day, I didn't see Liam until last period when I had study hall. My heart skipped a beat when he caught my eye outside the library. I was nervous about how he would react to my news. He waved and called, "Hold up, Miss Jessica."

I stopped at the door and held it open as he strolled over to me. He put his hand on the glass entryway and waved his hand in the air, indicating he was planning to follow me inside. I smiled shyly and led him to a quiet corner in the reference section, away from prying eyes or ears.

He didn't hesitate before asking, "So, did you ask your parents if I could take you out? I texted you last night."

I smiled disappointedly, "I wanted to talk in person," I explained, "I did ask my parents last night." I looked down and shuffled my feet, timidly wavering.

"And?"

"Sorry," I began, "My dad is over-protective and somewhat old-fashioned. He basically said I wasn't allowed to date yet. He thinks I'm too young."

I looked at him imploringly, hoping he wouldn't embarrass me.

He actually put his hand on my shoulder and nodded once, "That's what I was afraid of," Liam began in earnest, "I know who your dad is; he's pretty badass."

I just shrugged contritely.

"It's not your fault, pretty girl," Liam said good-naturedly. "I'll get over it…someday." He playfully put his hand over his heart and grinned. "Well, maybe in the future?" he asked.

I nodded, "Yeah, definitely. I'd like that." There was a slight pause in the conversation.

"Well, I need to reserve a table," I said, looking around the room, realizing the bell was about to ring, and I needed to find a quiet spot to work. I looked at my books and discovered I'd left my geometry textbook in my locker. "Oh no, I forgot my math book," I stated, eyeing a perfect table in a remote corner of the library.

"Why don't I walk with you to get it?" Liam asked. "I have gym this period, so I'm not in a hurry. You know how the phys. ed. teachers are when it comes to football players."

I laughed knowingly. Everyone knew the jocks didn't even have to participate in gym class, "Sure."

Liam gave me a genuine smile as we walked down the hall. "Would it be okay for us to be friends?" he inquired.

"That would be nice," I said, stopping at my locker, which, of course, happened to be adjacent to Jamey's. Jamey was standing with Mickey and Josh as he gathered books for his next class.

"Well, this is me," I joked, leaning against my locker. I saw Jamey staring at me, along with his friends, out of the corner of my eye.

Liam took my hand in his, brought it to his lips, and kissed it lightly, "See you later, sweetheart," he sang as he sauntered away.

Jamey stared at him as he passed by, but Liam again didn't notice.

I glanced at Jamey as Liam walked away. He scowled at me and shook his head disapprovingly.

Later that afternoon, while I was at cheerleading practice, I noticed my dad, Gerry Sullivan, and some of the other members of the athletic department walking through the football field's sidelines with the principal, vice principal, and head coach. It wasn't the first time I'd seen my dad on the field, so it didn't surprise me to spot him. His attention was focused on what the other men were discussing, but he smiled and waved in my direction when our eyes met.

When the group stopped to watch the junior varsity football players practice, I saw Jamey gesture to my dad. My father acknowledged him with a tip of his chin. I watched quizzically as Jamey stopped doing push-ups and whispered something to one of the coaches, who nodded his approval. Then Jamey jogged over to where my father was standing. My dad stepped aside from the other men and briefly conversed with Jamey. I noticed that Jamey had his back to me. Still, my father glanced in my direction while Jamey was talking, and when I met his eyes for the second time that afternoon, he tried to act nonchalant. He beamed in a way that was too friendly and a little fake. I found the whole thing peculiar and somewhat alarming, but I decided it wouldn't be worth asking my father or Jamey about because even if they were discussing me, neither of them would admit to it.

On Saturday morning, I woke up to the sound of my phone buzzing. I yawned and reached on my nightstand for my cell. There were about ten messages that I'd slept through from Kelly, Erin, Nikki, and Jenna. Apparently, I was the last one to wake up that morning, and it was only 9:00. It was about a week after Thanksgiving, almost time for Christmas, and everyone was feeling that holiday excitement. Kelly suggested we take the opportunity to go to the mall. We could Christmas shop and then see a movie. She proposed that afterward, we have a sleepover at her house and binge-watch a new show we were all eagerly anticipating, which was streaming that evening.

Everyone had agreed that we were overdue for a girls' day. It would be fun and felt almost necessary; it would be stress-free without the boys. Even Nikki remarked that she could use a break from Evan and all their togetherness. Kelly said she was staying at her mom's house. Her parents had joint custody. She was a very happy only child whose parents were both professionals. Her mom was a college professor, and her dad was a veterinarian. They had an amicable divorce and actually remained friends. They had no issues jointly attending parties and events for Kelly. It was relaxing to spend time at both of Kelly's houses because her parents let us basically do whatever we wanted. They were very lenient when it came to parenting.

Kelly's dad had once told my father that he believed human children needed fewer rules and supervision than animals because they were naturally independent. I overheard my father relaying the conversation to my mother and laughing about how he thought that idea was preposterous.

I could see the three dots on the screen of my phone, indicating that someone was in the middle of a text. My friends were in the midst of figuring out the specifics when I finally joined the conversation. "I'm in. Sounds fun. What time? Where exactly are we meeting?" Kelly wrote back that we should meet in mid-town Rosevalley at the Rosevalley Mall in a few hours.

I lazily got out of bed and sauntered into the kitchen. My father and sisters were already sitting around the dining room table. My mother was making pancakes, bacon, hard-boiled eggs, and toast. My mom always made big meals. She loved to cook and was a very talented chef. We were required to eat with the family during the week, but my parents were more relaxed about weekend meals.

My mother had a plate with a stack of blueberry pancakes in one hand and plain pancakes with butter in the other hand. "Who would like pancakes?" she asked, walking over to the table. She placed both dishes on trivets and pulled a spatula from a steel pipe strung along the wall with hooks holding pans and utensils in ready reach.

"Why don't you sit down, Anna?" my father suggested. "We can get our own food. You don't have to wait on us."

It seemed like they went through this same routine every Saturday morning. My mom always insisted that she wanted to serve us. She enjoyed it. My father would inevitably shrug as if he'd done his part in at least making the suggestion that she not act as cook and waitress.

I poured myself a cup of freshly squeezed orange juice and sat down at my usual spot, in between my sister Sara and my father. Both my sisters insisted on sitting next to my mother when they were younger, so we'd established this seating pattern many years ago, which never changed.

"So, what's the plan for today?" my dad asked, making conversation.

"I have to be at the barn at 12:00," Megan said, "I get to ride Ponyboy today."

Sara yawned and took a bite of her bacon, "I don't have to be at gymnastics until 12:30," she chimed in.

"Do you need me to drive one of the girls to her lesson?" my dad inquired. "Isn't that kind of cutting it close?"

My mom shook her head. "No, I already have it arranged. I'll drop Megan off early so she can help groom the horse before her lesson, and then I'll take Sara to the studio."

My dad nodded.

"I might need a ride to the mall," I said casually.

"The mall?" my father questioned. "When was the last time you went to the mall?"

I shrugged, "I guess over the summer to get school clothes."

"Why would you suddenly decide to go now?"

Everyone fell silent, stunned by my father's questions, which sounded surprisingly accusatory.

I cleared my throat and shrugged. "Um, Kelly suggested we all go Christmas shopping," I explained.

"Who?" my father continued. "Kelly suggested *who* go shopping?"

I was perplexed about why my father was interrogating me. I didn't respond for a moment as I looked around the table at my mom and sisters' surprised reactions.

"I asked you a question," my father stated authoritatively as he placed his fork on the table.

"Me, Kelly, obviously, and Nikki and Jenna," I answered in a small voice.

My father raised his eyebrows and widened his eyes. "Just girls?" he asked suspiciously.

"Yes," I began with reluctance, "Kelly thought it would be nice to have a girls' day, and then she asked if we wanted to sleep at her house?"

My father tapped his fingers on the table and stared at the ceiling.

"That sounds fine to me," my mother finally chimed in.

"Really?" my father asked in an almost sardonic voice, a tone he very rarely used when addressing my mother.

"Anthony, what is this about?" It was obvious by my mother's defensive tone that she did not appreciate the way my father had answered her.

My father gave my mother an apologetic half-smile. "Sorry, Anna. That was not meant to be directed at you."

My mother continued to eye him suspiciously.

My father turned towards me, and the irritated expression returned, "I just think it's..." he stopped as he cleared his throat, searching for the right word. It seems very *convenient* that you and your *girl*friends decide to take a trip to the mall without any of the boys a couple of days after you ask if you're allowed to date."

My mother's shoulders slumped. I could tell she wasn't in agreement with my father, but she usually allowed him to take the lead regarding rules and discipline. He was definitely the disciplinarian in the family. My mother was more like an older sister when it came to child-rearing.

My mouth had dropped open; I was shocked and hurt, and I didn't know how to respond.

My father stood up and placed his hands on his hips. "You know what?" he began, "I would like to see your cell phone, Jessica.

As a matter of fact, I would like to see ALL of your cell phones. I should be doing cell phone checks regularly, as a matter of fact."

We all sat frozen in our chairs. We had never been required to hand over our phones unless one of my sisters was being punished.

My father's mouth was set in a grim line. "You heard me," he was talking in a calm yet cross voice, "All of you, get up and get them- bring me your phones immediately. That means *now!*"

My mother shook her head, sighed audibly, and walked over to the coffee machine as we hurriedly got up from the table to retrieve our phones.

About an hour later, after my father had made a production of going through each of our phones, he was satisfied that I was telling the truth. There was some joking about my nine and twelve-year-old sisters' texts, which contained a lot of comments about how mean and unfair he was. He seemed to take it as a compliment and laughed good-naturedly about it. My sisters remained silent as he read through their immature, childish texts to friends.

My father decided to look through my sister Megan's phone first and read aloud some of the commentaries between her and her friends, mainly from the barn; she was an avid horseback rider and spent most of her free time at the stable where she took lessons. Megan's texts were all about horses, games she played at school with friends, and how she thought it was unfair that my father wouldn't let her spend more time with horses and less time on homework.

He read through Sara's texts next. They were basically complaints about all her friends, peers, and teachers, how mean my father was, and how she couldn't do anything because of him. She constantly complained about having to study because she'd get in trouble if she didn't get all A's.

By the time my father got to my phone, he was rather amused by my sisters' innocuous yet biting comments.

He looked at the texts between Jenna and me about Liam. They proved that I had indeed told Liam I was not allowed to date and had turned him down. Then he went through the group text Kelly had sent this morning, which proved that I was meeting my girlfriends at the mall and wasn't trying to sneak and get away with anything.

When he was done, he handed me my phone back. I was distraught at that point. I was hurt, angry, and anxious. My chest was tight, and I felt like I couldn't get enough air.

"Can I go now?" Sara asked, holding her phone. "Can I get ready for gymnastics? I'm not in trouble for saying you're mean, right?"

My father smirked and shook his head, "No, actually reading through you and Megan's texts proves to me that I'm doing my job as a parent. You know, by not allowing you to do poorly in school or go to parties without adult supervision."

Sara didn't react.

Megan was less acerbic than Sara. Therefore, she felt apologetic about all the grumbling she'd done. "Sorry, Dad," she replied softly, "I didn't mean it, really. It's just that when you're a kid, you're supposed to complain about your parents. And I really didn't have anything to say about Mom. You know she isn't strict like you."

My parents exchanged amused glances, and my father nodded and waved his hand in the air, communicating that he wasn't bothered by her comments in the least.

Neither of my sisters had been what my father would consider *disrespectful*. They were criticizing him for being the way he intended to be, so obviously, he didn't take it as an insult that they thought he was a strict, demanding parent.

"Come on, girls," my mother said to Megan and Sara, "get ready for horse and gymnastics. We have to leave in a little while. Anthony, will you take Jessica to the mall?" my mom asked as she ushered my sisters out of the kitchen.

"I don't even want to go anymore," I cried, standing up suddenly. I couldn't stop the tears in my eyes from falling down my cheeks.

My mom shooed my sisters out of the room and walked over to me. She ran her hand gently through my hair and then patted my shoulder. "It's okay, Jessica. Go have fun with your friends. Your father was just being over-protective."

My father shrugged unrepentantly, "Maybe I overreacted, but it's better for me as your father to be safe than sorry."

"Well, Anthony, you *did* overreact," my mother reproached.

"And it's not fair," I said, choking back sobs. "I have never done anything to make you not trust me. I've never disobeyed you."

I swallowed soundly as my dad stood up and poured himself a cup of coffee.

"Why don't you get ready, Anna?" my father suggested, "This is between Jessica and me."

My mom massaged my back and kissed my cheek. "It's okay, honey," she said before leaving the room.

"Don't you think you're being melodramatic?" my father asked in a level tone.

"No," I insisted. "You really hurt my feelings. I mean, I have always been honest and obedient. I didn't deserve for you to accuse me…" I put my face in my hands and wept. I had never talked to my father like that, but I couldn't control my emotions.

He came towards me and embraced me. He put his arms around my shoulders and patted my back. After a few seconds, he pulled away. "Okay, Jessica. You had your release. I understand that was what you needed, but that's enough. You need to pull yourself together now."

I took a deep breath and tugged at my short ponytail. I wiped my eyes with a tissue my father handed me.

"Listen, I know that you are a good girl. You have never given me any trouble," he began in a kind voice, "but everyone makes mistakes. No one is immune to impulse decisions, especially at your age."

I rubbed my fingers across my lips, unsure of how to respond.

"No one is perfect, Jessica," he continued. "I know you are pretty close to it, like your mother, but *no one* can always do the right thing. And it's my job as a parent to make sure I stay on top of things. Yes, I'm the mean one, and your mom isn't strict like I am. That's just who we are as people. We didn't choose those roles. They just naturally developed. But that sometimes puts me in a position where I must be the bad guy. My job is to protect you, not to be your friend."

I nodded and sighed, figuring that was the closest thing to an apology I'd get from my father.

"Now, why don't you get ready, and I'll take you to the mall."

I was about to leave the kitchen when my father gently took hold of my arm. "Jessica, you really don't have to take everything so personally. You shouldn't be so sensitive."

"Okay," I whispered.

As I walked to my room, I couldn't help thinking that my father didn't have to be so *in*sensitive. However, I obviously would never say those words out loud. It was undeniably in my best interest to keep that thought to myself.

Chapter Six: Consequences

To be honest, I liked many things about Jamey Russo besides his appearance. He was not only fun-loving but also a great deal of fun. In addition, he was outgoing, playful, and brave, and his solicitousness was sweet at times. He was formidable on the football field because he not only had innate talent but also worked harder than anybody else. I admired his tenacity. And Jamey Russo was hilarious. He could make us laugh so hard at times that our lunch table captured the attention of everyone within our vicinity.

However, Jamey possessed one trait that I loathed. To put it bluntly, he had a mean streak. He could be cruel and callous to people he perceived as weak or a threat to him somehow. He had a tendency to bully kids who were vulnerable or eccentric. Jamey was constantly trying to convince me to go out with him. He wanted to date exclusively. I refused. I wasn't ready to have a serious boyfriend, but more importantly, I disapproved of his mean-spiritedness and was candid about it.

We had the same conversation on several occasions, but he insisted that I was exaggerating. When he asked me for examples, I was unable to give him anything concrete. He would downplay certain incidences or flat-out lie and claim they never happened. The strange thing was he didn't really have a reputation for being a bully. He was identified as a popular, good-looking football player who was tough and robust. His "bullying" was seen by almost everyone as innocent entertainment. He was simply a jokester who liked to clown around.

One afternoon in early February, I was almost punished because of Jamey's cruel behavior. It was not surprising because that was how things were at Lomonoco Creek. The athletes, especially the football players, were given permission to engage in unruly behavior because they were considered more important than the rest of us.

When it happened, I was walking down one of the newly painted blue and gold checkered hallways with Kelly. Truth be told, if I hadn't been with Kelly, the incident might never have occurred. Kelly was one of those popular, pretty girls who was genuinely an empathetic and compassionate person. This, of course, made her a great friend. She was the one we all went to when we needed a shoulder to cry on. She was a good listener and always had comforting advice. Moreover, she went out of her way to be kind to her friends and everyone. Literally...*everyone*.

Kelly and I were both members of the freshman Student Council, and we were discussing an upcoming event. One of the art teachers, Miss Crinkle, was our advisor. When we were conferring about what we should do for February, I explained that The Sunshine Committee, which I was also a part of, was already doing romantic-type things. I suggested we do something helpful for society rather than sell flowers or deliver lollipops. Miss Crinkle thought it would be an excellent idea for us to do loving things for the community. We'd brainstormed and planned a bunch of humanitarian events. Then, the officers were each put in charge of one event to be worked on with the representatives.

Kelly and Josh were responsible for making bags for kids undergoing chemotherapy. Madeline Irene insisted on participating in a project that had to do with animals; therefore, she was organizing a campaign to persuade people to adopt pets from various shelters. I came up with an idea to support widows in nursing homes. I thought it might help women dealing with the loss of their husbands to receive care packages as Valentine's gifts. When I presented the concept, Jake Farrow requested that he work on it with me. Kelly, Josh, Madeline, and even Miss Crinkle snickered inconspicuously when Jake made the appeal because they all knew he had a crush on me. Kelly and Josh were always teasing me about it. Unfortunately, they would sometimes mention it in front of Jamey. His jaw would immediately tighten, and he would visibly flinch whenever he heard Jake's name. He didn't say much, but his irritation was evident by his facial expressions.

The hallway was somewhat busy as Kelly and I walked to first period. I was engrossed in our conversation, so I would not have noticed Caleb Collins if it hadn't been for Kelly.

"What's Caleb doing on the floor?" Kelly asked as she abruptly stopped walking and pointed to Caleb Collins, an undersized, scrawny kid. He had a reputation as a misfit, a weirdo with a highly annoying nasally voice. Furthermore, he was regrettably very good at drawing attention to himself by *constantly* raising his hand in class, challenging other students' opinions, and even questioning teachers about academics.

Although we weren't fond of Caleb, Kelly and I both became concerned when we noticed his current predicament. He was practically lying on the ground, surrounded by other students, who were either completely ignoring him or watching him with disgust; some were even stepping over him. He was laid out on the blue and gold tiled floor. There were books, pens, pencils, a calculator, a ruler, and a bunch of other items that I assumed belonged to Caleb strewn all over the hallway.

Kelly and I rushed over. "Caleb, what happened?" she asked with concern.

"Nothing. My books…um, they fell."

"We'll help," Kelly said, looking at me. I nodded.

"Caleb, Kelly, and I will help get your stuff together. You should probably get off the floor." I crinkled my eyebrows as I watched him stretch his arms and legs all over the floor as if he were playing a twister game.

"No, no," he insisted, "I've got it."

"Caleb, we don't mind helping!" I insisted.

Kelly looked at me and sighed. "Let's try to salvage the small things. The books will be easier to find." I bent over and started picking up highlighters, pencils, and pens.

"What are you doing?"

I jumped with alarm when I heard a furious male voice behind me. I stood up to find Jamey standing over me, scowling with Mickey in tow.

"I'm help…I'm helping."

"No!" Jamey said aggressively, "you're not. Get off the ground, Jessica."

I was initially confused. "I'm not…on the ground," I stuttered.

Jamey sucked in his cheeks and took hold of my arm. "Stop picking his crap up."

Kelly held out her hand, and I gave her the items I'd retrieved. She raised her eyebrows and gave Jamey a look of disapproval. "Did you do this?" she asked.

"No, I didn't do anything," Jamey said, smirking.

Caleb came rushing over. He looked at Jamey with a terrified expression on his lean face. "He didn't do it. I did. I dropped it all by accident."

We were all quiet for a second before Kelly turned towards Jamey and shook her head. "Yeah, right."

Mickey was silently sneering. He thought the whole thing was comical.

Caleb went back to picking his stuff up. Kelly continued to help him as the bell for the first period rang.

Jamey was staring at me, waiting for me to respond. He knew I disapproved of this kind of behavior. "Did you do this?" I finally said.

"I already said I didn't," Jamey said as he and Mickey exchanged an amused glance, "Caleb, did I have anything to do with this?"

Caleb stopped in his tracks. He'd recovered all his materials at that point. He was standing with a massive pile of books and other school supplies stacked up on top. He forcefully shook his head. "No, no! He didn't do it. It was all my fault."

I saw the fear on Caleb's face as he started to skip away. "Well, I have to get to class. Thanks for helping, Kelly and Jessica."

At this point, Kelly, Mickey, Jamey, and I were the only ones left in the hallway. None of us were concerned about being late for class.

Jamey shrugged, "I told you. Come on. Let's go. We're already late."

Suddenly, a rather foreign emotion overcame me. I had experienced it before, but not often. It was rage. I felt incensed that Jamey kept doing things like this. I began to undergo what seemed like an out-of-body experience because my fury was so overwhelming.

"You are such a jerk," I shouted at Jamey. "How would you like it if someone did that to you? Why do you enjoy being a bully? What makes you think you have the right?"

Jamey was standing in front of me with an unconcerned, almost entertained expression on his face, and it was evident he was trying not to laugh.

Before I could stop myself, I impulsively grabbed a stack of books from the pile in Jamey's hands and threw them across the hall.

Mickey doubled over; he was laughing hysterically.

Kelly pursed her lips and giggled.

Jamey grinned good-naturedly as he drawled, "Now, why'd you have to do that?"

Bobby, Mickey, Kelly, and I were alone in the hallway, or so we thought. I was still seething to the point that I couldn't see clearly. I felt dizzy, and I couldn't seem to catch my breath.

Kelly suddenly cleared her throat, "Oh no!" she began nervously, through gritted teeth, "here comes Mr. Vega."

We all turned to look in the direction in which Kelly was staring with a worried expression. When I spotted Mr. Vega, one of the physical education teachers at Lomonco Creek, my heart started to pound so quickly that I thought I might pass out. A lump formed in my throat as Mr. Vega strode over to us with his hands on his hips and a stern look directed at me.

I noticed Mickey and Jamey simultaneously shrug. Everyone knew that Mr. Vega favored the football players. He was the head phys. ed. teacher and created an environment among all the phys. ed. staff that the jocks were allowed to skip gym even if it wasn't football season. He gave special treatment to all male athletes, but the football players were his absolute favorites- especially players like Jamey, who won games for the team.

"All of you, follow me." he ordered, bending his finger in a "come hither" gesture and then pointing to the principal's office.

"Can I get my books first?" Jamey asked casually.

"No. Actually, Jamey, Miss Calabresi can get them for you!"

Jamey shook his head vehemently. "No way!" he stated, "She's NOT getting my books." His jaw was tight, and his hands were curled up in fists by his sides.

Mr. Vega nodded. He wouldn't dare defy Jamey. The rumor was that he was a closeted, misogynistic homosexual. He could be downright cruel to females and boys he thought were cowardly. Yet he practically revered muscular, courageous athletes like Jamey.

Jamey started picking his books up as Mr. Vega walked in the direction of the office. "Girls, follow me. Mickey, you can help with Jamey's books."

Mr. Vega probably assumed that Jamey was the type of boy who wouldn't allow a girl to pick his books up because he would see it as lowering himself. In actuality, I knew Jamey enough to understand that he wouldn't let Mr. Vega or anyone else humiliate me like that.

Kelly sighed and gave me a nervous glance as we followed Mr. Vega.

Mr. Vega swung the wooden door to the office open, not even bothering to hold it for Kelly and me. Kelly caught it before it smashed her in the face.

The administrative assistants stared wearily at us as Mr. Vega barged in like a bull in a china shop. "We need to see Mr. Blume immediately," he announced with authority.

Miss Lee, the youngest and newest secretary, nodded quickly and got up to knock on Mr. Blume's door. It was obvious she was intimidated by Mr. Vega.

"Miss Bachmann, what do you have to add to this situation?" Mr. Vega asked Kelly.

Kelly silently stared at the ground. I knew she wouldn't tell on me. She had too much integrity. She would rather take the fall or get herself in trouble. She was willing to risk anything in order to protect a friend- partially because she knew both her mom and dad would support her. I admittedly envied Kelly at times. Her parents made her life so easy and carefree. She was also so nice; it wasn't an act. She was genuinely a really good person. She went out of her way to be kind to even the most unpopular kids in school.

Mr. Vega cleared his throat with disgust. "You're of no use to me. Go to class." He waved his hand at her dismissively.

Kelly looked at me apologetically and did as she was told.

By the time Mickey and Jamey came into the office, Mr. Blume was ready to see us. Mr. Vega decided to also dismiss Mickey, realizing his testimony wasn't necessary. He had seen what had happened. He didn't need the spectators.

Mr. Vega pointed at Mrs. Noel, the red-headed secretary sitting closest to the door. "Write Mickey a pass to class, Karen," he commanded. "I actually don't need a witness. I saw what happened."

Mickey raised his eyebrows and shrugged as Mrs. Noel handed him a note excusing him for his tardiness. "Thanks for helping Jamey with his books," Mr. Vega said to Mickey as he ushered Jamey and me into Mr. Blume's expansive office.

When we were all inside, Mr. Vega closed the door soundly. "You won't believe what I just witnessed," he began, sounding outraged.

Mr. Blume rubbed his temples and sighed deeply. He was sitting behind his executive U-shaped desk; he looked not only uncomfortable but also very confused.

"Hi, Jessica," he said politely, "and how is your dad doing?"

Mr. Vega snorted. "He certainly wouldn't be happy with his daughter here, not after what I saw."

Mr. Blume raised his eyebrows in surprise. "That's hard to believe. Jessica is a stellar student. I can't imagine that she would do anything to change that."

"It was all a misunderstanding," Jamey began, "it wasn't Jessica's fault. Really"

"Well, then..." Mr. Blume began, standing up, about to give us permission to terminate the situation.

"Oh no, that is not the case. Jamey is being a gentleman. He is covering for Miss Jessica Calabresi here. If her father knew about what she did, he would be mortified."

Mr. Blume cleared his throat. "Well, as you know, Jessica's dad and I are good friends. We played football together in high school."

Mr. Vega nodded empathetically, "Yes, I know. And I'm sure you'll agree, once you hear about what this young lady did, that her father will not be a happy camper when he finds out about it."

I felt my heart sink as I looked down at the floor. My eyes automatically filled with tears at the thought of Mr. Vega telling my father about the temper tantrum he'd witnessed. My father would be not only mortified but also highly disappointed and incensed.

"Well, Mr. Vega, why don't you tell me what she did," Mr. Blume requested impatiently.

"Jamey, why don't you tell Mr. Blume what happened?"

"Nothing," Jamey asserted, "It was nothing! Can we just let it go?

Mr. Vega looked angry and startled.

"Well, that's okay with me," Mr. Blume said, sounding relieved.

"No, no way!" Mr. Vega sounded as if he might explode. "This young *lady,*" he used the term ironically, "threw Mr. Russo's books across the hall."

"That's only because..." I began in a contrite voice, but Mr. Vega cut me off.

"It really doesn't matter why. The fact is I saw you do it. And you at least need to apologize."

"Okay, I would really like to resolve this unfortunate situation," Mr. Blume began. "Jessica, you are a wonderful student. This was obviously an unusual occurrence. I'm sure nothing like this will ever happen again."

Mr. Vega cleared his throat and let out a dry, derisive laugh, "This little girl needs a consequence."

Mr. Blume pursed his lips and glared at Mr. Vega with a warning look. "I...will decide," he said through gritted teeth, "I, me, *the principal,* will be the one making the decisions here."

Mr. Vega and Mr. Blume looked fiercely at one another; it was a showdown. Jamey and I exchanged a quizzical glance before Mr. Vega finally conceded by lifting his head up and exhaling.

"Jessica, dear," Mr. Blume began in a pleasant tone, "we can let this situation go. We will NOT have to inform your father about it." He stopped and scrutinized Mr. Vega, who didn't flinch at this point. "Why don't you just apologize to Jamey, and we'll call it a day."

I was about to apologize to Jamey and be done with this whole situation, but Jamey decided he didn't want an apology. He wanted something else. I wasn't surprised by his request. As I listened to him speak, I thought back to the many conversations that foreshadowed his bizarre plea. Every situation had been subtle. Nothing I thought could be used against me. But who could have predicted that something like this would happen? This state of affairs just conveniently worked in Jamey's favor.

This was Jamey's chance to intervene in my completely platonic relationship with Jake Farrow, the president of the freshman Student Council. Jake liked me, and he made it obvious. He openly flirted with me. However, Jake flirted in a sweet, subtle way, not like Jamey. Jake was confident but not arrogant. He was athletic, but not in the traditional "manly" way that some jocks thought was superior. I liked Jake. He was a great guy. A friend. I didn't have feelings for him. I almost wished I did because he was intelligent, open-minded, and driven. He wasn't unattractive, just not my type. I didn't know what my type was- since Jamey was the lone person I'd sexually fantasized about. The only other boy I'd ever found appealing was Liam. Ultimately, I just knew that I could never be attracted to Jake.

Nevertheless, my insistence that there was absolutely nothing going on between Jake and me wasn't good enough for

Jamey. His jaw would inevitably tighten, and he'd angrily purse his lips whenever Jake's name was mentioned- usually at lunch or other social gatherings with our mutual friends. He would mumble something indecipherable but most likely unkind, making Mickey and Bobby laugh. Josh and Kelly always defended him. I would roll my eyes and refuse to discuss Jake beyond stating and restating that we were *just friends*.

The whole situation was perpetuated by Josh. He and Kelly noticed how Jake stared at me and always suggested we work together on projects in Student Council. In my opinion, Josh was passive-aggressive and would purposely make remarks because that's just the way Josh had always been. He would snidely make comments, which were purposeful to antagonize Jamey, and then innocently say, "Oh, but he's a nice guy. He's completely harmless."

Kelly would agree, look at me knowingly, and change the subject.

When Mr. Blume suggested that I apologize, Jamey had a strange reaction. He shook his head. "No. No. I don't want that." He sounded as if he thought a request for forgiveness would somehow offend him.

We all turned to him expectantly, waiting for him to continue.

"I don't want an apology, but I'd like something else instead."

I narrowed my eyes, knowing before he went on that, I would probably prefer to express regret than do whatever he was going to propose.

Therefore, when Jamey indicated what he would like in place of an apology, I wasn't surprised in the least. It was very convenient for him that things had worked out the way they did.

Jamey chewed on his finger as he told Mr. Vega and Mr. Blume what he would like from me in exchange for contrition. Although his request wasn't a surprise, I was utterly shocked when Mr. Blume went along with it. Mr. Vega would have agreed to anything- but Mr. Blume, on the other hand? I guess I had given him more credit.

"You know," Jamey began, looking away from me- staring directly at Mr. Vega because he knew he would agree with whatever he came up with, "football season is over, and baseball season doesn't start for a while, so I don't have much going on."

We were all quiet, waiting for him to carry on.

"I was thinking a lot lately about doing something...you know, something, um...good for people, I guess."

Mr. Vega forcefully nodded his head, urging him to continue.

"I know Jessica and I might have our little disagreements," he said, laughing good-naturedly, "but I admire the human...what's it called again, human help stuff...I can't remember the word......"

"Humanitarian?" Mr. Blume asked.

I suddenly knew where this was going, and I sighed with irritation.

Mr. Vega looked at me with something beyond anger, as if I had some nerve disrespecting a football player who had defended me.

"Do you have a problem, Miss Calabresi? I should hope not, considering what I just witnessed in the hallway?"

"No," I said, shaking my head.

"I wasn't finished," Mr. Vega shouted at me.

I noticed a look pass over Jamey's face. He furrowed his brows and stiffened. He didn't like the way Mr. Vega was speaking to me. He started to protest, but Mr. Blume stepped in first.

"Charlie...Mr. Vega, please let the boy continue!" Mr. Blume said through gritted teeth, "I...Me- *the principal* will lead this discussion." His voice had a warning tone to it.

"Jamey, get on with it," Mr. Blume encouraged a little impatiently.

"Well, I know I'm not on the Student Council. Jessica has been working with the other members on special projects for February. I know Farrow...Jake is the president, and he and Jessica have been working on making some kind of packages. Well, I mean, I was thinking Jake probably has a lot of other things he could be doing as president. So, I would love to step in and help Jessica- I mean replace Jake, to help them all out."

Mr. Blume nodded, "I don't see why that would be a problem. I know Miss Crinkle has complained that not enough people volunteer to help, and Jamey is right. I mean, Jake is the president. His role should be less hands-on. He can take on more of a leadership role if Jamey is available to help Jessica with her part in the February Student Council humanitarian activities."

"So, instead of an apology, you want to work with Jessica on this...this project?" Mr. Vega asked, sounding confused.

Jamey smirked and nodded. "Yeah, I'd like to basically take Jake's place, you know, to help him out."

At that point, Mr. Vega seemed to catch on. He leered at me, knowing this was a con. He liked the idea because he knew Jamey was being devious, and he'd probably figured out that Jamey thought Jake was trying to work his way into our relationship.

"Sounds good to me," Mr. Vega agreed, "and don't worry, I'll be glad to let Miss Crinkle know about it."

"Thank you." Mr. Blume said, looking at his colossal computer screen. I was sure that Mr. Vega would enjoy giving Miss Crinkle the news because she was a strong, independent woman who didn't pay any attention to him. I sensed that he had hostility towards her. At least, that's what I assumed because of the self-satisfied look on his face.

"Okay, all of you are dismissed," Mr. Blume stated definitively, "I have to get to work."

And just like that, Jamey became an honorary Student Council member.

Jamey insisted on going shopping with me to get the supplies for the care packages we were putting together for widows in nursing homes. That was part of the "February Student Council Valentine Give Back to the Community" activity I was supposed to be working on with Jake. I was irritated with Jamey, and for days, I found it impossible to even acknowledge his existence. I ignored him at lunch and avoided him- including his texts and phone calls.

He finally resorted to calling my landline, knowing one of my parents would pick up.

"Oh, it's Jamey," my mom chirped as she picked up the phone after glancing at the caller ID.

Jamey made polite small talk with my mother for a few minutes before she handed me the phone.

Since my parents were in the room, I forced myself to be civil to him. "Oh, hi, Jamey. Yeah, um, sorry I didn't see your text. I was busy doing homework. Oh, that's no problem. I'll get the supplies. My mom is going to take me on Saturday. Okay then. Sure. Yes, if your mom is that excited about taking us shopping, we can go together. Well, okay. Yes. See you tomorrow."

When I hung up the phone, my father asked what that was about. I explained how Jamey expressed interest in helping out with a Student Council event. Obviously, I neglected to mention the book-throwing part of the story.

"Hmmm, that's nice. Very impressive, Jessica," My father replied pleasantly as he typed something on his laptop. "You definitely have a positive influence on him- typically, football players his age wouldn't be interested in something like that."

"Josh is involved, too," I stated.

"Well, yes. Josh is well-rounded. He also wants to get into an Ivy League school, so he knows how to play his cards right," my father said absentmindedly. My parents had known Josh and his family since we were in pre-school, so my dad was aware of their familial expectations.

"Maybe he's just showing interest because he likes Jessica," Megan remarked casually from the couch. She was half listening as she watched some pre-teen show with simulated laughter.

"Well, either way. He is a polite young man," my mother chimed in.

Inwardly, I rolled my eyes and fantasized about throwing Jamey's books in his face, as opposed to the floor. "Well, I guess you don't have to take me to the store, Mom, since Ms. Russo wants to take us."

Everyone was quiet as I walked out of the room. They were all busy engaging in their own personal activities.

Later that week, Jamey and I planned to work together after school in the art room where the Student Council meetings were held. Needless to say, Miss Crinkle was not happy about this arrangement, yet she had no say in the matter. She was forced to kick Jake entirely off the project. She asked Mr. Vega why Jamey couldn't just work with Jake and me rather than in place of Jake. I'm assuming Jamey must have had a private conversation with Mr. Vega- asking that Jake be removed entirely. She requested a meeting with Mr. Blume. Mr. Vega reluctantly agreed. At said meeting, he told Mr. Blume that, in his opinion, the president of the Student Council should be delegating- not actively engaging in projects. Miss Crinkle told me that she flat-out asked Mr. Vega what experience he had running a Student Council. He, in turn, said it was really just common sense. They had a bit of an argument. Mr. Blume apparently chastised Mr. Vega for being rude but gave in and said that, under the circumstances, a decision had already been made. Jamey would substitute for Jake- but his consolation prize was that Mr. Vega and Jamey would not be allowed to have anything to do with the Student Council in the future.

Miss Crinkle privately told me she was fed up with favoritism towards athletes. Pragmatically, she understood that sports were an essential part of Lomonoco Creek. A lot of money was invested in them from various businesses (including my father's). Still, she and I agreed that it was just plain unfair.

I felt a great deal of hostility towards Jamey when we started the project. He had manipulated me and wronged Jake for his own selfish benefit. The worst part was that he couldn't care less about helping widows in nursing homes. He had done all this to force me to spend time with him. Actually, he did it to prevent me from working with Jake. His jealousy towards Jake and the lengths he went to remove him from this project made me feel incensed. His envy was completely unfounded. It was ridiculous. There was nothing between Jake and me, and I hated that Jamey acted like he had to find a way to come between us. I'd hardly spoken to him since the day we went shopping together.

Jake (but now Jamey) and I were going to put the bags together in Miss Crinkle's room Thursday after school. Miss Crinkle was going to distribute the bags on Valentine's Day to various nursing homes. She'd already arranged it with the staff at several places.

I had study hall last period, so I was able to start setting the art room up before Jamey came downstairs. The spacious, vibrant art room was in what was considered the basement of the school building. I had all the bags set out, along with the things we'd bought to store in the bags. We'd gotten candies, books of word searches, audiobooks, silk flowers, nail polish, and romance novels. We were going to arrange about one hundred bags. Miss Crinkle was planning to spread the bags out to four different nursing homes in Rosevalley and surrounding towns. There were approximately twenty-five widows in each nursing home the Student Council had contacted.

Jamey came to the art room at precisely 3:00, right after his last class. He smiled as he casually strode in with his book bag over his shoulder. He was taking a bite of a Kit Kat. He broke it in half and offered me the other half.

I shook my head and looked away from him, returning to what I'd been doing before he walked in, which was distributing all of the items we'd bought on the four rectangular, multi-colored tables so we could place one of each item in every bag.

"So, it looks like you've gotten a lot done already," he remarked cheerfully.

I nodded once, keeping the scowl on my face.

"Well, what should I do?" Jamey asked, "How can I help?"

I sighed heavily and slumped my shoulders. "Look, I don't even need your help," I said with disgust, "Why don't you just play a game on your phone or something."

"I WANT to help," Jamey insisted. He looked so earnest that it rattled me.

"Well, truthfully," I began, "I'd rather just do it myself. Just sit and make yourself comfortable. You can tell Mr. Vega and Mr. Blume that I was a good girl and let you work with me since it meant so much to you."

"Jeez," Jamey said, "how can you possibly be this mad at me? I wanted to work with you. Is that really so bad?"

"You totally screwed Jake over. For no reason!"

"Who cares about him?" Jamey waved his arm in the air as if Jake didn't matter.

I laughed without humor. 'Well, not you. Because you don't care about anyone but yourself."

"That's not true. I care about *you*," Jamey insisted empathetically.

I snorted with derision, "Yeah, right."

Jamey looked genuinely shocked and hurt. "Seriously? You don't think I care about you? Why would I go to all this trouble if I didn't?"

I glared at him. "If you *care* about me, then tell me why? Why do you care about me?"

"I just really, really, *really* like you...a lot."

"Why?" I placed my hands on my hips and stared at him as if this was an inquisition.

"Well, you have the perfect freaking face," he tilted his head and smiled deviously, "I love looking at you, and your body is so...just so adorable. I especially love your..."

"That's what I thought," I said, cutting him off.

"What does that mean?"

"You like the way I look, which is nice and all. But you can't really like someone just because you like the way they look. For instance, I do like the way you look."

Jamey raised his eyebrows and smiled like the Cheshire cat.

"But, I don't like the way you act. You're a bully. Why would you pick on Caleb for no reason? Why do you get pleasure in that? You're so shallow and sometimes just mean."

Jamey sighed. "Listen, you're right. I shouldn't pick on kids like Caleb. I know you don't like it. It was just fun and funny, I guess," he paused, chewing on his bottom lip for a few seconds, deep in thought. "Seriously, Jessica," if you give me a chance, I promise I will try not to do stuff like that anymore."

"Whatever, Jamey."

"Jessica, I would do anything to get you to go out with me. I mean, like *anything.*"

"Why?" I asked, throwing my hands up in the air. "What do you like about me besides the way I look?"

Jamey walked slowly toward me. I backed up, but he stopped when I leaned against a chair and could go no further. He cupped my chin. I looked away, but he gently moved my face so his eyes aligned with mine. We stared at each other for a few seconds.

"I like how smart you are. You are like the smartest girl or person I know," he began, "I like…no, I *love* how sassy you are. Like when you threw my books across the hall and told Bobby off. I've never met a girl who's so sweet and sort of innocent, but you also really have balls." He laughed at the irony of his statement. "And I like how you always raise your hand in class, especially if someone else is having trouble answering the question. Like you're trying to help them out. I love how you're so athletic. I can't believe the effort you put into cheerleading. Watching you cheer is like watching…I don't know…like watching a gymnast combined with a professional dancer. I could watch you forever. And you care so much about stuff. You feel stronger than anybody. You put like one hundred percent into everything you do."

He paused for a minute and ran his finger down my nose and mouth, "And you're fun. You seem uptight, and well, you are kind of a nervous girl sometimes. But you really are a lot of fun. You make the best conversation. At lunch, you're the one who usually brings up an interesting topic if there's ever like a pause in the conversation."

I took a deep breath and stared into his eyes. I thought about the things I liked about him. His loyalty towards Bobby and his other friends, his ability to apologize, his protectiveness- well, I guess that was a good and bad thing. As he moved his face closer to mine, I thought about how I liked his lips. His soft, full lips were about to meet mine.

I let him kiss me. And then all I could think about was how smooth and delicious his lips were. I got lost in the kiss and allowed him to move his warm, minty tongue slowly and smoothly around mine, and when he finished and took a step back, I smiled at him.

"Let's get started," I said casually, "Since you want to be an honorary member of the student council, you get to unwrap and untie all 100 bags." I threw the giant garbage bag filled with plastic-covered gift carriers at him. He caught it and winked at me. All was forgiven…for now.

Chapter Seven:
The Infamous School Dance

I basically found out that Jamey was taking me to the "St. Patrick's Day Spring Fling" from my father- before Jamey even asked me. When my dad informed me that Jamey had called to request his permission to invite me to be his date to the dance, I wasn't at all surprised. I knew Jamey well enough to recognize his motives. Jamey knew my father would not only be impressed but also flattered. Jamey understood that my father was the type to appreciate old-fashioned respect and chivalry.

Jamey was also aware that my father would encourage me to go to the dance with him. He knew my dad approved of him. Jamey was manipulative and deceitful but also very clever. He epitomized good manners and deference around the members of the athletic department. He was especially courteous to my father because of his crush on me.

Interestingly, I had seen Jamey in school the day before he called my father, and he never mentioned his interest in taking me to the dance. We were all sitting at our usual lunch table when Erin brought up the dance. The Sunshine Committee, of which Erin and I were members, was sponsoring the "St. Patrick's Day Spring Fling." With help from the Parent Teacher Association, we were not only paying to host the dance, using money earned through various activities we'd participated in throughout the school year, but also planning the event. Erin had asked our friends if they planned to attend, and everyone replied in the affirmative.

My mom, my Aunt Gina, and Jenna's mother were members of the Parent Teacher Association. We'd worked closely with them on rules, guidelines, and expectations for an underclassman dance. This was the first nighttime social event held primarily for freshmen and sophomores. The Sunshine Committee met with the PTA twice to work out the details before we could proceed with the plans.

The Sunshine Committee agreed to the gentle "suggestions" brought forth by the PTA, which consisted of all women- moms of many students who were underclassmen at Lomonoco Creek. Juniors and seniors were not allowed to attend because "the moms" were of the opinion that we really shouldn't be mixing with older students. Ironically, Rachel was the one to bring this up, even though Jenna had been dating upperclassmen since the beginning of the school year. They insisted that students from other schools would not be allowed to attend because of liability issues, everyone would need permission slips, and there had to be drop off and pick up times. There was some argument about the food and drink choices; in the end, we agreed to no soda. No one contested the fact that there would be allergen and gluten-free food options. We were informed that three adult chaperones from the PTA would supervise. My mom, aunt, and Rachel did not volunteer for that.

    I had been sleeping when Jamey called to ask my father about the dance. He knew I liked to sleep in on the weekends and that my dad got up early so he could drink his coffee peacefully before the rest of us joined him, and my mom made breakfast.

    As usual, I was the last one to come to the breakfast table on the Saturday of Jamey's call. Everyone else in my family was a morning person. I enjoyed sleeping in the one day a week I was allowed to. Weekdays were "alarm clock days" because of school, and we attended Mass on Sunday mornings. Therefore, I liked to think of Saturday as my guilty pleasure. Waking up late felt like a luxury to me.

    I yawned and stretched as I strolled into the dining room. Considering my mom loved to cook, she made a huge buffet for our family every Saturday morning. The kitchen always smelled of pancakes, eggs, toast, and coffee. It was not only aromatic but also festive. Around St. Patrick's Day, she would add green food coloring to the eggs and bagels. Plus, she'd trade corn beef hash to her menu rather than sausage and bacon.

    Before I could even take my usual seat at the table, my dad cheerfully announced Jamey's intention to take me to the dance. "Of course, I told him it was your decision. I gave him my blessing but said he would obviously have to ask you," my father claimed. "He was very polite about it. I think it was very respectful of him to ask me. You certainly don't see many boys behaving that way these days," my father continued with admiration.

    My mom smiled and nodded, "I have to say, he is a very well-mannered young man."

"Maybe he's just pretending 'cause he likes Jessica, and he wants you and Dad to like him," Megan chimed in as she took a bite of her corned beef.

"Megan, don't be so cynical. You should try and see the best in people," my father chided.

Megan shrugged as my mom piped in, "And don't talk with your mouth full."

My mother was very enthusiastic about me having a date for the dance. "Well, Jessica. What do you plan to say? Aren't you excited, especially considering that you're on the Sunshine Committee, which is sponsoring the dance? Are you going to call him back and say you'll go with him?" She was acting as if I'd received a marriage proposal.

"Are you on the Sunshine Committee, too?" Sara asked with thinly veiled contempt, "How many activities are you involved in? Student Council, school newspaper, cheerleading, art club…"

"Sara…" my father said through gritted teeth, "being involved in a lot of activities is a good thing. And I don't think I like your tone, young lady."

Sara looked down and mumbled, "I didn't mean to be rude."

My father stared at her expectantly until she looked up and formally apologized to me.

My mother quickly changed the subject to avoid the awkward silence that followed. "So, Jessica, honey, are you going to allow Jamey to take you to the dance?"

I sat at the table and poured myself a glass of orange juice as everyone in my family stared at me, waiting eagerly to hear my response.

I sighed as I twirled my fingers around my wavy, bobbed hair. I thought about my decision for a minute. Did I want to go to the dance with Jamey? I smiled, thinking about the kiss we'd shared, and noticed the flutter in my stomach as I pictured Jamey's heart-shaped, masculine face and his golden chestnut eyes…I couldn't deny that I was deeply attracted to him. The thought of slow dancing with him and his soft lips touching mine made me tingle all over.

"Jessica?" My father asked after a prolonged amount of time had gone by.

"Yes!" I declared, smiling, "Yes, I am."

Megan immediately went back to devouring her breakfast; Sara remained stone-faced, but my mom and dad seemed pleased about my decision.

I called Jamey later that morning and told him I would like to go to the dance with him.

"Really? You will? Crap, I thought you'd turn me down. Did your dad talk you into it?" he asked, sounding skeptical.

I shook my head, although I knew he couldn't see me through the cell phone. "No, I made the decision on my own."

"Hell yeah, I am so excited!"

I couldn't help but laugh at the way he expressed his zeal.

It was decided that Jamey's mom would drive us to and from the dance. She was adamant about it and called my mother three times before the night of the dance, expressing her exuberance at the fact that Jamey was taking such a pretty, respectable girl to his first high school dance.

My mother hardly got a word in during these conversations. She was always taken aback by Ms. Russo's lack of social intelligence.

"I avoid her calls, don't return them even after she leaves messages, but she still keeps calling back." I heard my mom telling my Aunt Gina over a glass of wine one night. My aunt frequently came by after dinner on weeknights and had a couple of drinks with my mom. She was sometimes accompanied by Rachel Sullivan.

"Well, are you surprised? My aunt asked with sarcasm. "It's obvious she doesn't respond to social cues."

"And she drones and on and on about the most trivial things…I 'yes, yes' her the whole conversation, and finally, come up with an excuse to hang up."

"I'm glad Evan's mother is too busy to call me," my aunt joked, "You wouldn't believe how many hours she works." Evan's mother worked as a doctor in an emergency room. His father was a psychiatrist, so they were rarely around. "Evan is such a nice boy- ALWAYS around our house, but I prefer that to being harassed."

They both chuckled and moved on to another topic.

Before the dance, Erin and I spent hours decorating with the other members of the Sunshine Committee. The dance was going to be held in one of the mini-auditoriums that had recently been added to the school. We were going with a St. Patrick's Day theme, so everything was green: shamrocks, leprechauns, four-leaf clovers.

While we were putting vases of seafoam-colored roses on each of the tables covered with emerald table clothes, Erin asked me how I felt about Jamey.

"I'm still not sure," I replied.

"Well, you *must* like him; otherwise, you wouldn't be going to the dance with him."

I nodded, "I do, but I just have an issue with his temper and his attitude sometimes."

Erin shrugged, "He's nice overall; he just likes to joke around; he's always been like that."

"I just don't understand why he sometimes has to be such a jerk."

"I've known him since pre-school, and he's never like that with his friends," Erin assured me, "He likes to get a laugh by making fun of people, but he's not really that bad. And his temper...well, he has a lot of testosterone...besides, he isn't the type who would ever hit a girl."

"But he can be nasty to girls at times," I said, recalling instances where he blatantly ignored girls who greeted him or snubbed friendly female peers in the hallway.

"I mean, he'd never *physically* hurt a girl, and he's always been protective when it comes to his friends." Erin continued, "Once in seventh grade, this idiot, I forgot his name...well, he was rude to me because I wouldn't give him the time of day, and Jamey pushed him against a locker and forced him to apologize to me."

I widened my eyes and tilted my head. I wasn't sure how I felt about that. I understood that Jamey was defending Erin, but I couldn't comprehend why he had to be violent about it.

Erin must have read my mind because she said, "Yes, Jessica, he can be aggressive, but that's the way boys are. Especially football players. It's just the way it is. Besides, I have never seen him treat a girl like he treats you. He like freaking adores you..." she paused, "You do know that lots and lots of girls are jealous of you because of Jamey, don't you?"

I had never really considered that before. I silently stared at Erin, contemplating my feelings about this tidbit of information.

Erin grinned, grabbed my arm, and pulled me towards the closet where the St. Patrick's Day confetti and other miscellaneous possessions were stored, "Relax, Jessica. Seriously, JUST RELAX! You are way too serious and tense sometimes. Just try to have fun and enjoy yourself. Stop thinking so much."

Maybe Erin was right, I decided. I would go to the dance with Jamey- see what happened, and try to have a nice, fun, and *relaxing* evening.

Ms. Russo decided to loudly beep the horn in a celebratory way as she and Jamey drove down my street to pick me up for the dance. She practically jumped out of her solid black Mercedes before turning off the ignition when pulling into our driveway. Jamey stepped out of the car with a grim expression on his face. Ms. Russo had her camera out and was eagerly jumping in the air with excitement. "This is so thrilling!" She announced to my parents and me as we walked over to greet her and Jamey.

My parents nodded, with awkward grins on their faces. "Yes. Yes, it is, Connie. How nice of you to drive the kids to the dance," my father sounded patronizing, but Ms. Russo didn't catch on.

"It sure is! Their first high-school dance. Don't you look stunning, Miss Jessica," she shrieked, pinching my cheek.

I giggled with unease and mumbled my gratitude.

Once again, it was evident that Ms. Russo was embarrassing Jamey, but he remained silent, choosing not to make a scene. "Well, let's get some pictures. Stand next to each other." She ordered.

Jamey sighed audibly, but I could tell he was pleased as his eyes swept over me. I wore a forest green sun dress with slender straps. It fell just above my knees; it fit snugly but wasn't tight enough to look trashy. It was unseasonably warm that night, so I could do without my scalloped lace shrug for pictures. Jamey had on tan slacks and a lime green button-down shirt. He looked…well, he looked *really* good. The unique color of his shirt brought out a hint of gold in his brown eyes. He'd done his hair in a faux hawk, and the blonde highlights stood out in the afternoon sun.

Jamey placed his arm around my waist, and we smiled. After about fifty pictures were taken by Ms. Russo, my mother suggested we leave so we would arrive on time for the dance.

"Okay, Anna. And I will text you the pictures," she said reassuringly before getting in the car and motioning for Jamey and me to follow suit.

The car ride was painful, to say the least. Ms. Russo blabbed the whole time about mundane things like the weather. Jamey sat mutely staring out the window while I mumbled an occasional assent, pretending I was listening. When we arrived at the school where the dance was being held, I felt an extreme sense of liberation. As Ms. Russo drove away, waving ecstatically, I breathed an audible sigh of relief.

"My mom is so extra," Jamey muttered as we causally walked toward the auditorium. He placed his hand on the small of my back as we strode into the building, weaving our way through the gold and green streamers hanging from the ceiling.

"Wow!" Jamey exclaimed as we walked into the dance, "This is impressive."

I had to admit the auditorium looked fantastic. It had taken us hours to decorate, but the end result was worth the effort we'd put in. The room was dimly lit yet illuminated by the strobe lights methodically placed throughout the room. Each table was covered with an emerald green tablecloth with a vase of seafoam roses mixed with baby breath. Gold confetti glitter was spread along the drink and snack stands. We'd also hung a St. Patrick's Day Celtic wooden wreath on each side of the auditorium, and there were banners of shamrocks and leprechauns covering the walls. It was very festive, to say the least.

Jamey and I immediately flocked to our friend group. We were the last ones to arrive. Our clique was standing in the corner of the room near the snack tables across from the entrance. Nikki and Evan were holding hands and seemed engrossed in a private conversation as Mickey and Bobby stuffed their faces with potato chips and laughed about...well, probably something inappropriate. Josh and Jenna decided to come to the dance with one another. They were still what Jenna referred to as "friends with benefits." Josh had his hand on Jenna's shoulder and was handing her a glass of punch as Jamey and I sauntered over. Kelly and Erin were engaged in conversation with the boys who had taken them to the dance. Interestingly, they were sophomore identical twins who were both on the wrestling team. Jamey and I chatted about trivial things while we waited for the DJ to start playing music.

We had managed to hire a popular local disc jockey who worked at restaurants and nightclubs in the area. He was a friend of a friend of Erin's older brother. He introduced himself and motivated everyone by talking about how well the football and basketball teams had done this year and how successful our wrestling team was. He also mentioned how excited the town was for baseball season to begin.

He played fast music for a while- typical songs that got people on the dance floor. A lot of girls danced to the pop music, and some boys joined in, but Jamey refused. Finally, a slow song came on, and he asked me to dance.

It felt contrived at first- as if we were acting. We basically did the standard "hands around the waist/arms settled on the shoulders," swaying back and forth to an old-fashioned yet timeless slow song.

Jamey smiled at me and said, "I don't really like dancing, but I am enjoying this."

I let out a small laugh. I was silent, unsure what to say. I looked around at all the other couples on the dance floor. Jenna and Josh looked comfortable, joking around as they danced. Nikki and Evan were staring at each other romantically. Eventually, everyone else seemed to blur as Jamey wrapped his arms tighter around my waist. He looked deep into my eyes, "You're the best-looking girl here, by far," he said with certainty.

I shook my head, "No, I'm not."

Jamey kept a serious expression on his face, "To me, you are. To me, you always are."

For a moment, I was certain he would kiss me, and I wasn't sure how I felt about that- because we were in public. Jamey sensed my unease because he brought his lips down to meet my forehead rather than my mouth. It was so sweet and pure, and at the time, it felt more pleasing than if he'd placed his smooth, full lips on mine. Shortly after, the song ended. He took my hand in his and led me off the dance floor.

Another fast song came on, and Mickey and Bobby simultaneously pulled out flasks as we all congregated at an empty table. "Who's in?"

"What, right here?" Jenna asked mischievously.

Mickey looked at her like she had two heads. "Of course not, duh…let's sneak out the back door. All the chaperones are gossiping on the other side of the aud," he pointed to the three volunteers who were deep in conversation and paying no attention whatsoever to us kids.

"Sounds good," Jamey immediately answered.

Everyone agreed to go except Erin because she was a member of the committee putting on the dance, and she was afraid her absence might be noticeable; Josh, because he didn't want to risk his academic career or the wrath of his parents and me...because I didn't take risks like that. Needless to say, no one was surprised in the least by my refusal.

At first, Nikki was skeptical, but Evan said, "We won't get caught, Nik; come on, it will be fun."

They all left, and another slow song came on.

"Hey, Joshie, want to dance?" Erin asked teasingly, "Jenna won't mind."

Josh shrugged. He had a flirtatious relationship with Jenna, Erin, and Kelly, and none of them was that committed to him to be jealous. He said, "Sure," and they stood up and started to move toward the dance floor.

"You don't mind, do you, Jess?" Erin asked.

"She's fine. Miss Popular will find someone to talk to," Josh said, pretending he was joking, but I knew he was serious.

"No, it's fine," I said casually, waving them away. I couldn't help wondering why my friends couldn't see past the allure of Josh's wide-set sky-blue eyes, sandy blonde hair, and slightly crooked nose. He was undeniably good-looking, but he was also so pretentious and conceited. Plus, it was hard to like someone who was always ridiculing you.

Just as Josh and Erin vanished, Sebastian Marx appeared out of nowhere. Sebastian was a handsome, red-headed, fair-skinned sophomore. He was on the wrestling team and was mainly popular with girls because of his strong, tall, muscular body and flawless complexion.

"Hey, Jessica. How ya doing?" he asked, standing too close for comfort. I tried to back away, but he inched closer. "What's the matter? You afraid your *friend* might not like us talking?"

"My friend?" I questioned.

"Your friend, yeah. Rumor is Jamey Russo isn't your boyfriend because you won't go out with him. That tells me that you're on the market, right?"

I looked at him gravely and said, "I am NOT for sale if that's what you're implying."

Sebastian laughed harder than necessary, as if I'd told the funniest joke he'd ever heard. "No, no, hon…that's not what I meant. It's just an expression. I meant that you were free to date…or dance, you know, with other guys. Like me, for instance."

"Well, Sebastian, my relationship with Jamey is really none of your business. And I did come to the dance with him, so I don't feel comfortable dancing with someone else. Sorry."

I tried to push past him, but he followed me. "Jessica, wait up," he yelled.

He followed me to the table, which held fruit punch and other healthy alternatives to soda and whatever was in the flasks Mickey and Bobby brought. "Here, I'll get you some punch," he said forcefully as he grabbed the ladle out of my hand and clumsily poured the nonalcoholic beverage into a paper cup. A few drips landed on my dress when he handed it to me. I sighed impatiently and grabbed a napkin, dabbing at the punch before it made a stain.

"Oh, I'm sorry," Sebastian said. "Here." He picked up a wad of napkins, grabbed a water bottle, and offered me both.

I looked at my dress and didn't see a mark. The punch must have missed me, but I decided to tell Sebastian I was going to the bathroom to wash off, just to have an excuse to get away from him. "I'm going to wipe it off in the girls' room," I announced with annoyance.

"There's nothing there," Sebastian insisted.

"I just want to make sure," I said as politely as possible.

Sebastian grabbed my arm, "Look, there's nothing there. Don't be afraid to dance with me because of Jamey. I'm not afraid of him, okay? He's just a freshman."

"That has nothing to do with it," I asserted.

"I know. Everyone knows that guys are afraid to ask you out 'cause you let Jamey Russo control you…"

"That's not true!" I proclaimed. "That's ridiculous."

I started at Sebastian's grip on my arm, "Please let go of me." I said, trying to remain calm.

He actually clenched even tighter when I said that and moved close to me so he was only inches away, "Look, Jessica, you have to stop letting boys like Jamey stop you from dating other guys. You let that guy manipulate you, and everyone knows it. You won't dance with me just because of him…" Sebastian went on and on, accidentally spitting in my face as I tried to move out of his grasp.

I noticed Josh and Erin looking in our direction. Erin whispered something to Josh; it must have been obvious that I needed to be rescued. They headed towards us.

"Hey, what's going on?" Josh asked angrily. He and Erin were standing beside me. I noticed Jamey and the others come in at that moment. I desperately wanted this to end. I didn't want there to be a scene, especially not a fight.

Sebastian pointed at Josh threateningly, "Look, why don't you leave us alone? I'm trying to have a private conversation with Jessica."

Josh shook his head, "It looks like she is trying to get away from you." I was nervously watching Jamey walk over as Josh and Sebastian exchanged words. I couldn't decipher what they were saying because I could see by the look on Jamey's face that he knew something was amiss.

"Get your hand off her," Josh demanded.

"No," Sebastian said defiantly.

"Just let go!" I pulled my arm, but he wouldn't loosen his grasp.

"What the hell is going on?" Jamey asked, looming over us.

"Sebastian here is harassing your date, Jame," Josh said in a provoking tone.

I felt my heart start racing. I knew this was going to turn into a majorly embarrassing scene.

"Get the hell away from her!" Jamey yelled at Sebastian. He came over to us and pulled me away from him.

Sebastian didn't back down. He got up in Jamey's face and started shouting at him. Then he began poking him in the chest. Jamey didn't hesitate. He punched Sebastian in the face. Sebastian fell back. He got a few punches in, but eventually, Jamey was on top of him on the floor, pummeling him. There was blood all over. Everyone stood around watching. I couldn't take it. I thought Jamey might kill Sebastian. Even though it was obvious he'd won the fight, Jamey would not back down. He continued to clobber Sebastian, and no one dared step in to stop him.

I started to have a massive anxiety attack. I walked away from the fight and out the doors of the school. I had to get out of there. I had to get home. No one noticed me leave because they were so engrossed in the brawl.

I was shaking and hyperventilating as I walked home from school that night. I lived nearby, about a twenty-minute walk and a five-minute drive. I took my time because my anxiety had inevitably led to a full-blown panic attack. I experienced a level of terror I hadn't previously known existed. My body was reacting as if someone was holding a gun to my head. My heart was beating so rapidly that I truly feared it would pop out of my chest. I felt incapable of having rational thoughts. I was dizzy and light-headed. I honestly believed I might have a nervous breakdown.

When I finally reached the driveway to my white Colonial, about an hour after leaving the dance, I noticed my dad pacing at the top of the stairs of our well-lit hallway. It suddenly occurred to me that Ms. Russo certainly would have notified my parents that I was nowhere to be found when she came to pick up Jamey and me. It was the first time since the fight that I had a clear, distinct thought. I felt bad that I had most definitely worried my mother and father.

When I opened the front door, I was about to mumble an apology, but I choked on my words when I noticed the look of fury on my father's face. I'd had never seen him so angry. His hands were in fists at his sides, his jaw was tight, his temple was pulsating, and his eyes were blazing with indignation. My mother stood at the top of the stairs by his side. She had her hand on his shoulder, obviously trying to placate him. My sisters were standing behind my parents. They looked frightened.

"Where have you been?" My father demanded to know as I hesitantly began walking up the stairs. My sisters quickly retreated in the direction of their respective rooms. They resembled mice scurrying away from a rapidly sweeping broom.

"I left the dance because…"

"We already know what happened! Ms. Russo filled us in," my father informed me. He was shouting. "She has been worried sick about you, and so have we!" I'd never heard him roar like this before. I was still in a daze, so confused I wasn't sure how to react.

"Anthony, please calm down," my mother said pleadingly, looking at me with sympathy.

"No, Anna! I will not calm down. Please call Connie and tell her Jessica is okay."

My mother sighed and walked to the kitchen to call Ms. Russo.

"What were you thinking?"

"You don't understand," I tried to explain, "I had to get out of there. You wouldn't believe what Jamey did."

I was now standing on the top step facing my father, who was still in the hall leading to the kitchen. I was scared to go up any further. I wasn't sure what he would do. He had never hit us, but I was afraid he might strike me at that moment.

He walked into the kitchen and watched me expectantly, ordering me to follow him with his eyes. My mother wasn't in the room. She must have brought the phone into the living room so Ms. Russo wouldn't hear the exchange.

I tried to explain to my father that I couldn't handle the blood, wasn't thinking straight, and didn't know what else to do. His face did not soften as I babbled on. In fact, he seemed to grow more incensed.

I stopped talking and looked down at the floor. His wrath was almost unbearable.

"You do know a girl is missing from Rosevalley?" he finally asked with an accusatory tone.

I nodded, "Yeah, but everyone knows she's a runaway. I mean, we live in a safe town. I didn't think anything could happen in Jamestown."

My father pursed his lips and turned his back to me. He circled to the right side of our kitchen nook. "Go to your room," he ordered, "I'm too angry to talk to you right now." He still had his back to me.

"But Dad, I…I'm sorry. I really didn't know…"

My father suddenly slammed his palms down on the counter, "Jessica, just go to your room!"

I stood for a moment, feeling frozen in place.

"Now! RIGHT NOW!" He bellowed, turning slightly and pointing in the direction of my room.

He started walking towards me, and for the first time in my life, I truly feared that he might physically harm me. I was desperate to explain myself, to find the words to make him understand why I'd *needed* to leave the dance. But I was afraid of what my father would do if I didn't obey him, so I turned on my heel and raced to my room. When I got there, I closed the door, leaned against it, and started sobbing.

It didn't take me long to get myself so worked up that I vomited. Three times. The nausea only dissipated because I'd completely emptied my stomach. All the contents of my intestines had been flushed down the toilet. I felt beside myself, and I still couldn't think clearly. My thoughts were hazy and incoherent. Images kept popping into my head- Sebastian's grip on my arm, Jamey's fists coming down repeatedly on Sebastian's face, all the blood, everyone watching and doing nothing to stop it, the wrathful expression on my father's face.

I sat numbly on the floor in my private bathroom. I was unsure how to feel or what to do. Shortly after I entered my room, I heard someone quietly knocking on my door. I don't know how long I'd been sitting against the ceramic tub. I didn't have a sense of time; my anxiety had completely taken over by that point- I felt as if it possessed me.

I was in a daze as I opened the door to let my mother in. I can't even remember the exact words that came from her mouth. I know I was completely silent during most of her visit. I felt mute. I only remember her telling me this would pass; my father would eventually calm down and forgive me. She said he was so angry because he couldn't bear the thought of something happening to me, and he had been so worried when I was missing. Then, she did the most helpful thing she possibly could at that time. She gave me a Xanax. I looked at her questioningly. I didn't have to say the words for her to decipher what I was thinking. She knew I was surprised she would have a benzodiazepine because she was such an easygoing person who let everything roll off her shoulders.

"This will help you sleep, honey. That's what you need right now. *Don't* tell your father!" she said as she handed me the pill and a glass of water.

As I swallowed the pill, she took a pair of pajamas out of my dresser drawer and handed them to me; this was something she hadn't done since I was six years old. "Change, get in bed, go to sleep. We can deal with this in the morning."

She put her hands on her hips and watched as I obeyed. She helped me unzip my dress and slip into a pair of satin pajamas.

I finally found my voice as I crawled into bed, "Why do you even have Xanax?" I asked curiously, "Have you ever taken it?"

"No," she replied, shrugging, "I don't need it, but I guess every woman my age has a handy bottle of Xanax around. I mean, you never know when you might need it."

She smiled and lightly closed the door. I closed my eyes and fell asleep within twenty minutes.

The next morning, both of my sisters came into my room to console me. Even Sara felt bad for me, which was very unusual. They both sat on my bed; Megan stroked my hair. Sara looked uncomfortable as she meekly asked, "Are you okay?"

I shook my head and whispered, No."

"What happened?" Megan asked curiously.

I didn't have time to answer her because my father burst into the room and roared, "Come with me, Jessica."

Before I even set foot on the ceramic tile floor in our kitchen, my father picked up our landline and held it for me. "You are going to call Jamey and Ms. Russo and apologize."

"Apologize to Jamey?" I was dumbfounded.

"You will obviously apologize to Ms. Russo for making her worry. And from what I understand, Jamey was trying to defend your honor. He was sticking up for you because that boy was harassing you."

My mother walked into the room at that moment. She had a no-nonsense look on her face, and her hands were planted firmly on her hips. "Jessica, will you please go to your room?" It was more of a command than a question. "Anthony, I need to talk to you," she said to my father in a very stern voice.

As I started to walk towards my room, I heard my mother say, "There is no way in hell my daughter is going to apologize to that boy- or any boy for that matter."

My father tried to speak, but my mother interrupted him.

"Jessica is naturally intelligent when it comes to boys. She is instinctually aware of how to *teach* boys to treat her. It comes naturally to her like all the women in my family, and I will not allow you to undermine that."

When I arrived at the entrance to my bedroom, I walked in and shut the door, afraid my parents might get upset with me for eavesdropping. Therefore, I couldn't hear the rest of the conversation. Besides, their voices were muffled because they started to whisper.

A few minutes later, my father came in and told me I did not have to express regret to Jamey. However, he was still going to call Ms. Russo, and I had to apologize to her.

It was a quick call. Ms. Russo started to babble on after I apologized, but my mother took the phone and said, "Sorry, Connie. Jessica has to go."

When the phone was placed back on the receiver, my father told me to return to my room because he was still too angry to talk to me and would be in later. I couldn't stop myself from sobbing and articulated my repentance, but my father replied, "You wouldn't be here to shed tears and show remorse if you'd been kidnapped. Go to your room."

I hung my head and did as I was told.

Later that night, my father knocked on my door and said he was ready to have a discussion with me. I opened the door and quickly sat on my bed, waiting for him to begin. I knew he would be doing most of the talking, and it would be in my best interest to make eye contact, listen, and nod at the appropriate times.

He had an austere expression on his face as he sat in my desk chair and folded his arms across his chest. He said he was disappointed in the impulsivity of my actions. He accused me of behaving impetuously at times.

"But, I…" I was going to say that he'd never reproached me for recklessness, that this was really the first time I'd gotten in any kind of trouble. I should have known he would shut me down.

"I am not done," he said harshly, "You sit and listen until I tell you it's okay to speak. Do you understand?"

I swallowed soundly and nodded.

I sat quietly and tried to focus on his lecture. I understood the gist of it, but I was too sensitive and anxious to listen explicitly to his words. I nodded as he spoke, feeling and, I'm sure, looking contrite.

He finally stood up when he was done. "So, Jessica, you need a consequence for this because, as I've said, it is very serious. You are grounded for the next two weeks. No electronics, no television, no phone, and no activities that don't involve school."

I whispered, "Okay, Dad," feeling a little shocked because I'd never been punished. I had witnessed my sisters receive the same harsh consequence on many occasions, but this was the first time I was on the receiving end.

As my father opened my door to leave the room, I couldn't stop myself from saying, "Dad, can you wait one second?"

He turned around and looked at me somewhat impatiently.

"Will you ever forgive me and trust me again?" I asked, starting to choke up. I felt tears stinging my eyes. I would be traumatized if he said no.

He half-smiled, but the grin didn't reach his eyes; obviously, he was still upset with me, "Yes. I already forgive you. And I trust that you learned your lesson. I don't think you'll make this kind of mistake again."

"I won't, I promise," I vowed with all sincerity.

He nodded once and walked out of the room, not looking back. I finally felt a sense of peace; serving my penance with dignity and acceptance would most likely assuage whatever residual distrust my father harbored.

Chapter Eight: Defense

Bobby was lingering by my locker on Monday morning following the fight. He anxiously stared down the hallway as I turned the corner, obviously waiting for my arrival. He had a worried expression on his face. He was rubbing his dimpled chin, and his amber eyes were dilated. He was rocking back and forth on his heels. When he saw me, he waved and smiled, a hesitant grin. I'm sure he was practicing his justification of what Jamey had done at the dance. Although they could be mean-spirited when it came to others, one thing I admired about Bobby and Jamey was their loyalty toward one another.

"Hi, Jess!" Bobby declared in an amplified voice as I approached him. It was apparent that he was tense on Jamey's behalf.

"Hi, Bobby," I said, sighing heavily and avoiding eye contact.

He decided to delve right in. "Listen, Jess, Jamey is SO sorry. He begged his mom not to call your father."

"Well, she DID call my father," I interrupted, "And I have never seen him so mad. He wouldn't even talk to me; he said he was too angry for almost two days, and now I'm grounded from everything for two weeks, and he's still..."

I saw the hopeless look on Bobby's face and stopped rambling. I thought of what he'd had to deal with at home with his abusive stepfather. "I'm sorry," I said contritely, "I know I shouldn't complain about being punished when your stepfather..."

It was Bobby's turn to cut me off, "He doesn't do that anymore," he exclaimed, "and it's because of, it's because of," his voice trailed off, "It's because of your father."

I nodded, sensing the uncomfortable tone in his voice.

We were quiet for a second before he continued, "Will you please just listen to me for a minute?" he asked gently.

I nodded, agreeing only because I felt guilty that I'd brought up such a sensitive topic in probably a patronizing and accidentally tactless manner.

"Jamey has a temper. Yes, I know he does. He knows he does. And he's over-protective of you because he cares about you. Sebastian was being really shitty to you, and that's what prompted Jamey to act the way he did."

"He didn't have to take it to that level. There was so much blood. He should have stopped. He has no self-control. I mean, he could have caused permanent damage."

Bobby shook his head, "Jessica, I know you're not used to violence, and yeah, Jamey beat the crap out of Sebastian. But, believe me- Sebastian will be fine. He deserved what he got."

I was not convinced, "I still don't think he needed to keep punching him over and over and over!"

"Maybe he did go too far," Bobby agreed, "but as someone experienced with violence, I can tell you, there's no chance he caused lasting injuries. Blood looks scarier than it really is."

I wasn't sure how to respond to that, so I remained silent, which gave Bobby a chance to resume. "Listen, Jamey REALLY likes you. This guy was harassing you. He put his hands on you, Jess. He wouldn't let go of you when you asked him to. Sebastian is the bad guy. Not Jamey. You have to give him a chance. He wants to be less, um, well, you know, he told me he wants to be nicer and not let his temper get the best of him- for *you*. But he can't just change overnight. How do you think it made him feel to see the girl he likes being disrespected physically and emotionally?"

I sighed again, this time in acquiescence. "Okay, I get it."

"You're going to be called to Mr. Blume's office," Bobby informed me.

"Why?" I asked, dumbfounded.

"The school was willing to let this slide. But Sebastian's mother, Mrs. Marx, made a big stink about it. She made such a huge deal out of it that they have to call you in as a witness to what happened to decide on Jamey's punishment. If he gets suspended, he won't be able to play baseball. Mr. Blume doesn't want that to happen, but after Mrs. Marx called the superintendent and threatened to go to the press, the administration told Jamey's mom that they have to investigate or things could get ugly. Mr. Blume asked Jamey to stay home today even though he's not suspended. I guess Blume has to have a meeting with you, the chaperones, Mrs. Marx, and Ms. Russo to determine the next course of action."

I threw my arms up in the air in exasperation, "Why ME? So many other people witnessed what happened!"

Bobby shrugged. "Because you were the reason for the fight. I mean, come on. You know how things work. Your mom is on the PTA, and your dad is involved in like *everything*. Your family is kind of important. You're the key to it all."

He widened his eyes and exhaled.

I pursed my lips and stared at the ceiling, "I get it."

The loudspeaker suddenly came on, as if on cue, "Jessica Calabresi, if you are in the building, please come to the office at your earliest convenience. Thank you in advance for your cooperation." It was Mr. Blume in a pleasant tone, making sure to send the message that I wasn't in trouble, that I was being summoned to the office for official business.

Bobby and I locked eyes before I slumped my shoulders and headed to whatever situation awaited me.

When I reached the office, Mr. Blume was waiting for me in the hallway. He had his hand on the door, holding it open. When he caught sight of me, he ushered me to him with a friendly smile.

I staggered towards him with trepidation. I had no idea what was in store for me. An interview? An interrogation? Hadn't I already been punished enough for something that wasn't even my fault?

"Jessica, dear. Thank you for coming so quickly," Mr. Blume said cordially- as if I'd had a choice.

I rubbed my lips together nervously and waited for him to carry on. "Come in," he gestured to the inside of the office and followed me as I entered.

I noticed all eyes on me as I crossed over into whatever unpleasant experience awaited me. The teachers, administrative assistants, and other staff quickly averted their eyes. They went back to whatever they'd been doing after Mr. Blume silently admonished them with an almost imperceptible shake of his head.

He sighed heavily and placed his hand on my shoulder in a fatherly way. "Let's talk privately in my office," he said as if it was a suggestion.

I silently followed, avoiding eye contact with everyone in the room.

I felt simultaneously relieved and claustrophobic as I settled into a seat opposite his desk.

"I'm sure you are aware of what this is about," he began hesitantly.

"The dance," I replied morosely.

"Yes," Mr. Blume nodded once and looked away. He seemed deep in thought, trying to find the words to explain what would happen next.

He sighed again, an even heftier exhalation than before. "Look, Jessica, I am very sorry to have to drag you into this. Obviously, you did nothing wrong where the school is concerned. As you probably already know, the rumor mill has been blazing with the news that you left the dance and walked home. I took the liberty of calling your dad before I called you in. I am aware he was not happy with you about that out of concern for your safety, but that is none of my business. "

He suddenly stopped talking and stared at me as if he was waiting for me to speak. I wasn't sure what I was supposed to say, so I just bowed my head, waiting for him to continue.

He placed his elbows on his desk and entwined his fingers. "Well, we thought we had this situation under control until early this morning. The chaperones and testimony from Jamey, Josh Kowalksi, Erin Johnassson, several other witnesses, and even Sebastian conclusively pointed to the fact that Sebastian had started the fight with Jamey after Jamey became aware that he was harassing you. Jamey did win the fight."

I couldn't help but snort at his choice of words.

A nervous look spread across Mr. Blume's face. "Um, Jessica, I did just speak to your father," he hesitated, then swallowed soundly and went on, "It is my understanding that you went to the dance with Jamey Russo as his date. Right?"

"Yes, we did go together."

Mr. Blume cleared his throat and continued, "Jamey was...well, according to Jamey and some of your other mutual friends, he was outside getting some fresh air when Sebastian basically accosted you. From what Josh and Erin said, he grabbed your arm and wouldn't let you go after you repeatedly asked him to stop. Jamey said he was defending you, and Sebastian started a physical fight with him. Is that true? From what your father told me, that was his perception."

I knew he was mentioning my father on purpose. He wanted me to know that my father didn't want Jamey to get in trouble; he wanted me to know that my father had agreed with whatever narrative Mr. Blume and the others had come up with.

"Jessica?" Mr. Blume asked when I didn't answer right away. I thought that, technically, everything he said was true. Jamey was protecting me. Yes, he went overboard, but he was defending me. And I had to admit Sebastian was being a bully. He was acting in a violent, aggressive way. Initially, he unquestionably was the culprit in the situation.

"Yes, that's what happened." I finally spoke.

"Look, Jessica," Mr. Blume said as he rubbed the back of his neck, obviously feeling tense, "Your father confided in me that the level of violence bothered you. But when you look at the situation in retrospect, do you understand that Jamey was the good guy here? Sebastian is a good wrestler, but wrestling season is over, and..." he stopped himself because he knew he was revealing the real reason he wanted me to "stretch" the truth.

"I get it," I said, feeling somewhat lightened now that it was all out in the open. I was being asked to leave out details to minimize Jamey's destruction. "Jamey will be starting baseball soon, and this kind of thing could hurt not only him but the team and the school if it's not handled correctly."

Mr. Blume looked relieved, "Yes, and your father understands that."

I nodded in acquiescence. I was basically being threatened by the fact that my father was a huge contributor to the sports programs at Lomonoco Creek and an athletic department member. Jamey was an asset to the baseball team.

"Okay, I'll get down to it because we're running out of time," Mr. Blume said quickly, glancing at the grandfather clock on his wall. "This situation had been settled. That is until Sebastian's mother decided to make a big deal out of it. When Mr. Marx picked Sebastian up, he was willing to sweep the unfortunate encounter under the rug. The Marxes are divorced. Sebastian was at his father's house until Sunday night. When he arrived at his mother's house, she saw the bruises and apparently blew the situation out of proportion. I've discussed the event with Mr. Marx and Sebastian. They would like this state of affairs to go away- disappear. It's embarrassing. Mrs. Marx doesn't realize that she is emasculating her son." He shook his head with disapproval.

"Well, anyway...she couldn't be persuaded to overlook it, so she called the superintendent and threatened to go to the press if a meeting wasn't held to reassess the incident."

I felt a wave of fear pass over me. "Who will be at the meeting?" I asked.

"Well, we decided, with the superintendent's approval, of course, that I will be there, Mrs. Hobbes, because she is the vice-principal, Ms. Russo, Mrs. Marx, and the three chaperones, who are all in agreement as to what happened since they already interviewed many students who witnessed the fight. We would also like you to be there since you were the reason for the fight. Obviously, your recollection of events is vital to our final decision about Jamey and Sebastian's consequences."

I swallowed soundly and rubbed my forehead, once again feeling anxiety wash over me.

Mr. Blume nervously glanced at the clock again, "Your father thought you might be panicky about this, and unfortunately, he has to be in court this morning, so he suggested your mother be a part of the meeting- in fairness to you."

I forcefully exhaled, feeling an immediate sense of relief at the mention of my mother. Her presence would definitely provide me with solace. She had a way of bringing comfort to tense situations.

Mr. Blume suddenly stood up, "You can wait here while I assemble everyone else in the conference room. I won't bring you in until your mom arrives, and I will ensure you are sitting next to her. Everyone is on your side- well, who knows what Mrs. Marx is thinking, but that's not for you to worry about. All you have to do is tell the...tell what we talked about, and it will be over before you know it. They should all be arriving shortly."

"We're good?" Mr. Blume asked pleasantly as he opened the door to his office.

I nodded, thinking about the irony of being asked to bend the truth by the adults in my life who were supposed to be role models. The sad thing was, I wasn't at all surprised.

The interview took place in a conference room adjacent to the main office. My father had taken my phone away, and I hadn't brought any books with me when I was summoned to the office, so I basically was made to sit twiddling my thumbs- literally, while I waited for all the participants to arrive. I was still nervous about having to tell my version of events to a room full of witnesses, but the fact that my mom would be there lessened my uneasiness.

Finally, after what I'm sure seemed much longer than it was, Mr. Blume opened the door and motioned for me to enter the conference room. It was painted pale yellow and had pictures of several historical buildings in Rosevalley from earlier times. It was meant to be a celebration of the history of our town. As I looked across the large, rectangular table that dominated the room, I thought that people in Rosevalley were generally very proud to be residents. I noticed how bright the overhead light was shining in the already bright room as Mr. Blume held the empty seat next to my mother out for me.

The moment I sat at the middle of the table, my mother patted my shoulder and then placed her hand on my arm. Mr. Blume was sitting at the head of the right side of the table, while Mrs. Hobbes sat diagonal from him on the left side. The three chaperones were all sitting crosswise with their hands folded. Ms. Russo was seated next to my mother. Mrs. Marx was strategically placed right across from me.

Mr. Blume cleared his throat and began the "discussion."

"We are here today to revisit the events of what happened on Saturday night at the dance," he announced as he looked around the table with authority.

Mrs. Marx was the only one in the room who didn't seem calm- she was obviously on edge- she was sitting hunched over in her chair and had a cross expression on her face. Her lips were pursed into a thin line, and her eyes were opened wide; she kept tapping her foot under the desk. The chaperones looked perfectly content; they had nothing to lose. Ms. Russo had a massive smile on her face; she knew this would end well for Jamey.

Mrs. Hobbes cleared her throat and smiled professionally. "We have already heard from the chaperones about what they witnessed that night, and we also have the testimony of many witnesses at the scene of the fight. I don't think we need to go over those."

"Well, maybe I do since my son was the victim here," Mrs. Marx interrupted. She was clearly upset and overly emotional.

"Your son was the victim?" Ms. Russo cut in sarcastically, "I think not. It was MY son who was tormented by YOUR son and had no choice but to defend himself."

"Your son did not come home with bruises all over his face and body." Mrs. Marx yelled, pointing at Ms. Russo and shaking her finger as she did so.

Ms. Russo remained composed, staying seated and speaking rather calmly, "Well, it's not Jamey's fault that he won the fight," she snorted with a laugh in her voice.

"That's the most ridiculous…"

My mother cleared her throat and sighed audibly, "Excuse me, but my daughter will not sit here and be a witness to a catfight. If she has to testify about what happened, fine, but we will not stay here and watch two grown women yell at one another."

Everyone was silent. My mother could take command of a room when she saw the need, and she had done just that.

Mr. Blume looked at my mom apprehensively- knowing he'd better take control of the situation or there'd be consequences. "Mrs. Calabresi is correct. Jessica has agreed to give her version of events even though this was settled. After hearing the testimony of all witnesses, you- Mrs. Marx saw fit to involve the superintendent and make threats. You wanted to have another meeting to clarify things. Well, you got your wish."

Mrs. Hobbes decided to step in, and she smiled in deference to my mother, "Mr. and Mrs. Calabresi have agreed to allow their daughter to further endure the hardship of having to relive this traumatic event. From here on out, I propose that we allow Jessica to speak without interruption."

Everyone except Mrs. Marx either nodded their head or murmured their consent.

Mr. Blume looked at Mrs. Marx and firmly asked, "Is that okay with you, Mrs. Marx? I hope so because she is the only witness we have not heard from. Your son and his father agreed with our decision, but you are the only one questioning the school, the boys involved, and, like I said- all the witnesses, including *your own son.*"

"We will leave right this minute if Mrs. Marx does not agree to let my daughter speak without interruption." My mother started to stand up and take my hand in hers.

Mrs. Marx nodded, "Okay then," she said through gritted teeth.

I told everyone about Sebastian harassing me, grabbing my arm, refusing to let me go, even after I told him to at least twice. I explained that he threatened Jamey and verbally attacked him. I was adamant about the fact that Sebastian had started the fight. He had. I wasn't lying about that. Mrs. Marx cringed when I blatantly described how her son held my arm against my will. She was silent until I was done talking.

When I was done, she held up her hands and said, "Okay, I understand that Sebastian was wrong in what he did, but how can Jamey just get away with beating him to a pulp?"

"He didn't even have to go to the hospital," Mr. Blume pointed out.

"Okay. I just want to ask one more thing if that's okay," Mrs. Marx began, backing down, "From what I understand, Jessica left the dance during the fight. I was told, through the grapevine, that she found it too violent, that she couldn't handle seeing all the blood- all of Sebastian's blood. If that's true- then obviously, Jamey went too far and should be punished."

Mrs. Hobbes cleared her throat, "Jamey has been punished for engaging in the fight. He has weight room detention for a week."

"If Jamey was so brutal that Jessica walked home alone from the dance...well, I don't think that's a severe enough punishment."

"Let's settle this right now," Mr. Blume said, puffing air from his nose, "Jessica, why don't you tell us why you left the dance, dear?"

At that point, I just wanted to put this situation behind me. Jamey did go too far, but he was protecting me. Sebastian was the one who'd crossed the line. He had manhandled me; he had harassed me- maybe he did deserve what he got. I pushed my guilt for telling a white lie aside and didn't hesitate as I straightened up, looked Mrs. Marx dead in the eye, and perjured myself, "I left the dance because of your son. I was so distraught by what he did to me. He really scared and upset me. I had to get away from the dance, so I walked home alone. And I did it because of Sebastian, not Jamey. I left because of Sebastian."

Chapter Nine: Spring, Summer, Italy, and the Barbecue

After the meeting, I decided to forgive Jamey, move on, and pretend the incident had never happened. I wanted everything to go back to normal- whatever that was. I soon realized there was no "normal" where Jamey and I were concerned. We had yet to establish *what* we were exactly. I knew I did not want a serious relationship, and Jamey initially wouldn't accept that. He was relentless. He constantly asked me- *begged* me to be his girlfriend. In fact, it felt like I spent the entire month of April warding off Jamey's appeals. At the beginning of May, I finally decided that I had to have a serious conversation with him about the fact that I wasn't ready for a commitment. I wanted to avoid revisiting the subject over and over again. It made me uncomfortable, and I started to dread his texts and spending time alone with him because he would inevitably bring the conversation around to us becoming romantic in a monogamous way.

One random afternoon, I decided to wait for him after baseball practice so we could have a meaningful discussion about my frame of mind regarding "us."

"Hey, you waited for me," Jamey said enthusiastically as he walked out of the locker room after showering and changing out of his practice clothes.

"Yeah," I started with an almost apologetic firmness in my voice, "We need to talk."

Jamey's face suddenly turned ashen as if he'd been informed about the death of a relative.

"It's not bad…well, not that bad." I swayed my head back and forth, laughing in an attempt to assuage his fear. I was sure he thought I was going to tell him I was seeing someone else or there was no hope for us in the future.

He looked somewhat relieved but still skeptical, "Then what is it?"

"I just want to be open and honest with you. Okay?"

"Okaaay," he stated hesitantly.

"Let's walk," I suggested, "My mom is picking me up soon, so I don't have much time."

"Okay, my grandmother is picking me up in front of the gym in about," he stopped and looked at his watch, "fifteen minutes."

We headed toward the recently reconstructed gymnasium, where all parents picked kids up after sports practices. My mom would also be arriving soon at the same location.

I didn't want to be negative and perseverate on my apprehension to date Jamey. So I told the truth, yet excluded some of the details.

"Can I just talk without interruption?" I asked with a pleading tone in my voice.

Jamey sighed and nodded his consent.

"Listen, I really like you, Jamey. I do. But I don't want a boyfriend right now. I'm just not ready. I really want you to stop asking me out. It makes me feel pressured, and it just creates this awkwardness between us. As I said, I *like* you, and I promise there isn't anyone else."

Jamey stopped walking and took my hand in his, "Are you sure?" he asked, looking deep into my eyes.

"Yes," I said with conviction, "I promise. There isn't."

Jamey exhaled and nodded rapidly, "I get it. As long as this isn't about another guy."

"Jamey," I began resolutely, "It's not."

"Okay, okay...I won't harass you anymore about being my girlfriend. You're a good girl. I get it. You need time. You're different from other girls, that's why I like you so much. I understand."

"I'm just not ready for a, you know...an actual significant other or anything physical."

Jamey smiled as we arrived at the spot where our respective rides would soon be coming. He turned to face me and put his hands on my shoulders, "I promise I will NEVER pressure you to do anything sexual that you are uncomfortable with, okay?"

I nodded, I could see the sincerity on his face, and I believed him.

"And I will wait," he continued, "I will wait until you're ready, and I promise to stop badgering you."

I bobbed my head, and a look of acknowledgment passed between us; we were on the same page...at last.

Once I decided to pause my romantic involvement with Jamey, I told Jenna that I desperately wished our friends would stop interrogating me. They were relentless, constantly asking me how I felt about him and what was happening between us. Jenna advised me to be honest with Nikki, Kelly, and Erin about it- she assured me they would understand if I clarified my feelings.

"It's your choice, Jess. Of course, Nikki will sympathize, and I'm sure Kelly and Erin will respect your wishes if you explain that you're just not ready," she informed me with confidence. Fortunately, her presumption was accurate. Nikki was my cousin, practically like a sister, so I was aware that she would always be on my side. Erin and Kelly had also proven to be loyal friends, although I hadn't known them for that long. We had all really grown close quickly and spent the majority of our time together.

Soon after my conversation with Jenna, Kelly invited us over for one of the many sleepovers we had that summer. It was the weekend after my talk with Jamey. I took Jenna's advice and decided to gently clarify the current state of my relationship with Jamey and my desire to let the subject go- at least for the time being.

Nikki shrugged and smiled supportively.

Erin looked up with a detached expression on her face. She'd been polishing her toenails a dark shade of blue. "That's cool," she said matter-of-factly.

Kelly nodded, "Of course, we support whatever you feel comfortable with," she replied in agreement as she continued French braiding Nikki's long black hair.

Jamey must have talked to Bobby and Mickey because they avoided the subject. Evan was pretty much oblivious. He was primarily concerned with Nikki. He had no interest in my relationship with Jamey.

Josh, on the other hand, as usual, was the one to stir the pot. He was our sole friend who brought up Jamey and my liaison, and it only happened once. We were all sitting in lunch one day in mid-May. We were having a civil conversation about the upcoming long weekend.

"My mom is planning on having another party," Jamey casually divulged.

We were cavalier as we discussed the spring festivity Ms. Russo was preparing. There was no tension, no discomfort until Josh decided to remark in a snarky way, "Hey, Jamey, I wonder if Jessica will get drunk and let you feel her up this time." He laughed mockingly, but no one else did. Everyone fell silent, and I noticed Jamey give Josh an almost murderous glare.

"Shut up, Josh!" Jenna exclaimed with disgust. "Stop being such an ass."

Josh shrugged, "Geez, I was just joking," he said, trying to lighten the tense mood he had created, "I just mentioned it because…"

"Never mind," Jamey said authoritatively, "Freaking drop it."

"Whatever," Josh said with a tilt of his head. Jamey shot him another venomous glance and changed the subject.

I smiled gratefully at Jamey as he continued talking about something irrelevant. He winked at me, and we all pretended nothing had broken the previous nonchalance of our conversation.

Generally speaking, nothing out of the ordinary occurred during the rest of the school year. It wasn't until June that things changed…for the worse. Jamey's whole family was going to Italy for the summer. He was leaving a week after the annual carnival on the Green. The Green was an area in the middle of Rosevalley where many events were held throughout the year. For instance, craft fairs, dog shows, concerts, and fireworks on Independence Day. My friends and family spent a lot of time participating in various activities in this particular area of town.

This was the first year my parents were allowing me to attend the carnival with my peers, although they would be there with my sisters, friends, and relatives. Almost every resident came to the festival at some point during the weekend it was held.

Jamey was being forced to go to Italy with his family because his mom didn't trust him to stay home alone, and there was no one else to reside with. His entire family spent June through August in Rome with relatives every summer. Jamey said he didn't want to go, but he had no choice. He had been somewhat depressed during the weeks following up to his trip. I noticed he was a little more solicitous toward me. He started asking strange questions. Out of the blue- he'd text and randomly ask if I was sure I didn't want to date *anyone* or if it was just him? He had Bobby, Erin, and Kelly question me about my "love life." I assured him I wasn't planning on getting romantically involved with any boys while he was gone. I sensed insecurity in Jamey because, with him being gone, he wouldn't be able to monitor my "comings and goings," so to speak.

Therefore, I wasn't shocked by how he behaved when we met at the carnival. We initially had a great time. I was in paradise after Jamey convinced me to eat normally forbidden foods like corn dogs, deep-fried pork on a stick, and cotton candy. I couldn't stop laughing while he spent almost an hour and probably $40.00 playing "Ball and Bucket Toss" so he could win a giant stuffed koala for me. I jumped up and down, cheering after beating him at "Balloon Dart," and he pretended to pout. It was thrilling to hold his hand on the roller coaster and scrambler. And even though he didn't like heights, he agreed to go on the Ferris Wheel with me. It was amusing because Jamey's fear of heights was astonishing, considering I'd never seen his vulnerable side before.

It wasn't until it got dim and the event was almost over that Jamey's possessive, mean-spirited side emerged. We were walking to one of the many ice cream stands with Nikki and Evan when I spotted a male, approximately our age- maybe a little older appraising me. He wasn't inconspicuous about his interest in me. I immediately tensed up, hoping that Jamey hadn't noticed. But he did. and he couldn't just let the incident slide. As the young man passed by, I detected Jamey's hands forming into fists. I saw his jaw tighten and his eyes narrow with anger.

"What the hell are you looking at?" he angrily shouted at the anonymous kid.

The boy seemed shocked as Jamey approached him.

"Nothing, I wasn't…I didn't mean to…" The kid was stuttering and obviously afraid. It was apparent he didn't mean to offend Jamey or me.

"Just don't freaking look at her," Jamey commanded with an incensed look.

"Okay…I'm sorry. I didn't mean to do anything wrong," the boy was still stammering, and he now looked terrified. It was the look on his face. The fear that Jamey had provoked made me feel so utterly disgusted with him that I could no longer bear to be in his presence.

As the boy practically ran away, I turned to face Jamey with a look of revulsion on my face. I was so livid with him at that moment that I wanted to say the most awful things. I wanted to express how completely sickened his actions had made me. But I had self-restraint, unlike Jamey, and I decided to tell him that.

I put my hands on my hips and glared at him, "There are so many things I want to say to you right now. But I'm not going to because, unlike you, I have self-control. I don't act like a toddler when I'm upset."

He instantaneously looked apologetic and attempted to make amends. Still, I held my arm out, "No," I stated with authority, "NO. You, once again, were out of line. What you did nauseates me. Why do you always have to ruin things?"

I turned to Nikki, "Please text our parents and ask if we can leave. I don't want to be here any longer. I'm going to wait in the parking lot."

Nikki nodded, "Of course. Evan and I will go with you."

Evan gave Jamey an apologetic look and shrugged. Everyone knew Nikki was the boss in their relationship, so Jamey was left at a loss for words.

"Have fun in Italy. Don't contact me before you leave," I exclaimed, looking away from Jamey. I started walking as fast as I could. I had my back to him as I said through gritted teeth, "And don't you dare follow me."

To his credit, Jamey was wise enough not to directly contact me before he left. He tried to communicate through Jenna, Nikki, and even Bobby, but I made it clear I needed a break from him- a long respite- like two and a half months, the duration of the summer break. Therefore, when he left for Italy, we had no interaction after the incident at the carnival. I was okay with that; in fact, I was somewhat relieved. I did need a pause from Jamey in an emotional, physical, and social way. I needed to clear my head; at the time, the only way I could do that was to not only be separated from him but also place him in a padlocked compartment in the back of my mind.

The summer before tenth grade was actually a relaxing, drama-free time for me. I had fun while Jamey was gone. I didn't feel the stress I'd felt since I'd first laid eyes on him a year prior. I felt young again- innocent, carefree. Whenever thoughts of Jamey came to mind, I immediately swept them away and deliberately repressed them.

The girls and I had sleepovers; we went to the Jamestown Country Club with our moms and swam and ate. We had biweekly manicures and pedicures. We all went to cheerleading camp for two weeks. We also spent time with our male friends. We met them at the beach, the mall, and the movies. No one mentioned Jamey- at least around me.

I felt tranquil and content *all* summer. Nevertheless, although I knew I was enjoying myself., deep in my subconscious mind, I couldn't pretend there wasn't something missing. The excitement...the longing, the passion.

Jamey...*Jamey* was missing.

During the last couple weeks in August, it was a tradition for my immediate family to visit relatives on my mom's side, the famous kinsfolk she didn't feel comfortable publicly discussing. My mother left Los Angeles to escape the spotlight when she was 18 years old. She chose to go to college in Monroe, the town that housed St. Padre Pio, the prestigious college she and my father attended. My mother had been a diligent and studious student and was accepted to many universities, but apparently, her first acceptance letter came from St. Padre Pio in Connecticut, which was on the other side of the country. As she tore open the envelope, she had already made up her mind without waiting to hear from all the other schools she'd applied to. She was intrigued with "the seasons," which we New Englanders take for granted. She also wanted to embark on an adventure- start over in a place where she knew no one, and no one knew her...or her famous family members. Although my mom left L.A., she stayed in close touch with her ancestors. The two weeks we spent with them every summer were probably the most enjoyable and exciting of the entire year. We went on nonstop adventures, which inevitably left us exhausted upon our return.

Jamey's family returned from their vacation around the same time we did. Ms. Russo decided to have another one of her famous parties to kick off the school year. We weren't planning to attend. My mother declined to answer Ms. Russo's texts and calls, begging her to come to the party. The decision to spend the Saturday evening of the party relaxing remained even after my Aunt Gina tried to cajole us into going. She kept saying how much fun we'd have and all the gossip the party would provide. My parents refused to give in. We were all drained from the trip. The jet lag crushed everyone in my family, mainly because of all the unforeseen layovers. There was a last-minute emergency with the airline, so we ended up having to wait for hours at the airport. The flight times kept changing, so we all sat in uncomfortable chairs, unable to sleep or relax.

I was okay with missing the party. In fact, I had managed to block Jamey from my mind while we were in L.A. We spent our time shopping, going to the beach, and watching movies my relatives had starred in. It was always a dream vacation- one that we all enjoyed tremendously. I wasn't ready to return to reality. I'd escaped into the life my mother had essentially fled from. She loved her famous family and spoke to them often, but she didn't want to live a life where she was constantly in the spotlight. It was as simple as that. Although, visiting once a year was a special treat for us all.

I was especially relieved about my parents' decision after my conversation the next morning with Nikki.

I sensed something was amiss when she called my cell early the following day. Nikki rarely phoned. She usually just texted me. She made small talk for a few minutes, asking questions we'd already discussed about my trip. After a few random inquiries, she was suspiciously quiet.

"Is something wrong?" I questioned with curiosity. I thought maybe she and Evan had had an argument.

She sighed audibly and stammered a bit, "Okay, well…um."

"What? Seriously, Nik- what is it?"

"Alright, Jess. I'll tell you. I have to, but let me ask you something first," she hesitated, then continued with trepidation, "You are over, Jamey, right?"

I needed to figure out where this conversation was headed, so I had to pause before I responded. "Yeah, why?"

"Well, before I tell you…are you 100% sure you are over him?"

"Yes!" I stated with conviction.

Nikki sighed, "Okay…well, he was bragging last night. You know, about the girls he hooked up with in Italy. I heard the guys laughing and congratulating him. I asked Evan about it afterward. He said Jamey had admitted to losing his virginity to some girl who worked as a waitress at a restaurant his family owns in Rome. After that, he apparently spent the summer…I guess you could say- adding notches to his belt."

I was silent for a minute as I contemplated this. Finally, I spoke up, "Is he planning to keep in contact with any of these girls?"

"No!" Nikki said enthusiastically, "He was bragging about the fact that he didn't even remember their names."

"What a jerk." I said, "He really is…" My voice trailed off. I realized with complete certainty that I was not jealous. I found it odd. After all the time and energy I'd put into my "relationship" with Jamey Russo- why wasn't I the least bit envious?

At that moment, I concluded that it was because I was over him. That was why I didn't feel an iota of envy. We were over. Done. I laughed and told Nikki, "Well, that ship has sailed."

Little did I know.

Part II.
Tenth Grade

Chapter Ten:
The Substitute

Before I began sophomore year, I made it clear that my relationship with Jamey was over. I accepted the fact that it wasn't meant to be, especially considering that I immediately felt relieved the minute he set foot on the plane to Italy. Moreover, when he came back, he boasted about his sexual conquests while overseas. In my mind, there was no more "Jamey and Jessica." On the other hand, Jamey needed convincing that I was no longer romantically interested in him. Hence, inquiries were made.

Evan asked Nikki to ask me about my feelings and intentions regarding Jamey.

Josh asked Kelly to ask me about my feelings and intentions regarding Jamey.

Mickey asked Jenna to ask me about my feelings and intentions regarding Jamey.

And so forth.

Therefore, in order to put a halt to the pestering, I instructed my friends to let Jamey know, in no uncertain terms, that I did not want him to pursue me. I just wanted to be friends. I was adamant and unyielding about my decision.

I must admit, I was appreciative that Jamey eventually relented and backed off. He didn't contact me. Our only communication occurred when we were with friends. He flirted a little, but not in an uncomfortable or aggressive manner. After a while, it seemed as if he had moved on, and I was thankful. After all, he was sought after. Girls threw themselves at him. He had one of those personalities that females found alluring. He was charming when he wanted to be, and he was extremely confident. Add to that his natural good looks, and unsurprisingly, girls found him irresistible.

No one told me if he was with other girls- it was a taboo subject. My friends knew I didn't want to know. They were respectful enough to keep quiet about Jamey's promiscuity. But I wasn't ignorant enough to believe that any guy who'd already had relations with numerous girls would suddenly become abstinent. I concluded that he was having sex regularly with the girls who chased after him. Interestingly, he never engaged in public displays of affection- the signs were subtle. A wink, a smirk, a sly glance. Jamey developed a reputation for not wanting to be monogamous. He made it clear to the girls he fooled around with that he wouldn't hold their hands in school, send them flowers, or even kiss them around other people. He was a player, and even though I had no proof of this, it was apparent.

In retrospect, I find it almost unbelievable that for nearly six months, I was able to repress the truth- to deny the reality that I was still intensely attracted to Jamey. I wouldn't allow myself to fantasize about him. Whenever I felt aroused by Jamey Russo, I would force myself to think about something else.

I managed to push my feelings for Jamey aside by immersing myself in various activities, even more so than I had as a freshman. I once again became a member of the Student Council. I was elected vice president this year, much to Josh's chagrin. He was treasurer again. I also stayed a member of the Sunshine Committee, the art club, and the school newspaper. Cheerleading remained my true passion, but I added the coordinator of the tutoring and babysitting programs to my list of obligations. Needless to say, I was very busy. Things remained this way until the beginning of December. The Student Council was in the midst of planning a holiday dance. The proceeds would be donated to a charity that aided impoverished families during the Christmas season. My thoughts predominantly revolved around getting straight A's and doing my part to make a difference. I was content and doing just fine. That was all before the incident with the substitute.

Things with Jamey were forever changed in early December because of the literal worst substitute teacher in the entire world- Mr. Harry.

During our sophomore year, we were required to take an elective about mental health, and there weren't many valuable choices offered. My friends and I all decided to take a ridiculous course called "Take a Look at Yourself." We chose this class so we could all spend at least one period together, and it seemed like the easiest of all selections. It dealt with bullying, sexual harassment, depression, anxiety, and expressing our feelings so we wouldn't become suicidal. At least that was the way Mrs. Spelling (our regular teacher) described the goal of the class...well, that was my understanding. I mainly studied for other classes or passed notes to my friends during this class. Phones were collected at the door so we wouldn't be distracted. I know Mrs. Spelling meant well, but the course seemed utterly useless. I don't think the kids in class were honest or open to the message she was trying to convey. It took place during the last period of the day. Basically, all we did was write journal entries and watch videos about teenage "issues." Every single one of the members of my friend group attended this class. We all agreed that the last minutes of the class, when Mrs. Spelling allowed us to socialize, was the best part of the class and probably the most productive.

Mrs. Spelling was rarely absent, so we were all surprised to find Mr. Harry sitting comfortably in her seat when we arrived at class one day at the beginning of December. I can't even remember the specific date, which is strange, considering it changed the shape of my entire life. I was genuinely sideswiped after the episode. Things were never the same. My life was transformed, and although I was an active participant, I felt like everything that happened next occurred without me truly consenting. It seemed like fate. Looking back, I realize that immediately after this incident, the way I reacted or failed to react indicated that I allowed myself to follow a path that seemed like destiny. At the time, I consented to the transformation without putting enough thought into how my life basically shifted overnight. I hadn't realized at the time that one event can alter virtually everything, and then- there's no going back.

The students at Lomonoco Creek were always taken aback when they walked in to find Mr. Harry would be replacing our regular teacher for the day. Some students would roll their eyes, others smirked, and there were also those who groaned. It probably depended on your latest experience with Mr. Harry because he literally had several different personalities. I often wondered if he had Dissociative Identity Disorder.

Mr. Harry was the person the school called when they were completely desperate- he was most definitely the last name on the substitute list. Unfortunately, our school was desperate quite often. Mr. Harry was hired to "teach" at Lomonoco Creek at least once a week. He'd been banned from the elementary and intermediate schools because those kids were young enough to go home and tell their parents the unusual things he did. High schoolers weren't as open with their parents. Everyone knows teenagers are less forthcoming because they have more important things to do than talk to their parents about their school day. Therefore, he was still welcome in our school because there hadn't been that many complaints.

When my friends and I walked into class that day, Jamey laughed and said, "Shit is going to get interesting."

Bobby and Mickey were standing on either side of him, and both started guffawing when they saw Mr. Harry. "Hell, yeah!" Mickey announced, "Entertainment last period of the day."

They haughtily walked to their seats because they found Mr. Harry entertaining; he generally didn't mess with the football players. On the days he was in a foul mood, he saved his ridicule and insults for the weaker kids who were too afraid to defend themselves.

On this particular day, he appeared relaxed...*very* relaxed. He had his feet on the desk, an old-fashioned newspaper in his hands, and a goofy grin on his elongated face. Once everyone was seated, he looked down at the notes Miss Bayer had apparently left and said, "O-k-a-y...it seems like we're going to be sharing today. Who wants to start?"

I immediately lost interest and opened up my math textbook. I decided to get a head start on my homework. Laurie Smithers was the only person to shoot her hand up, "I'd like to share!" she practically shouted in an almost defiant tone.

I sat between Nikki and Jenna; I noticed them exchange an amused glance. Laurie had a reputation for being an odd girl. She always had a scowl on her face. She was mad at the world and dressed in all black. She hung around with the goth crowd. She was outright rude to the cheerleaders and jocks- even when we tried to be friendly and polite. I'd held the door open for her on at least two occasions, and she would glide through without acknowledging me. Jenna had once shouted, "You're welcome!" when she was a witness. Laurie didn't look back- she kept walking as if we'd offended *her* somehow.

She was also constantly giving my friends and me dirty looks. One day in the library, Kelly asked her if something was wrong. We were sitting across from Laurie and her clan, but she was ignoring them and glaring at us with a look of pure hatred- she was practically shooting off daggers.

"No, nothing's wrong," Laurie spat and muttered, "bitch," under her breath.

"I'm sorry you're having a bad day," Kelly tilted her head and smiled at Laurie sympathetically.

At that point, Laurie growled like a dog, shot up, and stormed out of the library.

The boys I hung around with paid her no mind. She was not on their radar. She was invisible as far as they were concerned. I guess you could say that my opinion of Laurie before that day was unclear. I wasn't a fan of her all-black wardrobe, rainbow-colored hair, and the piercings spread over her face. Still, I didn't think her fashion sense was any of my business, and I rarely gave her a second thought. I didn't dislike her, even though it was apparent that she was one of those people who despised cheerleaders and anyone who conformed to the norms of society. That was all I knew about her before that day.

I was about to find out a lot more.

I tuned out after Laurie agreed to read her poem. I was engrossed in my math homework. I became startled when I realized the room had fallen silent, and all eyes were on me. Laurie was standing in front of the class with a piece of paper; she had taken a break from reading. I looked around and then turned toward Laurie. She was waiting until she had my attention to continue.

Laurie cleared her throat and glanced at me with defiance. The revulsion on her face that was unmistakably directed toward me was baffling. I felt as if she had slapped me across the face; her rage was so intense that I could feel it physically.

"I'd like to restate the name of my poem now that I have everyone's attention. My poem is called 'Little Red Riding Hood.'"

I gasped; my eyes flew open, and I put my hand across my chest. My heartbeat sped up, and I felt as if I might faint. She actually wrote this poem about me and was about to read it aloud in front of all our classmates. I realized at that moment that she must have overheard a private conversation I'd had with Nikki and Jenna a couple of weeks before.

I was annoyed one afternoon after experiencing two situations that made me uncomfortable. The first occurred in the morning after my mom dropped me off at school. I was hurrying into the building because I was about to be late due to the fact that I had unexpectedly gotten my period and missed the bus. As I was racing into the building, a group of senior boys drove into the parking lot about thirty miles over the speed limit. The driver slowed down when they saw me, and some stuck their heads out the window. They started making catcalls, whistling, and blowing kissing noises at me. I was infuriated but too embarrassed to address them. I refused to turn and face them, although I was red-faced with my fists clenched as I made my way through the doors just as the first bell rang.

The second incident happened during gym class. Unfortunately, my school had a pool. Therefore, we were required to pick one semester each year for swimming lessons. Every girl in school hated this class. I decided to get it over with my first semester of tenth grade. On the same day, I'd already been harassed. I was shocked when I walked out of the locker room with my bathing suit on, and an upperclassman- who I wasn't familiar with- simultaneously stepped out of the boys' room. He looked me up and down and raised his eyebrows with approval as if I were merely a picture in a dirty magazine. I gave him a disgusted look as he chuckled and quickly scooted away.

I recalled the incidents to Nikki and Jenna later as we were on our way to cheerleading practice.

"That's so gross!" Jenna hissed, "You should have flipped them off."

Nikki's reaction was more subtle, "Some boys just don't understand that girls don't want to be treated like objects."

"No, actually," Jenna began, "They don't care."

"I just hate being looked at like I'm, I don't know how to explain it- I guess like I'm 'Little Red Riding Hood,' and they're wolves who just want to eat me!" I stated angrily, "I'm not a piece of bacon or cake. It makes me feel subhuman."

Nikki and Jenna agreed as we continued, not realizing that Laurie Smithers had been eavesdropping on our conversation.

As Laurie read her poem, I thought about the fact that she had absolutely no right to target me this way. I couldn't recall ever having a conversation with her. I certainly had never harmed her. In fact, I didn't even laugh when my friends made mild jokes about how strange and creepy she was. I knew I wasn't as kind and sympathetic as Kelly, but I never made fun of people. I hated bullying and didn't even find mocking people who were "different" humorous.

And Laurie was the one who had always been cruel to me without provocation.

I'll never forget her accusations towards me. Someone she didn't know. Someone she clearly despised. She could have picked any pretty, popular girl in school, but she chose me. I couldn't figure out why- maybe because of what she'd heard me tell my friends?

To paraphrase, she accused me of pretending to be nice when in reality, I was a bitch. She wondered why I would wear make-up and dress in skinny jeans and skirts that showed off my "flawless" figure if I didn't want guys to notice me. She physically described me- otherwise, people might not have known who she was talking about. She cleared her throat before she began reading and adjusted the paper In her steady hands. Her voice was loud and clear as she read:

"Little Red Riding Hood"
Petite
Thin, hourglass figure
Silky honey-brown hair
Almond-shaped chocolate brown eyes
Oval shaped face
Pert nose
Symmetrical features
Looks just like famous movie stars
Why do you pretend?
Why do you pretend not to want attention?
When you want to be eaten by the big bad wolf?
You are a con artist. You are actually the wolf dressed in sheep's clothing.
Pretending to be nice
Overachiever
Cheerleader
Rich girl
I hate you

When she was done, every single person in the class was dead silent.

Finally, Jenna- who was never at a loss for words blurted out, "Seriously, you bitch! What are you in love with her? You are such a skank!"

"Seriously, sweetheart," Bobby began sarcastically, "This is OBVIOUSLY one mad girl crush. What the hell?"

"I can't say I blame you, Sis," Jamey chimed in, "But yeah…this is no doubt lesbo territory."

Kelly stood up and smiled with pity, "You poor thing. You must be so sad to write a poem like that."

Josh laughed out loud.

Mr. Harry sat with his feet on his desk, a smile on his face. I was thinking that he was definitely high.

Everyone was staring at me, wondering how I would respond, including Laurie.

This was one of those moments when I was overcome with justified rage. It only took a couple of seconds for me to tell Laurie precisely what I thought about her poetry.

I stood up, feeling enraged. I had become a volcano that was about to erupt. I was exhaling fire, puffing out smoke from my nose. I pointed my finger at Laurie and told her exactly what I thought of her and her poem. Akin to similar encounters, when I was overcome with fury, I experienced what felt like an out-of-body experience.

"You know what, Laurie? I am sorry that you are so unhappy with your life that you feel the need to write and then read aloud a poem that is so mean-spirited and hateful to a whole class of kids. A poem that is obviously about me. I have never done anything to you. I have never snubbed you, left you out, or even given you a dirty look. So, for you to target me- sorry, but that says more about you than it does about me. If you have something against me- that's all you! Not me! If you don't like me, for whatever reason, that's fine. I don't care less what you think about my clothes, the activities I'm involved in, or my relatives, although it's none of your damn business. I get that high school sucks for you. But you know what, that's not my fault. I have never been unkind to you or *anyone* in my entire life. I am NOT fake. Why should you care if I'm a cheerleader? Why do you care if I dress like most teenage girls in this school? Are you saying that because I don't want to be treated like an object, I'm supposed to dress like an Amish person? For the record, I don't show cleavage or wear skirts that look like underwear. The way I dress is normal. I shouldn't even have to say that because IT'S NONE OF YOUR BUSINESS. Like I said, I'm sorry you are so unhappy and angry- but don't you dare put that on me! You purposely tried to embarrass me in front of all my friends and peers. You're the villain here- no matter how popular or unpopular both of us are. You are the one who tried to hurt, embarrass, and shame me! And the comment I made about Little Red Riding Hood, guess what? I'm not ashamed of it. ***I own it.*** I don't like boys treating me like a piece of meat. I think I should be able to dress like a *normal* girl without being treated that way. I suggest you get therapy because your obvious hatred towards me is sick and perverse."

I noticed at that moment that my classmates were staring at me with their eyes and mouths agape. Their images all seemed to somehow amalgamate - it was an illusion. However, once I reached my finale, I looked around the room and noticed that everyone was as still as mannequins. The room was dead silent. I got scared for a minute and had an irrational thought- what if I had teleported into a horror movie, and everyone was dead?

Laurie huffed and puffed, and I was going to really lose it again if she tried to cry to make people feel sorry for her. But she didn't, and I was grateful for that. She just grabbed her poem and started walking back to her seat with an angry yet defeated look. "How do you know I was even talking about you?" she half whispered as she plunked down at her desk.

"Well, it's pretty obvious!" Jenna shouted sarcastically, "Seriously, girl – you need to just get a life!"

Everyone suddenly started clapping as I shrank back down in my seat. I was relieved when Kelly decided to intervene at that moment. I didn't want to create a situation where I was the reason people started to bully Laurie rather than make subtle, snarky remarks behind her back.

Kelly looked at me with a woeful expression and a question in her eyes. I nodded pleadingly. I knew she was the only one of my friends who would understand and fix this.

"Okay, guys," she said in a cheerful voice. Everyone listened because Kelly was a sweet as pie, super pretty cheerleader who was so popular and caring that she was a force to be reckoned with. "This is an unfortunate situation. This would not have occurred if Miss Bayer was here," she glanced apologetically at Mr. Harry, whom I deduced was so high he hadn't a clue what was going on because he was still sitting in the exact same position with the same look he'd had before Laurie read her poem. "Anyway," Kelly continued, "I think Jessica would agree...We should leave this alone. It's more of a ...um- well, a private matter. No grudges. The people involved will deal with this without being bullied."

No one responded. I think they were all still in shock. A situation like this was rare. It was hard to process.

Kelly was basically at a loss for words. She looked at me desperately.

"I agree," I sighed and glanced at Laurie, who was sitting with pursed lips and her arms folded against her chest protectively. She reminded me of an angry toddler. I stood up at that point and shook my head with disgust, "I won't hold a grudge against Laurie. I just want to let this go. With that being said, we should all sign a petition stating that Mr. Harry should never be allowed to sub in any class ever again! I mean seriously," I pointed to Mr. Harry, "You are obviously high on something, and you have NO business acting as a teacher. In reality, this is all your fault."

Mr. Harry giggled and nodded. I wasn't sure how to respond to that. My peers suddenly started to chuckle- and just like that, the whole room erupted into uncontrollable laughter. Then- it was Jamey's turn to take center stage.

Jamey suddenly dropped to his knees right in front of me and put his hands together as if in prayer. "This girl has spunk!" he announced as he looked around the class, nodding his head.

I am sure I turned the brightest shade of red possible. I tried to walk away, but Jamey grabbed my ankles. "Come on, Jess," he begged, "Give me a chance. I freaking love you! Go out with me. Please be my girlfriend. I am seriously begging you."

"Let go of me," I ordered through gritted teeth.

"I'll let go if you agree to go out with me."

I looked around and noticed that most everyone was laughing good-naturedly and shaking their heads in amusement. Jamey was one of those guys who could get away with insufferable behavior like this. He was popular with girls and guys; he was known for being funny, and he had one of those personalities that allowed him to get away with just about everything and anything.

Bobbly walked up and put his hand on Jamey's shoulder, "Come on, bro…the bell's going to ring." He looked at me with a benevolent smirk on his face.

"I want everyone to know that regardless of whether or not Jessica Calabresi agrees- she is MY girl!" Jamey went on as he started to stand up, leaning on Bobby for support.

"Jamey, just shut up!" I ordered, "I am not an object to be possessed. I don't appreciate you talking about me like that. You know- it's disrespectful."

He looked deeply into my eyes as he bit his bottom lip, "I would never disrespect you." He then shook his head in confusion and continued, "That doesn't even make sense."

"Damn, now she's definitely off limits," Tony Luciano said. He was a friend of Jamey's and a fellow football player.

"You bet she is," Jamey stated, looking in Tony's direction with an affable look on his face, "She belongs to me."

He turned his gaze back to me, "Seriously, Jess, if I can't have you, no one can." He winked, directing his statement at me but saying it loud enough for everyone else in class to hear.

Tony shrugged, "Okay, man. That sucks, but I got you."

"Shit," Matt Roarke, another football player and friend of Jamey's, said in a teasing tone, putting his hands up in the air as if he was surrendering, "One hot girl off the market; no disrespect."

Jamey widened his eyes, pointed at him light-heartedly, and shook his head, "She's off limits."

Tony and Matt came up and stood on either side of Jamey. Tony clapped him on the back, and Matt put his arm around him. "No one's going to mess with you, man," Matt assured him, "Or her."

Jamey nodded. He turned towards me and winked, "See you later, Baby," he said with what sounded almost like a twang.

Bobby shook his head and poked Jamey in the back, "You are too much, Jame. Take it down a notch."

The bell rang as if on cue, and they all started to walk out of the room together.

I surveyed the expressions on Jenna, Nikki, Kelly, and Erin's faces, who were surrounding me at that point, "What just happened?" I asked incredulously.

Nikki looked perplexed, "I don't know," she began, "But he is kind of out of his freaking mind."

Jenna shook her head with disdain, "He's an idiot. Don't let him get to you. He's so sexist!"

Kelly swirled her fingers through her wavy auburn hair and smiled good-naturedly, "He's not *really* sexist," she claimed, "He's just a typical jock. I mean, he just really, really likes you, Jess. He's half joking."

Jenna snorted and rolled her eyes, "Sorry, Kelly, but sometimes you're naïve."

Kelly, being Kelly, didn't get offended. She was always sweet even when being insulted, "It's just that I've known him since forever, right Erin? He's just a goofball sometimes. He's not a bad guy."

Jenna shrugged, "I didn't say he was a *bad* guy. He is a friend. But he IS a male chauvinist."

"We better get to our next class," Erin stated, leading us towards the door, "And Kelly's right," she asserted, turning her head to face the rest of us, "This isn't a big deal. Everyone knows how Jamey is. He certainly likes you, Jess, but obviously, he's half joking. He's just trying to make people laugh. No one is going to take him seriously."

Erin. Was. Dead…
WRONG.

Chapter Eleven:
Little Red Riding Hood

I honestly don't know what happened after the incident with Mr. Harry. I felt like I was in a whirlwind- as if everything, even my feelings about Jamey, were out of my control. I was in somewhat of a fog, going through the motions without feeling like I was even making decisions. I don't know when I decided or *if* I actually decided to give Jamey another chance.

Frankly, I was shocked that my classmates wasted any time and energy pondering our, for lack of a better word, *situation*. Everyone in school was interested. Some were even fascinated with the state of affairs between Jessica Calabresi and Jamey Russo. We were both constantly questioned about our "status." Was I his girlfriend? No. That was the standard answer from us both because I adamantly informed Jamey on many occasions that he was NOT my boyfriend. Our friends were inquisitive but knew our reluctance to relay information had nothing to do with us being secretive. We weren't trying to hide anything. In actuality, Jamey and I were cautious with our words because we weren't entirely sure about our relationship.

Oddly enough, it wasn't only the members of our peer group who were curious about us. It was literally the talk of the school for weeks. Needless to say, I was not only perplexed about this but also ill at ease and anxious that everyone was gossiping about Jamey and me. I loathed all the staring and whispering as I walked down the hallways from underclassmen and upperclassmen, which caused me to feel extremely intimidated.

Jenna and Nikki kept assuring me that, eventually, people would move on, like they always did, and lose interest. For the most part, that was true. However, it certainly took longer than expected. Plus, even after the hoopla died down, we were still considered an intriguing topic of interest.

Despite our uncertainty about *us*, Jamey and I did communicate. He made it clear that I was the only girl he truly desired. I was the only girl he wanted to be monogamous with. He wanted a bona fide, full-fledged "jump in with both feet" commitment. In retrospect, I was the one who sent mixed signals. It was my fault that we were unable to define our connection. I was also culpable for the curiosity among our classmates. I was the one who refused to make a decision. I wasn't trying to play hard to get or be spiteful. I truly felt confused, and I didn't know what to do. Therefore, I allowed our situation to remain complicated.

I was most definitely very, very much attracted to Jamey. We were physically involved, but I put limitations on our intimacy. I kept him from passing what some would call first base. He was allowed to kiss me- deep, passionate kisses, but nothing more. And even though we only had sensuous contact with our mouths, there was such strong chemistry between us- it was palpable. These moments were special, electric, and exquisite. I sometimes wanted to move beyond the kissing, but I always practiced self-control, and Jamey never tried to "cop a feel," he was incredibly respectful of my boundaries.

I found out the strangest thing about Jamey from Jenna. Apparently, Mickey told her that when Jamey hooked up with girls in Italy, he refused to kiss any of them. He felt it was too personal. And if they tried to kiss him, he'd move his face away and blatantly express that kissing wasn't allowed. I didn't understand why the girls he was with would agree with this arrangement, but according to what Jamey told Mickey, they almost always did.

Although Jamey knew he couldn't force me to be his girlfriend, he did make it known that I belonged to him. Even though I told him I wasn't ready for anything serious and disapproved of some of his personality traits, he still "claimed" me. He didn't care when I called him sexist. He would turn the situation around and start questioning me about why I was so offended. He would ask why it bothered me if I wasn't interested in dating anyone else. I would try to explain that I didn't like how he objectified me, but he would claim that he didn't even know what that meant and that he was just trying to protect me from "wolves." It eventually became a joke that I grudgingly had to laugh at.

When all was said and done, I was off limits. Upperclassmen had no interest in me. I was known as a straight-laced prude, as far as they were concerned. And boys around my age, who might have been interested, were scared to mess with Jamey- one of the strongest and toughest kids in school who was not afraid to start a fight. And Jamey had never lost a fight- whether he started it or finished it.

After a while, I became accustomed to our arrangement. I felt as if we'd both signed some kind of contract. There were many things that Jamey and I never discussed, although they somehow became guidelines. I guess the term "unspoken rules" originated from situations like this. We had expectations of each other, and we both followed them. The *rules* became known to our friends and peers. I can honestly say that I don't recall how our relationship eventually just took on a life of its own. We established this unusual understanding without ever sitting down and having a conversation about it. It just unraveled. After about a month, this inexplicable bond between Jamey and me felt normal. I accepted it- sometimes begrudgingly, but I didn't protest- at least not too vehemently or with sincerity. I became complacent and complicit- believing wholeheartedly that things would eventually change and develop into a monogamous relationship, which I just wasn't yet ready for.

The Rules:

- Jamey would try to change and become a better person. I would prepare myself to enter into a relationship if he did.
- Jamey could not pressure me when we had intimate moments. He knew I was reluctant to go beyond first base. He respected that. We made out nothing more. He never even tried to go further because he read my body language and knew I wasn't ready.
- Even though we weren't exclusive, I wasn't "allowed" to date. The reason was that I agreed Jamey was the only guy I was attracted to. I wasn't ready for a relationship, so why would I want to date another guy anyway? This rule didn't bother me because, truth be told, I had no interest in anyone other than Jamey. Besides, boys were too afraid of Jamey to speak to me, let alone ask me out.
- This wasn't really a rule. In fact, it was something no one ever dared mention. Jamey might have had physical encounters with other girls. He wanted to be with me exclusively, but I refused to commit. In light of this, I had my suspicions. I honestly wasn't jealous- because, in my mind, his possible sexual conquests were the equivalent of self-exploration. If there were other girls, I knew they meant nothing to him. Aside from me, he'd never publicly shown

affection towards any females. It was common knowledge that he pined after me and would never commit to anyone else. He also made it crystal clear that he wanted me to agree to be his girlfriend.

Although our relationship was atypical and unconventional, Jamey and I shared many special and intimate moments. He was always loving, respectful, and sweet to me. He made me smile wider than anyone else I'd ever known. He was unabashed when expressing his feelings for me. He had no shame. He didn't have to. He was Jamey Russo, after all. His name and reputation spoke for itself. Boys like him didn't have to be subtle or worry about embarrassing themselves. He could get away with virtually anything.

Sometimes, I wished I wasn't so attracted to him. He was dreadfully good-looking, and I loved his chiseled physique. I fantasized about him all the time- but I knew the things I daydreamed about were meant for the future. I was only fifteen, and I respected my body. I was also raised Catholic and knew "good girls" didn't let boys soil them. My friends would have thought that was old-fashioned, so I kept those views to myself. I didn't judge the promiscuity of other girls. I just knew that I had to be 100% ready when it came to allowing a boy to do anything besides kiss me.

Jamey and I kissed a lot. We snuck off together regularly. Never publicly. I was not a PDA sort of girl. We found ways to be alone. Usually, these times occurred when we were participating in a group activity. Our friend group frequently went to movies, dances, parties, basketball games, etc. On those occasions, Jamey would always find a way to make sure we spent time alone together. His kisses were so gentle…he was slow and methodical. He didn't slobber all over me. When he kissed me, his tongue was warm and soft. He would put his arms around my waist- never touching me in private places. He would always look me in the eyes and smile- taking me in. He'd tell me how beautiful I was, rub his finger across my lips, and grip my chin- just showing appreciation.

Jamey and I would also text- he would always be the one to initiate. His texts varied. He would sometimes write something sentimental- like "Hey, pretty girl- what's up?" Or sometimes he would let me know what was going on at home- "My mother is a freaking nut job. Can we please switch parents?" Other times, he would make a joke…he often would make me laugh out loud.

I would have been more likely to commit to Jamey if he had made a more serious attempt to change, but when all was said and done, he really didn't try hard enough. He still bullied weaker kids and made sexist remarks that annoyed me. He was too overprotective and grilled me about irrelevant events and nonexistent threats. He made unnecessary comments to ensure that other guys knew I was off-limits. For every good time we had together, there was an equal amount of bad behavior on Jamey's part.

The proverbial shit really hit the fan after the incident with "The Kissing Closet."

Chapter Twelve:
The Kissing Closet

For many students attending Lomonoco Creek, one of the main advantages was the numerous athletic opportunities it offered. Although they were mostly male-dominated, cheerleading, the physical activity I was passionate about, existed year-round. The most celebrated sports at my school were football, basketball, and baseball. Therefore, cheerleaders were deemed essential for only those particular sports. Although several kids played or participated in softball, soccer, wrestling, golf, track and field, etc., cheerleaders weren't provided for them. At my high school, those sports were considered less important. This seemed to be a common theme in most academic institutions.

Aside from cheerleading, one drawback to being involved in any sport at Lomonoco Creek was that you had to try out every season, regardless of how talented you were. Cheerleading didn't change the way other sports did. It didn't require a different set of skills like every other sport. Consequently, my friends and I were allowed to continue our favorite hobby throughout the school year. I was incredibly grateful and relieved that the pastime I felt especially zealous about didn't require you to prove yourself time and time again. Tryouts, in my opinion, were anxiety-provoking and exhausting. Therefore, I was incredibly relieved that I could remain a cheerleader for every noteworthy sport- the three biggest draws.

In retrospect, that was likely because, although cheerleading was considered a sport, and we were highly valued and respected, we were there to support the boys. That truthfully didn't cross my mind when I was in high school. The athletic department, school board, and administrators weren't involved in cheerleading and didn't care all that much about us. However, they expected us to be there to support the boys. Because of that, cheerleaders and our coaches could formulate our own rules. There were no formal policies put into place. As a result, we could do what we wanted.

Being young and admittedly naïve, I gave no mind to the fact that this was a sexist policy. I felt only gratitude for being chosen as a year-round cheerleader. Only about a dozen of us were allowed to remain in our positions throughout the entire school year. Most girls were considered mediocre and/or not as invested in the sport as the rest of us. They were obliged to go through the motions during each season, and the decisions of who made the squad were left to the coaches and head cheerleaders.

The only hardship about this tradition was what inevitably occurred at the end of each sophomore year. It didn't necessarily have to be negative, and sometimes it was considered enjoyable. It depended on the situation and who was in charge of making the rules. I don't know when this ritual began, but it had been going on for at least a decade.

Right before baseball season, the two future varsity cheerleading captains planned a gathering for the long-term sophomore cheerleaders to "welcome" them to varsity sports the following year. The sophomore and junior baseball players were also invited because, without boys, it wouldn't be a party and certainly wouldn't be any fun. The reality of the situation was that it never really turned into a welcoming but more of a hazing. Everyone knew that. It always involved forcing the cheerleaders to do uncomfortable things. In previous years, the cheerleaders had been cajoled into jumping in a pool without their clothes on, pouring large cups of cold beer over their heads, mooning cars driving by things like that. Humiliating.

Melissa Wilder and Michelle Banks, known as the "The Two M's," were juniors- and would soon be the varsity cheerleading captains. They were two of the most admired girls in the junior class and would inevitably be the most popular females in school. They were responsible for the event this year. They were always friendly and pleasant as far as I was concerned, but they had a joint reputation for being sneaky and devious at times.

In my sophomore year, we were all invited to a party at Michelle's house. No one knew what their "welcoming" gesture would entail. We were all justifiably nervous. Essentially, when all was said and done, I was the only one of the cheerleaders who was majorly embarrassed during the *celebration*.

Because of Jamey.

Once again, he made a major catastrophe out of a situation that could have been innocuous. And I was the one who had to suffer because of him.

There were several reasons I was panicky about going to Michelle's party. Before I asked permission, I anticipated my dad would forbid me from attending. He wasn't stupid. He obviously was aware that the availability and consumption of alcohol at most high school parties was a given.

He surprisingly granted me permission to attend because it was a sports-related event. He made it clear that I was allotted only one alcoholic beverage because I was almost sixteen years old. He knew that the other kids might mock or harass me if I chose to abstain. My mother shrugged and nonchalantly advised me to nurse the drink all night, and no one would notice or ask questions.

My friends and I were all very anxious about what Melissa and Michelle had in store for us cheerleaders. We had no idea if they were planning a somewhat stress-free initiation or if they had something horribly unpleasant in mind. Of course, we were hoping it would be as painless as possible. I certainly didn't anticipate that things would turn out as dreadful as they did- at least for ME. I was under the assumption that although we were all wary, it wouldn't be *that* bad, considering my best friends and I were all in this together.

Erin, Kelly, Jenna, Nikki, and I had discussed the party several times. We tried unsuccessfully to figure out what we thought the two "M's" were planning. Basically, it came down to the fact that we had no idea. It literally could entail anything, and we would never be able to guess, no matter how much we tried. Although we knew that to be the case, we continued trying to guess- right up until the party began.

My mom agreed to drive Nikki, Jenna, and me to the party. Our parents had collectively decided on a curfew of midnight. My Aunt Gina offered to pick us up. My father said it would be okay to text if an abstemious, trustworthy person offered to drive us home. He was adamant that the person be sober and someone we could rely on.

The get-together was being held at Michelle's house. She lived a few streets north of us, only about a five-minute drive. Her neighborhood had recently been built, so her house was brand new. She had lived down the street from Jamey before moving the previous year. Jamey and Michelle had played together as children. Although her new residence was about the same size as the homes in my neighborhood, it was a downgrade from where she'd lived before. According to my mom, her father had been the C.E.O. of a company and was fired a few years back. My mother explained that it was not unusual for heads of corporations to be let go or asked to resign because there was nowhere to go but down. Michelle's dad immediately got another job, which paid significantly less than his prior salary. If Michelle was insecure about the smaller size of her new house, she certainly never showed it. In fact, she was the most self-assured and confident person I knew.

Michelle lived in a large brown ranch-style house on a cul-de-sac. All the homes in her neighborhood looked identical except for their color. I figured the inside of each residence was also similarly designed. All the appliances in her house were pristine and contemporary. It was decorated with a colonial theme, similar to mine, which created a cozy, warm atmosphere. The ambiance was in direct opposition to how I was feeling on the inside. Michelle's house had only one floor, but we were relegated to the kitchen, dining room, backyard porch, and bathroom.

My closest friends and I had all arrived at Michelle's house by 8:00 that night. My crew mainly mingled with each other for about an hour. We were once again whispering about the "hazing ritual" Melissa and Michelle had come up with. At this point, we were beyond anxious and just curious and yearning to hear what it was and then get it over with. The sophomore boys had no interest in the event whatsoever. They eventually began their own conversation separate from ours, although we were all gathered in the same circle on the granite patio outside Michelle's house. It was dark out, but the hanging lanterns lit the area up.

Finally, after what seemed like hours, Melissa and Michelle called all of the sophomore girls and junior boys into the dining room. They ushered us in, explaining that the sophomore boys had to remain in either the kitchen or somewhere outside. They weren't allowed to participate in this part of the night. None of them seemed concerned. They were too busy getting drunk.

While announcing that it was time for the sophomore cheerleaders to become initiated, Michelle and Melissa acted so somber and mysterious you'd think they were running an actual inauguration. I thought it was somewhat ridiculous.

The two "M's" had all the girls sit down around the vast dining room table while the boys were to remain standing along the pale blue colored walls. Once we were settled, they explained what this year's welcome event would involve. Melissa told us they had come up with a game that we should be grateful for and appreciate because it wouldn't be painful or harsh like some of the expectations in the past.

She went on to say that we would be participating in what they called "The Kissing Closet." She explained that they had a list of all the junior boys' names and would be pulling them out of a Mason jar. The boy who was chosen would get to pick one of the sophomore cheerleaders to take into the hallway closet- which, according to Melissa, had remained empty during their move. She claimed it was wide and roomy- the girls would be required to stay in the closet for five minutes. No girl would be forced to do anything she didn't want to do, but it was mandatory that the female chosen accompany the boy into the closet.

I was suddenly nauseated and dizzy. I hoped I wouldn't be chosen- because I would not only feel embarrassed, but I was also terrified of Jamey's reaction.

The boys standing around the dining room in a semi-circle were practically salivating. They obviously loved the idea. Many of the girls squirmed in their seats- there was a mixed reaction among the females in the room. Aside from Nikki, my friends were perfectly comfortable with the idea. Nikki looked at me and raised her eyebrows. Then, she shrugged when she noticed the distressed look on my face. I wasn't sure if she was trying to make me feel better because of Jamey or if she was acknowledging that her actual boyfriend, the guy she was currently committed to, would have a mild reaction if she was chosen to accompany a guy in the closet because he trusted her. Ironically, Nikki's *boyfriend* was less of a threat than Jamey, a boy I refused to settle down with.

I felt like I was in a room occupied by statues as Melissa and Michelle prolonged the commencement of the game by whispering to each other while pretending not to surreptitiously scan the crowd. After what seemed like an eternity, Melissa picked up the cup containing all the boys' names and shook it. She closed her eyes and smirked as she put her hand in the jar and ruffled the names.

"Don't be silly, Melis," Michelle teased, "They will all get a chance- eventually."

The two "M's" giggled as everyone waited in anticipation.

"How about I pick the names, and you say them?" Melissa suggested, directing her attention to Michelle as if the rest of us weren't in the room.

Melissa slowly placed her fingers in the cup and drew out a name. "Hmm...who do we have here?" she asked with exaggerated curiosity.

Melissa widened her eyes and morphed her pink, glossed lips into a wide "O." She pointed at Gene Camillo. "Geeeeeeene Camilio, come on down!" she shouted as if she were a game show host on speed.

Gene clapped his hands and chuckled, "The luck of the...wait for it...Italian," he pronounced the "I" as eye, thinking he was very clever. He had a reputation for being very proud of his heritage and sometimes referred to himself as "The Italian Stallion."

"Shit, no fair. That prick gets first pick," one of the other baseball players said good-naturedly.

Gene ignored the comment. He was a handsome, fun-loving, and gregarious guy who had hooked up with Jenna. I had no idea what she saw in him. I found him obnoxious.

No one was surprised when he looked into Jenna's eyes and rubbed his lips together. I was almost positive he would pick her because he was the one who wanted to become a couple, while Jenna was only interested in screwing around with him. She would laughingly say, behind his back, that he was the type of guy who wanted what he couldn't have.

When she said this to all of us at lunch one day, Mickey joked, "Sounds like he's getting plenty to me."

Jenna looked at him as if he was an idiot, "That's not what I mean, jackass," she'd said condescendingly, "He thinks he wants me to be his girlfriend."

Mickey shrugged, "Maybe he does!" he said in exasperation. "I don't want you to go out with him...obviously, but what the hell? How do you know that's NOT what he wants?"

"You don't know anything about guys," Jenna informed him. Everyone burst into laughter when Jenna claimed to know more about the male of the species than another actual male.

Gene's eyes continued to linger on Jenna before Melissa said impatiently, "Come on, Gene- just pick already. The other guys are waiting."

Gene pointed at Jenna and winked, "I choose you, girl," he declared, with what I presume he thought was a seductive tone.

Jenna sighed and made a production of going into the closet with him- in typical Jenna fashion. She pranced over to him and slammed the door to the closet once they were both inside. When the five minutes were up, everyone laughed because Jenna and Gene didn't come out until Michelle knocked on the door three times and very fiercely the third time. Jenna raised her eyebrows in satisfaction, and Gene grinned sheepishly as they strolled out of the closet.

Aaron Justice was picked next. He was very attractive and had a reputation for being a player. He looked over all the girls as if we were sports cars, and he was allowed to purchase only one of us before his eyes landed on Erin. He made a comment about wanting to choose a sure thing as he pointed in her direction. Erin good-naturedly rolled her eyes. Surprisingly, she was not embarrassed by her promiscuous reputation at all. Erin willingly agreed.

I breathed a sigh of relief as I nervously rubbed my hands together and tapped my foot rapidly on the rug. During the entire five minutes that Erin and Aaron were in the closet, I prayed that I wouldn't get chosen during the entirety of the game. When they came out, they also appeared to have enjoyed their experience. Erin's lips were puffy, and her eyeliner was smudged. Aaron tapped her on the behind and winked as they parted ways.

Next up was Kyle Mansfield. Kyle was comical, attention-seeking, and too self-assured to actually be secure. I found him to be one of those overly confident people who was secretly hiding major insecurities. He wasn't particularly attractive but popular because of his athleticism.

I continued looking down as Kyle stood before us. I studied the fabric off my jeans as his eyes roamed over us like we were cattle. Pieces of meat. I couldn't fathom how the other girls failed to recognize how chauvinistic this ridiculous game was.

"Time to choose," Michelle finally said after Kyle hesitated for at least three minutes. Although I was still intensely staring at the faded blue denim on my skinny jeans, I could see through my peripheral vision that his finger was swaying back and forth as if he was about to make the most pertinent decision of his life.

"Hmmm, let's see..." he murmured mischievously. I panicked because I could feel his eyes on the top of my head. I adamantly refused to look up. I didn't know if I was imagining that he was staring at me. He was obviously building suspense because he continued to keep quiet.

"Come on, Kyle," Melissa said impatiently.

When he said my name, a hush fell over the crowd. I closed my eyes and blew out a long breath. I struggled to stop the tears from forming in my eyes. Everyone knew about my situation with Jamey, which made me feel nervous and humiliated.

"Jessica," Melissa said deviously, "You know the rules."

I pursed my lips and sighed heavily as I reluctantly stood up. I was panic-stricken, knowing that if Jamey found out, he would cause a scene.

The room was completely silent as I slowly ambled over to Kyle.

Melissa stood up suddenly with her cup in hand, "I need a refill," she informed us. I knew the keg was outside- on the patio where Jamey and his friends were hanging out, and I anticipated what would happen next.

I was reluctantly about to enter the closet with Kyle. He placed his hand on the small of my back as Jamey came storming into the room, followed by a smug-looking Michelle. She had obviously told him what was happening for entertainment's sake. I had also heard rumors that she had harbored a crush on Jamey when they were little kids and lived in the same neighborhood.

"Get your hand off of her," Jamey demanded. He immediately pulled me away from Kyle in a gentle way, but he had an irate expression on his face.

"Listen, Jamey," I said, my voice trembling, "The rules are that I must go in the closet with him. But I'm NOT going to do anything. I promise. Just trust me."

Jamey laughed without humor. "I DO trust you, but I sure as hell don't trust him," he said with disgust, jutting his chin in Kyle's direction.

I looked pleadingly at Michelle. She cast her eyes downward. Considering the two "M's" were in charge of the game, I was hoping at least one of them would intervene. But I was beginning to think they'd planned this. Melissa just shrugged sheepishly and raised her eyebrows as if there was nothing she could do about it.

"Listen, man," Kyle began impatiently, "You don't own her. You two aren't even a couple. And even if you were, these are the rules of the game."

"I don't give a crap what the rules are. Jessica is not going in the closet with you or any other guy in this room."

Kyle looked down and grinned with an amused expression on his face. When he looked up, he pointed at Jamey, "You think you can bully guys younger and smaller than you. But guess what? I'm not afraid of you." He continued pointing as he moved closer to Jamey, "You're not going to tell me what I can do during a game. This is a tradition; you don't get to mess with it."

Jamey stepped closer to Kyle so they were inches apart. "Do you want to make a bet?" he said, tilting his head with a threat in his voice.

As Jamey and Kyle continued to argue, and their words grew angrier and more heated, I moved away from them. I looked across the crowd and noticed that everyone was intently staring at the two, fixated, almost desperate to find out what would happen next. I felt the same way but for contradictory reasons. No one was going to interfere. The crowd was basically watching an entertaining reality show. It was *interesting* to them. Jamey was once again turning my life into pandemonium at the expense of my mental health.

When it became clear that this would inevitably get physical, Michelle said, "If you two are going to fight- you need to take it outside. You are not going to do damage to anything in my house. My parents will kill me."

"That's fine with me," Jamey declared.

Jamey walked quickly towards the door and swung it open. Kyle was close behind. Before Jamey could make it outside, Kyle pulled his fist back and attempted to punch him in the side of his face. Jamey dodged Kyle's fist. He then pushed him down the steps and onto the grass outside. Kyle fell but immediately got back up. He shoved Jamey, but Jamey stayed upright. Everyone ran towards the door, but I did the opposite. I moved as far away from the fight as I could. I could hear punches, grunts, cheers, and jeers from the crowd.

As the fight continued, I moved further into the house, feeling isolated and distressed. I was standing by myself in a corner of the room, picking at my cuticles, when Jenna came and found me. She grabbed my arm and said that Gene would drive me home. They were planning to leave- and spend some time together in his basement before Jenna's curfew. She told me the fight was being broken up. Jamey had won- no surprise. Jamey was tough and strong, but he also was more powerful because of how jealous and enraged he'd become. The other baseball players had pulled them apart after watching long enough to determine that Jamey was triumphant.

Jenna led me out a side door with Gene following behind us. I was once again angry and sickened by Jamey's actions. Gene tried to make a joke about it in the car, but Jenna shushed him. After that, we were all silent. I sat in the back seat and tried to stop the tears from spilling from my eyes. Jamey had humiliated me again, and I vowed I would never forgive him this time.

After that incident, no boy at school was courageous enough to even think about asking me out. For the rest of my sophomore year, guys were afraid to glance in my direction. That eventually changed- after about a year, but I won't go into that horrible ordeal until later.

I would say that the most infuriating part of the "Kissing Closet" was what it did to Jamey's reputation. He was seen as a hero after the confrontation at the party. He was considered macho and brave. People admired and even idolized him. However, I was furious with him for acting violently with no provocation.

I didn't want to cause contention within our circle of friends, so I was willing to act civilly toward Jamey, but I put our emotional and physical relationship on hold. I didn't spend time alone with him and refused to answer his personal texts.

I finally gave in and forgave Jamey when he offered to help me with a charitable event. I was still a member of the Sunshine Committee, and we were trying to raise money for a cause called "Homes for the Homeless." Their mission was to help impoverished people in inner cities build houses. For weeks, we tried cajoling our classmates into offering their support, but we weren't having much luck. Our efforts were futile until Jamey intervened. He convinced all the baseball players to volunteer. Jamey was persuasive, and almost everyone on the team offered their assistance. I don't know what he did to encourage his teammates to help- but whatever he said or did worked. Without their aid, we wouldn't have been able to achieve our goal. With their help, we actually exceeded our initial aspirations.

As a result, at the end of May, I conceded. Jamey was finally out of my *"dog house"* once again.

Chapter Thirteen: Equilibrium

There was no animosity between Jamey and me before he left to go to Italy again the summer before our junior year. His family did not trust him to stay home alone, although he profusely protested. They knew he'd inevitably get into trouble if left to his own devices for three months. He complained and even seemed depressed about the trip this time. He had each of his guy friends' parents appeal to his mom to allow Jamey to stay with them for the summer rather than travel, to no avail. Jamey's mother may have been foolish, but she wasn't foolish enough to trust her rebellious, underage son not to get into trouble- probably with the law, which would have dire consequences for the entire Russo family.

Before he left, he was particularly empathetic about wanting to date exclusively. He begged me to pledge my loyalty to him. I declined because I still did not wholly trust Jamey, and I didn't feel comfortable enough to make that kind of commitment. The thought of having an actual boyfriend made me extremely uneasy.

I sometimes wondered why I had a fretful disposition when my sisters and parents were so relaxed and capable of just going with the flow. My mom confided in me that, yes, anxiety disorders are inherited, but not every member of a family is burdened with it. She told me her mom and great-grandfather suffered from nervousness. I assumed it skipped a generation.

While I wouldn't commit to Jamey, I did interrogate him about his intentions while overseas. He assured me that he would think of me the whole time he was away, and he had no interest in looking at other girls. I rolled my eyes and laughed. He didn't grin in that mischievous way of his when he swore that he loved me. I could tell he was being completely honest and sincere. I almost felt bad about questioning him because he seemed offended by my nonchalance and what he considered an accusation.

For undetermined reasons, that June, I felt much differently when Jamey left than I had the previous summer. I was overcome with a sense of melancholy and emptiness. I really missed him. I knew he'd be back in the fall, yet I initially experienced an overwhelming sadness that I hadn't anticipated. Through good times and bad times, even when I was mad at him- he was still there- in my sphere, my space. He was in my life. When he flew overseas, our separation caused me to physically ache.

I was not only sorrowful because I knew I wouldn't see him for two and half months, but this year, I also worried about him meeting and cheating with other girls. I hid this from EVERYONE. I didn't want to talk about it. Not even with Jenna or Nikki. I spent the second half of June privately moping around while publicly pretending I was content. Finally, I decided at the beginning of July that I had to busy myself with activities to take my mind off Jamey.

I decided to put him in a space in the back of my mind, store his memory there, and lock it up until he returned home. I even went so far as to avoid our male friends for fear they'd casually mention him.

I went to cheer camp again with my girlfriends, took swimming lessons to become a certified lifeguard, and took a job as a junior camp counselor. I also volunteered every Sunday to help with the Children's Liturgy and taught the elementary students during Sunday Mass. I became so busy that the thoughts of Jamey were relegated to dreams. He showed up almost every night…I knew my subconscious refused to allow me to repress him.

The best part of the summer was how proud my father was of me. He constantly praised me and commented on how all the activities I was involved in would benefit me in the long run. They would all look good on a college application. He would use my experiences as teaching points for my sisters. Sara, of course, continued to resent what she considered his favoritism. And as far as Megan was concerned, my father's words went in one ear and out the other.

For the most part, Jamey stayed hidden in my imaginary vault. By August, I didn't have to pretend to be content because I actually was. Although I wasn't consciously thinking about it, I knew Jamey would be back soon, and time did fly when you busied yourself with an abundance of hobbies and obligations. Everything was fine and would have stayed that way if it hadn't been for a slip of the tongue from my cousin Nikki at one of our family gatherings. Nikki's accidental mention of Jamey created not only distress but also intense embarrassment for me. Unfortunately, those feelings were never completely alleviated.

For as long as I can remember, my family got together with Jenna and Nikki's families on the first Friday of every month for formal dinner parties. We'd always done it, and it was a guaranteed good time for all of us. Our moms alternated hosting, and after they each had a turn, we'd spend the fourth month at a restaurant for dinner, drinks, and dessert. Usually, we would go to the country club our families belonged to because they offered extra-curricular activities for all age groups. Our younger siblings would swim and go to the game room. Our dads would join a poker game, and our moms would go to the spa. Jenna, Nikki, and my endeavors fluctuated. Usually, we would swim in the heated pool and then sit outside by the fire pit and gossip. Occasionally, we would join our moms for massages and mani/pedis. It all depended on our moods that particular night.

On the first Friday in August, our families had dinner at the lavish country club we belonged to in Jamestown. It was a typical evening- nothing out of the ordinary. But a conversation occurred during dinner that disturbed and alarmed me. It probably would have been moderately upsetting for most people, but for me, it was semi-traumatic.

Before going our separate ways, our entire crew always sat down to eat together. That was not negotiable- our mothers insisted upon it. Because there were so many of us, and we were VIP members of The Jamestown Country Club, we were allowed access to one of the deluxe rooms with our own private waiters.

The conversation at dinner that evening began in a very light-hearted manner. Our moms discussed how they planned to spend time getting massages at the spa later that night. Nikki's dad said his back had been hurting, and he wouldn't mind having someone work on it.

That caused my dad and Jenna's dad to mock my uncle. In their opinion, it was not manly or acceptable for a male to go to the spa. Therefore, they ribbed my Uncle Phil mercilessly.

When my mom made a joke about luring my dad to the spa, my sister Megan actually laughed so hard she had to cover her mouth, almost spilling her drink. My father acted like he'd rather walk over hot coal than do such a thing.

"Jess- can you imagine if you asked Jamey to do that?" Nikki asked.

After her impulsive remark, she immediately covered her mouth and widened her eyes as if she'd made the hugest gaffe possible.

Initially, no one responded, but it did elicit a reaction from almost everyone at the table. My parents and Aunt Gina knowingly smirked, Jenna gasped, Megan giggled, and Sara rolled her eyes.

Nikki nervously laughed, "Um...not that there's any reason for me to bring him up. I mean, everyone knows you guys are just friends. Right? I just thought how it would be funny to imagine someone so...um- you know, masculine going to a spa. But, we all know that there's nothing," she snorted, "**Nothing, I mean nothing at all between you two...** I don't know why I even said that. So dumb!"

I was humiliated, and although I knew it was an accident, I was furious with Nikki for letting that comment slip. I looked down at my meal and prayed that the conversation would move in a different direction.

It didn't. I felt all eyes on me.

After several seconds, Jenna cleared her throat and attempted to change the subject, but my sister, Sara, was too quick for her.

"Everyone knows about you and Jamey," Sara said with disdain, "Why do we have to keep pretending it's a secret?"

I glared at her angrily and spoke through gritted teeth, "NOTHING is going on between us."

My mother chuckled with amusement and flipped her hair off her shoulder.

"I would LOVE to go out with Jamey," my sister Megan remarked, He's sooooooo cute!"

"That's why Megan is going to remain in Catholic school until she's 18," my father remarked dryly, and everyone laughed good-naturedly.

"He is handsome," my Aunt Gina chimed in with a mischievous wink in my direction.

Nikki anxiously tugged on her hair and looked at me apologetically. "I should not have said that," she stammered, "It was an accident. There is absolutely nothing going on between Jessica and Jamey."

"I wouldn't say *nothing*," my father remarked in a snarky tone.

"There is definitely *something* going on between you two," my mother teased.

My mother must have noticed that my face was a deep shade of crimson, and my eyes were brimming with tears. Her whole demeanor immediately transformed. The color flushed from her cheeks as she swallowed soundly and guiltily averted her gaze from mine. "Yet, I suppose, it's really none of our business." Her previously amused tone was now humorless and reeked of concern.

"Well, come on now," my dad began, but he halted when my mother gave him a warning glance.

Once again, the room fell quiet as my dad shifted in his seat and fiddled with his silverware.

I don't remember how, but the conversation finally shifted in another direction. I didn't participate in what our families spoke about for the rest of dinner because I was stuck inside my own head. I kept quiet.

I was not only surprised that my family was aware of my involvement with Jamey but also embarrassed that my private life-*my relationship,* if you could call it that, was public fodder, and even my parents found it entertaining.

Part III.
Eleventh Grade

Chapter Fourteen: The Back of the Bus

From the time we were freshmen, my girlfriends and I frequently had sleepovers. We rotated between houses, and our respective parents were almost always home during the course of the evening. It wasn't until junior year that any of us dared bring alcohol to one of these events. The first exception to this occurred when Kelly's dad started dating a new doctor at the veterinary hospital he owned.

Kelly's parents had been amicably divorced for at least seven years. They were both professionals with busy careers. Her mom was a college professor, and her dad was an animal specialist. They remained best friends after they split, which might have been why neither of them had hitherto developed a monogamous relationship. That all changed when Mr. Bachmann fell for his new colleague. Kelly wasn't bothered by her father's new paramour; instead, she immediately saw this as an opportunity to invite us over for what inevitably became a cliched "Girls' Night In."

Her dad planned to take his lady friend to a fancy restaurant in Desmond, a city located twenty minutes outside Rosevalley. He told Kelly if he drank too much, he would take an Uber to a hotel and spend the night. Kelly knew her dad well enough to recognize that when he used the term "if," he really meant "when," thus she planned the night accordingly.

The minute her dad left for his date, Kelly stole two bottles of wine and one container of gin from his liquor cabinet. She insisted that their cook take the night off so we'd be adult-free but coaxed her into leaving plenty of "fun food" for us in the refrigerator- the type of junk her mom would never allow her to eat. In fact, both her parents would have considered it garbage and forbade her from consuming it. Kelly had a passive-aggressive way of persuading people to capitulate, most likely because most folks found her too sweet to rebuff.

Therefore, the five of us would be on our own with plenty of alcohol, forbidden food, and no one to answer to. Of course, our parents didn't know the minute details of the sleepover, and there was no reason to tell them. As far as we were concerned, her dad was going on a date and would be home afterward. We didn't consider omissions to be lies.

I was the only one of my friends who didn't yet have a car because I had a late birthday. Nikki, Jenna, Kelly, and Erin had all already turned "sweet sixteen," and all of my friends received a party and vehicle as a gift for what our parents considered a special age. Jenna was the worst driver of the four of my closest comrades. It was a mystery among my friends and family how she persuaded the driving instructor to give her a license. Nikki, Erin, and I assumed it had to be excessive flirting. And Jenna didn't deny it. She loved driving, and although she was a danger to those on the road- especially the people in the car with her, she always offered to drive- no, she actually insisted on driving and told us when she'd be picking us up. Therefore, she was the one who drove us all to Kelly's that night. Although we were in the car for less than five minutes, we felt as if our lives had been spared by the time we arrived.

Kelly flung the door open and excitedly greeted us before we even reached the front door. Mr. Bachmann's residence was very basic and plain on the inside and outside. Her mother's taste was more extravagant. His home was the smallest in the upscale neighborhood where he moved after his separation. He jokingly referred to the lack of character as minimalistic. Kelly's mom shrugged when Kelly complained about how bland her dad's taste was. Mrs. Bachmann concurred that it didn't have a woman's touch. There were no frivolities- it was rudimentary.

Kelly prearranged the living room before we arrived. Mr. Bachmann's living room was comparable to what my mother would refer to as a lounge. It consisted of a leather couch and several armchairs spread across a faux wooden floor. The circular overhead lights made the room too bright, almost shrill, and fluorescent. It also contained a big-screen television and a coffee table. It looked even more casual than usual because Kelly had sprinkled it with sleeping bags, blankets, pillows, and bean bag chairs.

As we walked inside, Kelly insisted we all change into our pajamas right away before settling in and getting comfortable.

Jenna raised her eyebrows and sarcastically remarked, "O-key, DO-Key, Kel."

Kelly clapped her hands, "This is going to be so much fun. I love hanging with just the girls. I mean, sometimes. Not ALL the time; that would certainly get boring."

Erin nodded empathetically, "I agree," she exclaimed as we all made our way to whatever room we'd been designated to get changed in.

By the time we all arrived back in the living room, Kelly brought out cheese and crackers, mozzarella sticks, chicken wings with blue cheese, and a plate of homemade brownies (baked by their cook); she shrieked and proclaimed that she was positive her dad wouldn't be back, and therefore, we could all get drunk. She immediately produced the bottles of liquor she'd taken.

Even though we had a field trip to the Capitol the following day, I wasn't nervous about drinking. We weren't departing until 10:30, and I wasn't afraid of getting caught. I planned to take it slow and do what my mom had suggested when I went to "M and M's" party- sip slowly, eat as I drank, and drink twice as much water as booze.

Kelly opened a bottle of red wine first. She had elegant goblets that her father had apparently been granted in the divorce. She gave us all a massive serving of Cabernet and bottles of Pellegrino water. I was certain I would be fine while we gossiped, watched Netflix, and gossiped some more. We'd downed two bottles of wine between the five of us when Kelly suggested we play Truth or Dare.

That was when the trouble started.

I did not want to play Truth or Dare. I detested Truth or Dare. It was my least favorite game. I loathed dares and was afraid of telling the truth- well, I feared being honest about whatever question I might be asked, especially because I knew the inquiries would most definitely revolve around Jamey. I had no idea what answers would be demanded of me, and I really, really hated the unknown.

On the other hand, my friends didn't seem to have similar feelings- in fact, their attitude towards the game was obviously in direct opposition to mine.

"I'll start," Kelly announced, "But let's switch to the heavy stuff," she opened the bottle of gin she'd placed on the reclaimed wood coffee table. I still had about a quarter of a glass of wine left from before. I'd been drinking at a snail's pace until now. I quickly swallowed what I had left and greedily held my glass out for more.

"Seriously, Kelly- what about tonic?" Jenna questioned, with an edge in her voice, "We can't drink gin by itself. Only alcoholics do that. And we're too young to be drunks."

We all laughed at Jenna's dark joke.

Kelly sighed and stood up, "My father must have tonic somewhere," she said as she quickly left the room.

I was sitting a few feet away from Jenna, but she came and kneeled next to me when Kelly left the room. Nikki and Erin took Kelly's departure as an opportunity to fill their plates. "All that's missing is pizza," Erin said jovially, "We should have ordered pizza."

"We still can," Nikki replied, shrugging.

Nikki and Erin began a discussion about whether or not they should order pizza and then debated where to order from.

Jenna nudged me and whispered, "Don't be nervous; it's just a stupid game."

I laughed a little too loudly, "What makes you think I'm nervous?" I questioned.

Jenna tilted her head and widened her eyes with an amused expression, "I know you," was her only reply.

Kelly came back into the room with two liters of tonic water. "Now, we have some tonic; let the games begin!"

Once the game started, I lost track of time and my ability to use common sense. I wasn't accustomed to drinking alcohol, so obviously, my tolerance was low. I'd only had one glass of wine before my first glass of gin and tonic, and even though I had plenty to eat, the gin went to my head before I realized it. I poured a lot more tonic in my glass than gin, but in the long run, that didn't matter. It was especially excruciating that I had to wait to be chosen.

Kelly immediately began the game after making sure we all had refills. She bounced up and down on a bean bag as she pointed at Nikki, Truth or Dare?" she asked merrily.

Nikki shrugged good-naturedly and took a sip of her drink, "Truth," she said as she chewed on her bottom lip.

"Have you and Evan gone all the way?" Kelly asked excitedly.

Jenna clucked her tongue and sighed with disappointment, "Seriously? That's your question. That's an easy one. Come on."

"Yes, we have," Nikki quickly admitted.

Everyone wanted to know when, and Nikki said they'd finally decided to go all the way that summer. They had always intended to wait until they were sixteen. It happened the night of Nikki's birthday party.

"Kelly, you wasted a good Truth. Seriously!" Jenna reproached, "Everyone basically already knew that."

Kelly good-naturedly rolled her eyes, "Okay, now it's Nikki's turn."

Nikki giggled and turned to face Jenna. Nikki didn't even have to ask before Jenna chose Dare. Sometimes, I wondered how Jenna and I could be best friends when we were so different. Nikki dared Jenna to ask Mickey for his help on a math assignment. Jenna reluctantly did it, although we all knew Mickey was terrible at math, had a massive crush on Jenna, and would relentlessly harass her after she texted him.

Jenna picked Erin, and she chose to tell the truth. When asked how many boys she'd slept with, Erin had to contemplate it for a couple of minutes. "No, not him," she muttered to herself, "We only had oral. We all exchanged amused glances as she silently counted her conquests on her fingers before admitting she'd gone all the way with seven guys. She wasn't the least bit embarrassed about it. Erin owned her promiscuity, which was why no one ever mocked, bullied or shamed her for it.

After that, Erin turned in my direction. At that point, I was on my second gin and tonic and hadn't yet realized how buzzed I was. I had been holding my breath during the game thus far and had rapidly drained my first glass and a half of liquor. But even the fuzziness in my head couldn't stop my stomach from doing flip-flops as I waited to hear what Erin had to say. It was the moment I had been dreading. Before Erin spoke, I immediately chose Truth- that was much safer than taking a dare.

She asked me if I fantasized about Jamey and if I ever used self-exploration when I thought about him.

I was mortified. I took a huge gulp of my gin and tonic. I felt myself turn bright red- my cheeks were burning like I'd sat in the sun for too long. I couldn't even meet the eyes of my friends. I started chewing on my fingernail.

"Obviously, that means *yes*," Jenna said, trying to save me.

I looked up and nodded. They all giggled but didn't seem surprised. It wasn't nearly as big of a deal as I'd anticipated. They were so nonchalant about my response that I felt almost like a deflated balloon. Why had I thought my friends would ask me something humiliating? Why had I once again gotten myself so worked up that only the alcohol prevented me from experiencing a full-blown panic attack?

"It's your turn, Jess," Kelly began, snapping me out of my reverie. "Well, actually, it's my turn, and I chose Dare."

I sat silently, trying to figure out what I should dare Kelly to do. Erin finally suggested that I dare her to ask out Chandler Barrett- a senior that Kelly had a crush on. Kelly seemed all too eager to take the dare. I took a gulp of my water as Kelly snatched her cell phone and called Chandler.

I don't know what happened after that because I had to rush to the bathroom to throw up. I spent the next few hours puking up the food and alcohol I'd consumed while my friends finished the game. I found out later that they'd played a second round. I wasn't sure what was worse- puking for two hours or being asked to bare your soul.

The next morning, Kelly opened the door to the guest room where I'd passed out the night before and jokingly sang, "Wake up, sleepy head. It's time to get ready for our *amazing* field trip."

I was parched with a pounding headache and a feeling of lethargy more debilitating than when I'd had the flu a few years before. I had slept soundly and was so startled by Kelly's presence that I shot up like a pop-up doll. As she closed the door, I laid back down, groaning.

It took all my energy to get out of bed, shower, brush my hair and teeth, and get dressed. I wanted to feign sick, but I knew I would never get away with it. I had to grin and bear it. Before we left, Kelly handed me a giant cup of coffee and three aspirin.

Kelly drove us to school because the rest of us refused to allow Jenna to drive. I was the only one who had puked and passed out, but Erin, Kelly, and Nikki were also slightly hungover. Jenna felt fine because she was used to going to parties with older boys and drinking, and she was also savvy enough to drink at a steady pace.

"I'm going to tell you girls a secret. If you want to avoid a hangover, you have to take meds before you go to bed. That way, you wake up without a headache." Jenna advised.

"What the hell!" Erin protested angrily, "Why didn't you tell us that last night?"

Jenna shrugged, "I was going to, but you lightweights all passed out before me."

"You suck," Nikki murmured, "Seriously."

Jenna exhaled and nonchalantly replied, "Karma."

"What does karma have to do with anything?" Erin asked.

"Karma is working in my favor because you wouldn't let me drive."

"That happened today," Erin objected, "You didn't tell us about the aspirin before we refused to let you drive."

While they argued, I sat with my head against the window, feeling slightly dizzy and nauseous.

When we got to school, three Coach buses were waiting for us. The Parent Teacher Association held a fundraiser over the summer selling organic sunscreen to help Mrs. Oliver, one of the social studies teachers, and Miss Clement, the sophomore guidance counselor, pay for a field trip they had actually started planning in August. Mrs. Oliver always took her history classes to the Connecticut State Capitol building at the end of September. We re-learned how the three branches of government operated that year, and she was overzealous about us observing this process. The trip was about an hour, so it required a luxury vehicle, according to Mrs. Oliver. She wanted her students to be as comfortable as possible on the ride to witness the beauty of our democracy.

My friends and I were only concerned about whether we could ride on the same bus together. We all signed up for bus one the moment the lists came out. Actually, I signed us all up because I was considered the most responsible member of our crew, so Bobby suggested I get to the directory before class since I was always one of the first students to arrive and pencil in all of our names.

As Erin, Kelly, Jenna, and Nikki strode onto the extravagant vehicle, we noticed Evan and Josh seated in the middle of the bus on opposite sides of one another.

"Over here," Evan waved us towards them, "Look, there's an overhead compartment for bags and stuff."

He opened up the stowage bin located above his seat and the one behind it. He put his arm out, took each of our bags, and stored them for us as we placed ourselves in the cushioned seats.

"Such a gentleman," Jenna remarked, winking at Nikki.

Nikki grinned widely and kissed Evan on the cheek before sitting beside him.

"Are the rest of the guys here yet?" Erin asked.

Josh was sitting with his feet across the bench, and his possessions were sprawled all over the place. He yawned and said matter-of-factly, "No, and they're planning to sit in the back. They're bringing flasks. We can't risk getting kicked off Student Council, so we're sitting here with you ladies."

"Oh, aren't we lucky!" Jenna muttered sarcastically.

"Oh, and I want the seat to myself. I have work to do," Josh added in a dismissive tone.

Erin giggled, "No one said they wanted to sit with you anyway."

"Touche," Josh shot back.

I was desperate at that point to rest my head against the window. I remembered to bring a small traveling pillow with me, so I hopped in the seat behind Nikki and Evan, immediately placed my face against the smooth cotton headrest, and closed my eyes. Erin sat next to me, and Jenna and Kelly sat across from us. The three of them murmured as I felt myself falling back into a light sleep.

I didn't even notice Jamey and Bobby's presence on the bus. I was right at that beautiful moment between awake and asleep as they came on; I was milliseconds away from dreamland. I became aware they were standing next to my bench when I heard Jamey ask Nikki what was the matter with me.

"Is she hungover?" Bobby asked incredulously.

"No!" Jamey said, sounding amused yet surprised.

I didn't stir as I overheard Nikki explain that I had been inebriated the night before. It was most likely because we were playing a game of Truth or Dare, which led me to self-medicate in order to hide my uneasiness at being asked embarrassing questions. Those weren't her exact words, but the boys understood her insinuation. Bobby was obviously becoming bored with the conversation because he suddenly announced that he was heading to the back of the bus to claim his seat. "Come on, Jame. Let's go," he ordered impatiently.

Jamey hesitated, "No, I'm staying with Jessica."

I could practically hear Bobby rolling his eyes. He sighed heavily and good-naturedly drawled, "I don't think she's going to be a lot of fun in that condition."

"Erin," Jamey demanded, "Go sit with Josh."

"I wanted to sit by myself," Josh complained.

Jamey heavily blew air out his nose, "You're lonely, Josh. Erin, go sit with him."

Josh laughed at Jamey's insistence, "You are such a prick."

Erin whined half-heartedly, "You're so bossy."

I didn't look up as Erin got out of the seat we'd been sharing and moved across the aisle to sit with Josh. I was startled, however, when Jamey plopped down next to me, gently lifted me over his lap, and placed me on his other side. "Here, lean down, it will be more comfortable," he said as he tenderly pushed my head down on his upper limb and patted my hair. I obeyed because I was too tired to argue, and his muscular shoulder felt comfortable and secure. Jamey wrapped his arm around me, and I snuggled into him. Unfortunately, we didn't notice Mrs. Oliver come onto the bus.

I was completely startled when I heard Mrs. Oliver clear her throat and make a tsk sound. I swiftly jerked away from Jamey and gulped, feeling scolded before she even verbalized a reprimand for what would obviously be construed as PDA.

She pursed her lips before speaking. She was apparently trying to choose an appropriate response to her observation. "Mr. Russo," she began sternly, looking directly at Jamey and avoiding eye contact with me, "Make sure you are showing proper discretion, and…" she paused as she looked up at the ceiling.

"Umm, Jamey…there will be no disrespect on this bus. Do you understand?"

I was not surprised that she had been careful to place all of the blame on Jamey, although what she'd witnessed was clearly mutual. I had a reputation for being a "good girl," and Mrs. Oliver, along with all the other faculty and staff at Lomonoco Creek, held my family in high regard. They wouldn't jeopardize upsetting us.

Jamey did not have a reputation as a "good boy," in fact, the opposite was true, and his family had accepted that. Jamey didn't care about his naughty status. He sounded amused as he promised Mrs. Oliver that he would behave himself. "Believe me, Mrs. O- I would NEVER disrespect *Jessica.*"

Everyone within hearing distance laughed raucously except me. I knew what he was insinuating. I wasn't sure if I should consider his clever comment an insult or a compliment.

As Mrs. Oliver was called off the bus, I narrowed my eyes and shook my head at Jamey with a disapproving look. "It was a joke," he insisted, tickling my waist. I squirmed in my seat and ordered him to stop.

"You don't have to embarrass me like that, Jamey," I muttered.

Of course, as usual, Josh had to chime in, "You're the one who won't commit to him, Jess."

"What does that have to do with it?" I questioned Josh angrily.

"Everything," Josh said as if I was an idiot for even asking the question.

"Nothing," Jamey said through gritted teeth, giving Josh a warning glance, "Just let it go."

Josh shrugged and leaned back in his chair.

I sat openmouthed, dumbstruck by Josh's off-the-cuff remark. Jamey shrugged good-naturedly and beamed at me. He leaned in and brushed his lips across mine. "I love this adorable nose," he claimed, patting my nose lightly. I half-grinned and decided to let both Jamey and Josh's comments go.

Mrs. Oliver went back and forth between the three buses for about half an hour. She appeared stressed out and was making cantankerous statements under her breath. Our bus driver was commiserating with the other two while Mrs. Oliver, Miss Clement, and the additional volunteers dealt with whatever was holding up the trip.

I was having trouble focusing because my head was still pounding despite the aspirin, and I was overcome with exhaustion. Even the coffee I'd attempted to drink made me feel nauseous. I needed a shot of adrenaline because I felt as if exhaustion was spreading through my veins. Miss Clement finally came on the bus and announced that we would be leaving shortly, "There are just a few tiny kinks Mrs. Oliver is working out with the representative from the Capitol," she said cheerfully, "We will be departing soon. I'll tell the driver that we are almost ready."

She left the bus again, and once more, we were all alone without an adult chaperone.

"Hey, Jamey?" Mickey yelled for the third time, "Come back here with us, man!" Mickey had been trying to get Jamey to go to the back of the bus since he had come on about an hour before. Bobby finally gave up because he knew his efforts were futile.

"You said you were going to sit with us. What the hell?" Mickey continued.

Whenever Mrs. Oliver or Miss Clement left the bus, Jamey would put his arm around me.

He ignored Mickey's comment as he pulled me closer to him.

Josh sat forward in his seat and smirked, "He's not going anywhere," he told Mickey in an amused voice.

Erin giggled and nodded, "That's for sure. They look so cozy."

Mickey and Bobby simultaneously harrumphed.

"Leave me alone," Jamey said flippantly, "I'm sitting with my girl."

"I am NOT your girl," I retorted loud enough for those around us to hear.

Suddenly, a female voice rose above the snickers of my peers. I immediately knew it was Kayla O'Neill. Kayla had a major crush on Jamey. Everyone knew this. From what I'd observed, Kayla's feelings were not reciprocated. "She's his girl when she's around," Kayla proclaimed with what could only be interpreted as resentment and disgust.

I heard gasps and intense whispers throughout the crowd. The tension on the bus became so severe it could have been bowdlerized with a chainsaw.

Everyone waited for Jamey or me to respond.

Jamey immediately withdrew his arm from around my waist. I noticed that his jaw was clenched, and his nostrils began to flare. As he slowly and methodically stood up, his wrath was palpable. Every muscle in his body was tense as he addressed Kayla, "What did you say, you little bitch?" He was pointing at her with a look of pure fury.

I stood up to witness Kayla's reaction. She shrank in her seat, and tears started to form in her eyes. She seemed to immediately regret her impulsive comment.

I placed my hand on Jamey's arm, "Just let it go," I said through gritted teeth.

But Jamey remained in position, glaring at Kayla. His gaze somehow spoke to her, sending daggers into her because she flinched.

They continued the staring contest for seconds.

"Jamey," I warned, trying to pull him back into the seat.

Kayla finally gulped, "Nothing," she whispered meekly, "I...I didn't say anything." She turned towards the window and wiped at her nose.

"Yeah, that's what I thought," Jamey stated, narrowing his eyes and scowling at her as if she was a piece of trash.

I was appalled by the way that Jamey addressed Kayla. The vile tone, the total lack of respect for another human being. He treated her as if she were a degenerate. Her reaction was heartbreaking, even if I knew she insulted me with her bitter comment.

I sat back down in the seat, tilted my head forward, and put my face in my clammy, shaking hands. When I looked up, Jamey acted as if nothing had happened. He casually pulled a sports app up on his phone and was scrawling through it.

"Go sit with your friends," I ordered.

He looked at me wide-eyed with shock.

"Now!" I directed with finality.

"What?" he mouthed, unable to find his voice.

I pointed to the back of the bus, "I don't want to be near you right now." I was whispering because I didn't want anyone to hear me.

"Jess, listen..." he began.

"NO!" I cut him off, "I am not going to change my mind. Please just go."

He sighed and reluctantly stood up. He licked his lips and balled his hands into fists. "Please, Jessica," he began pleadingly, "Listen to me."

I shook my head, refusing to meet his eyes, "Go. NOW," I was gritting my teeth, and my tone was unyielding and austere. I needed him to realize that my demand was irrevocable.

In order to save face, Jamey chuckled loudly, "I guess I will join my boys, considering Jessica wants to rest," he announced.

Mickey and Bobby cheered as Jamey grabbed his bag from the overhead compartment and made his way toward them.

Mrs. Oliver cheerfully skipped up the steps of the luxury vehicle with the bus driver trailing her. She announced that we were ready for our trip to begin.

"Finally, man," Mickey proclaimed as the engine ignited and the seat belt sign shone overhead.

Before the bus departed, Jenna suddenly plopped down next to me while the bus driver was rambling about all the rules. She rolled her eyes and explained that Kelly had abandoned her. Kayla apparently started sobbing after Jamey berated her, and Kelly felt the need to soothe her. "She is such a bleeding heart," Jenna commented disapprovingly.

"Well, Jamey was brutal. He didn't have to be that awful."

"Did you make him leave?" Jenna questioned.

I nodded.

"You are too much," Jenna laughed, "She *was* insulting you. You do know that, right?"

I shrugged, "I don't care what she thinks. She has low self-esteem. She likes Jamey, and she's just jealous. I feel…"

"Whatever, Dr. Harris," Jenna cut me off, addressing me by the name of a popular psychologist who had her own talk show.

I closed my eyes and puckered my lips. And then smiled because no matter what, I could never be mad at Jenna.

"Looks like you will be using that headrest as a pillow because you're not lying on my arm," Jenna joked, nudging me playfully.

I grabbed my cushion, placed it on the window, and laid my head down.

"Just for the record," Jenna said, "I'm with Jamey on this one. Kayla is a little bitch."

I remained silent. Pleading the fifth.

Chapter Fifteen:
Uptight and Conceited

The night of the field trip, Mickey reluctantly hosted a party at his somewhat infamous residence. His renowned, well-to-do family owned a very successful chain of diners in Connecticut and lived in a huge Mediterranean-style house that overlooked the Connecticut sound. He had a lot of siblings and extended family members who frequently visited, so he was seldom home alone. He rarely had people over because he claimed his family was too loud and annoying. Everyone was intrigued by his unique living quarters. Therefore, when Jamey and Bobby found out his entire family was taking a trip to Greece, they harassed him until he agreed to throw a huge bash. Mickey threatened to kill them both with his bare hands if anything ended up broken or ruined. They promised that they and the other football players would act as "body guards" and kick anyone out who became too unruly.

My friends tried to persuade me to go to the party. Nikki insisted it would be amazing- we'd finally get to see the inside of Mickey's illustrious home. Jenna claimed that she would act as a shield between Jamey and me. She swore she wouldn't let him within ten feet of me. She initially suggested that I flirt with other guys as retaliation but immediately backtracked when she realized the consequences of doing something that foolish. Kelly and Erin tried to defend Jamey, like they always did, which was irritating.

"He just *really* likes you, Jess," Erin began, "He acted on impulse. I mean, she was being really freaking rude."

Kelly sighed and nodded, "Although I did feel very sorry for Kayla, I also am trying to see the situation from Jamey's point of view."

Jenna cut her off, "I am not a fan of Kayla's by any means, but let's just drop the topic. Okay? Obviously, Jessica doesn't want to go. Let's stop pestering her about it."

Fortunately, that put an end to my friends' attempts to cajole me into going to Mickey's shindig. So, I was practically the only junior at Lomonoco Creek to miss the party, and I didn't care. However, ALL my friends did attend and enjoy the social event of the year.

I pushed all thoughts of Jamey out of my head that night and fell asleep relatively early. I slept well while everyone else was partying. I actually went to bed right after dinner, feigning tiredness from the long day. When I awoke the next morning, I felt refreshed and more like myself. It was Sunday, so I got dressed for church. Nikki and Jenna were not present at Mass that morning. Their parents weren't as strict as my dad and even joked about the girls' absence being due to "sickness" from a late night of partying. I knew my dad wouldn't have allowed me to skip church. He was very concerned about appearances and required all three of his daughters to regularly attend Mass. I was involved in a number of charitable activities, so my father didn't demand that I go to youth group, but he did force my unenthusiastic sisters to attend once a week.

My friends were planning a trip to the Rosevalley Mall to do some clothes shopping later that morning. I was planning to meet them later because I assumed my father would force me to join our family for brunch at the Jamestown Country Club even though Jenna and Nikki wouldn't be there. I didn't even ask about bowing out until my aunt mentioned the excursion to the local mall as we were chatting outside the chapel.

"Jess, honey, aren't you meeting Nikki and the other girls?" she asked pointedly.

"I guess after breakfast," I replied, glancing towards my father.

Aunt Gina winked at me, "Anthony, the girls are all going shopping and plan to eat at the food court afterwards. Why don't you drop Jessica off at home so she can go with them?"

To my surprise, my dad nodded in agreement, "No problem, Jessica. If you want to go with your friends to the mall, that's fine. There's no harm in you missing one brunch, after all."

"Thanks, Dad," I stated, giving my aunt a grateful glance. I was relieved because I knew I'd be bored without my friends.

The trip would have been just another expedition to the mall if Kelly hadn't felt the need to mention a scenario she'd witnessed between Jamey and Kayla at the party.

After a few hours of gossip, trying on clothes, and making purchases, my friends and I concluded our afternoon with a visit to the food court. We were sitting around a large, secluded booth in the corner of the vast room filled with nothing but chain restaurants and florescent lights.

Erin, Kelly, Nikki, Jenna, and I occasionally treated ourselves to Chinese food after a few hours of bargain-hunting. We called our visits to the dining hall a treat because we didn't often eat that way. We usually regretted it later because we'd end up with stomachaches. Erin joked that the food was like crack. It was addicting but so horrible for you.

We were quiet as we ate until Kelly suddenly broke the comfortable silence. She cleared her throat and methodically placed the plastic fork she was holding on her perfectly folded paper napkin. "I noticed Jamey talking to Kayla at the party last night," she replied, shooting a glance in my direction.

I had been in a state of guilty pleasure after just finishing a carton of fried rice. I was about to take a bite of my fat-laden chicken but stopped when she said this. I looked at her expectantly, waiting for her to continue.

"Yeah, so?" Jenna said, with an edge to her voice.

Kelly shrugged nonchalantly, "I just thought it was interesting."

I was dumbfounded, uncertain of what Kelly was implying or why she was broaching this topic.

Jenna did the talking for me- although I wouldn't have been as rude and outspoken about it. "Kelly, what's your point? Why did you even bring this up? What are you implying?"

"I'm not *implying* anything," Kelly kept up the innocent charade.

"Are you saying they hooked up or something?" Jenna asked aggressively.

I nearly choked on the water I'd just taken a sip of. I started coughing and almost spit it out.

Kelly put a hand to her chest, "Of course not! I brought it up because I thought Jessica would be glad that Jamey was being civil to Kayla. She did get very upset when he was mean to her."

Erin decided to chime in at that time, "Jamey would never hook up with *her*."

"Why is she so fixated on him, then? I can't figure that out. I mean, why is she obsessed with Jamey?" I asked with curiosity. I was playing the events out in my head as I spoke, thinking out loud, basically.

Erin widened her eyes and looked at me like I was the most naïve person in the world, "Because she's nuts!"

Kelly nodded, "She is mentally unstable," she agreed, "That's why I feel sorry for her."

Jenna slammed her diet cola on the table a bit too harshly, "I still don't know why you'd even bring it up, Kelly. Do you really think Jessica wants to talk about *him* right now?"

Nikki was usually an observer during confrontational discussions like this, yet this time, she decided to weigh in. "I wonder if Kayla has feelings for Jamey because he, you know, leads her on or something."

"No," Erin insisted, "That is not it. He doesn't lead her on. She's just one of those girls who…"

Jenna finished the sentence for her, although not in the way Erin intended, "One of those girls that guys use for sex."

My head started spinning. Was Jamey sleeping with Kayla? Was that why she was so obsessed with him?

Nikki looked confused as if she was trying to put the pieces of a puzzle together, "But Jessica said Jamey was texting her all night, right, Jess?"

I sighed, "Yes, he texted me about twenty times. He kept saying he was sorry, and I don't know, I turned my phone off, but when I woke up, I noticed he'd sent me like a million texts all through the evening."

Erin cleared her throat and attempted to assuage the situation, "I'm sure that Jamey felt awful about how he treated Kayla and was most likely apologizing for his bad behavior."

"Yes!" Kelly declared, "That's exactly what I was thinking. That's why I mentioned it."

Jenna rolled her eyes at Kelly, "Like I said before, Kel- you shouldn't have brought it up."

Kelly held her hands up in surrender. "Geez, sorry. I didn't think it was a big deal. Let's change the subject," she suggested in typical Kelly fashion.

The following day, right before lunch, Erin and I were standing at my locker discussing an event the Sunshine Committee was organizing for Halloween. We were in the midst of planning a fundraiser. We had decided on a romantic/spooky theme. Erin was explaining that she thought we could sell lollipops shaped like ghosts and distribute them like Valentine's.

Erin was looking thoughtfully at me as I explained how I envisioned our proposal playing out, "I was thinking we could use white chocolate and formulate it into the structure of a heart, but put an "O" shaped mouth on the pops so they'd resemble a ghost."

I was about to continue but abruptly ceased speaking when I sensed someone behind me. I knew who it was before Erin confirmed my suspicion. "Hey, Jame," she casually remarked."

I turned around to find Jamey standing directly in the back of us with his hand stretched out flat on the solid blue wall next to my locker. He had a sheepish look on his handsome face, and his hooded chestnut eyes were opened slightly wider than usual; they were apologetic, remorseful. Although my stomach fluttered appreciatively, like it often did when we gazed at one another, I was about to tell him to go away. I opened my mouth to speak- to make him aware that I was in the middle of a conversation with Erin and that he shouldn't interrupt.

But Erin beat me to the punch.

"Well, I'm going to get going," Erin started, "I'll see you guys at lunch." I noticed an almost imperceptible look pass between them before Erin slunk away.

I didn't have a chance to ask about what I could have sworn was a secret glance between the two of them because Jamey started right in with apologies. "Listen, I am SO sorry, Jess, for acting like a jerk on the bus. I know I promised I would try to change, but she just got me so mad. She can be so…just, such a…"

I interrupted him, "Okay, Jamey. Whatever. You don't need to continue."

"So you forgive me?" He asked. I couldn't help but stare at his beautiful, full lips as they curved upward into a grin.

I rolled my eyes. "No," I said without conviction.

He continued smiling because he could tell I was lying.

We were quiet for a second while I contemplated whether or not I should question him about Kelly's disclaimer at the food court. Nevertheless, I heard the words escaping my lips even before I made the decision to voice them, "I heard you were alone with Kayla at the party last night." I looked at him blankly, curious as to how he'd respond.

He nodded without batting an eye. "Yeah, I apologized to her. I said I was sorry because I knew that's what you wanted me to do. NOT because I felt like I needed to apologize to her after how she treated you. I did it for YOU."

"Well, Kelly mentioned it, and at first I thought…"

"You thought what?"

"I thought you hooked up with her," I reluctantly admitted.

Jamey laughed with disbelief, "Why would I hook up with her when I can't stand her?"

I shrugged, "I don't know; she just acts so in love with you all the time. It makes me think maybe you lead her on."

Jamey snorted and cleared his throat. "No!" he insisted, "That's ridiculous. I'm not attracted to her AT ALL!"

Although I felt relief wash over me, I pursed my lips and narrowed my eyes, "Well, I know you're not celibate."

Jamey put his hands on either side of my locker and leaned in so we were merely inches apart, "You are the only girl I want. The only girl I feel *anything* for. The only girl I freaking LOVE!"

"But I'm not the only girl you are attracted to," I said, searching his face for clues, fishing for information.

Jamey's eyes looked as if they might bulge out of his head, and he threw his arms in the air in frustration.

I refused to budge. I wanted an answer. Was he or wasn't he fooling around with other girls? I needed to know.

"Be my girlfriend," he whispered, brushing his lips against mine, "If you would commit to me, we wouldn't have these absurd discussions."

I shook my head. "Not until you change."

Jamey sighed impatiently, "I'm trying, but when some little…"

I gave him a warning glance.

"When some chick," he spat out the word with disgust, "insults the girl I love, I can't help but get angry."

I looked down. "I bet you'd lose interest in me the minute I committed to you." I accused.

Jamey stepped back and looked at me open-mouthed, "Is that why you won't go out with me? Is that what you're afraid of?"

I shook my head vigorously. "No. I'm not afraid of anything," I said defensively.

"Then be my girlfriend," he leaned in and really kissed me this time, and I let him even though we were in the middle of the hallway and people were passing us by. I let him and got lost in the warmth of his lips for a moment.

I finally pulled away, "We're going to be late for lunch."

"So?" Jamey said, grinning. "You still haven't answered me. Will you?"

"You already know the answer," I began as I playfully pushed him, "No. Not until you change and start treating people like Kayla in a nicer way. Not until you stop bullying people."

Jamey rolled his eyes but gently took my hand in his. As we started walking hand in hand to lunch, he said, "You know she hates you, right?"

"Who?" I asked.

Jamey guffawed as if he couldn't believe I didn't know who he was referring to, "Kayla," he said definitively, "She tells everyone she thinks you're uptight and conceited."

I waved my hand in the air as if I was shooing away a fly, "I don't care. I feel sorry for people like her who are so insecure about themselves that they have to judge others. I read that only miserable people, people who aren't content, feel the need to put other people down in order to make themselves feel better."

Jamey cleared his throat and lightly swatted me on the behind as we walked into the cafeteria, "Okay, whatever. I love to hear you talk no matter what you're saying, but when you get started with the psychobabble, it sounds like Russian to me."

When Jamey and I walked into the immense, recently renovated cafeteria, I headed to "our" table. The room had been sectioned off into four squares. Each grade level had its own subdivision. The Student Council of each class and the Parent Teacher Association had worked together the previous summer to create a very unique room that was basically transformed into four separate quarters.

Of course, all of the walls were painted our school colors- blue and gold, but there were different designs on each division. The junior partitions were solid blue, with a painting of each of the seasons strategically displayed in the center of each wall. A local artist had volunteered to decorate the eleventh-grade section because she was a friend of my mom's. She apparently had a connection to my grandmother. Everyone agreed that she did an amazing job. The images appeared so realistic they could have been mistaken for photographs. Her work definitely paid off because she had become an overnight sensation after the room was revealed in the newspaper.

I began to head in the direction of a table in the back of the junior area- the booth where my friends and I always sat. We basically claimed a table every year- just like most of the other kids at Lomonoco Creek. I slowly pulled my hand away from Jamey's.

"Oh, you're not buying lunch?" he asked jokingly. He knew I hated the school lunches and never bought them. It had become a joke between us. They were disgusting, in my opinion- fattening with no nutritional value. As a member of the PTA, my mother had been fighting for healthier school lunches since my freshmen year.

Kayla happened to be standing a few feet in front of us. When she heard us giggling about how I wouldn't eat the school lunch if my life depended on it, she instinctively turned around. When she caught Jamey's eye, she immediately made an about-face.

I licked my lips, feeling awkward, "Okay, I'm going to sit down."

Jamey nodded, but he had a grim expression on his face.

I casually walked over to the table. Everyone else was there already.

"So, did you and Jamey make up?" Josh asked in a curious but also semi-mocking tone as I took a spot next to Jenna.

I shrugged, "I guess."

"That's good," Josh stated as if he actually cared.

We continued our conversation, which revolved around trivial things, nothing out of the ordinary. Jamey came and sat down next to me after a few minutes with his tray of disgusting-looking chicken nuggets, greasy French fries, and what appeared to be smooshed-up strawberries. I grimaced when I observed what he was about to consume. He didn't notice the look on my face as he squeezed my leg and kissed the side of my cheek.

Erin smiled brightly, "So sweet."

Mickey smirked, and Bobby jokingly rolled his eyes.

Suddenly, the table fell quiet. Everyone across from me was looking at something or someone in the back of me. I abruptly turned around to find a remorseful-looking Kayla standing directly behind me.

My eyes widened, and I gulped, unsure of how this was going to play out.

She had a contrite expression on her almost but not quite pretty face, and she was folding and unfolding her hands, which appeared sweaty. I was thinking she could have been more attractive if she wore less black eyeliner and applied a pinker shade of blush and lipstick, as opposed to the bright red she'd chosen. She mumbled something, but I had to ask her to repeat herself because I was caught up in mentally giving her a makeover.

"Oh, I was just saying sorry for what I said on the bus, and I hope I didn't make you feel uncomfortable in the lunch line when I looked at you."

I was startled into silence. I couldn't believe she was apologizing to me. "Um, okay, but you don't have...it's not necessary..." my voice trailed off because I was at a loss for words.

Kelly cleared her throat and spoke up, which I was grateful for. "It's all water under the bridge," she chimed cheerfully.

I nodded, "And anyway, you shouldn't be apologizing to me," I seemed to have found my voice, "Jamey should apologize to you."

Kayla nodded, "Oh, he already did," she looked at Jamey and licked her lips. He nodded once as she continued, "At the party."

"I told you," Jamey said to me definitively.

We were all quiet for a minute- quiet as in awkward, a *very awkward* silence.

"Bye, Kayla," Jenna said in an irritated tone, "You can go now."

Kayla tentatively put her hand up as if she was waving and crept away.

When she was out of earshot, Josh said, "That was weird."

"Creepy," Nikki agreed.

"Did you tell her to do that?" I asked Jamey.

He shook his head vigorously, "No!"

Jenna flung her hair off her shoulder, "She is a pitiful girl."

"I think it was nice of her to apologize," Kelly began, "And seriously, Jenna, you don't have to be so mean-spirited."

Kelly and Jenna continued to banter back and forth. Everyone else went back to talking about football, cheerleading, math homework, Halloween- but I watched Kayla out of the corner of my eye.

I witnessed her slowly walking back to her table, muttering something to her friends as she grabbed her tray of food. They glanced over at our table, but I was the only one who noticed. She sauntered over to the garbage bin, and even though she was staring at the ground, I detected tears in her eyes. She was slumped over and wouldn't look up as she threw her uneaten food away. In fact, she almost bumped into the garbage bin. She then practically flew out of the cafeteria.

Jamey nudged me playfully. "What's up?"

I shrugged, "I guess I just feel sorry for her."

"Jess, come on," Jamey began in a voice louder than he'd anticipated, "She can't stand you. She thinks you're a bitch. She hates your guts!"

The rest of our friends heard his comment and burst out laughing.

"I just don't get why she apologized then," I said.

Erin looked from Jamey to me and threw her arms up in the air, "She apologized because she doesn't want any bad blood."

"I don't think she *hates* Jessica," Kelly said.

"Yes. She does," Josh stated flatly.

"Maybe she felt bad about how she treated you after I apologized to her at the party," Jamey said, shrugging.

Jenna cleared her throat, "You are all full of shit. She apologized because of Jamey. She's dumb enough to think this will make Jamey...I don't know, treat her nicer or something."

We were all silent because everyone knew Jenna was right.

Nikki finally broke the silence, "Jess, seriously, of course, Kayla would never talk about you to ME. But it is common knowledge that she thinks you're...I don't know how to put it really. I mean, she certainly isn't fond of you. She does think you're..."

Jamey finished for her, "She thinks you're uptight and conceited. End of story."

The bell rang, signaling this conversation had run its course.

Chapter Sixteen: Tailbones, Threats, and Ice

I never would have predicted that a collapse during cheerleading practice would result in two key shifts in the dynamics of my relationship with Jamey. Yet my unfortunate plummet caused our partnership to change- permanently. The transformation was positive. But also negative. And, it's honestly still unclear if the good outweighed the bad or vice versa. The only thing I can definitely attest to is the events that followed my fall foreshadowed our future together.

The afternoon started out like every other Friday before an away basketball game. The games alternated between Lomonoco Creek and other high schools, which meant that when we didn't have a home game at our school, the cheerleaders and basketball players had to travel on a bus together to another educational institution where we'd use their auditorium to cheer and compete.

We were practicing a first heel stretch with me, being the smallest and lightest, at the top of the pyramid. I had done so many cheerleading stunts over the years that I was in no way worried about falling. I'd had a few semi-serious injuries throughout my life, but none while cheerleading. This would actually be my first and last wound acquired while participating in my favorite activity.

The bus had arrived, and we were waiting for the basketball players to emerge from the locker rooms to load the automobile. We were traveling to Fairfield, which was about an hour away, so we would be spending the night in a motel after the game. Coach Lisa, who had been our head instructor since we were freshmen, was running late as always. She was a perfectionist and instilled fear in almost everyone but me because I was similarly fanatical. We were like-minded. She also had an anxious disposition, which I could relate to. However, she was the type to express her nervousness in a loud, antagonistic way- while I kept mine bottled up inside my own overcrowded head.

If truth be told, it was Coach Lisa's fault that I tumbled to the ground that day. We had practiced the shoulder stand too many times. It was unnecessary for us to perform it again. We technically should have been making our way onto the bus because the cheerleaders were supposed to be waiting for the basketball players when they were ready, as the head basketball coach constantly reminded Lisa. They frequently argued about her tardiness.

None of us cheerleaders had the audacity to question Lisa, but one of the junior coaches mentioned we were behind schedule after she ordered the three bases and me, the flyer, to practice the basket toss.

"Lisa, Joe is going to have a conniption if we are not on the bus when they come through," Coach Becky reminded Lisa gently.

Lisa grumbled, "I don't give a crap about Joe. We're doing it once more."

And we did…only this time when I was at the pinnacle. Marabelle Chamberlain, one of the trio of girls holding me up, lost her concentration when she heard the basketball players begin to enter the gymnasium. Her hand wavered, and that was all it took for me to come crashing to the ground.

Even though I didn't lose consciousness, I was so disassociated that it felt like I did. I was in a state of complete shock when I realized I was lying on the hardwood maple floor with Coach Lisa, Coach Becky, and several cheerleaders surrounding me. They were all asking me various versions of, "Are you okay?" Initially, I wasn't sure what parts of my body had hit the surface. Hands were grasping at me, coming from all directions. Some were encouraging me to stay down, and others were trying to help me sit up. I was in such a daze, and panic overcame me. My heart was racing. I was sweating and felt like I couldn't breathe. I started waving my arms in the air, shooing everyone away.

"Give her some space!" Coach Becky yelled. She sat down next to me and stared into my eyes.

She started shooting questions at me, but I couldn't focus because I heard Coach Lisa and Coach Angolo arguing.

"What the hell is going on?" Coach Angolo shouted.

"Jessica just fell," Josh said, sounding concerned. He cut through the crowd of cheerleaders and sat next to me. "Geez, Jess. I saw you fall. Are you okay? You need to get to the hospital."

I panicked when I heard the word hospital. I vehemently shook my head.

He laughed, "I know you are afraid of doctors, honey. And I'm sorry to tell you this, but you need to get checked out."

I was trying to assess the situation, but the pain in my head, which I realized was already pounding as I placed my hand on the back of it, was starting to spread into my temples due to the roaring voices of both coaches.

"Every time we have a game, your girls are late getting on that damn bus. You do it on purpose, Lisa. I know you!"

"Why don't you shut the hell up, Joe? You don't intimidate me!"

No one was surprised by this screaming match because a version of it happened before every away game, but today, there was additional chaos. And that was because of me. They now had a bigger problem because I'd fallen, and that had to be addressed.

"We need to be on the bus ten minutes ago!" Coach Angolo yelled.

"Well, I have a girl down," Coach Lisa spat, "I am dealing with this."

"Deal with it fast, Lisa! Because that bus is leaving when I say it is leaving, and if we have to go without you, we will."

"You wouldn't dare!"

"Boys, get on the bus!" Coach Angolo ordered.

The basketball players did as they were told. They started marching like soldiers out of the gym and onto the awaiting vehicle. They weren't stupid enough to defy Coach Angolo, whose explosive temper was infamous.

The cheerleaders were either watching me, looking to Coach Lisa for direction, or rushing to gather their stuff.

Coach Lisa finally turned to Coach Becky and threw her hands up in the air, "What the hell are we supposed to do? We've got to go!"

"Should I take her to the doctor?" Becky asked.

"No, we need you for the halftime routine, Becky," Lisa insisted, "They can't pull that off without you. You taught them the whole thing."

"I can take her," Erin said, shrugging. In the midst of all the confusion and pandemonium, Erin finally came up with the perfect solution. She had been sick with the flu for a week and hadn't been at practice. Therefore, she wasn't even able to participate in the halftime routine. Her presence wouldn't be missed. Both coaches immediately agreed.

"Get her to the doctor, Erin," Coach Becky commanded before leaving the gym.

Coach Lisa, on the other hand, was mumbling about how they'd have to figure out what to do about all the planned stunts now that I wouldn't be there to perform the task as a designated flyer.

"Feel better, Jessica," she shouted, emotionless, without even turning to face me, "I could wring Marabelle's neck for this," she muttered angrily as she walked through the glass, garage-like doors.

And then there were two.

Erin helped me to my feet and asked if I needed assistance walking to the car. I shook my head and assured her I was fine. I knew my next task was to convince Erin to allow me to skip the doctor part of this. If any of my friends could be swayed, it would be her. I silently thanked God that Erin was the one who'd had the flu and consequently was put in charge of babysitting me.

Once we were sitting, buckled up in her brand new silver Lexus, Erin said, "Alright then, I guess I'll take you to the clinic in South Rosevalley."

"No," I said with conviction.

Erin's eyebrows creased with surprise, "Okay, we can go somewhere else."

I shook my head with a vengeance, "Erin, I CAN NOT go to the doctor's."

Erin looked at me wide-eyed, "You have to. I promised Coach Becky I would take you."

"Listen, I am fine," I insisted, "I don't need to be seen. I have a few scratches."

Erin persevered, "I saw you fall, Jess. You bashed your head on the ground, and you fell really hard on your butt. You could have a concussion or broken your tailbone."

"Well, even if I did, which I'm sure I didn't, tailbones fix themselves."

"Jess, I have to. I'm sorry."

My eyes filled with tears. I was terrified of doctors. Seeing a physician was my biggest fear. Since my traumatic childhood experience, I have avoided medical facilities at all costs. "Please, Erin," I begged, "I promise I'm okay. I am fine. No one will ever have to know. We will pretend I went to the doctor. It will all be forgotten. I don't even feel like I'm in that much pain," I lied.

Erin looked at me imploringly.

I grabbed her hands and squeezed them, "Please! Why don't we just go to Jamey's party."

Josh and Evan were the only boys in our friend group who were basketball players. Jamey, Bobby, and Mickey played football and baseball. Typically, most of the student population went to home and away games, but not when it was such a long commute. Therefore, since Jamey's mother was away and his entire extended family was in Italy, he was having a huge bash at his house. Jamey was now at an advantage. His grandparents retired and moved semi-permanently to Italy the year before. His mother had been a somewhat attentive parent when her folks were around to monitor her. When they left, she lost interest. She started traveling- a lot. She had no responsibilities and an unlimited amount of money. Therefore, she took off every weekend, leaving Jamey to his own devices.

Jamey's get-togethers were always invitation only. Freshmen and sophomores were only welcome if one of his bouncers (basically all of his football buddies) was interested in a younger girl. If someone showed up uninvited, he or she was immediately made to leave. At around 1:00 A.M., Jamey, Bobby, and Mickey started kicking people out.

This night would be similar to all his previous gatherings, except our squad was planning to spend the day after the party hanging out in Jamey's rec room. We were all excited about watching a popular horror series that was finally streaming on AirTV.

I could tell my tears were breaking down Erin's resolve to take me to the emergency room. I had also piqued her interest by mentioning the party, but she still needed convincing. "Isn't Jamey going to wonder why we're there?" she asked hesitantly.

I shrugged, "We'll just say I had a slight fall."

Erin sighed and turned to face the steering wheel, "Are you sure?"

"Absolutely!"

"Okay, I guess it's fine if you are absolutely sure you're okay," she replied tentatively, "I hope I don't regret this."

"You won't," I assured her. I didn't tell her that I was thinking if anyone would end up regretting this, it would be me.

The party was in full swing when we got to Jamey's. I had begun to relax a little. Now that my attention was averted from my fear of physicians, my mind was starting to register pain. My behind, right upper thigh, wrist, and head were throbbing. I knew I had to find some aspirin ASAP and self-medicate all night to diminish the pain.

Jamey was not only drunk but also high by the time we arrived; in fact, almost everyone had already downed a few drinks. Jamey seemed satisfied with my explanation that I'd had a minor fall and Coach Lisa was being overly protective. He didn't appear concerned in the least. I winked at Erin and asked her to get me a shot while I stole some pharmaceuticals from the bathroom.

"Of what?" she asked.

"Anything!"

After taking three pain pills, I gulped down whatever liquor Erin handed me as quickly as possible and instantly started coughing afterward.

"What's wrong?" Jamey said, coming up behind me and placing his arm around my shoulder.

"I had a shot," I explained as I watched Erin walk over and sit on a very willing senior's lap. His name escaped me, but he might have been the catalyst for why it had been relatively easy to convince her to skip the walk-in clinic.

"Are you okay?" Jamey asked, looking slightly concerned.

"Yes, I'm fine," I replied, trying to sound nonchalant, "Is there any more...."

Jamey looked at me, waiting for me to continue.

"Pot?" I asked weakly, feeling myself blush.

He smiled deviously. I usually shied away from weed because it made me tired, but I thought it would probably be the best way to self-medicate without making myself vomit.

Jamey found someone to find someone to find someone who had more weed, and after that, the night became a blur.

I woke up the next morning on the couch in Jamey's rec room, wrapped in his arms.

I had been in an almost coma-like state before waking up beside Jamey. After all, I had downed a shot, smoked pot, and consumed two beers. I had spent the evening in a blissful daze, oblivious to the pain shielded by the drugs and alcohol. I didn't even remember falling asleep next to Jamey. After initially opening my eyes, I had to orient myself to my surroundings. It took me several seconds to recall the events of the previous afternoon.

For some reason, the intense pain I felt in my upper thigh and backside didn't register right away. It might have been blotted out by the pounding of my head from the crash and possibly a hangover. I seemed to only be able to notice one injured part of my body at a time. First, my behind, then my head. After that, I realized my wrist was also aching so much that it was tender to the touch.

Once I ceased feeling disassociated, I slowly got up from the coach, careful not to wake Jamey. I surveyed the room and noticed that Erin was sound asleep on one of the love seats covered with a fleece comforter, and Mickey was on the floor with a pillow and sleeping bag. I tiptoed past them, holding my head in my hands and wondering where I could find some aspirin to dull all the discomfort coursing through my body.

I made it to the other side of Jamey's gigantic estate before I found Bobby in the kitchen. He was cleaning up. There had been so many people at the party that it was impossible to contain them in Jamey's quarter of the house. But Jamey wasn't concerned about that because, after all his parties, he would hire a maid service to clean up.

"Hey," I said in an anguished voice when I caught sight of Bobby putting dishes in the dishwasher.

He looked startled to see me. "What are you doing up?" he asked inquisitively.

"What are *you* doing up?" I asked, trying to sound lighthearted, even though I was finding it almost impossible to deal with the enormous amount of distress I was experiencing.

Bobby shrugged casually, "I am an insomniac," he admitted. "I hardly ever sleep."

"Oh," I whispered, unintentionally closing my eyes and massaging the bone around my right hand.

"What happened?" Bobby asked incredulously when he caught sight of my wrist. "Holy shit, did you sprain it?"

"I don't know," I acknowledged, "I hurt it yesterday during cheerleading practice. That's why Erin and I didn't go to the game. I fell and was supposed to go to the doctor, but…."

Bobby emitted an elongated exhalation, "Yeah, I know. You're afraid of doctors."

I nodded glumly, "Bobby, I am in agony right now. I don't know what to do," I knew I could trust Bobby. He wouldn't judge me, and he would help me figure out a solution.

"Let me look at your wrist," he said gently.

I held my hand out, and he tenderly took it in his, "I have had enough injuries playing football to be able to tell whether it's sprained or broken," he replied as he looked it over. After a couple of seconds, he continued, "The good news is it's not broken. The bad news is it is mildly sprained. You must have landed on it just right- enough to hurt like hell but not enough to need a cast. It can be wrapped up with a Figure 8 elastic bandage. So you don't have to worry about the wrist. Did you hurt anything else?"

I nodded reluctantly, "Yes, I fell on my upper thigh and behind. I am so sore back here," I rubbed my hands along my tailbone, feeling self-conscious but not mortified because it was Bobby. He could be intimidating to other people, but he was always kindhearted with me.

Bobby smiled and licked his lips, looking down at the ground. It was apparent he was trying not to snicker because it was an embarrassing place to have an injury.

"I also…hit the back of my skull."

Bobby tilted his head and gave me an affectionate but semi-chastising look.

"I know, I know," I said, "but the doctor. I just can't. The thought of going freaks me out. Even thinking about it makes me nauseated and out of breath and…."

"I get it," Bobby said, "Let me look in your eyes." I came closer to him, and he peered into my eyeballs as if he were an actual doctor, "They aren't dilated," he informed me before he began shelling out questions, "Are you dizzy? Are you nauseous? Are your ears ringing? You can walk straight without wobbling, right?"

"Yes, and I don't have any of those symptoms."

"Well, I am almost positive you don't have a concussion, then," he replied reassuringly. "You know, I do have some pain pills. Heavy-duty ones I stole from my mom. That would help."

I was just beginning to feel tremendous relief as if an enormous weight had been lifted from my shoulders. "Yes. Yes! Please," I shouted happily, as a colossal grin began to spread across my face.

But before I could breathe a mammoth sigh of relief, I became distracted by the thunderous commotion coming from the other side of the house. Bobby and I were so startled by the sudden ruckus we practically jumped out of our skin. We stared at one another, perplexed as loud, indignant voices and stomping feet headed our way.

"What the hell, Jess?" Josh said as he and Jamey stormed into the room. "Are you kidding me? You didn't go to the doctor?" He turned towards Jamey, "You should have seen how she fell. She smashed her head against the ground. She could have had a concussion. She could have broken her hip."

I was silent because I didn't know what to say. Technically, Josh was right. I logically knew that, but no matter what, I couldn't get past my phobia of doctors.

Jamey decided to join in with the reprimanding, "You could have damaged your tailbone. You could have cracked your freaking wrist, Jess. I can't believe you came here and basically lied to me. You said you had a minor fall. That's certainly not MINOR!"

"The worst thing about this is you do things like this all the time. This is like the seventy-fifth time you've hurt yourself and pretended it was nothing." Josh started rattling off all the times I'd fibbed about injuries. He didn't stop until Erin and Mickey entered the room, wondering what all the fuss was about.

"What's going on?" Erin asked, her china-blue eyes wide with concern.

Mickey was running his hands over his chin and pulling at his thin lips, "What the..? You guys woke us up!"

Erin looked around the room before inquiring where everyone else was.

Josh waved his hand aimlessly as if that wasn't important, "Evan's in the rec room. Jenna and Kelly are freshening up. They'll be here soon."

"Erin, weren't you supposed to take Jessica to the doctor?" Jamey exclaimed as he threw his arms up in the air.

Josh gave her a reproachful look, "You shouldn't have let her talk you out of it. You saw how badly she was hurt."

Erin looked down at the floor guiltily, "She swore she was okay."

"I'm still trying to wrap my head around the fact that Josh and Evan are here," Mickey said, cutting her off, "When did you get here, and why didn't we hear you come in?"

"You were both passed out cold!" Josh explained, "Jamey and I had a conversation right in front of you, and neither of you woke up.

Erin started to giggle, and Mickey followed suit, "We did too many shots," I guess," he replied sheepishly.

Jamey rolled his eyes and sighed, "Who cares about that? We all know you two are both lightweights. That doesn't matter right now."

Erin tilted her head as if she accepted this, but Mickey looked offended, "I am NOT a lightweight."

Jamey's jaw tightened, and he swallowed soundly; it was becoming evident that his anger was increasing. "Go to the rec room, both of you. Wait for us there. We need to figure out what to do with Jessica. She might need to go to the emergency room, and you are talking about B.S. that doesn't matter."

"No!" I shouted, "I am NOT going to the emergency room. I am not."

Erin looked at me sympathetically. "She wouldn't go last night. That's why we came here. She's afraid because of what happened."

Josh shook his head as if he was shaking away a heap of nonsense, "Jess, seriously. You need to grow up and get over your irrational paranoia of doctors. That's what therapy is for."

Bobby finally placed himself in the middle of our circle of friends, demanding that he be heard. He didn't often do things like that, so everyone was quiet, waiting for him to speak, "Listen, Jessica told me she was hurt before you came storming up here. Everyone knows that I have had enough injuries from football- probably even more than Jamey, to be able to tell if a person has a concussion. Jessica doesn't. End of story. I also checked her wrist. It's sprained, but mildly. It will heal just fine. The only issue...."

He looked at me, almost apologetically, "Is her thigh and behind? She would know if she broke her hip. That's stupid." He glared at Josh with an almost imperceptible look of disapproval, which made me happy despite all the craziness.

"What if she broke her tailbone?" Jamey asked; he seemed calmer after his best friend took charge of the situation.

"First of all, we both know that it will heal itself. Plus, she'd be in more pain. I would guess it's just an acute contusion."

Jamey blew out a sigh of frustration, "How severe is the bruise, Jessica?"

"It's not that bad. I'll be fine if Bobby gives me pain pills. He says he has some. I'm fine, really. Like I said, it's not that bad." I blurted all this out, eager for Josh and Jamey to stop harassing me, but also feeling desperate to get my hands on the pills.

Josh snorted derisively, "If it's not that bad, why would you need prescription pain pills Bobby stole from his mother?"

"Good point," Jamey said reproachfully; he pointed his finger at me as if I were an errant child, "I still think you might need to be seen."

"No! No! I told you I am not going!"

"What if your dad found out about this?" Jamey threatened. "Maybe we should let him know, then he can decide."

I panicked; I couldn't believe he was playing this card. I thought he was bluffing, but I wasn't sure. Even though I was very much afraid he might follow through, I stared at him- looking him directly in the eyes, "If you do that, I promise you, I will never forgive you."

Jamey licked his lips and scratched at his head. He knew I was serious because of how calmly and deliberately I'd delivered my message.

Everyone fell silent until Bobby once again became the voice of reason, "Let's just get down to it. Bruises rarely need medical attention. She needs ice and pain pills. She'll be fine."

Jamey nodded and pursed his lips. "Okay," he surrendered, "no doctor if you let me check it out."

I furrowed my eyebrows. "What? What do you mean?"

"I just want to make sure it's not infected or anything. I'm not trying to *check **you** out*. Don't even accuse me of that. I just want to make sure. If you let me, then Bobby can give you the pills, and we'll ice it."

I felt my eyes start to fill with mortified tears, but I tried to hold them back. The thought of Jamey examining my behind was beyond embarrassing, but I knew I had no choice.

"Okay," I whispered.

"I guess we'll go to the rec room," Erin said.

I'd forgotten Erin and Mickey were still in the room. They had both been silent during most of the exchange.

"Yeah, the cleaning crew will be here soon anyway to clean upstairs," Jamey agreed, "But I can tell Bobby helped them out as usual." He playfully nudged Bobby with his arm.

Bobby blew out a puff of air, "Maybe I should get started downstairs. It's a mess down there, too."

"I don't want to hang out in a dump," Mickey blankly stated, "Let's go surface clean, as my mom calls it."

Josh chimed in, "Well, I'm not helping because I wasn't here to make the mess."

Erin laughed and good-naturedly punched Josh on the arm, "Don't be so lazy," she ordered.

While they were getting ready to leave to go to the rec room, Jamey looked at me with a smirk on his face. "You're lucky you have a bruised ass because if you didn't, I'd put you over my knee for being so irresponsible."

I turned beet red, and my mouth fell open as the rest of my friends laughed at Jamey's sexist comment.

"You better not touch me," I said firmly.

"Oh Jess," Erin began lightly, "He's just joking."

"Who said I was joking?" Jamey teased.

"Then I'm leaving," I asserted.

"Really?" Jamey asked, sounding almost as if he was daring me. "Don't you want Bobby's pills? Or would you rather…"

"Just shut up, Jamey," I said, my voice cracking.

"Aw, leave her alone," Bobby said sympathetically, "Just check her out, let me give her the freaking pills, and get some ice. Get on with it."

"Jamey's right," Josh added, "She did act like a child. She deserves to be treated like one."

That almost set me off. I wanted to tell Josh where to go, but I was too distracted. I was desperate for the pills, ice, and the alleviation of pain that continued to course through my body.

Erin took hold of Josh's arm, "Come on, Josh. Let's go. Stop picking on Jessica."

I watched as he followed the rest of them out of the room. And then I burst into tears.

Jamey immediately came over and put his arms around me. "Don't cry, baby. Stop. It's okay." The tears were flowing now, and my body started heaving as Jamey held me close and soothed me. "I love you; that's why I acted like that. I care about you. I was upset because I was afraid you were hurt."

He held me until I stopped sobbing and shaking. When I calmed down, he patted my back as if I was an infant in need of burping. When I lifted my face up, he wiped away my tears and gingerly kissed my forehead. After that, he placed his warm lips on mine. When he pulled away, he cupped my cheeks in his hands, "It's okay. I promise. Let's get this over with."

I swallowed soundly and nodded as he led me to one of the many upstairs bathrooms. This one was located on the left side of the kitchen. We never really ventured toward that part of his mini-mansion.

I realized that in all the times I'd been in Jamey's house, I'd never actually been in this particular room. It had the same minimalist style as the rest of the house. The walls were painted white, with a mahogany vanity cabinet and a silver waste bucket. White towels were hanging from the wall and a circular accent mirror. Jamey nudged me over to stand on a gray and white checkered chenille rug. He told me to place my hands on the vanity and to pull my skirt up.

"I could do it, but I think you'd feel more comfortable. I promise I'm not enjoying this, Jess," he claimed, "I know how uncomfortable you are."

I did as he said, and he asked permission to pull my underwear forward. I said he could.

He did it quickly. I was stiff as a board, holding my breath. He released them after a couple of seconds and whistled. "Okay," he said slowly, "It does look bad and painful. You need to let me ice it today, or it will swell and get worse, okay?"

"Why do *you* have to ice it?" I gulped as he placed his hands on my shoulders and guided me to turn around

He moved his face close to mine and kissed me again on the lips, "Because I want to. And after Bobby gives you the pills, you will most likely pass out. Let me get a pail of ice, you can lay next to me, and I'll cover you with a blanket. It will feel good, believe me. Tomorrow and for the next few days, you'll have to do it yourself. Okay? I have some ice packs I can give you, or sometimes frozen vegetables work even better. Okay?"

I nodded.

Jamey took my hand, "Let's get you those pills."

When Jamey and I eventually made our way into the rec room, which hadn't changed much since we were freshmen, our friends were all scattered around and involved in various activities. Mickey and Josh were sitting on the sectional couch playing violent video games. Jenna had her feet up on the chair recliner, texting someone- probably her new college boyfriend. And Evan was sitting on an ottoman with Nikki on his lap, and they were predictably making out. Erin and Kelly had their feet stretched out on an Oriental rug covering the hardwood floor, painting their toenails.

No one paid much mind to us when we entered, but I did notice Bobby's eyes scan the room, giving everyone a threatening look. I assumed he'd ordered all of them to mind their own business and pretend the incident hadn't happened.

Bobby was playing the part of den mother, still cleaning up while the rest of the gang played. "Are we ready to watch the first episode?" he asked Jamey and me as he put the broom he'd been holding in a custodial closet.

Jamey nodded, "Yeah, but come here first."

Bobby walked toward us," Want me to give her the pills?"

Jamey nodded, "Yeah, thanks, man."

Bobby escorted me to another part of the house I'd never seen before. It was a guest room that apparently belonged to Bobby. It made sense for him to have his own chamber because he frequently stayed overnight at Jamey's. Bobby's private room was attached to the rec room. It was small but somewhat impressive. It was painted a dark blue with football decals covering the ceiling. He also had posters of sports figures on the walls and a double bed with a football comforter.

Once we were inside, he opened the first drawer of a mahogany dresser, took out a pill bottle, poured a couple of white tablets into his palm, and handed them to me. "Be careful with these," he ordered, "Take two now. They'll knock you out. Take half when you're around your parents. You'll probably need them Monday and possibly Tuesday- take one before school and two at night. You can switch to aspirin on Wednesday. I'll give you the rest before you leave. Okay?"

I nodded as he looked at me with a serious expression, making sure I was taking all of this in. I was so anxious to get the pain relievers into my system that I threw them in my mouth and swallowed them down without water.

"Impressive," Bobby said, grinning.

When we walked back into the rec room, I noticed Erin and Kelly were now relaxing on beanbag chairs while everyone else was seated comfortably in the spots they'd been in when I left the room with Bobby. They were in a semi-circle around the television, which was almost the size of the entire wall. Jamey had taken a spot on the velvet loveseat placed outside the circle but still within view of the television. He was sitting on the edge with his arms in between his legs. He had a bulky pillow with a satin case over it and a faux fur blanket placed next to him.

"You good?" he asked Bobby and me as we walked into the room.

"Yup," Bobby said, "She'll be out cold in a few."

"Feel better, Jess," Erin murmured.

Kelly, Jenna, and Nikki muttered similar words of sympathy.

"Let's start this!" Mickey commanded, "Come on."

Jamey waved me over as Bobby began fiddling with remotes. Once again, he was playing host even though it wasn't actually his house.

I noticed there was a steel bucket of what I assumed was ice on the oval end table next to the loveseat Jamey was sitting on. He had removed the cushions so we could comfortably fit on it. "Come lay on my lap," Jamey instructed.

As I walked toward him, he smirked and added, "You should get used to this position."

Jamey and Josh started laughing.

I stopped in my tracks and glared at Jamey.

Jenna came to my defense, "Jamey, just shut up, seriously. Stop being a dick so we can watch the show."

Once again, Josh felt the need to pipe in, "She deserves it."

"Mind your own business," Nikki told Josh.

Jamey waved me over, "Come on, babe. I'm playing with you. Look, I have ice, and it will definitely help."

I refused to budge because I was not only embarrassed by Jamey threatening to spank me but also angry.

"Jess, don't be so defensive. I was just being funny."

"Well, you're not funny." Jenna retorted.

"Sorry," Jamey mumbled, "Come on. I actually want to make you feel better."

I sighed and reluctantly tiptoed over to him. He took my hand and helped me finagle myself over his lap so my back was pressed against his chest. He covered me with the blanket, and I laid my head on the pillow. My stomach did a flip as he lifted my skirt, which I'd never changed out of. I sucked in a breath as he pulled my underwear down, "You okay?" he whispered, asking for my consent.

I purred my approval; the pills were kicking in, and I was suddenly beginning to feel somewhat elated.

The advertisements ended, and the show started. I was feeling a combination of euphoria and sluggishness from the meds. I closed my eyes and felt Jamey gently rubbing the ice over my bottom and upturned thigh. It did feel good, *very* good. While he used one hand to diminish the pain of my injury, he used the other to run his fingers through my hair and gently massage my neck. I felt safe and calm and cozy, forgetting entirely that this was an awkward situation. It was sensual and erotic yet simultaneously wholesome and pure. Jamey was alleviating my pain with one hand and showing his love for me with the other in the most innocuous way. I contemplated my paradoxical emotions as I drifted off into a blissful sleep.

Chapter Seventeen: Kevin LaFontaine

Lomonoco Creek offered a wide variety of electives, and we were allowed to choose new ones every trimester. I had been interested in learning about photography and was planning to take an introductory class about the art of snapping pictures. My plans were altered when Miss Clement, my guidance counselor, summoned me to her office.

I could tell she was excited as I sauntered into her bright, lively-looking workspace. Miss Clement's room was reflective of her personality. The buttery beige walls were covered with paintings of modern art and canvases with meditative sayings on them. She also had several pictures displayed on her desk of nieces and nephews and a formal engagement photo of her with her fiancé.

"Guess what?" she asked enthusiastically.

I arched my eyebrows curiously, waiting for her to continue.

"I was able to get you into a college-level class as your elective this trimester."

"What class?" I asked, immediately feeling disappointed because I had been looking forward to the photography class.

"It's being taught by Dr. Brown- a college professor," Miss Clement told me, her voice rose an octave when she enunciated the word "college."

"Dr. Brown teaches at St. Padre Pio, the school your parents went to, right?"

I nodded.

"Well, she is writing a book, so she decided to take a sabbatical, and because she is an alumnus, she agreed to teach a class here about the benefits of persuasive dispute. Isn't that exciting?"

Miss Clement sounded so thrilled that I didn't have the heart to tell her I wasn't really interested in debate. She went on to explain that she pulled strings to get me into the class. She knew on a personal level that I was passionate about many controversial topics. She verified my ability as a junior to take a class meant for college freshmen by speaking with other teachers who agreed that I was not afraid to communicate my feelings on paper or verbally.

While this was true, I had discovered in the past that debating tended to make me anxious and flustered. I had been a member of the debate club but decided not to rejoin. There were other extra-curricular activities I was more interested in, and I honestly felt like I wasn't particularly strong at arguing in an eloquent yet confrontational way. My anxiety got in the way and prevented me from truly expressing myself. Yet, I agreed to take the class because I didn't want to disappoint Miss Clement, and I knew it was an honor to be considered for it, bearing in mind that it was being taught by a prestigious college professor. Additionally, I was eager to tell my dad about it because I knew he'd be proud of me; after all, I would be earning college credit by taking this elective.

It didn't take long for Dr. Brown to discover that putting my thoughts on paper was more of a strength for me than verbally conveying them- at least when it involved contentious topics. I wasn't afraid to speak my mind, especially when it came to defending myself, but I didn't always feel 100% comfortable about quarreling over provocative subjects like abortion or the death penalty.

Dr. Brown asked me to stay after class one day and offered me words of encouragement. She claimed to be incredibly impressed with my writing skills. "Jessica, your thoughts and feelings are so strong. You have talent," she told me, "But you have to develop more confidence when expressing yourself in an actual debate."

I nodded knowingly.

"It's not that you aren't good at debating. You are. However, my concern is that your ability to defend your opinions through the written word doesn't match your ability to defend your opinions through the spoken word."

"That's always been the case," I informed her solemnly.

"Don't fret, dear," she said soothingly, "I have some advice for you."

Dr. Brown gave me a handout on meditation. She also suggested that I try yoga, breathing exercises, and journal writing. She assured me these calming exercises could alleviate my anxiety and prevent me from becoming rattled when it came to orally contesting an opposing view.

In the midst of my interaction with Dr. Brown, I noticed that a boy in class had taken an interest in me. Kevin LaFontaine was a good-looking and personable senior. He didn't really run in the same circles as I did. He hung around with the soccer and lacrosse crowd. I didn't know much about him, but he was popular enough for me to be aware of who he was.

Kevin and I initially had no contact. We were allowed to sit anywhere we wanted in Dr. Brown's class. It was run like a college seminar. Kevin made sure to sit in front of me, in the back of me, or next to me every day- whatever seat was available. He was not at all discreet in the way he stared at me. I avoided eye contact, and when I accidentally caught his gaze, I quickly looked away. Even though I never turned to face him, the flirtatious smile he had plastered on his face was noticeable through my peripheral vision.

This wouldn't have been a problem if Kevin didn't happen to be captain of the varsity debate club. Although I tried all of Dr. Brown's suggestions, I still tensed up before I had to debate someone in class. I would lose my train of thought, say "um" too many times, and sometimes even begin hyperventilating. I certainly wasn't the worst debater in the class. I wasn't really that bad. Nevertheless, Dr. Brown had taken an interest in me because she thought I had promised and went out of her way to try to help. Unfortunately, through no fault of her own, she ended up doing the opposite. She suggested that Kevin work with me to help my debating skills.

When Dr. Brown once again asked me to stay after class, she seemed as excited as Miss Clement had been when she told me about the class, "I have a wonderful proposal, Jessica," she began animatedly, "Actually, I have to admit, it wasn't *my* idea."

I waited silently to hear what she had to say.

"Kevin...Kevin LaFontaine offered to help tutor you,"

I started to stutter a response, but before I could protest, she clapped her hands together and said merrily, "I know! I know! I understand. You don't even have to respond. This is so kind of him. He has so many extra-curricular activities and not much free time- I would assume. But he can help during class and study hall. He actually came to me and said he'd like to work with you because he also sees a lot of potential in you. And just think, he is the captain of the varsity debate club!"

I knew it was a bad idea. I wanted to protest, but I had been taught to respect adults, especially someone like Dr. Brown, so I reluctantly agreed.

Knowing how jealous Jamey could be, I was slightly nervous he would find out about my being partnered up with Kevin. I was afraid he would threaten him or cause a scene if he discovered I'd been coerced into working with him. Fortunately, that didn't pose a threat because Dr. Brown arranged for us to work together during her class and the study hall she ran the very next period. I was obviously relieved that our affiliation would not become public knowledge.

Considering that Kevin had been nonverbally flirting with me since the course began, I was worried that he'd take it a step further once we began our tutoring sessions. The first time we entered the high-tech computer lab, which was connected to Dr. Brown's classroom, I felt my chest tighten as we were directed to a table in a private corner of the vast room.

"The two of you can work here. Is this private enough?" Dr. Brown asked amiably.

There were other people in the room with us, but they were all seated at least eighteen feet away. We would definitely have privacy.

"This is perfect," Kevin stated politely.

I simply nodded half-heartedly as I plopped myself down on a cushioned rolling chair. My heartbeat quickened as I watched Dr. Brown abandon us, knowing I'd soon be essentially alone with Kevin.

We made small talk for a few minutes about what I hoped to achieve and how he could help me. I thought I was in the clear as I scrolled through my Chrome Book. I had a debate coming up. Thus, I highlighted a few passages in my notes that I planned to review with Kevin.

"So, Jessica, can I ask you something?" He drawled the words out in a tone that I recognized well. It was the tone people used before they asked you something personal, insulting, or both. I froze and sucked in a breath because I knew what was coming.

"Maybe it's none of my business," Kevin began hesitantly, "But I was just wondering if you were…you know, available? I'm not sure if you're in a relationship with Jamey Russo. Is he your boyfriend?"

"Um…It's complicated."

Kevin snickered, 'It can't be *that* complicated. Is he your boyfriend or not?"

I paused, trying to think of how to explain.

"So, he's not your boyfriend?" Obviously, Kevin took my silence as a denial.

I tilted my head and sucked on my finger nail. I was still feeling not only uncomfortable but also confused. I wasn't sure how much I wanted to disclose.

"He's not my boyfriend," I finally admitted.

"That would mean you're available, then?" Kevin inquired in a frisky, playful manner

"No!" I stated firmly.

Kevin placed his cheek in his palm and chewed on his bottom lip. "That doesn't make sense. Are you dating someone besides Jamey Russo? From what I hear, he is a pretty possessive guy when it comes to you."

"Listen," I replied, trying to sound as no-nonsense as possible, "It's complex, and I don't want to talk about it. I *really* don't want to talk about it."

Kevin brushed his hands through his hair and shrugged, "I get it," he replied good-naturedly, "Your relationship status is off-limits."

I breathed a sigh of relief as he changed the subject to something less distressing and "debatable," like whether or not plastic straws should be banned in order to protect sea turtles.

For the next couple of weeks, things between Kevin and me were harmonious and relaxed. He did refrain from probing me about Jamey. Instead, he spent the time we were supposed to be discussing debate, enquiring information about me. He was also very complimentary about my appearance. He constantly told me how pretty I was. He claimed that I looked almost identical to my great-grandmothers, who had been famous actresses. When he mentioned them, I humbly averted my eyes and changed the subject. Unlike my sisters, my mom and I were self-conscious about our renowned kin and avoided the topic.

In hindsight, I realize Kevin and I never really discussed my debating ability. We didn't get around to it. At the time, I didn't even realize we talked about anything and everything else because, truthfully, I wasn't all that passionate about strengthening my skills.

Although our connection was completely platonic, I started to feel as if Kevin knew everything about me- except my feelings about Jamey. I also realized that I knew an awful lot about him. He offered the information because I rarely questioned him about his family, friends, or interests.

After about a week of this, Dr. Brown asked how things were going. I had an actual debate coming up soon that would be graded; it was about delicate and complex environmental issues, and we hadn't practiced at all.

"Things are going well. I think she's ready." Kevin lied, considering he had no idea if I was prepared or not. We'd never even talked about it.

"That's wonderful!" Dr. Brown exclaimed, "I love seeing you two motivated, promising young people work together. It brightens my day to watch you interact."

Kevin seemed quite pleased by her words, "Well, we love working together, don't we, Jessica? We make a good team."

I nodded, although his words made me squirm.

Dr. Brown clapped her hands and giggled. She was acting as if we'd announced our engagement. There was a part of me that wondered if she wanted Kevin and me to start dating. She seemed to have taken a liking to both of us and obviously thought we'd make a good pair. She knew how ambitious I was, and I have to admit, Kevin was not only a very good debater, but he was also quite charming and polite when it suited him.

Unfortunately, Dr. Brown's enthusiasm was the catalyst for Kevin's attempt to once again take our relationship to the next level. When she sashayed out of the room, I turned to Kevin with a serious and somewhat nervous look on my face, "We really haven't talked about my upcoming debate at all. I hope I'm prepared. I think we should concentrate on that from now on."

"Or you could come to my house this weekend, and we could work on it?" Kevin suggested.

I shook my head, "No, I can't. I'm busy. Maybe we should actually practice instead of talking about other things."

"But I really like talking to you. I can't help it if we veer off topic."

I wanted to say that I wasn't the one who veered off-topic. He was. I'd let him lead the way, which was why I hadn't really noticed that we never discussed my upcoming debate. After all, he was supposed to be tutoring me. As a mentor myself, I knew the teacher was the one who was supposed to lead the discussions.

"I think we should concentrate on discussing academics from now on," I said rather firmly, "So I'll be prepared for next week."

Kevin grinned as he moved his face closer to mine. I turned away from him, which only brought his lips closer to my ear. "There's an easy solution. We can just meet on the weekend. Anytime. I'm available. Then we can continue to talk during study hall." He was whispering in a conspiratorial way.

"I really am very busy on the weekends. I can't, and my dad won't let me go to your house. He's strict."

Kevin raised both his hands in the air, palms out, in mock defeat, "Okay. There's an easy solution to that, too. We can go to your house and work."

"Kevin, we have a week to practice," I reminded him, "We can do that during study hall. We don't need to meet outside of school."

"Maybe I'd like to meet outside of school. Are you saying you wouldn't?" His tone was good-humored, but I was sensing a shift in the dynamics of our relationship.

I was quiet for a while, and Kevin finally said, "So…?"

I looked up into his eyes, and in a very definitive tone, I pronounced, "Listen, I think you are a nice guy. I really do. But I have a lot going on, and I am very busy. I would prefer that we practice during study hall. I don't have time to meet any other time. Sorry."

"I know I agreed not to bring it up," Kevin said in a much less friendly tone of voice, "But I have to say that I think this has something to do with Jamey Russo. I mean, you're not dating anyone else. Everyone knows there's something between you. I feel like whatever is going on between you two is rather strange."

I blew out an enormous breath and tried one last attempt to keep things civil between us, "I don't want to talk about it. Like I said before, it's complicated. Please, let's just change the subject."

"Are you afraid of him or something?"

"No, of course not."

"Well, it doesn't make any sense," He started to soften. "Talk to me."

"I don't want to."

Why?" he asked gently.

I sighed and lifted my shoulders in a wary way.

Kevin flashed me a toothy grin, "I'm a good listener."

"I'm not a good talker." I said with irritation, "And it's really none of your business."

"Well, then..." Kevin said through gritted teeth, and I knew our genial association was coming to an end.

Subsequently, Kevin seemed to change overnight- literally. The next day after class, I strode over to the table in the computer lab where we always sat and took out the notes I'd typed up the night before. Kevin swung open the door connecting the two rooms and took three expansive, exaggerated steps over to me. He then proceeded to slam his books down. I tapped my fingers on my books impatiently as he aggressively stated, "Okay, I guess I need to help you prepare for your debate."

I decided to feign ignorance and flipped to the highlighted part of my notes on the dangers imposed on sea turtles from plastic straws. I pointed to something I had a question about and started to ask Kevin how he thought I should respond if my opponent asked about the monetary problems associated with paper straws.

Before I was even able to open my mouth to speak, Kevin loudly cleared his throat, "So this is how it's going to be?"

I looked at him with a perplexed expression on my face.

"Don't look at me like that. Stop playing innocent. You know exactly what I'm talking about."

I licked my lips and looked down. I was not afraid or intimidated by Kevin LaFontaine. I actually found all of this to be an inconvenience. "No," I said through gritted teeth, "I don't."

"Well, let me explain," Kevin began heatedly, "We have become friends these past couple of weeks. All I wanted was to get to know you a little bit. Is that really so much to ask after I agreed to work with you? I could see...Dr. Brown and I could both see potential in you. I was trying to be nice, and you treat me like..."

"I haven't done anything to you," I declared, "In fact, if you are going to continue talking to me like this, then I don't want to work with you anymore. I'll tell Dr. Brown it isn't working out."

I started to stand up and collect my books, but Kevin firmly placed his hand over mine.

"Don't touch me!" I ordered.

Kevin changed his tune, possibly recognizing that I would not respond to his gaslighting. "I'm sorry," he replied apologetically, "I shouldn't have spoken to you like that." He put his hands up in surrender, "I am just really disappointed. I wanted to know what was going on between you and Jamey because I like you. I don't know why you can't just explain."

I looked Kevin squarely in the eyes with a serious expression on my face, "I will not tolerate you or anyone else talking to me or treating me with disrespect. Like I said before, Jamey and my situation is none of your business. If you can't honor that, then we can't work together."

"I understand," Kevin promised, "I get it. Now, please sit back down, and we'll discuss your notes."

But Kevin didn't understand. He started off each session pretending he was interested in helping me, and at some point, he would inevitably ask me on a date. When I would tell him I couldn't go with him to the movies or out to eat, he would say something to the tune of, "Oh, is it because of Jamey? Are you seeing him on Friday night? That's why you won't go out with me?"

I would give him a death stare, and he'd express regret and go back to giving me advice about my debate.

After a week of this insane routine, I'd had enough. I realized it was time to drop the class. It was an elective, and I knew debate really wasn't something I wanted to pursue. I contemplated talking to Dr. Brown, but I decided against it because she seemed to be very impressed with Kevin, and I didn't want to start trouble. I wasn't sure how my parents would feel about me abandoning the course, so I chose to tell them a "version" of the truth. I would need one of them to call the school in order for me to be allowed to switch to something else a month into the trimester.

My parents were understanding about the situation, and my dad even communicated how impressed he was with all the classes and activities I was currently involved with.

"You are incredibly active already, Jessica. We know how driven you are. Maybe you could switch to a pass/fail class that isn't academic." I was surprised by my dad's words but also relieved.

My mom agreed to call the school the next day and have me removed from the course. I naively thought this would be the end of my problems with Kevin when, in fact, my decision to withdraw from the debate only made things worse.

Kevin took my dropping the class very, very personally- even more personally than Dr. Brown. He took it as an affront. Although I didn't see him as a threat, I was aware he was narcissistic and antagonistic. He seemed to be the type of person to overreact and become obsessed when he took an interest in something or *someone,* and that someone, in this case, was me. I started to wonder if there was a reason why guys like Kevin were attracted to me. What was it about me that made mean boys interested in me, and not just interested, but fanatical? I did not see Jamey as falling into this category. Jamey was over-protective of me like Kevin had said, but he was never emotionally abusive or controlling. He always respected my boundaries.

Jenna and Nikki were the only people I originally told about Kevin's harassment. I expressed my concern about this type of thing happening to me over Sunday brunch. We were sitting off to the side so no one else could eavesdrop on our conversation.

Jenna put it into perspective for me. "Everyone knows that there's a...*thing* between you and Jamey. Normal guys wouldn't want to get involved in something like that. They leave you alone because they aren't trouble makers. Boys like Kevin enjoy conflict and confrontation. That's probably why he likes debating so much."

Nikki chimed in, "Maybe boys like Kevin enjoy a challenge."

I nodded, taking in what they were suggesting.

"Anyway," Nikki continued, "If Kevin keeps bothering you, you should tell your parents and get Mr. Blume involved."

I agreed but hoped it wouldn't come to that.

Unfortunately, it did.

When Kevin and Dr. Brown first found out that I had decided to abandon the class, they approached me in the hallway while I was at my locker after my new elective ended.

"Why did you drop debate?" Kevin asked. Although there was definitely an irritated tone to his voice, he wasn't overly aggressive because he was with Dr. Brown.

"What happened, Jessica? I thought things were going well," Dr. Brown chimed in. "Why did you decide to switch courses?"

I felt uncomfortable being accosted in this way. I had every right to withdraw from an elective if I wanted to.

I cleared my throat and turned my back to them, "I discussed it with my parents, and we decided that debate wasn't something I wanted to pursue in the future. I tried it and lost interest. My mom spoke to Miss Clement, and she agreed that I could transfer to photography since it's a pass/fail course."

My voice had an edge to it, and I think Dr. Brown detected that and did not wish to discuss it further. "Okay," she began, sounding disappointed. "Well, I guess there's no way we can persuade you to change your mind."

"No," I stately firmly. I spun around to face Dr. Brown and Kevin, holding my books firmly in front of me; they acted partially as a shield between me and them.

Kevin started to say more, but the bell rang, and Dr. Brown told him it was time to get to study hall. He obeyed, but as he followed her, his head was twisted, so he was looking directly at me.

After that, he started stalking me. He was never threatening or overtly cruel, which was why I allowed it to continue longer than I should have. His harassment involved texting and phone calls. I was civil at first, but when he continued the same line of questions and statements he'd been making in class, I blocked his number. He then began purposely passing me in the hallway and trying to force me to engage in a conversation. I avoided him at all costs. He wouldn't approach me when Jamey was around, but he did one time when I was with Nikki.

Nikki ended up telling my Aunt Gina about what was going on, and she convinced me to tell my dad. She reminded me that my dad was friends with the principal and could easily fix this situation.

I agreed. My dad was a little upset with me for not telling him sooner, but I explained that I was trying to be independent and handle it myself. I also voiced my feeling of humiliation about being pestered in this way.

My father sighed and nodded grimly, "I understand. These types of situations can be awkward and unnerving. Boys certainly shouldn't ever give girls unwanted attention. Obviously, this Kevin has no appropriate male role models in his life. I will call Harry, and I'm sure he'll take care of it."

Harry was Mr. Blume- the principal; he and my dad had been friends for years. In addition to them being buddies, my father was also a huge financial contributor to the school in many ways, so I felt assured that Mr. Blume would feel obligated to do what he could to put a stop to this.

The next day, I was standing at my locker right before lunch with Jenna. We were deep in conversation about a new college guy she was dating. I was listening intently to her description of the hot sex they'd had over the weekend. Although I was nowhere near ready to do it myself, I, like every teenage girl, was interested in details about it. It was something I knew I would someday experience, and Jenna made it seem so exciting and fun. I guess I was being naïve because I was at peace, under the misconception that my dad and Mr. Blume would be able to assuage the situation with Kevin. I assumed it would be over and done with after Kevin was scolded by the principal.

I was sorely mistaken.

Jenna and I were blindsided when the door to the office swung open, and Kevin barged out like a sky rocket. He had an incensed expression on his face as he headed toward my locker. It was apparent by the wild look in his eyes that the meeting with Mr. Blume triggered a response I was not expecting. I was so startled that I, once again, felt disassociated. Obviously, that was often my reaction when I became extremely surprised or anxious. In that moment, I genuinely felt as if I was looming over us, observing the scene as a spectator, not as a participant.

Although Kevin had not yet spoken, Jenna stood in front of me protectively.

His demonstrative hand gestures and irritated accusations made me so nervous at first that I couldn't concentrate on the precise words pouring from his mouth, only the meaning behind them. In his mind, I had wronged him by fighting back against his harassment. He accused me of tattling. He said I should've come to him before having my father call his friend, the principal. He berated my dad for using his influence to get his daughter out of perfectly natural situations. He also reproached my father for constantly throwing his power around.

"Get the hell out of here, you lunatic!" Jenna finally demanded when there was a pause in Kevin's diatribe.

Her irate voice pulled me out of my reverie. It was similar to a hypnotist snapping her fingers and awakening you from a trance.

"It doesn't matter how good you are at playing soccer or lacrosse around here," Kevin bellowed, ignoring her, "The only frigging athletes who are respected at this stupid school are the damn football players."

Jenna had her hands on her hips and was glaring at Kevin with venom, "I told you to get away from us, Kevin LaFontaine. We don't give a shit what you think."

If looks could kill, Kevin would have already murdered Jenna, but she stood her ground. She didn't even flinch as he pointed at her and proclaimed, "I'm not talking to you. I'm talking to Jessica."

"I don't want to talk to you!" I shouted, inadvertently drawing attention to myself, which inevitably provoked Jamey to come and see what was going on. I should have known he wasn't far away.

"We were friends," Kevin insisted, "That's all. I deserved to know why you dropped the class and why you stopped talking to me."

I vehemently shook my head, "No. You were harassing me. I told you to leave me alone."

Before Kevin could protest, Mr. Blume and Mr. Vega came out of the office. They must have overheard the commotion. They each took one of Kevin's arms and dragged him away from me, back towards the office. A crowd of people had gathered around and were animatedly discussing what had occurred, so I couldn't hear what they said to him as they carried him away.

Jamey pushed through the crowd and stood before me, "What's going on?" he asked with concern.

I sighed and reluctantly told him that my dad had called the school because Kevin had been bothering me.

"Well, I'm glad you told your dad, Jess," he said, "That was the right thing to do. But why didn't you tell me?"

I tilted my head, pursed my lips, and threw my hands up in the air, "Why do you think?"

Jamey couldn't help but smirk. "Well, at least you told your dad," he muttered. Then his mood shifted, an angry look spread across his face, "I'm going to kill that son of a bitch."

"No, you're not," I insisted, "Jamey, let it go. You don't need to get involved. It's taken care of."

I looked around and noticed that it was just the two of us standing there. Everyone had cleared out, even Jenna.

"Okay?" I asked.

"Let's go to lunch," Jamey said good-naturedly, taking my hand in his, "So you dropped that debate class?" he asked, purposely changing the subject.

"Yeah."

"What are you taking instead?"

I started telling Jamey about the photography class I was able to get into, and before I realized what had happened, I forgot to revisit the topic of Kevin LaFontaine.

Kevin had been suspended that day and sent home immediately. Therefore, Jamey never had the chance to confront him. He did, however, take a trip to his house, and when Kevin was taking the garbage out, he threatened him- he apparently told him he'd beat the living shit out of him if he ever bothered me again. Then, before he left, he punched him in the face.

I'm ashamed to admit that Jamey's violence in this situation didn't elicit an angry response- at least not from me; in fact, I was secretly pleased that Kevin got what I saw as his comeuppance.

Chapter Eighteen: The Vow

Alexa Parker's highly anticipated party took place approximately three weeks after the incident at my locker with Kevin. Once my dad made Mr. Blume aware of Kevin's harassment, and he subsequently accosted me in the hallway, Kevin had been suspended for three days, and in addition, he was given a week of after-school detentions. My father was irate when he found out about Kevin's reaction to being reprimanded by the principal. Mr. Blume phoned him immediately after it happened. I'm sure he was being cautious, knowing how influential and protective my father was.

When I got home that day, I was surprised to find that my father had left work early and was anxious to speak to me about the confrontation. He assured me that Kevin's behavior was being taken very seriously and it would not be tolerated. He informed me that Kevin had been given an ultimatum: if he bothered me again, he would face expulsion.

My dad sensed that I not only felt somewhat embarrassed about the situation but also nervous that Kevin's badgering would continue. "Jessica, you know you can trust me, right?" he asked.

I nodded vigorously, "Of course."

He smiled with encouragement, "Harry is an efficient principal. He runs a safe school, and under his leadership, Lomonoco Creek has a zero-tolerance policy for bullying." I couldn't help but silently scoff at that, considering what I knew about Jamey, yet I remained silent as my father continued. "I have known Mr. Blume for a long time. You know we've been friends since I was your age. And sometimes, it's acceptable to use relationships to your advantage. When it comes to my daughter, if I have to pull strings, I certainly will."

He put his hands on my shoulders and looked into my eyes as he went on, "You don't have to worry about that degenerate anymore. Okay? Do you understand?"

"Yes," I replied, breathing a sigh of relief. I knew my father would never make a promise he couldn't keep.

"But," he articulated with a note of caution in his voice, "You have to tell me if this boy calls you, texts you, tries to talk to you…if he even looks in your direction. And when you see him at school, look away. Do not make eye contact with him." He paused, watching me.

I was silent until he spoke again, "Jessica, I am being serious- very serious. I am going to ask you this one more time. Do you understand me?"

I swallowed soundly because even though I knew this wasn't meant as an admonishment, I still felt uneasy when my dad was stern with me. I slowly bobbed my head up and down.

"I want to hear you say it."

"Yes, Dad. I understand."

He was satisfied with my response because he smiled and patted me on the head before walking away.

I never mentioned to Jamey that I'd found out about his assault and the threat he'd made to Kevin. I decided it wasn't worth it. I wasn't angry with him, even though I felt like I should be. I couldn't bring myself to feel cross. This was the first time I ignored Jamey's violent behavior- especially when it was a result of something he'd done in my honor. In all honesty, I felt gratification and a sense of justice. I believed Kevin deserved the consequences he'd received because of his harassment and egotistical sense of entitlement.

After a few weeks, I assumed the unfortunate state of affairs with Kevin was over and done with. I hadn't heard a peep from him. I'd even passed him in the hallway a few times, and his eyes never steered my way. I was under the false pretense that he learned his lesson. All evidence pointed to the fact that he'd moved on.

Unfortunately, Alexa Parker's party changed everything. I did not want to attend Alexa Parker's party. I was completely against it, as a matter of fact. If I had refused to acquiesce, if I had stuck to my guns- the night wouldn't have turned out the way it did. Most importantly, it wouldn't have set off a chain of events that changed the pleasant and content course my life was on up until that point. Oddly enough, the incidents that occurred this particular evening had nothing to do with Jamey. As a matter of fact, Jamey wasn't even in the state at the time. Every year, during spring break, he went away to baseball camp in New York with Mickey and Bobby in order to strengthen their athletic skills during baseball season.

I didn't want to go to the party for two very important reasons. The first being that the Sunshine Committee was gathering at 8:00 the next morning in order to plan an annual spring event that we were in no way prepared for. We were all so busy with other activities, both social and academic, that we hadn't convened in a month. I was adamant about us getting together to at least brainstorm ideas. My anxiety was sky-high, considering that we were starting to get pressure from the administration and guidance counselors. Although there was no president of the Sunshine Committee, I had somehow been designated the leader of the group. Therefore, I felt responsible for making sure we garnered results at our meeting the morning after the party.

There was no alternative to assembling so early because Erin and I had to be in southern Connecticut at 11:00 A.M. Many juniors had signed up for a seminar being held in Fairfield County, which would help us master skills for a mathematical entrance exam we'd soon have the opportunity to take if we were interested in early college admissions. Everyone in my friend group was going except the boys attending baseball camp. In fact, Josh was planning to drive us all because he'd been given a Mercedes SVU for his sixteenth birthday. His vehicle was large enough to fit everyone; he was going to pick up Evan, Nikki, and Jenna and then swing by the high school to gather Erin and me.

Erin was the reason I ended up going to the party. She practically forced me to attend. Although there wasn't a specific reason Erin needed to go to this shindig, she acted like her absence would be a major catastrophe. Truth be told, Erin loved any and all social gatherings. She literally behaved as if her lack of attendance at Alexa's party was equivalent to missing her own wedding. This was partially because Alexa was promoting her get-together as the party of the year- *a celebration of spring.*

"Jessica, everyone is going to be there. EVERYONE!" Erin informed me, with panic in her voice, after I'd casually informed her I wasn't planning to go.

"Jamey won't be there. Mickey won't be there. Bobby won't be there. In fact, half the baseball team won't be there- they're at camp," I replied teasingly.

Erin sighed with exasperation, "Well, everyone else will be there. It will be so much fun. Come on! We can't miss it."

"Why do I have to go? You can go without me."

We were chatting on the phone the night before the party. We had started out talking through text, but Erin immediately called me when I casually mentioned that I didn't plan to attend.

"I can't go without you!" she announced.

"Why not?" I asked, feeling perplexed. I was aware that Erin had social anxiety, which was ironic, considering she was one of the most popular girls in school. And she was very attached to our clique and felt nervous attending anything that required socialization without one of us. But in this case, many of our friends would be there, so I couldn't figure out why she needed me to go. "Everyone else will be there," I reminded her.

"I know, but you know how it is with Nikki and Evan. Once they start drinking, they'll be all over each other. And Josh will be flirting and eventually hooking up with whoever turns out to be his flavor of the night."

"What about Kelly and Jenna?"

Erin blew out a sizeable breath, "That's the thing. Jenna refuses to go now that she's *dating* that college guy. This monogamy stuff with her makes me crazy." She paused, and I could almost hear her shaking her head with disgust. Erin didn't believe girls our age should settle down with just one boy. "And Kelly is all into Steve Sands. He's all she's been talking about. They've been texting, and he's going to the party. He's driving her there. She'll be hanging with him all night, and I'll be...."

"Alone?" I asked, rolling my eyes, "What if you end up flirting with some random guy? Then what? I'll be stuck."

"I absolutely promise I will not abandon you. I solemnly swear, and you know I never break promises."

I couldn't argue with that. There were two admirable traits that Erin possessed more so than any of our other friends. She could keep a secret, and she never broke a promise.

"Listen, Erin, why don't you just plan on having one drink? You can drive yourself, and if you feel left out or whatever, you can just leave."

"That's the thing. I can't drive. My parents grounded me because I came home high the other night."

I laughed without humor, "Well, I can't drive you. I don't have my license yet." The fact that I wasn't a good enough driver to even attempt to take the driver's exam was somewhat embarrassing for me. My mother refused to drive in the same car with me because the one and only time she did, she claimed I almost gave her a heart attack. My dad had given me a few driving lessons, but he was overly critical, and his constant instructions gave ME an anxiety attack. The only adult who'd been helpful was my Aunt Gina, and in a kind-hearted way, she basically made it clear that it was going to take me a while to become an adept driver.

"Listen, my brother said he'd drop us off..." Erin began.

"I never said I would go, Erin," I cut off her, feeling aggravated.

"Please hear me out, Jess."

I was silent, waiting for her to continue.

"I promise I will be ready to leave when you are."

"Well, that's good," I said somewhat sarcastically, "But how are we going to get home?"

Erin clicked her tongue against the roof of her mouth, "Seriously? We have like a million options."

"Like who?" I threw my arms in the air for emphasis, even though Erin couldn't see me.

"Josh probably won't stay late because he's driving us to the class tomorrow. You know him. His goal is to probably get a better score than you."

I snickered derisively. I was glad other people were catching on to Josh's competitiveness.

Erin went on, "And if not Josh, then we can always convince Nikki or Evan to drive us home."

"I don't trust either of them."

"Okay, if we have no other options, I will force my brother to pick us up."

I finally relented because Erin's older brother was a responsible college student. He wasn't into partying and was always studying. I felt confident that we could rely on John. "Erin, I'll go if you make John promise to pick us up if we're stuck."

"Thank you so much, Jess! You're the best. You know we can count on him. He'll probably be at the library or something."

"Fine," I said, sighing with reluctance, and I then hung up without saying goodbye just to let her know that even though I was conceding, I wasn't happy about it.

By the time Erin and I arrived at Alexa's, there were close to one hundred people there. Overall, this particular party was comparable to every other huge bash I'd attended during high school- except the atmosphere was more impressive. Alexa's enormous Victorian estate rivaled Jamey's in size, and it had a lot more character. Its décor was reminiscent of the Romanesque era- bright colors, stained glass, and decorative woodwork. I must have heard at least twenty females comment on how vintage and cool the house was. I had to agree. In fact, I spent most of the night admiring it while I nursed a lukewarm beer. I wasn't in the mood to socialize. I had my mind set against coming to this party and couldn't keep my nervous thoughts about my early wake-up time at bay. Erin, on the other hand, hadn't a care in the world, a complete social butterfly. She certainly didn't need me to be there as her safety net, although she did keep her promise and attempt to drag me along with her as she went from group to group, chatting up a storm. I felt like I wanted to wring her neck, but I also realized that was a result of my grumpiness. I was usually more animated during social gatherings, but I basically kept to myself most of the night, engaging in trivial, light conversations with people throughout the course of the evening.

I spent the first hour of the party chatting with Nikki, Evan, and some of our other classmates. However, after Nikki and Evan had a few drinks, they began cooing at one another, and then the caresses and smooches started. I abandoned them after Nikki climbed on Evan's lap, straddling him, and they started making out.

Kelly arrived fashionably late with Steve Sands. When she spotted Erin and I, she looked excited and smiled brightly at us. "Hi!" she exclaimed, widening her cornflower blue eyes and trying without success to discreetly shift her head in Steve's direction as if to say, "Look, who I'm with! Can you believe it?" Her attempt at obscurity was so transparent that Erin rolled her eyes at me, and I laughed out loud as we skulked away. They spent the rest of the evening huddled in an inconspicuous crook in the kitchen by themselves.

By the time the minute hand on Alexa's grandfather clock hit twelve and the hour hand was placed on the ten- I quickly scanned the room for Erin. She was standing with a group of lacrosse players in the corner of the enormous living room. I made my way over to her, planning to ignore the boys she was chit-chatting with. The only thing I cared about was getting home and going to bed.

"Hey, Jessica," Kevin LaFontaine said as I grabbed Erin's arm.

I was startled- taken completely off guard. I'd had no idea he was even at the party, let alone engaged in a conversation with Erin. When Erin turned to face me, I narrowed my eyes and gave her an injured look. She appeared confused until Kevin spoke again, "Jessica and I were in debate class together. She might have told you about me. I'm Kevin."

Erin's mouth formed a perfect "O" as recognition spread across her face. She'd known a little about Kevin's harassment, but she wasn't aware of who he was until that moment.

I sighed with disgust and ignored Kevin as I pulled Erin from the group. She allowed me to steer her away after giving a smile and wave to the guys.

"What time is it?" she asked.

"Time to go," I stated flatly.

Erin shrugged, "Okay. Fine. Let's see who we can get to drive us home."

We made our way over to Evan and Nikki, but Evan said he wasn't sober enough to drive yet.

Josh was playing beer pong with a bunch of tenth-grade girls when we found him in the kitchen.

They were staring at him as if he was an Adonis. He, of course, was lapping up the adoration like an over-indulged lap dog.

"Can you drive us home?" Erin asked him, getting right to the point.

The girls glared at Erin like she was attempting to steal precious jewels right from under their noses.

Josh shook his head. "Can't you see I'm in the middle of something?"

"We have an early morning. Aren't you planning to leave soon?" I asked anxiously.

Josh looked at me and smirked, "Relax, Jess. It's only ten o'clock. I'm not leaving for at least two hours."

The girl appeared relieved.

"But...what about the class?" I questioned.

"Listen, I don't have to get up until like 9:30. I don't have some dumb sunshiny thing to go to at like seven o'clock in the morning. I'm having fun. I am not leaving for a while."

"I'll text my brother," Erin said as she led me toward the door, "Let's wait outside. I'm sure he'll pick us up."

Fifteen minutes later, Erin and I were standing outside, waiting for a response from John.

I was pacing back and forth. We were the only ones outdoors because it was chilly, and it had started to drizzle. "You said your brother would pick us up!" I cried.

"He said he would," Erin replied defensively. I don't know why he isn't answering."

Erin tried his number again. "I sent him like five texts. This isn't like him."

I blew out a heavy breath and threw my hands up in the air, "I knew it!" I began, lividly, "I knew I should not have come."

"Hey, what's going on?" A male voice asked with concern.

It was Kevin. He was standing by the front door; he seemed to have appeared out of nowhere.

"Nothing," I mumbled.

"Why are you standing in the rain?" he asked.

Erin cleared her throat, "We're just waiting for a ride."

"Oh, is someone picking you up?"

When neither of us said anything, Kevin looked at me and then Erin, searching our faces, said, "I can drive you home."

I wet my lips, "No thanks. I don't think that's a good idea."

Kevin laughed, "Come on. It's all in the past. Bygones! I'm sorry I acted like a dick. I...I liked you and let things go too far." He put his hand on his heart, "I promise, I am not normally like that. You can trust me. I'm leaving. Let me drive you home."

Erin looked at me and shrugged.

Kevin tossed his keys in the air and caught them before walking towards his car. I remained in place, "Let's go. Come on!"

Erin started to follow Kevin, "I think he's harmless. He never actually DID anything," she whispered.

I gave her a cautious look, and she continued, "It's not like we have any other options."

Kevin smiled at me, "Jessica, I don't bite. I am just going to drive you ladies home."

Erin continued trailing him, and I slowly stepped in their direction.

When we arrived at his car, which was parked along the road, Kevin opened the back door and escorted Erin inside. I was about to step in, but he slammed the door shut before I could enter.

I looked at him questioningly as he opened the front passenger side, "Climb in," he said.

I was reluctant. I stood still a beat too long for things to remain comfortable, "Come on, Jess. My car is pretty small. And the seats up front aren't even attached. It's a sports car, so there's really only room for one person in the back. It's made for three people, tops."

I was still reluctant. Until Erin chirped, "Come on, Jess. Let's go. It will be fine."

Kevin tilted his head and raised his eyebrows, asking without words what I was waiting for.

So, I got in the car because sometimes we don't follow our instincts. We give in to pressure. We regret it later and learn from our mistakes. If only I realized that plans for the Sunshine Committee were trivial compared to the repercussions of getting in the car with Kevin LaFontaine.

The minute I set foot in Kevin's antique blood-red Corvette, I knew I'd made a mistake. I contemplated escaping- I almost leapt out, but Kevin was too quick. Before I could flee, he climbed into the driver's seat and secured the doors. Although his car was a classic, he'd had modern conveniences installed, like automatic locks. I tried to lift the handle and discovered I was trapped. I immediately felt claustrophobic; the luxury vehicle was so compact that it gave me the false sense that it didn't contain enough air. My fight-or-flight response immediately set in.

"You bolted the doors? Why? Why would you do that?" I asked Kevin, my voice shaky.

He laughed gregariously and patted my knee in a patronizing way, "To keep you safe."

"Why would that keep us safe?"

"I wouldn't want you lovely ladies to fall out now, would I?" He began humming as he adjusted the rear-view mirror.

I stared at him with suspicion as he put the car in gear. "RELAX!" He exclaimed in a tone that was too manic and high-pitched to be appropriate. Within seconds, it seemed like his personality had taken a three hundred and sixty-degree turn. I had known he was creepy and unpredictable, yet I still made the idiotic decision to get in a car with him. I immediately realized how impulsive I'd been.

I turned to face Erin, but she was oblivious to Kevin's strange behavior. She was tapping away on her phone, completely focused on the screen in front of her. She was in her own world at the moment- muttering to herself something about how annoyed she was with her brother.

"What road does Erin live on?" Kevin asked, "I'll drop her off first."

I cleared my throat, "No, actually, she lives a couple of streets past mine. I'm on…"

"Prudence Crandall?" Kevin flashed me a toothy grin, "Yeah, I know where you live."

I nodded, "Erin is on Candle Cove, which is five minutes past me."

"Not if I take a short cut. I can go through the roundabout on Main Street, and it will lead me to Candle, then I'll swoop back around and drop you off on P.C."

"That doesn't make any sense," I shrieked, "Why would you do that?"

Kevin shrugged, "That way, I get to spend a little more time with you. You'd like that, right? I mean, I was the only one around who could rescue you little princesses. I'm like a knight in shining armor."

"Kevin," I said through gritted teeth, "I am really sorry, but I don't have the time. I have to get up super early…"

Kevin threw his arms up in the air in a melodramatic way, "So you're using me? Again? I am nice enough to drive you home when no one else is willing to. But, instead of being appreciative, you just want to get rid of me." The fact that his voice sounded syrupy and sweet made his words even more frightening.

"No, that's not what I'm saying," I kept my voice soft and even as if I was trying to placate an unstable person- which, in truth, was the reality of the situation.

"Okay," Kevin replied, shrugging, "then I'll stick with my original plan." He turned, winked at me, and patted me on the head in such a condescending way that my fear turned to anger. I became incensed, and that emotion dominated any other sentiment that might try to slither its way into my over-stimulated brain.

"Just drive me home, Kevin!" I screamed. "Now!"

"What's going on?" Erin questioned. I could hear the concern in her voice. She must have been alarmed by the high-pitched, harsh tone of my voice.

Kevin ignored Erin and looked straight at me, "Jeez, Jessica. Calm down. You're hysterical. Are you on your period or something?"

"No! I just want you to take us home. That's what you promised you would do back at Alexa's house."

Kevin's lips curved up into a spine-chilling grin; his voice remained facetiously affable, "I never said I wouldn't take you home. So, stop being so silly."

At this point, I was having a full-blown panic attack. My thoughts were so unclear- I don't know if my anger outweighed my fear or vice versa. I felt disconnected, focusing on the tightness in my chest, my swiftly beating heart, and my rapid breathing. I was at a loss for words. I didn't know how to address Kevin. Was it even possible to reason with someone in his state of mind? I couldn't stop myself from studying him with a quizzical expression.

When Kevin noticed my gaping mouth and widened eyes, he collapsed into maniacal laughter, "What's wrong, honey? You look like you've seen a...ghost!" He lunged towards me as he said the word "ghost."

I jumped and actually hit my head on the window.

"Watch out!" Erin shouted. I turned towards the road and noticed that because Kevin had been staring at me rather than the road, he'd almost run over a cat.

Although the cat had already made it safely across the street, Kevin made a theatrical gesture of swerving to the right and ended up turning down a random side street.

"Now, we're on Parker Street, which is a cul-de-sac," Erin pointed out indignantly, "Why the hell did you do that?"

Kevin blew out a slow, casual breath, "Oops, my bad."

"Listen, Kevin," Erin spat with disgust, "Stop playing games and take us home."

"Oh, I'll take you home," Kevin responded, "But...I'll go MY way since I'm the one driving."

Erin's phone buzzed. "It's my brother. He was at his friend's house, and he didn't realize his phone was dead. He said he can pick us up now."

"Well, he's obviously too late," Kevin sang.

I had my head in my lap; I was hyperventilating. I couldn't watch Kevin or the road because they were both making me nauseated.

This is why I was surprised when Erin called out, "You're going down another dead-end street, you asshole! This is bullshit!"

Kevin snickered, "Oh jeez, oops again. I guess I'm just not so good with directions."

"Will you please just take us home?" I pleaded.

"Of course I will," Kevin replied soothingly, "I was just playing around. You girls need to get a better sense of humor. Maybe you can both buy yourselves one since your families have so much money."

"You don't know anything about us. Don't judge," Erin spat out.

"I know a lot about Jessica," Kevin said wistfully, "You see, we were friends..."

I lifted my head up and watched as he turned onto Main Street. We were now headed in the right direction and were less than ten minutes from my house, "I missed talking to you," he whispered, "I have to say I *really* enjoyed all the time we spent together."

He put his foot slowly down on the brake, "I think I might be going too fast."

Erin sighed with exasperation, "No, you are going about ten freaking miles UNDER the speed limit."

"I just think you're special, Jessica," he continued, sliding his hand closer and closer to my leg, "Very special."

I wasn't sure how to respond as he continued. His voice was like white noise; his words were spoken in a kind, pleasant way- yet I knew that could change in a flash. I looked away from him, out the window as we drove, praying he would just get us home safely and as soon as possible. He remained calm and drove steadily. I was just about to breathe a major sigh of relief as he finally, *finally* approached my street, "Here we are!" I cried about three roads before mine.

Nevertheless, Kevin drove right past Prudence Crandall.

"You passed me," I bellowed.

"That's okay, I'll just swing back around like I said after I drop off Erin."

"Why did you do that, Kevin? You did that on purpose, didn't you?" Erin interrogated, "She warned you ahead of time that her street was coming up. Why didn't you stop?"

I suddenly felt Kevin's hand start to sneak up my thigh, and before I knew what was happening, it was headed between my legs. I jerked away. "Don't touch me!" I shouted.

I grabbed my phone, "I'm calling my dad," I said and started to tap in his number.

"No, you're not," Kevin declared as he grabbed my phone and started swinging it in the air. I tried to seize it back, but he held it out of reach and giggled like a child. "You sure are a dick tease." he accused. There was still no malice in his voice- only saccharine sweet honey.

"Erin, call my dad," I ordered, yelling out the digits of his cell. "Tell him what's happening."

"Nothing's happening," Kevin said firmly.

Erin started dialing, "I'm about to hit 'call,'" Erin threatened.

Kevin stomped on the brakes, and we all went flying forward. We would have gone through the windshield if it wasn't for our seat belts. I looked around the road, hoping there was a police officer around.

"Fine, if that's what you want. If that will make you happy. I'll take you home, Jessica." He said my name with such venom it was clear he was so delusional that he truly believed I deliberately set out to break his heart.

"Give me my phone," I ordered through gritted teeth.

Kevin reluctantly handed me my phone back, and I called my dad. Except I didn't tell him what was happening. Instead, I explained that I'd be sleeping at Erin's house because we had an early morning. I kept my voice calm, and level so he wouldn't detect that anything was wrong. He would not only be irate with Kevin if he found out about this but also with me for being so foolish by accepting a ride from him.

When I hung up, Erin spoke up, "My street is the next one on the left. If you drive past it, I'm calling the police."

"Oh, I won't drive past it. Don't you worry," Kevin hissed with disdain.

He pulled onto Erin's road and suddenly started to speed up.

"Slow down," Erin and I shouted in unison, but he didn't. In fact, he was driving hurriedly and swerving all over the road.

He skidded to an abrupt halt when Erin shouted, "That's my house, 233. The one on the right."

Erin's brother, John, was walking towards their front door when we pulled up along the side of Erin's house. He spun around, obviously shocked by the sound of screeching tires. Erin and I both shot out of the car as quickly as we could when Kevin unlocked the doors. John began walking towards us. "What is going on?" he asked angrily.

Before John had a chance to confront Kevin, he drove off just as swiftly as he'd pulled up.

"What the hell!" John sputtered; this time, it was more of a statement than a question.

Erin and I stared at one another, silent as church mice.

"Who was that? Why was he driving like a maniac?"

Erin looked at me to explain.

I shrugged, "Nothing. He was just fooling around."

"Fooling around? Seriously? That's not funny or safe. You girls shouldn't get in the car with punks like that. Was he drunk? He better not have been. Mom and Dad would be pissed if they found out…"

"He wasn't drunk, John. He was just being…I don't know-*jokey*. He didn't start driving like that until we pulled onto our street. He was just doing that because no other cars were on the road."

"Erin, seriously. You and your friends need to be careful." He turned to face me with a pointed, admonishing look on his face, "You know your father would kill you if he knew you were driving around with guys like that."

I looked down sheepishly.

"Please let it go," Erin begged, "and don't be a freaking tattle tale."

John glared at both of us and then pointed his finger in our direction, "You promise me you'll be more careful in the future?"

"Yes, and it was actually your fault we had to get a ride home with him. If you hadn't let your phone die, we would've had a ride. Because of you, he was the only one we could find to drive us home."

John looked semi-ashamed as he put his hands up in surrender, "Who was that anyway?"

Erin and I exchanged a glance, "Just some guy from Jessica's debate class. No one you know."

As if on cue, John's phone buzzed, and he walked away from us as he answered it, leaving Erin and me alone.

Erin and I were quiet for a few seconds, processing what had just happened.

"That was bizarre," Erin finally said, breaking the silence, "Not to mention scary. I mean, WOW! I certainly didn't think your stalker was that much of a psycho."

"Me neither," I agreed, "I knew he was narcissistic and...I don't know, *weird,* but I didn't think he was dangerous."

"He's like a semi-rapist or something," Erin pronounced with emphasis.

I almost chuckled at the term "semi-rapist," but I was too overwhelmed in a numb, exhausted sort of way. Now that I knew we were safe, I was beginning to crash from the rush of adrenaline.

Erin tilted her head in the direction of her front door, "Let's go inside."

"Wait!" I commanded as a feeling of uneasiness came over me.

Erin chewed on her bottom lip and waited for me to carry on.

"Listen, Erin," I began, in an attempt to sound as serious as I possibly could, "This is really important, okay?"

She continued to stare at me with wide eyes.

"This was a dumb thing for me to do. Really dumb. I should not have let Kevin drive us home after he harassed me. If my dad or Jamey found out about this, my dad would be so mad at me, and Jamey would flip out!"

Erin's eyes grew to the size of saucers, "I can't even imagine!"

"We can't let them or anyone find out. We have to keep this to ourselves."

Erin nodded, "Yeah, I think you're right."

"I am completely one hundred percent right, Erin. We can't tell anyone about this ever! NOBODY! If we even tell one person, all hell will break loose. You know how easily gossip spreads."

"I won't tell anyone," Erin promised.

"Not even Kelly."

Erin nodded, "Not even Kelly." She said, sticking out her pinky. "Pinky swear?"

I twisted my pinky around hers like we were in grade school, and we both giggled.

I breathed a sigh of relief as I followed Erin indoors because I trusted her. I knew she could keep a secret. I knew she wouldn't tell anybody, not even Kelly- her best friend. She made a vow, and Erin always kept her promises. She'd pretend this never happened. She'd keep her mouth shut about it.

Unfortunately, she wasn't the one I had to worry about.

Chapter Nineteen: Alpha Males

I actually slept soundly that evening despite the stressful events that led up to me spending the night at Erin's. She had a guest room, but we decided to share her king-size bed. I don't think either of us wanted to be alone after dealing with Kevin's manic and incredibly scary behavior. I slept with my back to Erin, and she put her arm around my shoulder after running her fingers through my hair in an attempt to relax me. It was the first time that I had fallen asleep that way since my mother soothed me when I was a small child.

Erin had promised to keep my secret. That was the main reason why I felt untroubled. It would be putting it mildly to say that I was now convinced avoiding Kevin at all costs was a necessity. I wasn't afraid he'd seek revenge or start stalking me again. Considering the obvious consequences, I was certain he wasn't stupid enough to continue his harassment. According to my dad, Mr. Blume had made it clear to Kevin that our family would take legal action if necessary.

Erin and I were able to get up early, feeling refreshed. However, we both admitted we were still somewhat shaken by the experience. I found some solace considering that I genuinely believed the unfortunate incident was over and done with and that Kevin would never again play any part in my life.

Everything was actually going well. We made progress during our Sunshine meeting. A local florist had been in contact with Mrs. Garrison, our facilitator. The flower shop had offered to make floral donations if we agreed to donate the money to a hospital that treated children with cancer. We decided to have a plant sale as our annual end-of-the-year charitable event. We also planned to have a rose sale. Students could pay to send roses to one another throughout a school day in May, and the proceeds would also benefit the kids' infirmary. It was an easy solution to our inability to come up with a spring project.

Josh picked us up after the meeting, and all of us, aside from Jamey, Bobby, Mickey, and Jenna, attended the seminar in southern Connecticut. Jenna had bowed out at the last minute. Her parents and little sister, Ashlynn, were away at a spa for the weekend; therefore, she took advantage of the situation and spent the evening with her college man, Connor McQueen.

On the way home from the seminar, we all agreed the professor had been very helpful in preparing us for the exam we'd soon be taking- an extremely important assessment that could grant us early college admission. We planned to order a late pizza lunch at Josh's house that afternoon. Jenna was planning to meet us at Josh's because I promised to fill her in on what we'd learned. We all felt it was imperative to study as much as possible on Saturday because the exam was being offered on Wednesday afternoon, and the various activities we were involved in would stifle our ability to review our notes afterward.

Saturday was the one day my friends and I had to ourselves. Most of us were Catholic and had to attend Mass with our families on Sundays. Although my dad was stricter than Nikki's and Jenna's parents, they were still usually required to be present at church and Sunday brunch. I assumed Jenna's parents, Rachel and Gerry, felt obligated to "save face" because, in every other way, they were very lenient with their girls. Although my dad and Gerry Sullivan were best friends, they had very different parenting views.

Jenna showed up at Josh's large farm-style home about a half hour after the rest of us. We were all sitting around the enclosed porch attached to the main house with our Chrome books, pizza, and soda. We were fairly quiet as we ate and studied the information we'd gathered.

When she walked in, Josh couldn't resist making a snide comment. He and Jenna had formerly been somewhat flirtatious with one another. It bothered him when she became distant after she started dating her Connor.

"Wow, Jenna," Josh began, "I can't believe you're gracing us with your presence outside of school. Normally, we only see you at lunch."

Jenna sighed and rolled her eyes. "Shut up, Josh. It's getting old."

Josh snickered, "I guess you're just used to more *mature* boys now."

Jenna ignored him as she sat on the wooden floor and took out her computer. "Can we just get this over with? I have plans tonight."

"Of course you do," Josh drawled out his words for emphasis.

"What was it that the professor said about the periodic table? I didn't get all the notes about that," I asked, semi-distracted. I was looking through my computer at the highlighted notes I'd taken about the relationship between math and science and how it would most likely be presented on the exam.

Josh snorted, "You probably weren't able to take down the notes because you asked so many questions. I think you asked more questions than anyone there."

I glared at Josh and was about to retort, but Jenna responded before I could.

"Josh, seriously. Stop being an asshole. We already know you have a talent for being a dick. You don't have to put so much damn effort into proving it."

Everyone laughed- even Josh and the conversation became more light-hearted and focused on academia until Josh's phone buzzed with an unexpected text.

I never would have expected that Josh's text message had anything to do with me. I was sitting cross-legged on the floor, engrossed in studying the material I'd learned when Josh gasped loud enough for us all to look up questioningly. He kept reading while we waited for him to fill us in on whatever "news" he'd just received.

"How did you two get home the other night?" Josh asked Erin and me, his eyes darting between the two of us. Erin was sitting next to me in a wicker chair with her legs splayed over the side.

Erin and I exchanged a slightly nervous glance, "Why?" she asked hesitantly.

"I just got a text...." Josh stopped and shook his head, "How did you get home? You didn't answer."

"My...my brother drove us," Erin stammered.

I nodded vigorously.

Josh laughed without humor and raised his eyebrows, "Well, then somebody is making up lies about you."

"What do you mean?" Erin asked, jumping to her feet.

"According to Nathan Stewart, you got a ride with Kevin LaFontaine, and he...."

Before Josh could finish, Erin grabbed the phone from him. Although he was taller and more robust than she was, she had taken him by surprise. He watched with amusement as she scanned over the text.

I felt my stomach plunge when I noticed Erin's mouth drop open and the color drain from her face. This couldn't be happening. Did someone see us get in the car with Kevin? No one else was outside. I was in complete denial that anyone could have found out about this. I had been positive the horrible incident would stay between Erin, me, and Kevin for eternity.

"Holy shit!" Erin shouted after finishing the text.

Josh and Erin were both looking at me, Josh accusingly, Erin apologetically.

"What is it?" I demanded to know, "What does it say?"

Erin sighed heavily and reluctantly handed me Josh's phone.

"Who is Nathan Stewart, anyway?" Jenna asked; her nose was scrunched up, and she looked perplexed.

"He plays lacrosse with Kevin," Josh told her.

"Kevin? Who is Kevin?" Kelly asked, "What is going on?"

"The guy who was harassing Jessica," Nikki filled her in.

"Oh yeah," Kelly replied, "I kind of forgot about that."

I overlooked the fact that I had Josh's phone in my hand as I listened to the conversation among my friends.

"You better read it," Erin gently informed me.

I looked down at the phone. It read: "Hey J- your friend, Jamey, is going to flip out. He's with Jessica Calabresi still, right? Well…Kevin Lafontaine he plays lacrosse with me. He's bragging that he gave her and Erin Johansson a ride home. He says he made the moves on her in his car and grabbed her…you know, between the legs. He's calling her a dick tease. He says she's been leading him on. I mean, WTF?"

I was in a state of disbelief as I read the text. I couldn't believe Kevin was bragging about what he'd done. Never in a million years would I think Kevin would go around telling people about what happened.

I closed my eyes and squeezed the bridge of my nose. As I began to process what was happening, my friends' phones started buzzing. Their voices became white noise. They were all alerted to a version of our car ride with Kevin. The story didn't vary too far from the truth- there were added details, but the main idea- the fact that Kevin claimed I was a tease and that he'd violated me, remained the same.

I felt defeated. Deflated. I knew I'd made a mistake. I knew I shouldn't have gotten in the car with Kevin. It was stupid, and of course- Josh couldn't wait to point that out in the midst of all the texts- my phone was also humming, but I refused to look at it. My friends were filling me in on details as I sat on the floor with my back against the cushioned sofa. Their words all blended together. The information was basically the same, but its delivery was different.

Nikki and Jenna were protective and angry. Kelly was sympathetic. Erin was guilt-ridden because she felt complicit. Evan was silent. Josh was not only accusatory but also unafraid to say what everyone else was avoiding.

"I hope your dad doesn't find out about this," he said, "Because he will kill you right after he kills Kevin. But at least there's a chance HE won't find out. Jamey, on the other hand...." Josh snickered antagonistically.

I looked up at him, waiting for him to continue. Was there a chance this could be kept from Jamey? No. Of course not.

"You don't have to worry about ME telling him," Josh informed me, "I don't have to tell him. Someone else will definitely beat me to it or probably already has."

For the next ten minutes, I quietly listened to my friends speculate about MY situation. I was silent because I felt crushed. I was honestly too exhausted and numb to experience physical anxiety. My nervousness had manifested itself into despair. I couldn't handle the inevitability of all the gossip that would encompass me once school started, but then I realized that I didn't have to wait until Monday. It had started already.

Although it seemed longer, it was literally only ten minutes before Jamey showed up at Josh's house. Until his arrival, my biggest worry was what Jamey planned to do to Kevin. I didn't think I had to worry about what he planned to do to me.

Everyone except Josh gasped when we heard a car come screeching to a halt outside Josh's house. I looked up and saw Jamey's brand-new black Audi parked alongside the porch. I exhaled deeply and placed my face in my hands.

"How did he know she was here, Josh?" Jenna asked with disgust, "You are such a troublemaker."

Josh shrugged. "He asked, and I told him." He certainly didn't sound remorseful. If anything, his voice was prideful.

Jamey's car door swung open, and he leaped out of the car; Bobby and Mickey trailed behind him.

As the three boys walked onto the porch, I first noticed Bobby's inability to make eye contact with me and the sympathetic look plastered on Mickey's face.

I was still sitting cross-legged on the floor. Jamey came and towered over me. I tapped my fingers on the floor, refusing to meet his gaze.

He cleared his throat, "Did he touch you?"

"No," I said in a small voice.

"Are you sure about that?" His hands were clenched into fists.

"Yes."

Jamey looked towards Erin, who had come and sat next to me on the ground when Jamey arrived- to show solidarity.

"Erin?" His voice had an edge, although he remained calm. He reminded me at that moment of my father when he was angry about something.

Erin vehemently shook her head, "No, Jamey. He didn't do anything to Jessica."

Jamey nodded once; he most likely trusted we were telling the truth because Kevin's "source" acknowledged that Kevin had been unsuccessful in attempting to molest me.

"But he tried?" Jamey's question was more of a statement. He already knew.

Erin and I remained silent.

"That's a 'yes.'" Jamey said, blowing out an exaggerated breath.

"Well, I'm going to find him and kill him," Jamey said matter-of-factly.

The silence in the room was stifling. Josh finally asked what we were all wondering, "Why are you acting so calm about all of this?"

Jamey lifted his shoulders up and threw his hands in the air, "You know why," he began through gritted teeth, "Because Jessica keeps saying she wants me to watch my temper. My temper. She doesn't like the fact that I have a bad *temper*. So. I am doing what she asked me all these years. I'm remaining CALM."

'But you said you were going to kill Kevin," Kelly began with a perplexed expression. "That's not really...."

"I'm not literally going to KILL Kevin, Kelly," Jamey informed Kelly in a somewhat condescending tone, "And, yes, I can beat the shit out of him without losing my *temper.*" Whenever he uttered the word "temper," his voice rose an octave.

Josh was leaning forward in a lounge chair, his hands placed on his knees. He was obviously entertained by the situation, watching as if he was at a play. "He's probably not surprised, right, Jame? Our Jessica does things like this all the time. It was just a matter of time before she made another," he paused, searching for the right word, "Um...*impulsive,* or possibly *foolish* decision, and that's putting it kindly."

"Mind your own business, Josh!" Jenna ordered.

"Actually, Josh is partially right." Jamey began, "I'm not surprised. I knew there was a chance that freak was just waiting for an opportunity, a chance to get to you." He looked at me with a distraught expression. "And for the life of me, I really can't believe you gave it to him. I mean, that's where Josh is wrong. I know you do impulsive shit, but this- I really didn't think you were capable of doing something this dangerous. I mean, seriously. What would your father say?"

I stood up, "Don't you dare tell my father. I made a mistake. *A mistake.* I wasn't the one who did something wrong."

"Are you serious?" Josh asked, chortling sarcastically, "Yeah, Kevin shouldn't have done whatever the hell he did to you, but you got in his car. I'm not saying you were asking for it," he put his hands up, palms out flat, "That would be wrong for me to say. But, you should have known better."

"Don't talk to her like she's a child," Nikki chided.

Josh harrumphed as if she'd said the most ridiculous thing in the world, "Why shouldn't I talk to her like a child if that's how she acts."

"Screw you, Josh," Jenna retorted.

Jamey's eyes rested on me, "You did act like a child, Jess. Seriously."

I didn't want to argue with him. I was drained. I didn't think he'd go so far as to tell my father- he knew I would never forgive him if he did, but I was still slightly afraid he might be considering it. "You seriously better not tell my dad about this."

"He does need to know that Kevin's still harassing you, Jess," Bobby chimed in. "He doesn't have to know that you got in the car with him, but he's a threat...obviously. Something has to be done about this."

Jamey nodded grimly.

"You can't tell him I got into his car, please," I begged, "He told me not to go near him- to stay as far away as I could, and...."

"And yet, you actually got in his freaking car. Unbelievable." Josh snorted.

Jamey rubbed his lips together and then looked down at the ground. He sighed heavily and raised his eyes to meet mine, "I just honestly CAN NOT for the life of me understand WHY you would do that. What the hell were you thinking? I mean, you could have gotten raped! Do you understand that? Why would you put yourself in such a vulnerable situation? Why would you get in an enclosed vehicle with a maniac...a maniac who had been harassing you?"

"It was my fault, "Erin's voice sounded desperate, "I pressured her into it. If anyone is to blame, it's me."

"Erin, stop defending her. Just shut it," Josh commanded, but his tone wasn't mean-spirited.

"What were you thinking, Jessica, honestly? Please tell me what the hell you were thinking?" Jamey ignored Erin and Josh and continued to address me as if no one else was in the room.

I felt my eyes fill up with tears because I knew Jamey was right. It had been a stupid thing to do for a trivial reason. I ran my fingers through my hair and turned away from Jamey because I didn't know how to respond.

"Remember what you said you would do if she did something reckless like this again?" Josh reminded Jamey snidely.

"Josh, mind your own business!" Jenna ordered.

Suddenly, I felt Jamey tugging at my arm, pulling me alongside him. He plopped down on the wicker chair that Erin had previously been sitting in, threw me over his lap, and before I knew what was happening, I felt his hand swiftly come down on my behind multiple times. Even though I had pants on, he was hitting me hard enough for it to hurt. At first, I was in complete shock. I just laid there, immobile.

I don't know how many times he slapped me before I heard Jenna yell, "Stop him. Someone do something."

"She deserves it." This was Josh, of course.

"Bobby!" Jenna shrieked.

240

When I finally became cognizant of what was happening, I struggled to remove myself from Jamey's grasp, but he had trapped my legs with his much stronger one and was holding my hands behind my back. For a split second, I honestly felt confined, which made me panic. A feeling of claustrophobia came over me, and I started to hyperventilate.

"Jamey, come on, man, let her go," Bobby said in a pacifying voice.

"Bobby, stop him," Jenna ordered.

After what seemed like an eternity, I felt Bobby's muscular arm wrap around my waist and lift me off Jamey's lap.

As he released me and I got to my feet, Bobby placed himself between Jamey and me. Jamey gulped and nodded at Bobby, acquiescing. He looked out of breath from exerting himself- while spanking me. He had sweat on his brow, and he was breathing heavily.

I was overcome with so many negative emotions at that moment- anger, humiliation, and shame. I was unable to process what Jamey had done. It was unfathomable that he thought it was acceptable to spank me. The worst part, ironically, was that he hadn't even done it in anger. He was such a male chauvinist that he truly believed it was acceptable to "discipline" me in such an egregious way.

"I'm done," Jamey told Bobby so he'd move out of the way.

Bobby stepped aside so I was face to face with Jamey. He was flustered but not contrite. He attempted to say something, but before he could, I raised my hand in the air and slapped him as hard as I could across the face. "Don't ever freaking touch me again!" I shouted at him; I was so infuriated I imagined smoke emitting from my ears and nostrils, from every orifice in my body.

Although Jamey was much stronger than me, I'd hit him so severely that his head swung to the side. When he looked up, he had a shocked expression on his face.

There was a collective gasp amongst my friends. It was so quiet; you could literally hear a pin drop.

Josh finally broke the uncomfortable silence, "Wow, I never heard her use that kind of language before," he was mumbling, speaking without sarcasm for the first time that day.

"Jamey, you are a sexist pig!" Jenna accused, "Let's get the hell out of here."

I glared at Jamey as I pointed my finger in his direction, "Don't ever talk to me again. Don't call me. Don't text me." I paused, noticing the stricken, tormented expression on his face. I don't think I'd ever seen him look dejected or hurt in all the years I'd known him. The fact that my reaction to him manhandling me upset and surprised him made me even angrier than I'd initially been. I shook my head in disgust. "I hate you," I articulated in an even, menacing tone.

"Come on, let's go," Jenna said, grabbing her books.

I noticed Nikki exchange a glance with Evan; she shrugged apologetically because she obviously felt the need to side with me. She started picking up all my stuff. Evan waved her away with a tight grin, "I'll drop your stuff off after," he told her in a soft voice.

"I'm coming too," Nikki stated, throwing an irate glance in Jamey's direction.

Jenna put her hand on my back, and Nikki patted my shoulder. We marched out the door that way in unity.

"I hate him so much," I exclaimed when we were in the car, "I am seriously never going to speak to him again."

Jenna exhaled noisily, "I don't blame you. He's an asshole."

Nikki clucked her tongue against the roof of her mouth, "Yup, totally agree."

"I'm so done with high-school guys in general. They're sooooo immature," Jenna turned to face Nikki, who was sitting in the back seat, "Except Evan. He's a good guy."

"Yeah," was all Nikki said. I knew she didn't want to throw her relationship status in my face.

"Where do you want to go?" Jenna asked.

I sighed and shook my head, "I'm really tired. I just want to go home. Sorry, you left, Nikki. You could have stayed with Evan."

"No problem," Nikki replied amiably, "I am going to see him tonight anyway."

"Listen, Jen," I began guiltily, "I'll give you the notes tomorrow. I'm sorry I didn't get a chance today."

Jenna waved her hand in the air dismissively, "That's fine. No worries."

I leaned my head back in the chair, "UGH as if this situation with Jamey isn't bad enough. I also have to deal with the fact that everyone will be talking about me…and stupid Kevin. This is a nightmare."

"It will last a day, and then people will move on like they always do," Nikki assured me.

I knew she was right, but I was still dreading Monday. Everyone would be looking at me and gossiping about me.

"We'll be your bodyguards," Nikki said, giggling to ease the tension.

Jenna nodded in agreement, "You know we have your back."

We fell into a comfortable silence for a couple of minutes before Jenna looked at me with a mischievous grin, "I'm going out with Connor tonight."

I wasn't sure where this was going, so I simply said, "That's nice. I'm glad you guys are hitting it off. It seems like it's getting serious."

"Um, he has a really cute friend. I think you'd like him. His name is LaVonn Brooks. He's super smart, mature, ambitious, and easy to talk to."

I groaned, "He sounds great, but seriously, I don't want anything to do with any boys! Not for a long time."

Jenna pulled into my driveway, "Are you sure you're okay?" she asked as I started to open the car door.

"No," I said honestly, but I laughed a little as I got out of the car.

"We'll talk tomorrow, okay?"

I nodded.

"Bye, Jess. Love you," Nikki declared, blowing me a kiss.

"I love you both. I don't know what I'd do without you," I told them as Nikki got out of the back seat and gave me a hug.

Jenna winked at me, "Connor and I are going to a party tonight, and LaVonn will be there. I'll show him your picture."

I vehemently shook my head, "No! No boys!"

"He's not a boy," Jenna said, smirking, "You don't need another boy. What you need, my friend, is a man."

And before I could reply, she waved and drove away.

Chapter Nineteen: Alpha Males (Part Two)

As I walked through my front door that afternoon, I realized how utterly exhausted I was. I'd been through so many unpleasant events over the past few days, and it was all catching up to me. As I climbed the stairs that led to my kitchen, I noticed the heaviness of my head, and I was beginning to feel intense tension in my temples.

"What's wrong, honey?" My mom asked. She was standing by the stove, preparing dinner. "You look fatigued. You have dark circles under your eyes," there was concern in her voice.

I yawned and placed my hand over my mouth, "Just a lot of studying, I guess," I tried to sound nonchalant, not wanting to be questioned about the *other* reasons I was so drained.

My dad walked into the room, followed by my sister, Sara. "I thought I was just grounded from nighttime activities," she was saying in a pleading voice, "Why can't I go to dance class? That's a requirement. Right, Mom?"

"I don't see how dance class is mandatory. When you're grounded, you're grounded from all fun events...."

"Anthony, actually, Sara's right, "my mom's voice was deferential yet firm, "She is going to be in a recital soon, and if she misses a dance practice, she needs to have a valid reason."

My father narrowed his eyes suspiciously and pursed his lips. Obviously, he was doubtful.

"Okay," my mom went on, placing her silicon cooking glove on the kitchen counter, "It would be like missing a football practice right before a game. That would be irresponsible, right?"

My dad rolled his eyes, "Fine. I'll drop Sara off at dance after I pick Megan up from horseback riding. Go get ready," his voice was stern as he addressed my sister.

My mom smiled and shrugged as Sara left the room.

"I don't know why your sisters can't be more like you," my dad said as he gently squeezed my shoulder.

"Anthony, you know you shouldn't say things like that," my mother scolded.

"Well, they're out of earshot."

When my dad took a good look at me, unease crept into his green irises, "What's wrong, Jessica?"

I attempted to smile, but the lids of my eyes felt as if they were beginning to close against my will, "Just tired. I've been so busy the past couple of days."

He nodded and beamed at me, "You are such a hard worker, Jessica. Why don't you get some rest? I'm so proud of you, especially when I have to deal with your sisters' misbehavior. I certainly don't take you for granted."

Sara came into the room as he was speaking, and because my dad's back was to her, she rolled her eyes at me.

My father made no resolve to conceal his words of praise even after he noticed Sara standing with her duffel bag in hand, ready for dance class. In fact, he went so far as to admonish Sara again for getting a B on a math test that she claimed she was prepared for. "You really should attempt to emulate your sister's work ethic, Sara. She is able to have an active social life and still maintains acceptable grades. If I didn't think you were capable of getting all A's, I wouldn't expect it, but as you know, your report cards always say that you need to put more effort into your work."

Sara looked down at the floor and nodded. "Okay, Dad," was all she said in a rather defeated voice. She knew arguing would only get her in more trouble.

Before he left with my sister, my dad suggested I get some sleep. I eagerly agreed that that was precisely what I needed.

Hours later, I heard a knock on the door. I wasn't sure where I was or what time it was when I was startled out of a deep slumber. I jumped up in bed.

I had to consider my surroundings before I was aware of the fact that I had fallen asleep and there was someone at my door.

My mom tentatively opened the door to my room and snapped the lights on as I came to.

She informed me that I had visitors and my dad wanted me to join him, Jamey, and Bobby in his study.

"What? Why?" I exclaimed in a panicked tone.

"What's wrong?" My mom inquired.

I gave her a brief synopsis of what happened, leaving out the humiliating spanking. I expressed that I was afraid they'd told my father about me willingly getting in the car with Kevin after his dire warnings.

My mom sat down on my bed and patted my head, "I'm sure they didn't say anything about any wrongdoing on your part," she promised.

I was unconvinced, "How do you know?"

"Because I know your father," she began, "He expressed no anger towards you whatsoever when he asked me to come fetch you. In fact, he seemed in good spirits."

I apprehensively tiptoed to my father's study. Although I felt somewhat relieved by my mother's reassurance, my stomach was still doing flip-flops. I was about to rap on the door, even though the fact that I felt the need for an invitation seemed ironic, considering Jamey and Bobby were already in there with MY father.

I turned my fingers inward, forming a knocking gesture. I hesitated when I heard my father say, "How dare that degenerate piece of shit harass *my* daughter. Who does he think he is?"

"He obviously isn't smart enough to know who he's...." I heard Bobby's voice trail off.

"Screwing with," my father filled in for him, laughing despite the severity of the situation. I couldn't help but think of how strange it was to hear my father use that kind of language. Of course, I had heard him talk like that when he was in the company of his male friends when he assumed the females were out of earshot. Yet, he would never speak like that in front of my mom, sisters, and me. I shrugged, assuming it was a generational thing. He was raised to be respectful around women.

I finally got the nerve to knock while Bobby and Jamey chuckled a little too loudly at my father's choice of words.

"Come in," my dad called in a pleasant tone.

As I walked in, I noticed that my father was sitting comfortably behind his vintage executive desk with Bobby and Jamey placed in the two high-back leather chairs facing him. Although my mother had decorated almost every room in our house, my father designed the plans for his study. He wanted to replicate an old-fashioned room straight out of an episode of Mad Men, and he'd achieved that desire. He had a corner bar filled with tumblers of liquor, a bookshelf filled with law books, a framed photo of John F. Kennedy, who was his hero, and a detailed red, white, and black

Oriental rug that gave the room a bit of color. It was very ornate and business-like.

All three males stood up as I walked through the door. My father took a cushioned chair placed next to a round table on the other side of the room. He brought it over to his desk and tilted his chin as he locked eyes with me, an indication for me to come and sit. He then nodded at the boys, encouraging them to also sit back down.

"Well, Jessica," he began with trepidation, "Unfortunately, your friends are here for...." He sighed and placed his fingers on the bridge of his nose. He looked extremely uncomfortable. "The boys came here out of concern for you. They just spent the past half hour filling me in on some unfortunate events that have taken place involving Kevin LaFontaine. Apparently, he's been spreading rumors about you, making up lies, threatening to do reprehensible things, and making disparaging comments."

When he was finished explaining what Jamey and Bobby had told him, he was silent for a few seconds, possibly to allow me to digest his words and the meaning behind them. I didn't know how to react, so I sat and waited in silence for him to continue.

My father cleared his throat when he was done and looked at me with sympathy. "I know you must feel humiliated about all this, honey," he said, "But there's nothing for you to be embarrassed about. You are a beautiful girl. I am somewhat surprised something like this hasn't already happened." Then he turned toward Bobby and Jamey with a look of gratitude, "I suppose it hasn't because of friends like these two. Loyal friends who look out for you. And it certainly doesn't hurt that they're..." he paused, trying to find the right words, "football players, who know how to protect themselves, and aren't afraid to use their strength to protect people they care about."

Jamey swallowed soundly with a slightly abashed expression, and Bobby humbly turned his face downward.

My dad guffawed with humor and irony. "In fact, Bobby said he had to stop Jamey from *killing* this piece of garbage."

The boys chuckled along with my father. I sat straight-faced, my back arched. I not only felt highly uncomfortable but also aggravated. This whole conversation was unbearable.

"It comes down to this," my father asserted, placing his hands flat down on his desk, "There will be no repercussions for Jamey...."

"For what?" I asked.

My father shook his head, "It doesn't matter."

"What did he...."

My dad cut me off, and I understood that it would be futile to try to get more information from him, "What matters is that I will take care of this situation, and none of you have to worry about it. Okay?"

He was looking at me because I assumed he'd already made it clear to Jamey and Bobby that he was now in control. He was taking this predicament out of our hands. Therefore, it would go away like smoke sprayed with a fire extinguisher. I knew my father well enough to realize he had enough influence to do exactly what he was promising. I had no doubt that I would never see or hear from Kevin again. I also knew that inquiring about my father's methods would only irritate him.

My dad cleared his throat, stood up, and took a step away from his mahogany swivel chair, "Jessica, I wanted to let you know about this because the boys are afraid there might be gossip. You have to ignore it. Kevin won't be around; I can assure you of that. And we all know that you are a good girl."

"And people won't believe the gossip," Bobby assured me.

"Everyone knows you're a good girl, Jess," Jamey added.

My father nodded and smiled, "Why don't you walk the boys out, Jessica?" He clapped them both on the back. "It's good to see you two; hopefully, it will be under better circumstances next time."

And then he walked out of the room, leaving the three of us alone- placing me in the position to escort them out. I certainly didn't have a problem with that.

When I was alone with Jamey and Bobby, I noticed the look of caution on Jamey's face. His chestnut eyes were wide with uncertainty. I felt nothing for him at that moment- no compassion, no desire; actually, I didn't feel *nothing*...I felt *something*, but it was dark, like a swirling gray volcano. It was deeper than mere anger.

"We would never have told on you," Bobby said, looking back and forth between Jamey and me.

"Yay, thanks for that," I muttered, "I appreciate you not tattling on me," Although I was grateful that they omitted information that would have caused my father to be furious with me, my voice was dripping with sarcasm.

"You aren't mad at us for telling your dad, right Jess?" Bobby asked. "I mean, we had to. He would have tried again, and your dad needs to put a stop to...."

"Yes, I get it," I interrupted, "and for the record, I'm not mad at *you*, Bobby." I turned to face Jamey and narrowed my eyes, scowling.

"If looks could kill," Jamey said good-naturedly.

Jamey and Bobby simultaneously began to awkwardly laugh.

"Let's go," I snapped. I followed them out of my dad's study and slammed the door for emphasis. I practically pushed them aside and acted as their tour guide once we were outside the room. I strode quickly towards the front door- steering them out of my house.

Once we arrived at the foyer, Bobby quickly swung around Jamey and me so he was facing us. He unbolted the door before I could get to it. I noticed a look pass between Jamey and Bobby. I knew exactly what they were communicating to one another with that "look."

"See you later, Jess," Bobby sang as he headed towards his car, speed walking in order to leave Jamey and me alone.

Jamey and I were still standing in the vestibule, but I had been too quick for Bobby; I'd caught the door before it closed. I was holding it wide open, "Goodbye, Jamey," I stated coldly.

"Listen, please," he pleaded with a look of desperation.

I sighed heavily and stepped outside, gripping the handle of the door in the palm of my hand. I waved my arm in the air, indicating that I wanted him to follow me. He reluctantly stepped outside.

Once he was standing on my doorstep, I immediately stepped backward so I was inside.

"Jess, please. I'm begging you. Listen to me. I need to talk to you. You have to hear me out. It's just that I care so much about you. I love you! I really didn't have bad...."

I didn't hear what else he had to say because I slammed the door in his face- mid-sentence.

Checkmate.

Chapter Twenty: Pretty and Sad

It goes without saying that I dreaded going to school on Monday. I was aware that everyone at Lomonoco Creek was in some way familiar with the events of my encounter with Kevin LaFontaine, and even I had to admit it made for some interesting gossip, especially because no one knew what had actually happened. In effect, there was chatter being spewed all weekend about Kevin, *and* Kevin and me, *and* Erin and Kevin and me, *and* Jamey and me, *and* Jamey and Kevin and me.

My friends were sympathetic enough to downplay the intensity of the rumor mill. Kelly was sweet about it; I would have been irritated by her trivialization of the events, but I knew she was inherently good-hearted and honestly wanted to assuage my feelings of angst. Besides, it was hard for anyone to be mad at Kelly. Erin felt so guilty about encouraging me to get in the car with Kevin that she literally wanted to punish herself. She assured me that there was just as much gossip about her as there was about me. I panicked at that and started interrogating her about the possibility of people accusing us of having a threesome. Erin promised me that that was not the case. I didn't believe her until I confided in Jenna- my best and most straightforward friend, who was loyal to a fault but also honest- sometimes too honest, if there's such a thing.

After I expressed my fears to Nikki and Jenna at Sunday brunch, making sure no one else was in earshot, they exchanged an almost amused glance, and I noticed an imperceptible smirk on Nikki's face as Jenna began speaking.

"No offense, Jess," she casually whispered so only Nikki and I could hear her, "But you do have kind of…" she paused, pursing her lips and staring up at the ceiling in what appeared to be an attempt to find the right words. Finally, she continued, "Well, you have a 'too good to be true' reputation. A lot of people think you're a 'goody two shoes.' There's no way anyone would think to even start a rumor like that about you. And if they did, no one would believe them."

We were all silent for a second as I took in Jenna's words. They were somewhat insulting, but in spite of that, her frankness had basically lifted at least one of the weights from my heavily burdened shoulders. I pulled on my chin as I grasped at the authenticity of what she'd said.

"You're not mad?" Jenna asked sheepishly.

I shook my head and smiled, "No."

Nikki giggled good-naturedly and shrugged, "Well, you know. She has a point."

I scrunched up my face and puffed out my cheeks, "I guess that makes me feel better," I replied indecisively, and we tried to laugh indiscreetly so as not to attract attention- especially from our nosy little sisters.

It turned out to be less awful than I'd expected, which was probably because I'd had so much anticipatory anxiety that the reality of the situation paled in comparison.

As I walked through the halls and sat in class during my first three periods that Monday morning, I did notice groups of girls begin whispering after catching sight of me. Most of them tried unsuccessfully to be subtle. There were also a couple of senior mean girls who were audacious about looking me square in the eyes and raising their eyebrows as if to say...well, to be honest, I don't know what they were "saying." I only know it wasn't anything nice. I ignored them. The boys were all very well-behaved. They went out of their way not to look at me, which made their fear or respect or whatever it was they felt for Jamey all the more obvious.

I was able to avoid Jamey until the third period when we had music class together. The whole student body was required to take an arts elective every year at Lomonoco Creek. I partially blamed my mother for this because, as a member of the Parent Teacher Association, she was always promoting what she referred to as the "traditional subdivision of the arts." She was adamant about the school putting more emphasis on acting, painting, singing, playing musical instruments, etc. She insisted our educational institution offer more opportunities for students to get involved in modules like theatre and culinary skills. My friends and I weren't really interested in any of those things, so we chose the most undemanding and least interactive arts elective we could- The History of European Opera. In all honesty, this course would not have been painless if Mrs. York was not the teacher. Mrs. Madeline York had been a rigorous instructor who expected a lot from her students until she became a grandmother the year before. After that, she lost all interest in the education of her pupils and started counting down the days until she could retire.

Every semester, my friend group tried to plan at least one period when we were free for classes like this because most of our curricula weren't comparable. We had all managed to finagle our way into this particular tutorial, mainly because it was so unpopular. Our interests lie in sports and activities that were either humanitarian or advantageous to our future. Yet many of our peers yearned for the arts, so they fancied chorus, drama, guitar, sculpture, or one of the numerous other programs my mother had helped make available at our high-school. Although none of us were remotely interested in opera, we decided on this class because we were all free during the third period and knew our teacher had a reputation for showing videos, assigning hardly any work, and handing out A's like they were going out of style.

Over the summer, the art director had the entire area stationed off for artistic electives painted a deep shade of purple. She was under the assumption that the instructors would jazz their rooms up with creative posters or portraits flaunting their craft. Needless to say, that didn't happen in Mrs. York's room, which left it devoid of sunshine and consequently bleak and ominous. Since the birth of her daughter's son, Mrs. York has put little to no effort into making her room an inviting learning area. The dark, bare walls created a rather sinister atmosphere. A bunch of pictures of her new grandbaby adorned her desk; they were the only personal effects she had added this year. Mrs. York's classroom normally made me feel gloomy, but on this particular day, it was somewhat refreshing because it matched my already melancholy mood.

Interestingly, as I entered her class that morning, I felt a deep sense of gratitude towards her because she didn't have an enforced seating policy. Therefore, we weren't made to occupy the same cheap, plastic chair everyday like most of my other classes. This would make it easier for me to avoid contact with Jamey.

Jenna, Nikki, and I arrived early and took seats in the corner of the room. They sat on either side of me, so Jamey wouldn't be able to even make an attempt at sitting near me. When he walked into class with Bobby, just as the bell rang, I saw him glance around the vast teaching space, obviously searching for me with his eyes. I usually sat in the front row. I detected a note of confusion passed over him when he surveyed the desk I typically occupied. He finally found me and half-smiled, with a look of contrition on his face. I quickly shot him a disgusted, ireful glare and turned away.

Mrs. York was late that day, as usual. She sauntered in with a DVD in her hand and explained what it was by reading the label to us. She immediately placed it in her habitual "babysitter"- the antiquated DVD player and began scrolling through her phone. I couldn't believe she got paid to do this, probably because none of us complained. It was almost too good to be true.

I wasn't paying any attention to what was going on in class, I was stewing about Jamey's chauvinism and how much I hated him until Mrs. York's cell phone rang. She answered it, even though teachers weren't supposed to take personal calls while they were with students.

"Oh no, hold on," she spoke nervously into the phone, "Does he have a fever? Is he warm? My phone is breaking up. I don't get good service in this stupid room. Hold on…Jessica…Jessica Calabresi, come here, please."

I was shocked. Why was she calling my name? I sat motionless, feeling as if I was standing naked in front of the class. Everyone was staring at me.

"Jessica?" Mrs. York sounded impatient now, "I am talking to you."

"Y..yes?" I asked timidly.

"I need you to…" she stopped mid-sentence, "Why are you sitting back there, dear? You always sit in front? Please come here."

I remained frozen.

Mrs. York looked perplexed, "Please come here, Jessica. What is the matter with you today? I hope you're not sick, dear. But I really don't have time for this. I need you to watch the class while I speak to my daughter. It is an emergency."

When I stayed in my seat, Mrs. York clenched her teeth and slammed her hand on the table, "You are the most responsible student in class. I need you to come up here now. I won't get in trouble if I leave you in charge. Mr. Blume trusts you. I can't hear my daughter. It's about my grandson."

Jenna stood up and grabbed my arm, she tried lifting me out of my seat, "Get up," she muttered, "Come on."

I obediently lifted my legs and mounted myself off the chair, "Okay," I whispered as Jenna led me to the front of the room.

Mrs. York ran out of the room. I was in such a fog as Jenna sat me down in Mrs. York's large, leather swivel chair that I couldn't comprehend the voices of my fellow classmates. There was some animosity about Jenna accompanying me to the "teacher area" when Mrs. York had only given me that privilege. Jenna claimed she had ADHD and needed special accommodations, which made no sense. I knew her parents had taken her to a neurologist when she was a child to see if she had that disorder, but it turned out she was just lazy. I felt such complete disorientation that I missed most of the exchange between Jenna and another female student.

The only thing I remember before Jenna plopped down across from me in Mrs. York's straight-back supplemental seat was her raucous laugh after Nikki told our argumentative classmate to go screw herself.

Mrs. York was probably only gone for a few minutes, but it seemed much longer. It took what felt like forever to stop my rapidly beating heart, shaking hands, and the dizziness that had overcome me.

I was attempting to calm myself by taking long breaths in through my nose and slowly exhaling through my mouth while I massaged my temples. I was still feeling disassociated, which seemed to be a common occurrence since I'd met Jamey Russo.

"Are you okay?" Jenna asked, snapping her fingers in my face.

She giggled as I looked up at her, feeling as if I was waking from a bad dream.

"Everyone is looking at me," I whispered, "I am so embarrassed."

Jenna shook her head nonchalantly, "Nope. They're not. They've all moved on." She turned to gaze over the class, then back at me. She nodded, "Believe me, technology has shortened this generation's attention span. They are all on their phones or tablets. Our moms would be devastated if they witnessed the lack of communication going on in this classroom."

I stifled a cackle that brought me back to reality.

"Speaking of phones, let me show you something," she said as she pounded the screen of her bedazzled, designer-covered cell. After a second, she showed me a picture of an extremely attractive guy who looked to be about twenty years old. He had huge brown eyes with lashes long enough to make it appear as if he had eyeliner on; they were the perfect length. He might have looked feminine if it weren't for his hard, angular chin and wide jawline. His umber skin was so smooth and glossy that I almost thought the picture was photoshopped.

"Is this the guy you were telling me about?" I asked eagerly, although I was still hesitant about allowing myself to be attracted to any and all boys.

"Yes, and he likes you."

I tilted my head in disbelief, "That's not true," I said assertively, "You sound like a kid on the playground in fifth grade."

Jenna chuckled mischievously, "I'm serious!"

"Why would he like me?"

Jenna snorted and rolled her eyes, "Because you're gorgeous, stupid," she began, "and smart and ambitious and…"

I cut her off, "But he doesn't even know me."

Jenna had a twinkle in her eyes, "Well…I showed him your picture, and he thinks you're beautiful."

I swallowed soundly, feeling hopeful despite myself.

Jenna went on, "Plus, I told him all about you. He's Connor's BEST friend. I've known him for a while. He's amazing. He is SO different from *him.*" She leaned her head in Jamey's direction, "The only similarity is that they're both athletic. But they don't even play the same sports, which is good because you need as much distance from 'he who shall not be named' as possible. LaVonn plays basketball, and he's really good. But he's not all macho about it. You guys would totally hit it off. You would have so much to talk about."

I sighed heavily, "I'm just not ready to; I don't know if I even want to date."

"Jess, it's not like you're going to marry him- just meet him. This weekend. We can all hang out. Casually. You, me, Connor, and LaVonn."

I was quiet, mulling it over.

"What harm can it do?" Jenna asked, throwing her hands in the air.

When I looked down at the desk and mumbled, "I just need to be alone right now. I can't handle dating. I just need to deal with my anger towards Jamey. I don't know. I am just so mad at him."

"Your dad would love LaVonn," Jenna said with an impish grin, "Can you imagine how that would make Jamey feel?"

She had me.

A gorgeous, intelligent college student. One I couldn't help but find incredibly attractive. My dad's approval. Jamey's jealousy. Retaliation.

I nodded once, "Okay, but it's not a date, just hanging out."

"Just hanging out," Jenna agreed. Then she turned in Jamey's direction once again, and when she looked back at me, she was smirking, "I'm not saying it doesn't work."

I looked at her quizzically, arching my eyebrows.

"I mean the whole pretty and sad thing. It definitely works for you," she pronounced with a playful wink.

I sighed, waiting for her to continue.

"But…that gets old, and it's no fun," Jenna informed me, I think it's time for you to move on from that *persona*. Because now it's time for you to be a hot bitch."

Chapter Twenty-one: LaVonn Brooks and Kayla O'Neil

After my first encounter with LaVonn Brooks, I could tell that he was one of the most impressive and interesting people I'd ever met. The shallow part of me was attracted to him because of his striking physical appearance. He had the right amount of everything and was even more good-looking in person than on social media. He was tall, but he didn't tower over me. He was muscular in a lean, fit way. His sable eyes were illuminated by long lashes that were just shy of appearing feminine. His prominent chin and squared jawline gave him an overall masculine appearance.

A few days after agreeing to Jenna's proposal, I mustered up the courage to ask my parents if it would be alright for me to go out with Jenna and a couple of her college friends. We'd just finished dinner, and my mom and dad were relaxing in the living room. They were comfortably sitting on the sofa enjoying after-supper drinks. They were both reading; my mom was sipping Pinot Grigio with a suspense novel on her lap while my dad perused an autobiography of a popular political figure.

"What about Jamey?" my mom asked, crinkling up her nose. "You want to go out with another guy. And Jamey won't be there? It will only be Jenna, her boyfriend, and another *boy?* I'm confused. Did something happen with Jamey?" She exchanged quizzical glances with my dad.

I should have prepared myself for an inquisition, considering that since my freshman year, I'd never expressed interest in engaging in social activities with anyone outside my immediate circle.

I cleared my throat and looked nervously down at the floor. I didn't want to explain anything about my situation with Jamey. I was hoping to avoid the topic by claiming it was a group of friends hanging out innocent, platonic. "Honestly, we're just going as friends," I stammered, peering up but avoiding eye contact, "And Jamey and I have never been an official couple, I mean. This is just, it's just as friends."

Upon noticing my tense reaction to what felt like an interrogation, my mom had a somewhat guilty expression. My parents could sense that my mother's questions made me highly uncomfortable. Consequently, they both tried to feign nonchalance.

My mother smiled cheerfully, "Okay, that's fine. I just thought it was peculiar because you've never done that before. I mean, you always go out with your group from school. You've never been interested in tagging along with Jenna."

My dad was quietly staring at me with a neutral expression. I turned my gaze to him because I knew, ultimately, he would be the one to make the decision about whether or not I'd be allowed to go. That's just the way it was in my family. "Is it okay with you, Dad?" I asked. There was a part of me that wished he would say no.

He shrugged and glanced at my mom, "Sure. I certainly trust Jenna's opinion; she's like a niece to me, and I know Gerry adores Connor. He thinks he's the best thing that's ever happened to Jenna. He's tamed her rebellious side. If LaVonn is Connor's best friend, I'm okay with it. I can tell you don't want to discuss Jamey, so we..." he turned towards my mom. He widened his eyes as if acknowledging they both needed to surrender that subject, "So we won't ask what happened there, but considering LaVonn is in college. I know you *say* it isn't a date, but I want to meet him." He cleared his throat before adding, "I mean, your mom and I would both like to meet him."

I gulped and felt my stomach churn, "But it really isn't a date. I told Jenna to tell LaVonn that I only wanted to go out as friends. You won't, you know, question him like he's taking me out, right? I don't want him to get the wrong idea."

My dad took a long sip of his beer, and I noticed an amused expression on his face, which he tried to conceal. He thought a moment before replying, "Well, I certainly don't want you to be uncomfortable, honey. Why don't you have Jenna bring both boys here before you go out? We could just chat a bit. I won't give him the third degree or anything. We can just have a friendly conversation."

I nodded and smiled gratefully.

LaVonn was very relaxed when he arrived at my house that Friday evening with Jenna and Connor. It was apparent that he wasn't intimidated by adults and found it easy to engage in mature conversation. He was obviously not only "book smart" but also socially intelligent, as well. Jenna was a master at lessening tension in any given situation. Her presence and her sense of humor made the whole event not only stress-free but also surprisingly enjoyable. I could tell my dad appreciated LaVonn's academic ambition and social awareness. My mom was captivated by his interest in modern art and foreign films. I don't think my mother knew many people who shared her adoration for films with subtitles. My famous relatives had passed on their love of all things artistic to my mother. She always seemed just a little disappointed that the interest didn't extend to my sisters and me. Ultimately, it was an ideal meeting. My parents not only approved of LaVonn but were impressed by him.

Considering the circumstances, I was somewhat taken aback when LaVonn agreed to meet my parents before our initial meeting. I was incredibly nervous he'd think it was a double date. I made Jenna show me proof (texts) that she explained I was only interested in friendship. Apparently, he accepted that and aspired to eventually win me over. I have to say that he instantly put me at ease.

He was polite but made no attempt at physical contact. He held the door for me, insisted on paying for the food and entertainment, and listened attentively while I spoke. He was, in essence, the perfect gentleman. I was immediately drawn to him, but despite that, I continued to feel tense and nervous about "dating." The only guy I had ever been interested in was Jamey. I had no previous experience in this area- mainly because Jamey had pursued me. I basically just went along for the ride. This was foreign to me- I didn't know how to do *this*. I kept stressing the fact that I only wanted to be friends.

After three double dates, Jenna claimed that it was apparent I was attracted to LaVonn, and it was time for us to rendezvous alone. She reminded me of the intense conversations I'd had with him all three times we'd been out. She maintained that we were perfectly compatible. I had to admit it was refreshing to have discussions with someone like LaVonn. We were both interested in social issues like Black Lives Matter and the Me Too movement. Jamey wasn't against those things- but I couldn't have intelligent conversations about important issues with him either. He just wanted to talk about sports, social media, and television.

Before LaVonn and I went out solo, I made Jenna speak to him about my inhibitions. She was our go-between. She assured me that he was willing to take it slow. He found me to be gorgeous, intelligent, and highly ambitious. According to Jenna, he also appreciated the fact that I wasn't the type of girl to throw herself at him just because he was athletic, good-looking, and smart. He wasn't interested in the chase; he was willing to be patient because he felt like he'd found what he had been searching for.

We had a wonderful time on our first official date. He took me to an opening at an art studio. My mother was thrilled that he was able to get tickets to this spectacular event. Afterward, he made reservations at a restaurant that was swanky but not over the top. We had a great time talking about the unique portraits painted by an up-and-coming local artist. At dinner, we naturally fell into a comfortable dialogue.

At the night's end, he walked me to my door and kissed me very politely on my doorstep. I found myself wanting more, which was a first for me. But after a cross between a caress and a deep kiss, LaVonn smiled widely and said he'd call me- then he backed away and headed towards his car. I rubbed my lips together and grinned- even though I wished he'd come back and kiss me properly.

The dynamics changed somewhat in our friend group because of the situation with Jamey and me. My girlfriends felt obligated to sit with me at lunch, and the boys remained loyal to Jamey. That's not to say alliances weren't formed outside of school. It was apparent that Erin and Kelly were in contact with Jamey on a regular basis but limited the information they planned to convey based on my reaction. I knew they felt sorry for him; that much was clear. Yet, they both were treading lightly because they knew I was still furious with him.

Every day, one of them would broach the topic and inevitably end up editing "messages" after realizing I was nowhere close to forgiving him. According to Erin and Kelly, Jamey was beside himself. In the weeks following our falling out, at some point during lunch, one of them would find a way to finagle the subject of Jamey into our conversation. They literally managed to tell me, on a daily basis, how much he missed me and how depressed he felt.

For instance, one Monday afternoon, Kelly sighed and sadly shook her head, "Oh, Jess," she began despondently, "I talked to Jamey last night, and he is just so miserable. He doesn't know how he'll go on."

Nikki snorted, "He didn't look that sad at Ted's party Saturday night," she remarked derisively.

"Oh, you know how he is; he's good at acting all macho," Erin chimed in.

"But behind closed doors, he's a wreck," Kelly added.

Jenna guffawed. "Behind closed doors," she mocked, taking a bite out of her French fry, "Seriously, Kelly. Tell him to man up and stop getting you two to pass on his messages."

None of the other members of our clan mentioned Jamey. Jenna and Nikki wouldn't even give him the time of day. Evan knew better than to discuss the topic. I was avoiding Josh for obvious reasons. That left Mickey and Bobby. Mickey was dealing with issues I didn't understand at the time. I knew there'd been rumors about him engaging in questionable sexual activities. Still, I wasn't interested in hearing what they were. Jenna confided that Mickey had admitted he'd had a threesome with a girl and another guy. Mickey's proclivities became a cause for gossip for a while, but like everything else, people moved on.

Bobby did approach me after I blocked Jamey's calls and refused to even look at him at school. I immediately shut him down. "Look, Bobby, I know you have good intentions. I'm not mad at you, but I am done with him. He needs to get that through his thick skull."

Bobby looked hopeless as I shrugged apologetically and walked away.

After a few weeks, Jamey told Jenna he was desperate. He claimed he was going crazy and needed to talk to me. "Good luck," Jenna advised him with a sneer.

I wasn't prepared when he cornered me at my locker the next day. "Look, Jess," Jamey began hesitantly, "I know you've been dating some college guy."

I tried to swerve away from him, but he was too quick; when I moved to the right, he placed his hand on the wall beside my locker so I couldn't get past him. I attempted to escape the other way, but I stopped when he announced in a voice loud enough to attract some attention, "I'll make a scene if you don't hear me out."

I sighed audibly with irritation, "What? What do you have to say?"

He batted his eyes, and his face softened, "I know you're mad at me, but I can't believe you would actually start dating someone else. How could you do this to me?"

I laughed without humor and placed my hands on my hips, "Are you serious?"

Jamey looked almost exasperated, "Yes, of course, I am."

I stood there for a few seconds, unable to form the words to express my anger at his audacity, "What about 'leave me alone, and I don't want anything to do with you,' don't you understand?"

"Geez Jessica," Jamey muttered, "I mean, you know you're overreacting? Everyone thinks you're overreacting!"

I harrumphed, "Don't try to gaslight me, Jamey."

Jamey shook his head, "I don't even know what that means."

"Look it up," I ordered, "and leave me alone."

"I can't BELIEVE you are acting so melodramatic. Dating someone else. I've been trying to be patient about this. But I have to say, I'm starting to lose my patience. I'm getting sick of this shit."

I smirked as I looked him square in the eyes, 'Oh yeah, well, what are you going to do about it?"

Jamey made an attempt to speak, stopped, and then opened his mouth again. He was obviously having a difficult time deciding what to say.

"Are you going to try to beat him up?" I taunted, "Because I know that's your answer to everything, isn't it?"

Jamey didn't flinch; he was silent, watching me, so I continued, "LaVonn isn't the type to stoop to that level; he's not a boy. He is adult enough to behave like a civilized human being. He's not a neanderthal like you."

"That's low. That is uncalled for," Jamey said in a pleading tone. "I've never treated you disrespectfully. Ever."

"Do you really think what you did was okay?" I questioned, disbelieving.

Jamey threw his arms in the air, "I was upset, and I warned you."

I pursued my lips and closed my eyes, "I...I honestly have nothing else to say to you."

"Please, be reasonable."

"Listen, Jamey. I have to go. Don't contact me. I don't want to talk to you; I don't want to hear from you. I've moved on, and you're just going to have to deal with it," I took pleasure in the pain I saw in his eyes but pushed it aside as I continued, "And for the record, my dad loves LaVonn. They really hit it off. Both of us have moved on. You should, too. Why don't you ask Kayla out? I'm sure she'd be thrilled."

His mouth dropped open, and he stood staring at me in grief-stricken disbelief as I sashayed away from him.

Unfortunately, for Jamey, that wasn't the only time that week I left him distressed and speechless. That Friday, as part of an upcoming Student Council event, all of the officers were assigned to speak during Social Emotional Learning classes. The SEL teachers apparently were the only ones who willingly offered to allow us to take up precious time from their designated courses to promote a humanitarian cause we were sponsoring. Big surprise.

We were all paired up with another officer and appointed to classes that fit our schedules. Nikki and I were put together because our courses were similar; our curricula were all upper-level, so our study hall matched the lower-level SEL courses. Therefore, we were slated to speak at Jamey's Psych 101 class that day. I could have declined. After all, Josh and Evan were also available at that time since they had the same course load as us, but I didn't because I knew Kayla O'Neill was also in Jamey's class. And I saw the perfect opportunity to retaliate against him.

After their teacher announced to the class that Nikki and I were there to speak about an event for Student Council, one of Kayla's friends made an offensive comment about how ridiculous it was that I belonged to so many clubs.

Nikki tilted her head and retorted, "Well, some people have other hobbies besides vaping and chasing boys who are out of their league."

That got a snicker from the class and shut the girl up.

I went on to explain that we had formed an alliance with the local cinema to benefit a women's shelter that had opened in Desmond, which was the closest thing we had to a city near Rosevalley. The Student Council was selling film tickets, and the movie theatre was willing to donate a third of the profits to the shelter.

In order to make it fun, we'd come up with the idea that couples or want-to-be couples could buy tickets for one another. Nikki explained that because she and Evan were already dating, she would buy a ticket for him, and he would reciprocate. Any two people who bought tickets for one another would get half price on a soda and large popcorn.

"Nikki and Evan are an obvious example because they're already dating. Of course, they'll buy tickets for each other," I piped in, "But there might be other people who are interested in one another but aren't officially a couple," I continued with a sarcastic edge to my voice, "like Jamey Russo and Kayla O'Neill, for example."

The class went silent, but all eyes were on me, anxiously waiting for me to continue. The dynamics between the three of us were well known, although the gossip was old news.

"So, if Jamey decided to buy Kayla a movie ticket…."

Jamey cut me off with gritted teeth, "Not gonna happen."

Kayla looked down in embarrassment.

I continued, despite Jamey's protestations, "And Kayla bought a ticket for him too. Well, then they could go together and share a jumbo soda and a hefty popcorn for half the price."

The class came alive; that is - everyone but Jamey and Kayla. Kayla was still looking down with her hand placed on her forehead. I would have felt sorry for her if my fury towards Jamey wasn't dominating any and every other emotion I could possibly experience.

Nikki glanced at me and smirked, "So, does anyone have any questions?"

The room was abuzz at this point because the idea of a movie and half-price movie theatre "cuisine" was enticing. As Nikki fielded the inquiries, Jamey and I made eye contact. He tried to no avail to give me an intimidating glare, but I gracefully crossed my arms, kept the sparkle in my eyes, and met his gaze. I don't know what I was goading him to do, but it seemed like he did, and he looked away. Ashamed. Embarrassed. Defeated. I wasn't fully aware of what I'd wanted to achieve. However, I did know- I accomplished what I'd set out to do.

Chapter Twenty-two: Prom

At the end of April, all anyone in school could talk about was Prom. It wasn't our first major high-school dance, but it was definitely the most hyped-up and significant. I had been so excited at the beginning of the year before Homecoming. I loved every minute I spent helping the cheerleaders and athletic department plan all the festivities. My feelings during the Prom preparation were in direct opposition. Jamey and I were a "couple" at the beginning of my junior year or at least that was everyone's impression. We actually were voted Homecoming king and queen. There were pictures of us in the local newspaper with crowns on our heads; in one, we held hands with wide smiles. In the other, he is dipping me while planting a kiss on my lips. I was afraid my dad might get mad when he saw that, but he had only grinned and remarked to my mom, "I wonder when she's going to finally admit he's her boyfriend, for God's sake." I'd been eavesdropping outside the kitchen, but he caught me standing there and winked. He deemed it acceptable for me to be seen kissing a boy who was my unofficial mate.

Even though LaVonn and I had been dating for a few weeks, I was nervous and uncertain about asking him to be my Prom date. I also avoided the topic with my friends until Jenna, never one to shy away from a touchy subject, finally blurted out, "So, what's the deal, Jess? When are you going to ask him?"

We were sitting cross-legged together on the floor of my bedroom while I helped her with chemistry homework, even though I didn't think she was going to pass this particular exam. "You know you're going to fail this test, right?" I said, dodging her question.

"Yeah, well. I'll still pass the class. I have a few A's, mostly B's and C's. This will be the first test I fail. And I am seriously so done with this class. I don't care anymore."

"If we study tonight and tomorrow, I can help you get a C...."

"Jessica," Jenna began in a stern, matronly voice, unlike her normal tone, "Stop changing the subject. When are you going to ask him? **Are you going to ask him?** What's the plan here?"

I nodded with resignation. "Yes, I'm just not good at this stuff."

"Call him and ask him now while I'm here. If you do, I'll let you tutor me, and that will take your mind off of…everything," she spread her arms out as if "everything" was actually laid out in front of her. I grudgingly agreed, thinking it odd that she was bribing me by allowing me to help her study for a test she wasn't even concerned about.

LaVonn was ecstatic when I asked him to my Prom, almost as if he wasn't expecting it, which was odd because we had been seeing one another for nearly a month.

"I'd love to be your date," he proclaimed, "I'm so honored that you invited me."

To be honest, it was strange to hear him reveal that he was flattered by my invitation. I thought that I was the one who should be honored to have him as a date. Sometimes, I felt as if he was almost too perfect. He was everything most girls would want in a guy. He was a little more than ideal in all the ways that mattered. He was not just handsome but striking. His IQ was obviously above average, and his social skills were impeccable. He was athletic in a healthy way and had a wide variety of interests. He was the most versatile person I knew.

Besides all that, he was the epitome of a gentleman, and I couldn't have been more appreciative. I certainly didn't take it for granted. In addition to being respectful, he was also chivalrous. He treated me like an equal yet insisted on paying for meals and holding doors open. He was one of the good guys. I wasn't accustomed to *good* guys. I hadn't been the type of girl to seek out a bad boy, but I couldn't help the fact that one had been chasing me since before freshmen year. Although to be fair, I had fallen for Jamey, and the onus for that was all on me.

The best thing about dating LaVonn was that he was patient. He knew I wanted to take things slow and was willing to wait. Yet, so had Jamey. Whenever I tried to convince myself that I should take my relationship with LaVonn one step further, thoughts like that would creep into my head. The truth was, no matter how angry I was with Jamey, I couldn't stop obsessing about him. Sometimes, when I was kissing LaVonn, images of Jamey would pop into my head, and I'd anxiously try to push them away. Inevitably, I ended up starting to dread our intimate moments because they became a source of tension. I didn't want to fixate on Jamey, but I couldn't help it. He became like the proverbial white elephant.

It was as if there was an invisible wall I couldn't shatter. I'd been locked in this cocoon- Jamey had been the only boy I'd ever had romantic feelings for, and I wasn't sure if my emotions regarding LaVonn were sexual in nature. I'd go through an obsessive-compulsive spiral whenever I tried to rationalize it. The situation was maddening. Nevertheless, before Prom, I decided that I would get past it. I convinced myself I needed to be through with Jamey. I had found the perfect guy, and I was going to fall for him whether my heart and libido wanted it or not.

Planning for Prom went by in a blur. Two of the committees I was a part of- Student Council and Sunshine were the ones doing all the preparation as far as invitations, caterers, photographers, decorations, and a theme were concerned. I was truly only present in the physical sense during all of the organization involved, which was highly unusual for me. My friends on both committees understood and covered for me. Even Josh, who was then vice-president of the Student Council, wasn't mean-spirited about my lack of participation. Everyone, even the other members who weren't close friends, seemed to understand that my "break up" with Jamey had taken a toll on me- even if I was dating someone else. What made matters worse was that I literally felt, at that time, as if everything said about my situations with guys was verbalized with air quotes.

I wasn't the least bit surprised or upset when Kelly requested my permission to accompany Jamey to the Prom. She pleaded with me to be honest with her and interrogated me about my feelings in regard to them going together. I knew they'd been friends since pre-school. She had already made it obvious she felt sorry for him because he was so crestfallen about my dismissal of our relationship. I gave her my blessing only because she asked for it, and I explained that I understood.

After promising her I was okay with it in five hundred different ways, Kelly said, "He still loves you, Jess, that's why he wants to go with me because we're just friends. He isn't interested in anyone else romantically. He can't even bring himself to ask any other girl to go with him in case she gets the wrong idea, you know?"

I sighed and muttered, "Yup, sure. I get it."

The plan was for Jenna, Nikki, and I to attend the Prom together in a rented limousine with our respective dates. Together with our mothers, we did all the typical Prom groundwork. Jenna's mom, my Aunt Gina, my mom, along with my cousin and best friend were all very cautious around me while we were Prom shopping and setting up arrangements. I noticed looks pass between them, and they all handled me with kid gloves. I was too confused and consumed with my thoughts to be offended, thankful, or both. I felt like I was in a trance, just going along for the ride.

When the day of our Prom finally arrived, I woke up feeling vacant and numb. I went to the salon with my friends to get our hair and make-up done; my mom helped me get dressed and let me borrow an expensive necklace and bracelet that was a family heirloom. We stood across from the full-length mirror in her room as she attached the clasp to the designer diamond studded choker. She had a wide smile on her beautiful face, and all I could think was that I couldn't wait for the night to be over.

When our limo dropped us off at 7:00 on the dot, I allowed LaVonn to take my hand and guide me out of the vehicle. Our hands remained clasped as I blindly followed Jenna, Connor, Nikki, and Evan to the Prom entryway. I barely noticed the adornments or how beautifully everything was decorated in honor of the Prom's theme- "The Red Carpet." I tried to smile and wave as I walked with LaVonn across the extensive crimson runner into the auditorium. When we walked inside, I was blinded by the silvery fluorescent lights hanging from the blackened ceiling and the continuous flashing of bulbs meant to mimic the paparazzi. As we stepped inside, we were immediately greeted with a huge black and white "Lights, Camera, Action" sign to our left and, on the opposite side, a silver star with "Hollywood" emblazoned across the top. I felt like I was sleepwalking through the event and numbly murmured in agreement when anyone mentioned what a cool idea it was to display statues of celebrities around the room, or the originality of the fake palm trees, or how the entire wall covered with an actual panorama of Hollywood Boulevard made it feel so authentic. I found it beyond difficult to appreciate any of it.

I didn't come alive until I was on the black and white checkered dance floor with LaVonn. It was then that I noticed Jamey dancing with Kelly. He was staring at me with a possessive expression. I spontaneously decided at that moment to knock that controlling look right off his cocky face. I looked up into LaVonn's dark eyes and whispered, "Kiss me."

And he did.

It was soft and smooth and lingered for just the right amount of time. It felt really good, especially because I inconspicuously turned towards Jamey when it was over and noticed his forlorn, dejected countenance. I'd never seen such defeat in his eyes.

Prom Court was the most difficult part of the evening and the one I dreaded most. Jamey and I were both in the running for king and queen. I was anxious about having to stand on stage with him. The whole Prom Court thing was interesting because it forced me to consider the nuances and complexity of popularity in high school. My closest friends were part of a clique that was deemed Prom Court material. We were cheerleaders and football players- attractive and involved in activities that made us stand out. Although, in reality- we weren't really *popular*. In the traditional sense, we were, but not literally. I wagered that just as many people disliked us as those who admired us. I wasn't naïve. I knew a lot of girls found me to be annoying. Yet, we were the type to be elected to positions like this. And the fact that Jamey and I had been Homecoming king and queen made me deathly afraid that we'd be elected Prom king and queen, too.

I felt a lump in my throat, and my stomach started to churn as we were all called onto the stage. I nearly tripped on my heels as I walked up the rose-carpeted stairs and pushed past the heavy gold curtains. Naturally, I was placed next to Jamey. He kept surreptitiously sneaking glances at me while we waited for the winning names to be called. I refused to look up from the floor and placed my hands on one of the stanchions to steady myself. I was dying for this moment to be over. I couldn't imagine the awkwardness of having to pose with Jamey if we won.

I puffed out an extended sigh of gratitude when Nikki and Evan's names were announced as Prom king and queen. I had never felt more relieved in my life.

After being on stage with Jamey, my mood shifted. I didn't feel apathetic any longer or even angry. I started to feel melancholy. I knew that I was still livid with Jamey. In fact, I understood with complete certainty that I hated him with every ounce of my being. How dare he treat me like I was his property, someone he could give directives to and then punish for disobedience. The worst part was that he didn't recognize that he was wrong. Yes, he missed me. Yes, he was miserable, wounded, and distraught. Nonetheless, what he wasn't- was *contrite*, and because of that, I could not forgive him.

So, why wasn't I happy when I was at the Prom with the ideal guy? I realized that I should have been grateful, excited, even blissful, but I was unable to experience any of those emotions. For the rest of the evening, I tried to force myself to feel the way I knew I was supposed to. Unsurprisingly, that was an exercise in futility. Obviously, no matter how hard we try, we can't choose how we respond to certain things. We can't just make ourselves feel joy or even contentment. I was unsettled and extremely tense. And the more I tried to force myself to feel what I definitely wanted to, the worse it got. Before Prom was over, I became despondent. I wished I could just go home, but I couldn't do that either.

Jenna and I had promised Sammy Bollock we would attend the after Prom celebration he was throwing at his house. Mickey was also having a party that night. Although he had begged Jenna to come, she refused because Jamey would be in attendance. I knew Mickey was going through something and had been confiding in Jenna about it. However, I was too preoccupied with my own problems to pry. I was aware that Jenna seemed to be talking to him more than usual, and although I assumed it was platonic, I did question her about it.

"You're not like…interested in him, are you?" I asked one night when she told me they'd been texting.

She simply replied, "I hope you're not serious. Have you met Connor? Have you met Mickey? Is that like even a possibility?"

Most of the juniors longed to go to Mickey's party, which would inevitably be more glamorous and hedonistic, and more popular kids in school would be in attendance. Mickey was once again coaxed into having a colossal party because his parents were visiting Greece. Because Mickey's opulent home held such appeal to most attendees of the Prom, he made it an invitation only. He was anxious about his peers destroying his property. Therefore, Sammy Bollocks, another rather popular junior, and the Student Councils' historian, decided to have his own fiesta. When Sammy invited Jenna and me to his party, we reluctantly agreed. All of our friends were going to Mickey's, although Nikki was originally dead set against it. I finally talked her into it because I knew Evan wanted to be with his friends. Evan was willing to go along with Nikki- she wore the pants in that relationship, but I didn't think it would be fair to him. Nikki grudgingly gave in, which left Jenna, who had initially planned to bow out of both parties.

Jenna wanted to go somewhere with just Connor, LaVonn, and me, but I told her we should at least show our faces at Sammy's. I totally regretted that decision the night of the Prom. I wished I had not assured Sammy we would make an appearance because that promise left me feeling obligated. After standing in such close proximity to Jamey, the last thing I wanted was to celebrate. I wanted to go home. I contemplated feigning sick, but I didn't have the nerve to lie. Although I actually did feel unwell, just not in the physical sense- nevertheless, I forced myself to go along with our original plans.

Once we got there, I realized it was not just a mistake but probably the WORST decision I had ever made in my life. Everyone was celebrating, while I felt crestfallen. I obviously had not the slightest interest in partying, so instead, I chose to self-medicate. I ended up drinking myself into oblivion as the night passed in a blur. LaVonn noticed that I was over-indulging and tried to kindly suggest I slow down. I didn't listen.

Predictably, later that night, I ended up getting sick. As Jenna held my hair in Sammy Bollock's bathroom, I cried. When she asked me why, all I could tell her was the truth- I didn't know.

On the car ride home to Jenna's, I was too exhausted and drunk to be embarrassed. LaVonn was much nicer than he should have been. At the time, I didn't appreciate his kindness. I was incapable of feeling anything aside from sadness. Sometimes, the most challenging part about being miserable is being unaware of what exactly is making us so sad. I was fully cognizant of the fact that LaVonn was the perfect guy and Jamey was NOT. Despite this, my feelings were scrambled and confused. I wanted to control them, but it was pointless.

Once we got to Jenna's house, LaVonn took my hand as I stepped out of the car. He looked me in the eyes and said, "I'll call you tomorrow," yet it was more of a question than a statement.

"Yes," I whispered, "I'm sorry I ruined your night."

LaVonn laughed, "It was supposed to be *your* night."

I just shrugged and waved as I followed Jenna up her driveway. I planned to ask her to steal one of her mother's Xanax, so I could fall into a dreamless, anxiety-free sleep and escape the inexplicable emotions I was experiencing.

Chapter Twenty-three: Desperation

After the Prom, I continued to feel despondent. My thoughts were indistinct and muddled. My mind was in a perpetual state of chaos. This alien sense of upheaval was maddening. My brain was comparable to a jammed copy machine. I couldn't move forward; I had no intention of resuming my relationship with Jamey or breaking things off with LaVonn. I was stuck.

I began to literally feel depressed, and I wasn't one to throw that word around haphazardly. I loathed it when friends, peers, and the worst culprit, my sister Sara, misused it. I had taken psychology classes and was aware of what true depression looked like- it wasn't feeling sad because your mom didn't cook your favorite food for dinner or your boyfriend was absent from school. It was so much more serious and dangerous than that. I felt myself slipping into hopelessness and despair. I'd actually never felt so incredibly downcast before. I didn't know how to deal with this emotion. It was foreign to me.

For days, my friends and family continued to treat me like a China doll; they could tell I was delicate and fragile. They avoided the topic of boys and went out of their way to find other subjects to discuss. I was grateful that they were respecting my privacy but also a little hurt by their thinly veiled pity. After about a week of this, Jenna finally sent me a text asking if we could go to brunch and talk. I agreed- with both reluctance and relief.

Jenna had her license, and although she was a reckless driver (surprise, surprise), I had to give her credit because at least she'd passed the test. I still wasn't even brave enough to take it. She picked me up the Saturday after Prom, and we drove to a somewhat remote diner in Desmond. Jenna did an internet search of isolated, semi-derelict places nearby. Therefore, we didn't run the risk of encountering anyone we knew. We drove in relative silence because we were both reflecting on what we wanted to say.

The diner was definitely what my mom would refer to as a "dive," not the typical place we'd frequent, but obviously, that was the point. It was shaped like a white shoe box and hadn't been painted in at least a decade. The flashing "Jane's" sign had a lopsided "e," and the "a" had lost its luster when the battery ran out; it was the only letter that didn't light up.

It looked clean and efficient inside, although it hadn't been renovated since the 70's. The turquoise plastic booths were frayed and raggedy, and the walls were painted a sunshine yellow. There were a small number of people spread throughout the place, but overall, it was pretty empty.

After we'd sat at a booth in a far corner near the "Doll's" room, the waitress came right over to take our order. She was also dressed as if she'd stepped out of a time machine with a yellow and white zip-front dress, hip pockets, and practical platform shoes.

Jenna immediately decided on the lumberjack breakfast, while my order consisted of a fruit cup and coffee; my gloominess had suppressed my appetite.

After the waitress took our menus and walked away, Jenna began speaking, "Listen, Jess," she uttered with hesitation, "It's obvious that you're not happy."

She looked at me, waiting to see if I objected. I only nodded with a glum expression.

"You know I love you like a sister." She laughed wickedly, "Actually, that's a bad analogy. I love you more than either of us love our own sisters."

Jenna had a talent for lessening the tension during strained situations. Once again, she found a way to break the ice, so to speak. We both giggled at her joke-not-really-a-joke. In actuality, Jenna had no use for her younger sister, Ashlynn. And it was obvious to everyone that there had always been friction between Sara and me. I got along with my youngest sister, Megan, but she was an anomaly to me. We weren't close.

Jenna took a long sip of coffee before she continued, "It's obvious you are in…um, well. It's obvious that even if you don't want to feel the way you do," she stared up at the ceiling as if she was willing the right words to come forth, "I know you don't want to feel the way you do, and I don't understand it, but it's clear you still have feelings for Jamey."

I felt my eyes start to fill up with tears as the waitress brought our food over. I noticed a sympathetic look spread across the middle-aged woman's weathered face and automatically became embarrassed. She hurried away, not wanting to pry, as I took my napkin and wiped at my eyes. "I just can't help it, Jen. I am trying so hard to force myself to feel something for LaVonn. He's so perfect. I know that. I'm not stupid. I mean, I like him. He's smart and polite, and he has so many wonderful qualities. I want so much to feel for him what I feel for Jamey. I am really, really TRYING...."

"But, it's not working," Jenna finished for me with a deadpan, "it is what it is" tone of voice.

I nodded. "I am just so confused about Jamey. I can't get past it. I don't know what to do."

Jenna took a deep breath. "Even though I wish this wasn't the case, I think the first thing you need to do is break up with LaVonn."

"You're not mad at me, are you? I know you went to all the trouble to set us up." I looked at Jenna pleadingly. I couldn't handle it if she was upset. She was the closest person to me in the world, and I needed her approval- almost in the same way I needed my father's.

Jenna vigorously shook her head, "No, Jess. It was no trouble. And I could never be mad at you."

I smiled gratefully and held a hand to my chest, feeling a little of the weight on my shoulders being lifted. A part of me had been terribly afraid this uncomfortable situation would affect our friendship.

"Are you going to forgive Jamey?" Jenna asked, taking a huge bite of her waffles.

I sighed, "I don't know. I guess. But I can't until he realizes what he did was wrong."

"He called me," Jenna admitted.

"He did?" I inquired, surprised that Jamey would dare to approach Jenna.

She nodded, "He wanted advice. I told him he needed to figure it out for himself."

"Ugh, I don't know why I am such an idiot," I exclaimed.

Jenna gently shook her head, "No, you're not an idiot. In fact, you're one of the smartest people I know."

"Jenna, thank you for understanding. You don't know how much that means to me."

Jenna arched an eyebrow and tilted her head, "Well, I didn't say I understood. I just...love you no matter what, and I will always have your back."

"I love you," I declared, "much more than my sisters."

Jenna let out a guffaw and then nonchalantly replied, "I just wish you had better taste in boys."

Ever since my falling out with Jamey, my girlfriends felt obligated to support me when my crew was all together- like during lunch. The males and females were previously interspersed, but after Jamey assaulted me, the girls sat on one side of the long table we inhabited, and the boys assembled on the other.

During lunch on Monday, I noticed Kelly sneaking covert glances at Jamey before she once again broached the subject of our break up.

"Jess, can I ask you something?" She began cautiously.

I shrugged, knowing that her question would inevitably involve Jamey.

"Are you ever going to forgive Jamey? Or is it definitely over between you?"

I sighed, a drawn-out, audible sigh, "I'm not sure."

"Well, he keeps asking us to talk to you," Erin chimed in.

"You know he loves you, and he feels bad…."

"Does he feel sorry?" I said, cutting Kelly off, "Is he sorry for what he did? Or does he just feel sorry for himself? It certainly doesn't seem like it."

At this point, I was surprised because Jenna actually spoke up in Jamey's defense, "Well, Jessica, maybe you need to give him a chance."

Erin, Kelly, Jenna, and Nikki were all staring at me at that point, waiting for me to respond.

Nikki glanced over at Jamey, pursed her lips, and nodded once, "Yeah, Jess. I think it's time."

We all fell silent and went back to eating our food. Everyone knew that the fact that Jenna and Nikki were on team Jamey meant it wouldn't be long before we made up unless he screwed up again.

The first thing I did in making amends with Jamey was to allow him access to my phone number. About two minutes later, I clicked "unblock," I got a text from him. He'd written in bold, uppercase letters, "YOU UNBLOCKED ME!!!! Yes."

I was doing homework when it came through. I picked it up, half smiled, then threw the phone back on the bed. A few seconds later, another text came through. This one was from LaVonn, asking if I was available to chat. I quickly replied that I was doing homework and would try to call him later, even though I knew I wouldn't.

My phone buzzed once more...Jamey again, "Can we talk tomorrow?"

I waited, deciding how to reply. Luckily, I was working on a simple grammar assignment, so the fact that I was having trouble concentrating didn't create a problem.

About a half hour later, I responded. "Maybe," I typed and added, "Leave me alone for now. I'm trying to do my work."

He wrote "K" and added a happy face and thumbs-up emoji.

Little did I know what "Can we talk?" would entail.

The next day, I was feeling some anticipatory anxiety about *talking* to Jamey. It wasn't until lunch that he approached me. He was the last to arrive at the table where we normally all sat. The "separation" had instantly discontinued after my talk with the girls. I was slightly surprised when I entered the cafeteria and noticed Jenna sitting with Mickey in the far corner near the wall. What was that about? Nikki was snuggling with Evan; they were lost in their own little world, and Kelly, Erin, Josh, and Bobby were engaged in a conversation, which had them all laughing hysterically. I put my tray down and started arranging the food from my lunch tote when Jamey plopped down across from me.

I pursed my lips and started tapping my fingers on the table.

"I just have one thing to say to you," he began earnestly.

I waited silently, unwilling to give him anything.

Then he got down on one knee and shouted, "Please take me back!"

Everyone in the cafeteria was staring at us. I looked around, feeling mortified. Only Jamey would be able to get away with this type of behavior and still be seen as an admired alpha male.

"Jamey, stop!"

He grabbed my ankles as I tried to get up from the table, "Forgive me." he cried.

"Let go of me," I demanded.

"Not until you forgive me."

He was talking quieter now, so only I could hear him. "Please, I shouldn't have done..."

I cut him off and said through gritted teeth, "I don't believe you. You're only saying that because Kelly told you to."

"No! That's not true," his voice was loud again, which caused everyone to giggle and continue whispering about us.

"Jamey, you're embarrassing me. I will never forgive you if you don't get up right now."

Jamey gulped and then slowly rose to his feet. His eyes never left mine; he was looking at me with those beautiful metallic brown eyes. Without words, he was begging me to at least give an inch.

"I'll think about it," I replied in a stoic voice as I rose from the table, "I have to go to the bathroom," I added, feeling desperate to be alone- away from Jamey and all the prying eyes.

Although I didn't turn around, I could feel his stare boring into me as I power-walked toward the lavatory.

I practically dove into the empty restroom and murmured a prayer of gratitude for the privacy I so desperately needed. Once I was by myself- safely inside one of the stalls, I couldn't help but smile.

Later that evening, my cell started ringing while I was eating dinner with my family. I realized I'd forgotten to leave it in my room.

"Oops," I said absent-mindedly, "I forgot to take my phone out of my pocket." My mom was adamant about us not using electronics during family time. I couldn't help but look at the screen as I removed the device from the pocket of my jeans and turned it to silent mode.

"Who is it?" Megan asked teasingly, "Is it LaVonn?"

"No," I replied without thinking, "It's Jamey."

Both my parents' eyebrows shot up. "Interesting," my father said neutrally.

"I'd probably get grounded if I 'accidentally' brought my phone to the table," Sara grumbled.

"That's not true, Sara," my mother said dismissively.

I placed my phone on the counter, and it buzzed. As I sat back down, it hummed again.

I smiled awkwardly at my mom. "Should I just bring it to my room?"

She nodded good-naturedly.

Before placing it on my desk, I noticed Jamey's text, which stated, "Call me. Please. I love you!! We need to talk."

I was grinning as I walked back into the kitchen.

"You look happy, Jessica," my mom remarked as I sat back down in my chair.

My dad nodded, "You haven't looked cheerful in quite a while."

"Really?" I was perplexed. I didn't think my misery had been that apparent.

My parents and sisters all nodded at once.

"Are you glad that Jamey's back in the picture?" Sara asked with an edge to her voice.

"LaVonn is a very nice boy," my mom said, "but I don't think he's...."

My dad finished for her, "Right for you, and I only say that because ever since your break up with Jamey and your interest in LaVonn, you seem distant and rather melancholy."

I was quiet because I felt uncomfortable discussing my personal life with my family. I wanted to keep it private; regardless, it always appeared as if they were aware of literally *everything*.

"How come you're so secretive? What's the big deal?" Megan asked. If it was Sara, the tone would have been snarky, and she probably would have gotten into trouble.

I just shrugged, unsure of how to answer. I did recognize that I was more guarded than most girls my age, but I couldn't help it. My romantic relationships made me self-conscious and somewhat embarrassed. I felt awkward discussing boyfriend-type stuff with my parents and sisters.

Megan went on, "When I start dating, I'm going to talk about boys all the time. I wish I could start now."

My father jokingly put his face in his hands and rocked his head back and forth. We all laughed, and then my mom started to ask my sisters about their day. I was relieved by the change in subject.

Later that night, I decided to set things in motion once and for all. I texted Jamey and told him I needed space. I alluded to the fact that I was planning to end things with LaVonn, but I was vague and noncommittal. Then, before phoning LaVonn, I called Jenna for moral support. She confirmed that ending things was the right thing to do. I agreed; I couldn't continue to lead him on. Jenna assured me that he already sensed something was amiss so he wouldn't be caught off guard or surprised.

When it came down to it, I didn't have to initiate the "discussion." LaVonn did it for me. He could tell I wasn't content, especially after my encounter with Jamey at the prom.

"Jessica, I think we need to talk," he said in a serious but gentle tone.

"Jenna didn't say anything to you, did she?" I asked. This time, I didn't want Jenna fixing things for me. I wanted to be mature enough to do this on my own.

"She didn't have to."

LaVonn ended up doing all the talking, and I really didn't have to add anything. It was probably the easiest split-up in the history of split-ups. I had no experience in this area, but I watched my girlfriends fret for days over how to break a guy's heart- especially Kelly. She always felt remorseful about it. On the other hand, I felt tremendously guilty that LaVonn made it so easy for me.

"Look," he began in an even-keeled tone, "I can tell that you still carry a torch for your ex-boyfriend...."

"He was never really my boyfriend," I interrupted.

LaVonn exhaled a little impatiently, "Yeah, we've been down this road before."

I decided to ignore his comment. I was accustomed to people making similar remarks.

"I don't know what you want to call him, 'boyfriend' or whatever. Anyway, it's clear that you have feelings for him. You don't feel the same way about me. While I am disappointed about that, it's been over a month now, and well...you've never seemed as into me as I am into you. You've tried, but it's not happening. To be honest, I think we're both wasting our time."

"I'm sorry."

LaVonn chuckled in a kind way, but it was without humor, "There's nothing to be sorry about. You didn't do anything wrong."

"I'm sorry if I led you on."

"I don't think that's the case," LaVonn stated, "These things happen. I just want you to know you're too good for that guy. I hope I'm wrong because I care about you. I really do wish you well."

"Thanks," I said sheepishly, "You do know you are being way too nice about all of this."

"Why wouldn't I be nice about it?" He sounded genuinely perplexed.

I was silent for a few seconds, contemplating where I got the notion that separations had to be contentious. "I guess it's just my lack of experience," I said.

We talked a little bit longer in a casual way. Before we hung up, LaVonn said, "Well, I do hope things work out for you, Jessica. I wish you good luck," but he didn't sound hopeful that restoring things would Jamey would bring me any luck at all.

I felt like I needed some time before I completely forgave Jamey and went back to whatever it was we had been to one another. Although I kept denying he was my boyfriend, I was aware that we had belonged to each other in our own strange, unique way. It was not traditional because I wasn't ready to commit to him. Josh had once accused me of being commitment-phobic. Although I denied it, I was beginning to think his accusation was partially accurate. If truth be told, I was reluctant because I knew that if I did concede, there would be no going back. I just wasn't willing to accept his flaws, even though, deep in my heart, I knew they were part of what attracted me to him.

After ending things with LaVonn and making peace with Jamey, I was determined to remain single for a while- to reflect and mull things over. I had a lot of questions about the state of our union and where I wanted it to go next. That was my plan. Little did I know that things would take a different turn and ultimately bring us back to where we'd been before. In retrospect, if I had had more time to think things through, I might have made different choices rather than just going with the flow of our already-established relationship.

The next morning, I got separate vague texts from Jenna and Nikki stating that they couldn't drive me to school- I usually got a ride with one of them, but apparently, they both had "something come up" at the last minute. I thought this was rather odd; it had never happened before, but I quickly dismissed it and started preparing for the school day.

Sara was a freshman, so none of her friends had driver's licenses, and she refused to take the bus. Megan, on the other hand, loved the bus, so every morning, my mom made sure Megan safely climbed into the big yellow van and then drove Sara to school.

Sara couldn't resist making a rude comment when I climbed into the back seat of my mom's Audi. "Oh, you're slumming it today?" she asked sardonically.

"What does that even mean, Sara?" my mom questioned.

"Nothing," Sara remarked.

She then proceeded to complain about all her teachers, and my mom made soothing noises and comments, although I wanted to tell Sara to shut up. This was the main reason why my sister refused a ride from anyone else. She wanted to whine about her non-existent problems, and my mom was the only person who could tolerate her numerous grievances. Personally, I thought my mother enabled her.

When I stepped out of my mom's car, I felt a headache coming on, although I'd only been forced to endure my sister's unpleasantness for five minutes. I was pensive as I staggered through the sliding glass doors that led to my locker. I remained lost in thought as I strolled to the hallway, which was designated for the junior class. It wasn't until I was only a few feet away that I noticed all my books spread out on the floor by my locker. I was utterly confused and stared at them for a moment with a baffled expression. When I looked up and took in my surroundings, I noticed my friends, acquaintances, and peers scattered around my space. Jenna, Nikki, Kelly, and Erin stood in a semi-circle with sly smiles.

"What's going on? Are you guys playing a prank on me or something?" I asked with irritation. I certainly wasn't in the mood for shenanigans.

"Just open your locker!" Jenna ordered playfully.

They backed up as I lifted the latch on my solid blue metal locker and cautiously opened it. I wasn't sure what to expect. Was a fake snake going to pop out or something?

When I did look inside, I noticed a massive vase of purple and pink roses- my favorite colors. A piece of loose leaf paper was attached that had been folded in half. I took a deep breath as I reached in to retrieve it. My hands were shaking as I spread it out. In what was unmistakably Jamey's scrappy handwriting was written, "I am SO sorry! I was wrong. Please forgive me."

I gulped and felt my eyes start to fill with tears. This was what I had been waiting for. This was what I needed to get past his atrocious offense.

An apology.

An admission that he was wrong.

For a few seconds, I couldn't move. I was overcome with emotion. I felt a surge of relief. I could forgive him now. I forgot about needing space and time to think. I started to fiddle with my hair nervously until I remembered that I was standing in the middle of the hallway. It was dead silent because everyone was waiting to see my reaction.

I anxiously turned around, unsure of what I would see. I noticed Jamey standing across the hall, surrounded by Evan, Mickey, Bobby, and even Josh. Jamey had his arms crossed and a huge smile on his face. A huge rush of unexpected euphoria came over me. I forgot about all the people standing around and rushed over to him. He put his arms around me as I initiated a lengthy kiss. The kiss was different from all the times I made out with LaVonn. They were both good kissers, but I felt something with Jamey that I was unable to feel with LaVonn. There was no tension. It was familiar, comfortable, and stirred feelings that made me blush. We made out for a long time while our classmates either cheered or jeered. I felt like I had returned home again.

Chapter Twenty-four: Mickey's Secret and College Visits

My junior year ended with a significant revelation that caught me by surprise. My "involvement" started with a phone call from Nikki.

When I heard my cell humming, as opposed to a rapid typescript, I presumed something important must have occurred. My friends typically texted rather than phoned me. Jamey was the only person I spoke to regularly on my mobile, and I had just hung up with him a few minutes before, so I knew he most likely wasn't the one ringing.

I noticed Nikki's name flash on the screen as I accepted the call.

Nikki began without a greeting, "Did you hear about Mickey?" she asked, sounding astonished.

"No, what about him?" I assumed he'd done something else sexually adventurous or stupid or both.

"People are saying he's gay."

I gasped, not because I had anything against anyone's sexual preferences. I was initially shocked because I never would have made the connection with Mickey. In fact, for years, he'd always claimed to have a crush on Jenna.

"Do you think it's true?" I questioned, "It could just be a rumor."

Nikki cleared her throat and sighed, "From what I understand, he's not denying it. Evan called him to offer support, and he didn't say either way, which means...."

I finished for her, "Which means it's true."

I was silent for a few seconds, contemplating Jenna's recent correspondence with Mickey. I pondered this and wondered if, perhaps, Mickey had been confiding in her. Jenna was outwardly liberal and had even tried to object to attending the Catholic church because of their stance on gay marriage. Jenna's parents, along with mine and Nikki's, dismissed Jenna's protestations by joking about being "Cafeteria Catholics." My Aunt Gina explained, "Most

Catholics these days basically pick and choose what they believe. We just, you know- don't have to agree with everything the church says. And none of us has anything against homosexuality."

My mom agreed, claiming that even the Pope was lightening up on the divisive topic.

This occurred a couple of years ago while we were eating brunch at the country club after Mass. I was not surprised that Jenna had the audacity to protest being forced to attend services at an institution she didn't believe in. She was bold and outspoken, and everyone was aware of that. She actually claimed that she felt it was unfair to be made to do something against her will. And she verbalized it in a loud enough voice for *everyone* to hear- all our parents and siblings. Nikki and I exchanged amused glances. Neither of us would have the nerve to make declarations like that in front of our entire families. Jenna was in a league of her own. Even if I had the inclination to be so bold, I wouldn't because my dad would have been livid. Jenna's father, Gerry, didn't seem to have the energy to discipline his daughters. Rachel and Gerry griped about their daughters' misdeeds but did nothing about their disobedience beyond grumbling.

After Jenna's outburst, her parents looked annoyed rather than embarrassed. We were all close enough not to judge. Jenna's parents were not blood-related but might as well have been.

I thought back to that incident, and all the other times I'd witnessed Jenna publicly defend the LGBTQ2 community. She had joined the debate team just to be able to argue her point. Everyone in our friend group knew how she felt. Therefore, if Mickey was struggling with his sexuality, she would definitely be the one he would go to.

When I hung up with Nikki, I immediately called Jenna, who confirmed my suspicions. Mickey had explored his sexual proclivities by having threesomes and discovered that he was predominantly attracted to boys. He'd communicated this to Jenna before anyone else because he knew she would be supportive. He hadn't come out and told anyone else yet. He was afraid of their reaction. It baffled me that even in this day and age, sexuality was still a controversial issue.

I asked Jenna why she hadn't told me; I was a little hurt. "You know you can trust me, right?"

"Of course," she insisted, "It's just that you were dealing with your own issues at the time, and I never had a chance. Plus, it isn't my truth to tell, you know? It's Mickey's."

"I get it." I said, feeling a little guilty for treating the information as if it was gossip, "Sorry," I replied, "It's just surprising. I mean, he had a crush on you for years. Was that real?

Jenna snickered, "I don't know. Maybe it was a non-sexual crush. Maybe he was using me as his beard. He doesn't even fully understand. He's trying to figure things out."

"Yeah. I wonder how his friends feel. Wait! What about Jamey?" I blurted out, "Does he know?"

"I'm sure he does," Jenna declared, "Everyone does."

"I wonder how he'll respond," I said tentatively.

"We don't have to wait long to find out," Jenna told me, "Mickey won't be in school for a few days. He can't face the gossip. I'm sure everyone's *true* feelings about it will come out in his absence."

Jenna was right about that. In fact, the school was abuzz with rumors and gossip. Our classmates were shocked. It didn't seem possible that Mickey- the class clown, the serial sexual adventurer, the infamous keg stand champion was attracted to guys. Frankly, our peers were mainly astonished because he was muscular and athletic- a jock. He was a phenomenal football and baseball player. I was flabbergasted to hear my classmates' ignorant comments throughout the morning. I found it hard to believe that teenagers, who considered themselves enlightened, could be so ill-informed and oblivious. The stereotypes strewn about were mind-boggling. All day, I heard remarks like: he doesn't look gay, he doesn't dress like a girl, he doesn't have a feminine voice …I rolled my eyes and glared at people but didn't say anything, not wanting to add fuel to the fire. How could so many of my peers think all gay people fit into the same box?

I anxiously awaited lunch that day to see how the conversation would unfold. I already knew how Jenna and Nikki felt, but I honestly couldn't anticipate the reaction of my other friends. I was aware Jamey had been friends with Mickey since grammar school. Still, I was uncertain how he would respond to Mickey's recently exposed sexuality. Would he feel threatened? Would it make him uncomfortable? Would it evoke feelings of disgust? I tried to recall any conversations I'd ever had with Jamey involving the provocative subject, but nothing came to mind, which did seem strange to me.

I was mainly apprehensive because I knew that Jamey's stance could be a game-changer when it came to the status of our relationship. And at this point, I was finally feeling content. I didn't want that to change.

Fortunately, I was not only somewhat surprised and proud but also relieved by Jamey's reaction to the news about Mickey.

Later that day, we were all sitting at our usual lunch table. Everyone was there except Josh and Mickey...no one was saying much, and the quiet was strange. We were making small talk, which was unusual. Typically, we all had much to discuss.

"Yeah, Josh had to stay after to talk to Mr. Killingly," Evan remarked, explaining Josh's absence.

Everyone seemed to nod robotically in unison.

Josh's sudden presence startled us all because he plopped himself down in the middle of the group and loudly slammed his tray on the plastic table top. "Mr. Killingly needs me to tutor someone else," he replied in a faux, nonchalant tone, watching me out of the corner of his eye, "I'm surprised he didn't ask you, Jessica. Don't you have a higher average than I do in calculus?"

I sighed and rolled my eyes. The competition was never-ending and exhausting where he was concerned. "I'm already tutoring five kids," I stated smugly. I couldn't resist trying to one-up Josh.

Josh looked around the table, "Hmmm, where's Mickey?" he asked with an amused tone, "He can't handle the pressure of being out of the closet?"

Everyone was silent.

"Well, I mean, he's not denying it," Josh went on, "It has to be true."

Jenna glared at him, "Who cares if it is?"

Josh threw his hands in the air. "I'm just saying..."

"Just saying what?" Jenna interrogated.

"Do you have a problem with it?" Jamey asked through gritted teeth.

Josh looked uneasy and a little confused as if he wasn't sure how to respond.

Bobby tilted his head and raised his eyebrows, "Well, Josh, why don't you answer the question?"

Josh remained silent, expressionless. It appeared as if he was about to speak but couldn't find the right words.

"Because if you do have a problem with it, then you also have a problem with us," Jamey spat, pointing from him to Bobby.

Josh laughed. "No, I don't have a problem with it. It's not 1950."

Jamey and Bobby were glowering at Josh, their eyes narrowed, synchronized. "Good, because he's our friend, and it doesn't matter if he's gay or not," Jamey proclaimed, "And when he comes back, if anyone gives him a hard time- *anyone*...."

"We have his back," Bobby finished for him.

I found out later that Jamey and Bobby kept their word- and the most impressive part about it was they didn't use violence. Some of the guys on the baseball team mocked Mickey when he finally found the courage to return to school. Jamey let them know that, in no uncertain terms, he and Bobby were standing by Mickey, regardless of his sexual orientation. Their devotion led the other players to accept Mickey for who he was. The rumors and gossip ended abruptly, and everyone inevitably moved on to the next "newsflash."

Later that week, when Jamey and I were conversing on the phone, I brought up Mickey and how I was somewhat surprised by his perspective. "It's just that I always thought...well, to be honest, I guess I never really did think about it because it's never come up, but I would have assumed you'd be uncomfortable with guys being, you know? Guys are attracted to other guys. I guess I'm trying to say that I'm glad you're standing by Mickey."

Jamey seemed taken aback and rather stunned by my response to his reaction, "Why wouldn't I stand by him? He's one of my best friends. Who gives a shit if he's gay? Why should I care?"

"I'm just relieved, I guess, to see how open-minded you are. I never knew...."

Jamey cut me off, "I don't know about being open-minded. I just know what's right. You don't turn your back on your friends. Loyalty is everything."

I agreed, and we were both silent for a minute; there was nothing left to say, and neither of us had an immediate idea of how to segue into a new topic. Finally, I asked Jamey about what colleges he planned to apply to. As he rattled off an answer, I tuned out, thinking that although I was happily surprised by Jamey's devotion to Mickey, I couldn't help wondering how he would react in a situation where a baseball player he wasn't close with or just a casual acquaintance came out of the closet.

    Although I was fairly certain I would attend the same college my parents had- Padre Pio, which was located close to home and deemed one of the most prestigious universities in the country, I had the desire to weigh all my options before making a final decision. I didn't want to have any regrets. I felt it was necessary to visit all of the other secondary schools I was considering based on copious notes I'd written down after extensive research. I had made a list of prospects and knew I would only be satisfied if I ruled all of them out before ultimately choosing Padre Pio.

    My parents were in complete agreement. Therefore, that summer, my father suggested we travel the country as a family and visit all the universities in what he jokingly referred to as my "portfolio." My guidance counselor had met with my parents and me in June before school ended to discuss the possibility for me to graduate early. She said I had enough credits to begin college during the second half of my senior year. I was excited and proud to hear that I had the opportunity to receive my high school diploma in December. However, I was certain I wasn't interested in moving on to the next chapter of my life without fully finishing the one I was still in.

    Shockingly, my dad decided to suspend his professional obligations for the summer, which was basically unheard of in my family. His law partner, Gerry, agreed to take over all my father's cases. After all, my dad was usually the one covering for him, so it was only fair. My mother claimed that my father had earned it, considering he usually only took two weeks off a year- this would be the first year he'd ever taken a real vacation.

    Therefore, I rarely saw Jamey the summer before my senior year. Of course, we texted and spoke on the phone, but while I was traipsing around the states visiting universities, he did what he normally did over the summer- partying while his mom vacationed.

    We visited New York City, Boston, and Rhode Island in July. Even though we went shopping, saw plays, perused museums, etc., on our tour of college campuses, my sisters complained because they would have preferred being home with their friends. Megan especially missed horseback riding, and Sara constantly moaned about falling behind in gymnastics. My father finally threatened to take away all their technology if they didn't stop whining.

It wasn't until August, when we took a two-week vacation to Los Angeles, that all the members of my immediate family were content. We visited my mom's relatives on many occasions throughout the year- Christmas, spring break, and during summer. My maternal grandparents all lived in close vicinity to L.A. My mom was practically the only member of her extended family who had chosen to stay as far away from the spotlight as possible. My grandmother was away that summer promoting a new clothing line she'd developed. My grandfather, the head of a production company at one time, was retired but still had connections. He entertained my dad during our two-week vacation. They had a lot in common, including a love of golf, poker, and expensive scotch. My dad spent all his free time, when he wasn't with me, touring The University of Los Angeles- a college I had become especially interested in, either on the golf course or engaged in high-stakes card games.

We stayed with my great-grandmother, Nona Jessica, that summer. She lived in a lavish stucco mansion with an illuminated waterfall, several heated pools both inside and outside, a sauna, a tennis court, and basically every comfort imaginable. She had been a very famous child and teen actress in the 1940s and 50s. As an adult, she continued her career on a much smaller scale but permanently retired after her husband's death. She developed an aversion to the paparazzi after being harassed during a very painful time in her life. Regardless, she also still had many friends in the industry and was able to provide exciting experiences for my mom and sisters. They visited movie sets at University Studios, went to film premieres at Grauman's Chinese Theater, and dined at Spago and Musso and Frank Grill. They shopped on Rodeo Drive. They had the time of their lives. Nona Jessica had tired of those extravagances. Although she was happy to oblige my mom and sisters, she bowed out of attending. I was focused on college, so although I would have ordinarily enjoyed indulging in such activities, I had to make the most critical decision of my young life and couldn't think about anything other than my immediate future- would I go to college in Los Angeles or attend St. Padre Pio?

My dad took me to tour The University of Los Angeles three times while we were in California. The college provided us with a guide during each visit. As a result of my 4.0 average, SAT scores, and the impressive amount of college credits I'd already secured, the college representatives seemed eager to entice and impress me. The dean mentioned the possibility of early admission. She suggested I might be able to begin my freshman year in January. I only needed two more classes to have enough credits for my first trimester.

  I was definitely tempted. I loved the school. Interestingly, it was not a well-known institution. I would never have heard of it if it wasn't for my great-grandmother and her connections. The university president wanted it that way. He did not want to attract attention like other Ivy League schools did. My dad and I were told that the students who attended were meant to receive special attention. The academy actually did no marketing whatsoever. One of the admissions officers, Dr. Keller, explained, "We only want the best of the best. And that means girls like you, Jessica. Not only are you academically and socially suited for our school, but we…to be blunt, are looking for students with prominent familial backgrounds. You fit all the criteria of the almost infinitesimal number of students we will accept."

  Even though I was almost sure I wouldn't have the courage to leave literally *everything* behind and travel across the country for college, I had to admit that I felt extremely tempted to do so. The truth was The University of Los Angeles stirred much excitement and enthusiasm in me. It was posh and rather cozy. It resided on private property and looked almost like a wealthy neighborhood with buildings that resembled Victorian homes. The dorms were like suites. The grounds were covered with either bright green synthetic grass or stone walkways, surrounded by colorful angel trumpets and birds of paradise. There were strategically placed palm and gold medallion trees strewn around campus. It reminded me of Fantasy Island. It felt like paradise. I also adored the warm California weather and knew it would be easy to become accustomed to it.

  My feelings were mixed. On the one hand, I couldn't imagine a world where my friends, parents, and Jamey were absent. Not to mention that St. Padre Pio was also an extremely elite, state-of-the-art, notable university. Yet I had to admit, it wasn't as beautiful or enticing as The University of Los Angeles. It had phenomenal academic programs, but it wasn't known for its focus on mental health, like ULA. Considering that I wanted to be a psychologist, realistically, I knew that ULA was a perfect fit for me.

My parents didn't tell me their opinion about what I should do, but assessing their thoughts through their comments wasn't difficult. My dad wanted me to stay home, even though he was generous with his time and kept taking me back to ULA. He made offhanded comments about St. Padre Pio while we were there. For instance, while we were walking on the grounds and I commented on how ultramodern and stunning the buildings and walkways were, my father would make an off-the-cuff remark about the numerous benefactors who contributed to keeping up the campus at Padre Pio.

On the other hand, my mom never accompanied me to the university but made animated statements about the excitement of living in L.A., how fortunate I'd be to have Nona Jessica close by, and how I'd love the year-round warm weather.

Nona Jessica was not at all subtle about her feelings and thoughts on the matter. She made it perfectly clear that she believed I should come to California, live with her, and attend The University of Los Angeles. She assured me that with her connections, I'd have no trouble getting in. She also offered- **insisted,** actually, on paying for my entire college tuition. Although my dad was never intimidated or offended by the extraordinary wealth and generosity of my mom's family, it was apparent he found that proposal somewhat insulting and unnecessary. Granted, he was respectful enough of Nona Jessica to keep his feelings to himself.

All of my family members were aware of my uncertainty. My sisters made it obvious they could care less what I did, with the exception of Sara alluding to the fact that she wouldn't be heartbroken if I chose to go to L.A. My parents' stances were subtle, although I had a sense of what they thought. Nona Jessica was the only one who voiced her opinion on a daily basis.

She could sense that I was feeling reluctant about moving across the country. Therefore, in order to persuade me to choose ULA, she invited me on a private outing so we could "discuss" the situation. My mom and sisters were shopping. My dad was at a prestigious country club with my grandfather the day Nona Jessica unexpectedly approached me. I assumed she enquired without warning so I wouldn't have the opportunity to decline.

I had just showered and was about to have a late breakfast when she approached me in her spacious kitchen. I noticed she was dressed a little more formally than usual. "There's this special place I'd like to bring you," she informed me. I was about to tell the cook

I wanted eggs and toast for brunch, but Nona Jessica dismissed her before I could.

When we were alone, she continued, "My first boyfriend used to take me to this...well, it used to be a diner. It's much different now. It's not a place I would normally go to, but for some reason, I have the urge to go back and see what they've done to the place. Would you do me the honor of accompanying me?" she asked in a jokingly ceremonious tone.

"Your first boyfriend? Who was he? I had never heard about him? Seriously, who WAS he?" I interrogated. She had succeeded in capturing my attention.

"Oh, it doesn't matter who he was. He, well, he met a sad demise. It was inevitable," her face took on a faraway, slightly dreamy look as she continued, "Yes, I was secretly dating him against my father's wishes. One night, I got into trouble when he found out I had snuck out and met him at this discreet dive." She chuckled at the memory and tossed her trademark raven hair off her shoulder, "I can laugh now, but I certainly didn't think it was funny back then. My father was very strict, and the public was very interested in all of us-considering my mother, and I were both famous actresses, and he was one of the most celebrated baseball players of all time. The whole situation became public knowledge, and I was humiliated."

I looked at her inquisitively, waiting for her to carry on, but she shook her head dismissively and clapped her hands, "It's close by; we won't run into any paparazzi, and we can talk in peace. Okay?"

"Okay," I said, smiling with trepidation.

About forty-five minutes later, after Nona Jessica's driver dropped us off at a small, quaint teahouse, the two of us were sitting in a hidden corner booth in the farthest corner of the parlor, away from any other patrons. Apparently, Nona had called ahead to make arrangements. She was highly protective of her privacy. The hostess was happy to assist and promised to ensure my great-grandmother would remain inconspicuous.

"Well, this place is much different than I remember," Nona Jessica said after we'd been served the finest Asian tea in decorative glass mugs. After stirring in a pinch of cream, she tapped her swizzle stick on her linen napkin. It was evident that she was thinking of how to continue.

I looked around, taking in the extravagantly fancy and delicate ambiance, "Yeah, it doesn't look like a place you'd sneak off to with a secret lover," I lightheartedly replied.

"It was MUCH different back then," she announced with a chuckle. Her demeanor suddenly changed, and she became quite serious: " I asked you to come with me today because I wanted to ask you why you're hesitant about coming to L.A. I don't want to pressure you...."

She stopped speaking as I raised my eyebrows and tilted my head- calling her bluff. We both smiled because we knew that was a fib- she had most certainly been pressuring me for weeks.

Nona Jessica shrugged sheepishly, "I am sorry, dear. It's just that I...to be honest, I have always had a special feeling about you. You remind me of myself in a lot of ways. I was always close with your mom, but she takes after her father's side of the family. The nerves...well, they come from my side."

"My mom is really laid back," I said knowingly, "Not like me."

"Or me," Nona Jessica added. "You're driven. I was also...driven."

I smiled politely, waiting for her to go on.

"Jessica, I was just curious about the relationship you're in, this boy you're involved with. Is he the reason you don't want to leave Connecticut?"

I was shocked into silence. I didn't even know Nona Jessica knew about Jamey. I wasn't sure how to respond.

"How did you know about Jamey?"

Nona looked down at the table, somewhat guiltily, "Well, your mom. She's confided in me about him. She said you've been seeing him for quite a while."

I nodded and sighed. I was so sick and tired of explaining and justifying personal information about myself. It made me highly uncomfortable.

"Yes, we've been...well, not really dating, but kind of...I don't know...."

"Go on, honey," Nona encouraged.

"He's never really been, my boyfriend." I admitted, "I don't know how to explain it. I've just been reluctant to commit."

Nona Jessica looked me in the eyes with a deadpan expression on her aged yet still beautiful face, "Jessica," she began,

"If you really loved this boy or cared about him enough to remain in Connecticut...if he was special enough to stop you from going to the college of your dreams, don't you think, my dear that you would have made a commitment to him a long time ago? If he is important enough to alter your entire future, shouldn't he at least be important enough for you to call him your boyfriend?"

My mouth dropped open, and I placed my hand over my heart. "Well, I mean, it's not just him. There are other reasons and things..."

"Like what, darling?"

I gulped soundly and cleared my throat. Her words had impacted me enough to leave me speechless.

"I don't know what to say," I whispered, finally finding my voice.

She smiled a little smugly and patted my hand, "Then don't say anything, dear. Just think about it. Okay?

I nodded and took a gulp of my tea.

I still had not made up my mind about what college I should attend when we were ready to leave California and travel back to Connecticut. I obsessively reflected on my great-grandmother's words, knowing in my heart she had a valid point. Why wasn't I willing to commit to Jamey? Did he mean as much to me as I thought he did? Was I ready to step out of my comfort zone and take a leap into new terrain? Yes, I would be leaving my friends, parents, and Jamey behind...but I would have my extended family, and I could make new friends. Plus, I could visit, text, talk on the phone, and FaceTime. It wasn't like they'd completely disappear from my life. I pondered, making the most significant choice for weeks before finally coming to the conclusion that I wasn't brave enough. I didn't have the courage to move across the country and leave everything behind. It all came down to cowardice; I was self-aware enough to realize that. I decided to finish my senior year at Lomonoco Creek, accumulate more college credits, and then attend Padre Pio with my friends the following year.

Part IV.
Twelfth Grade

Chapter Twenty-five: Daydreams

The rest of the summer passed by in a blur. Before I knew it, I found myself sitting in English class the first week of senior year. I couldn't believe how quickly the last three years had passed by. I was reflecting upon my magnificent visit to Los Angeles and the lovely ULA campus. I realized I'd be missing out on the phenomenal psychology program the school offered and the individualized instruction that Padre Pio would not be able to provide. I was daydreaming about the beautiful Victorian buildings and the delicious smells of the flowers unique to California, such as the sticky monkey and redwood sorrel. I knew I would have loved spending time with Nona Jessica, possibly even living with her. Maybe she'd open up to me more about her first boyfriend and what it had been like to be a movie star in the 1950s- when Hollywood was glamorous and magical. I wished I was brave- brave enough to leave everything behind and take a risk.

I was taken completely by surprise when Dr. Brennan, the professor teaching "Female Writers of the 19th Century," chanted my name.

"Sorry?" I asked, "What was that?"

She grinned in a good-natured way, "You were paying attention, Miss Jessica, weren't you? I can't imagine you were off in Lalaland during *my* class.."

"Sorry," I repeated, but this time, I said it as a statement rather than a question. She was a prestigious instructor who also taught at one of the local colleges, and I was obviously embarrassed. It was an honor to be allowed entrance into her class.

"I guess I'll let this one transgression go," she joked, "I was discussing the endings of Edith Wharton's The Age of Innocence in contrast to Jane Austen's Emma. They are both celebrated female authors with very different ideas about how to conclude their novels. They have extraordinarily opposing views on what one might call 'closure.' Austen believed in 'happily ever after' endings, whereas Wharton was quite the opposite. You could argue that Wharton's books and short stories had a 'miserably ever after' theme. I'm interested to hear what you think about that, Jessica."

I was quiet, contemplating an answer. I suppose I was silent for an uncomfortable amount of time, although I was typically able to form opinions at a speedy pace. Josh- who was only taking the class because he wanted to be seen as open-minded and socially aware when he filled out college applications- couldn't wait to point out in his typical obnoxious fashion that I was struggling for a response.

"This is odd," he began sarcastically, "Usually, it's hard to get her to shut up."

I turned around and glared at Josh as a few female students giggled and batted their eyes at him. It was both irritating and perplexing to me that anyone would be attracted to an arrogant narcissist like Josh.

"Shut up, Josh!" Nikki said through gritted teeth. She didn't even turn around to face him when she said it. She just looked at me and rolled her narrowed eyes.

"Josh and Nikki, please," Mrs. Brennan said sternly, "You're both out of line.

There was an uncomfortable silence in the room for a few seconds before I cleared my throat, realizing I had an answer, "Actually," I began, sitting up straighter in my chair, "I think that in real life, neither ending is realistic. In real life, I think there are no *happily or miserably ever afters*. Real life is more like **contentedly** ever after."

"Continue," Mrs. Brennan responded. I could tell I'd intrigued her.

"I twirled my finger around my hair and ran my fingers over my lips, pondering how to clearly convey my thoughts, "Well, most people don't fall in love and live an ecstatic life…the endings of *happily ever afters* basically end on the high note. After that, life becomes more complicated and boring. I've never seen a couple who's been married for decades fawn all over each other constantly. I think they become content but not blissful like they might have been at the beginning of their relationships. On the other hand, I don't believe many people would have to live in misery for the entirety of their existence because of one mistake."

Mrs. Brennan smiled and nodded once, looking pleased, "Good answer, Jessica." I felt a sense of pride as she raised her eyebrows and pointed at Josh, "What do you think about that, Mr. Kowalski?"

I smiled knowingly, this was Mrs. Brennan's way of embarrassing Josh. She was all about girl power in a healthy, not "reverse sexist" way, and it was obvious she didn't appreciate the way Josh treated girls.

Josh shrugged and rolled his eyes, "Whatever," he mumbled.

I sneered at him and arched my eyebrows as if to say, "Don't mess with me."

I was *content* at that moment, knowing I'd won this round in my ongoing feud with Josh.

Chapter Twenty-six: Kara

About a week after I was caught daydreaming in class in early September, my parents had a dinner party for my dad's work colleagues and their families. Nikki and Jenna were in attendance since our fathers were partners in the same law firm. My mom planned and executed this annual gathering at the end of every summer. It was a way for Gerry, Uncle Phil, and my dad to thank their employees for another lucrative year. Aunt Gina and Rachel always offered to take a turn, but my mother insisted on hosting. My father constantly claimed that his wife had the talent and dedication to be a party planner, and everyone who knew her agreed. It was another artistic trait she inherited from our relatives. My sisters and I always had the most fantastic birthday parties as children because my mom could take any theme and turn it into a pleasurable, chic, and classy celebration. While my friends' parents usually hired professionals to organize the significant events in their lives, my mother basically designed and coordinated all of our special occasions.

As far as my mom was concerned, the event was a success- scrumptious appetizers, a delicious and gourmet multi-course meal, a formal yet intimate atmosphere, and special drinks for guests of all ages. Almost everyone had a spectacular time and raved about what an amazing hostess my mother was. Unfortunately for Nikki and me, it was a relatively lackluster event. We felt as if we spent the entire evening trying unsuccessfully to politely reject the advances of some older boys in attendance. Jenna, on the other hand, had the time of her life.

Many of the attendees brought their children to the get-together. A couple of lawyers brought along their college-aged sons. Interestingly, they were all single, which was probably why they decided to accompany their parents. In previous years, we discovered that that was the case when mature offspring tagged along. Our dad's employees knew they had seventeen-year-old daughters and obviously passed that information on to their unattached kids.

Jenna had literally flirted with one of the guys the entire evening. I could tell they'd immediately connected the second he walked in the door. I noticed that seductive smile my best friend plastered on whenever she was in the company of an attractive male who had the potential to become…well, her mate in some capacity, whether it was a one-night stand, a solitary date, or a long-term boyfriend. Nikki and I were friendly and courteous but basically kept to ourselves- even though the other boys tried to no avail to chat us up.

On Monday morning, as I was at my locker getting ready for lunch, that night was the furthest thing from my mind. I was stacking my books neatly, lost in thought- interestingly, I was ruminating on a conversation I'd had with Nona Jessica the night before. She was still unsuccessfully attempting to get me to change my mind about coming to school in L.A. It had become a family joke. She called every weekend, and after conversing with my mom, saying a quick "hello" to my dad and sisters, she would ask to speak to me. She'd begin each conversation by drawling on about a wonderful event that was taking place close to the college, or she'd mention how an impressive celebrity's child would be going to ULA in the fall. I was always gracious and respectful, of course. Still, I'd ultimately end up reminding her that I was positive at that point that I had made the right choice and wasn't planning to change my mind. She'd then express disappointment but wouldn't push the topic any further.

I was lost in a dreamlike state when I suddenly felt strong, muscular arms wrapped tightly around my waist. I was so startled I literally hopped in the air. Before I could turn around, I heard Jamey chuckling as he tickled my abdomen. He continued to laugh as I wriggled away from him.

"What are you doing?" I asked good-naturedly, turning to face him.

"Hey babe," he greeted me. He tapped my nose playfully and kissed me tenderly on the lips. As always, I felt a beating in my chest as his lips brushed mine. It surprised me that I was still magnetized by him. Just the sight of him made my heart flutter, and a warmth spread over my entire body from head to toe. My intense attraction for him not only excited me, but it was also scary at times.

As he pulled away, he had a mock stern expression on his handsome face, "So young lady," he began, "I heard you were hanging out with older college assholes this weekend."

I put my hand on my hip and tilted my head, "How do you know they were assholes?"

Jamey pursed his lips and puffed out his brawny chest. "Did you talk to any of them? Or flirt?"

I giggled, "Are you jealous?"

"Should I be?" he questioned.

"Maybe," I said teasingly, drawing the word out.

"Oh yeah?" Jamey inquired as he put his hands on my shoulders, gently pushing me back against my locker, "You better not be flirting with other guys because you belong to me."

"I told you before I don't *belong* to anyone. I'm not an object."

Jamey waved his hand in the air dismissively, "Stop with the feminist crap. You know what I mean."

I sighed and rolled my eyes, "Whatever. Anyway, how do you even know who I was hanging out with?"

"Kelly. I guess Jenna told her she met a new guy. I'm just glad she's done with that other douchebag."

I chose to ignore that comment, considering LaVonn's connection to Connor was obviously still a sore spot.

"I don't have any reason to worry, right?" Jamey inquired, sounding just slightly nervous.

I shook my head, "No. Nikki and I didn't bother with them. We were basically bored all night," I bit my lip, watching him.

"Good," he whispered as he leaned in to kiss me longer and more passionately this time. I knew that no matter how often our lips became one, I would never tire of feeling his mouth on mine.

"So, how was Caleb Flannery's party?" I asked, spinning around to face my locker so I could finish arranging my books.

"Fine," Jamey replied apathetically, "Kind of boring, not as much fun as my parties."

"Yeah, that's because you have a lot more...." I shut my locker, satisfied that my books were arranged efficiently, and then rotated. I spread my palms out and simulated that I was running them over the perimeter of Jamey's property, "You have a lot more toys and things," I stated, alluding to the fact that Jamey's family had immense wealth and their home was proof of that. In and outdoor heated pools, a bowling alley, a mini movie theatre, two bars, a tennis court, a field to practice sports; the list went on and on.

Jamey pulled me in for a side hug, "You know, I am having a huge celebration this weekend. I mean, it's our senior year. Our last year in high school. We need to really start the year off right!"

"What about your mom?" I asked as we started walking hand-in-hand to the cafeteria for lunch.

Jamey scoffed, "She's going to be away with her latest gigolo. They're going to the Bahamas."

We walked in a comfortable silence for a second before Jamey added with trepidation, "She was actually just asking about you."

"Your mom?"

Jamey nodded, "She wants to know if we're a couple yet."

"What did you tell her?"

Jamey sounded semi-frustrated, "I didn't know what to tell her. I mean, what the hell am I supposed to say? Because you still won't...you STILL won't commit."

I stopped suddenly, alarmed but not completely surprised by Jamey's accusation. I inhaled a huge gulp of air and slowly blew it out as I pulled Jamey to the edge of the hallway. We were standing in a private nook, a secluded space, away from prying eyes and curious ears. I looked deeply and sincerely into his eyes. I squeezed both his hands- gently yet firmly as if I could convey the truth and authenticity in my words, "Soon, Jamey. Soon. I promise."

He bit his top lip and gently whisked a piece of hair off my face. "I can wait," he murmured, "I can wait because I know that I'm going to marry you one day, and we're going to have beautiful kids. And they will have your looks AND your brains."

I laughed out loud. "Let's not get ahead of ourselves."

Jamey subtly shook his head and placed his forehead against mine, "I'm not getting ahead of myself. I knew I was going to marry you before we even started ninth grade, the first time I saw your gorgeous face and hot body on the football field."

A part of me wanted to protest that he shouldn't say things like "hot body," but truth be told, I was human, which meant I was also flawed, and statements like that from the one and only guy I'd ever been majorly attracted to were flattering- so I remained silent.

"AND, I know one day, hopefully, sooner rather than later, I will be your loyal *boyfriend*," he informed me as he tenderly patted my hand and led me back to the center of the hallway.

As Jamey and I entered the cafeteria, I was startled when I noticed a girl in the junior class fixedly watching us. I initially couldn't read her expression. She was standing towards the end of the lunch line, oddly facing the opposing direction of everyone else in the procession before her. For seconds, she boldly looked us up and down and continued to undress us with her cat-like turquoise eyes. She was immobile as other students passed her in line. I briefly met her eyes but abruptly looked away after noticing the disgusted look her pretty, angular face took on as she shook her head back and forth.

"Why is she looking at us like that, Jamey?" I asked, certain he'd noticed.

I remained standing, refusing to make my way further into the room. However, Jamey was still headed in the direction of the table our friends occupied. I needed an explanation. He wouldn't look directly at me, although I'm sure the glare on my face was boring into him.

"Can we please go sit down?" Jamey beseeched, practically pulling on my arm.

I refused to move. My feet were planted in place, "No," I retorted, "Not until you answer me."

"It's nothing," Jamey said in a voice that was too strained to sound as casual as he'd intended.

I swallowed soundly, noticing that the girl was still stationed in the same position in line- encouraging other kids to go ahead of her, and she kept watching us. "It is NOT nothing. That's bull," I was starting to get angry. It was evident that something was amiss.

Jamey glanced in the girl's direction and shrugged, "I don't even know her."

"Are you sure about that?" I was challenging him because it didn't take a genius to know he was lying.

Jamey rolled his eyes and threw his hands in the air- in a gesture of defeat, "Look, I don't know why she's looking at us or what her problem is."

I poked my finger into his chest, "Did something happen between you two at Caleb's party? I interrogated, "I'm not stupid, you know? There's no reason why she would be staring at us like that. Something must have happened."

Jamey sighed a long, drawn-out sigh and ran his fingers through his hair, "Look, Jess, I swear nothing happened between us. These little sluts...."

"Jamey!" I cut him off, "Don't talk like that. That's misogynistic."

Jamey clucked his tongue, "What does that even mean?"

"Seriously!"

"Sorry, I shouldn't have said that," he began apologetically, "Anyway, these girls hit on me, and they're jealous of you because they know that you," he stopped and placed his hand on his chest, "I'm not trying to be corny, but my heart belongs to you. It has for years. You know that. And so do they."

I narrowed my eyes, "So, you're saying she hit on you?"

"I don't know. Maybe," Jamey said noncommittally.

My mouth dropped, "How can you not know? Come on, Jamey!"

Jamey threw his hands in the air in exasperation, "You know what, Jessica?" I was taken aback. Jamey rarely called me by my full name. It was like a parent using his child's middle name when addressing her because she was in trouble. "If you would go out with me and be my official girlfriend, this wouldn't keep happening."

I looked down and licked my lips, feeling as if I'd been rightfully chastised. Besides, I was desperate not to have this conversation and go down this rabbit hole. Instead, I decided to accept Jamey's explanation by nodding once. "Let's go," I said, tugging on his bicep.

As we started to walk past the girl to our table, she gave us a nasty smirk and remarked, "Pathetic," in a voice loud enough for only us and a few of our other classmates to hear.

The kids standing within earshot pretended not to witness the scene she was creating.

Jamey looked pointedly at me, "Okay, for your sake, I'm going to keep my cool."

I watched him without speaking because I wasn't sure what to say or do or what he was going to say or do.

Jamey walked right up to her and calmly said, "Don't look at her...or us." I had to admit, he was being much nicer than he would have been in the past.

She waved her hand in the air and exclaimed, "Wow! Whatever."

"I'm serious, Kara. Just leave us alone," Jamey continued.

The expression on her face went from anger to astonishment to resignation in a matter of seconds. Her mouth shaped into a perfect "O," She brazenly stuck her middle finger up and practically shoved it in Jamey's face. He actually took a step back, and I was briefly afraid he'd verbally attack her. I was actually impressed that he didn't react at all.

After Jamey walked away from her, she finally turned around and started moving forward in the lunch line.

"I don't know what that was about," Jamey said, his voice sounding slightly surprised, "I thought I was decent about it. She didn't have to flip me off."

"Well, Jamey," I began in a somewhat amused tone, "She might have been offended because you called her the wrong name."

"No, I didn't."

"Her name isn't Kara."

He scrunched up his nose in confusion, "Yeah, it is."

"No," I replied with certainty, "Her name is Tara."

Jamey put his hand on his chin and looked up at the ceiling, "Really?" he looked genuinely confused, "I really thought she was named Kara."

I shook my head and watched him.

Finally, he shrugged and let out a chortle, "Kara. Tara, who cares? The only girl's name I give a crap about is yours."

Chapter Twenty-seven: Rope Climbing, Volleyball, and Jamey's Hot Tub

I thought a lot about my relationship with Jamey after the situation with Tara in the cafeteria. I couldn't deny that Jamey was right when he claimed girls would probably stop hitting on him if I would officially become his girlfriend. It did seem like all our classmates were aware that we were dating/not dating- to some capacity. I was cognizant of the fact that our business was public knowledge because we chose to be involved in activities like sports and Student Council. People knew who we were, and they cared about the gossip that revolved around us. I couldn't deny that I'd placed myself in a position of *popularity*, for lack of a better word. It sounded shallow, but that was high school. I had to be honest with myself- I mean, no one is humble enough to deny being in the spotlight isn't flattering, although there were times when I wished I was more anonymous.

I came to the conclusion that Jamey and I had fallen into a rather comfortable arrangement.

It felt as if we were both perfectly content with the unique relationship we'd established. I foresaw a future with Jamey- I felt strongly that we would eventually be committed to one another. I continued to have reservations about calling him my boyfriend. I still thought he had some maturing to do- he sometimes did engage in mild taunting of younger classmates. I always chided him on this kind of behavior, but he'd brush me off, claiming that he wasn't nearly as callous as he'd been in the past. He'd promise to eventually stop what he referred to as "teasing"- he claimed he'd be able to resist the urge when I agreed to become his official girlfriend. He said he longed for me to belong to him. When I scolded him for making such a chauvinistic comment, he replied, "Well, I want to belong to you just as much as I want you to belong to me."

I really couldn't argue with that, so I kept quiet. I didn't tell him that the idea of being a part of a couple terrified me, although I didn't know exactly why that was. I wanted it…*eventually*, but I wasn't ready yet. I think part of me knew that once I committed, there would be no going back. We were going to the same college. We'd definitely be dating by then. We'd graduate and, in due course, get married. I was petrified at even the idea of taking that first step because I knew it would be the beginning of the rest of my life. A life I was excited about but still not ready to begin.

If Jamey had pushed things- if he was as adamant our senior year as he'd previously been, I might have conceded and agreed to become a couple. Yet, he was very patient and understanding about my feelings. In fact, he was complacent with the way things were between us. He constantly promised that he would never try to take advantage of me- that he wouldn't rush things. He said he'd wait as long as I wanted. I was shocked by this, considering we'd never done anything beyond kissing.

I felt like I needed all my closest friends to understand. Yet whenever I attempted to discuss the situation, I was unsettled by their responses. Although they were always polite, Kelly and Erin made it obvious that my feelings perplexed them. Erin would silently widen her eyes and raise her eyebrows. And at one point, Kelly scrunched up her nose in confusion and proclaimed, "But it's been three years!"

I shook my head, "No. Not really. We were never…you know…" my voice trailed off because I didn't know how to verbalize my thoughts.

Jenna and Nikki always had my back and supported my feelings, but when I asked them directly what they thought about Jamey's willingness to wait, they were both semi-vague. They'd make comments about how strongly he felt about me or how he was inclined to hang on because he knew we'd eventually be together. Before the conversation would continue- either I would change the subject or they would- it definitely seemed like we were all avoiding something, but I wanted to keep it that way. I wasn't willing to admit it, but I subconsciously was aware that all my friends thought my reluctance to commit to Jamey was bizarre, and they were sparing my feelings by not coming out and acknowledging it.

Jamey started having huge bashes at what used to be his grandparent's home at the beginning of our senior year, and it soon turned into a weekly ritual. When Jamey's grandparents retired, they rarely set foot in Connecticut. They spent their time in either Florida or Italy. Therefore, they decided to gift their home to Jamey's mom. Ms. Russo was even more of a hot mess than she'd been our freshman year. She went through boyfriends like mechanics go through screwdrivers. Every weekend, she traveled to some exotic location with her latest piece of arm candy- which left Jamey essentially alone most of the time. In his mind, this was basically an invitation to celebrate.

All of my friends, aside from Jenna, were planning to go to what he was referring to as "The Selected Senior Shindig" because it was his first invitation-only party. Bobby jokingly told him that was the corniest thing he'd ever heard come out of Jamey's mouth, but Jamey wasn't fazed by Bobby's insult. He thought his use of alliteration was very clever.

Jenna scrunched up her nose and shook her head with disgust when Jamey told us all about it at lunch. She told me afterwards, on our ride home from school, that even if she wasn't dating the new college guy she'd met the weekend before at the gathering at my house, she wouldn't go because the trite, goofy label violated her principles. I laughed knowingly and said, "Jamey does have some maturing to do. That's why I'm, you know, waiting."

She raised her eyebrows in a somewhat dubious manner but eventually told me she was glad Jamey and I were getting along so well, and maybe our coupling was meant to be after all.

I nodded in agreement, "I really think it is," I informed her joyfully, "I feel good about things, better than I ever have, actually. I've been thinking a lot about the future, and I don't know, I think we'll…I think we'll end up together."

Jenna smiled and squeezed my shoulder, "I'm happy you're happy."

Unfortunately, the night of Jamey's "Selected Senior Shindig," I was in a lot of pain. I'd strained my muscles in phys. ed class because of the horrible, chauvinistic gym teacher who had been assigned to the senior class. He made a comment that sent me over the edge and on a mission to prove him wrong.

Lomonoco Creek had an annual rope climbing contest. It was taken very seriously by the jocks in school- males and females. The contest was split because it was deemed unfair for the girls to compete with the boys. Therefore, there were two categories- one for the top three fastest girls and one for the top three fastest boys. Medals and gift cards were provided based on student achievement. One of the football players always won the boys' contest- usually, in our class, it was either Jamey or Bobby. I had never been victorious because I'd failed to scale my way all the way up to the ceiling, which was considered the "pinnacle." This year, I was determined to be triumphant. Sadly, I did not rank. I actually came in eleventh place, BUT I did make it all the way to the top of that damn rope.

This year, I was unwavering in my resolve to succeed- especially after our teacher, Mr. Rexes, who we sarcastically called Mr. Sexist- because he WAS, snidely commented that he doubted any girl in *our* class would be able to hike up the twenty-foot cable. He made a remark about cheerleading not really being a sport.

This was particularly insulting because physical education at Lomonoco Creek was set up in such a way that students who participated in certain sports were assigned to the same class. The athletic department, including my father, thought gym classes should be planned according to each individual's strengths and interests. Therefore, the entirety of my class consisted of cheerleaders.

When Mr. Rexes made that sexist, offensive comment, I knew I had to prove him wrong. I pushed myself- using all the strength I could muster in my arms, legs, back, thighs- basically, EVERY part of my body, while my classmates cheered me on, and I did it! Even Mr. Rexes was impressed. He had a jovial smirk on his face as he clapped in a purposefully slow and exaggerated manner.

I was so proud when I came down that I did a little bow and pretended to tip my hat, "I guess you were wrong," I stated sarcastically, "Maybe you should give cheerleaders more credit."

"I guess I was. Cheerleaders are stronger than I thought," Mr. Rexes admitted, "But if I were you, I'd make sure I had a bottle of Advil on hand. You're going to need it."

I harrumphed, "I doubt it," I muttered, although I already knew he was right.

By the time Nikki, Evan, and I arrived at Jamey's, the party was in full swing. It was a warm evening, and Jamey made it clear that under no circumstances was anyone allowed inside. He didn't want the responsibility of cleaning up after such a huge gathering. About one-third of the senior class was in attendance and some fortunate juniors whom Jamey had specially selected. Lower-classmen were not allowed. Jamey and Bobby had ostracized the athletes who'd mocked Mickey and made it clear they were unwelcome. The popularity and respect for both of them trumped any discrimination against Mickey, and everyone mainly accepted him at that point. Mickey was still getting accustomed to his newfound sexuality. As far as I knew, he did act on his feelings but wasn't comfortable with public displays of affection.

Jamey and his mom presently inhabited his grandparents' picturesque Georgian Colonial manor. Although it was more traditional and subtle than the excessive residence he'd previously lived in, it was most definitely a mansion, considering it was four levels high and over 10,000 square feet wide.

I felt like I was in an outdoor casino as Nikki, Evan, and I perused our way through the perimeter of Jamey's estate. Floodlights illuminated the patio, and spotlighted plants and trees were strewn about the yard, making it easier to see in the dark. There was an unlimited amount of activity and partying transpiring as we made our way through the crowd. Jamey and several other attendees were involved in an intense volleyball game. Tons of people were swimming in the heated outdoor pool while others were relaxing in sun loungers or standing around the stamped concrete deck, engaged in conversation. Another handful of kids were drinking and vaping by the firepit.

While the three of us were getting beer from the keg, I noticed Kelly, Josh, and three other football players relaxing in the rectangular stainless steel hot tub, which is where I immediately longed to be. Although I had taken four pain killers before leaving for the party, my entire body ached. I was still high from the adrenaline of proving Mr. Rexes wrong. I had shown him that cheerleaders were capable of intense physical exercise. I felt damn good about that, but my body felt…well, it felt like I'd climbed up a rope using and straining every muscle in my legs, arms, shoulders, and back in the process.

Nikki happened to notice the newly installed whirlpool at the exact same time as I did, "Let's go in the hot tub!" she exclaimed.

"That is precisely what I was thinking," I said enthusiastically as I finished pouring beer into my plastic cup.

"Come on!" Nikki directed, tugging on Evan's arm and nearly spilling his beer in the process.

"I'm in," I announced, trailing behind Nikki and Evan.

Although there were already five people lounging inside the jacuzzi-style spa, it was large enough to fit at least five more people. Once Evan and Nikki noticed that everyone was in their underclothes, they looked at each other, shrugged, and immediately started stripping down.

I froze when I realized I didn't have a bathing suit, and my only option would be to go in wearing just my bra and panties. "I wish I had brought a bathing suit," I said in a somewhat whiny voice as I sat down on the porcelain tiles surrounding the hot tub and folded my legs under my bottom.

Kelly smiled good-naturedly, "Just shed your halter and capris and come in in your undies like the rest of us," she suggested.

"I don't wear *undies*," Josh scoffed.

Kelly giggled, "Whatever."

Josh met my eyes and smirked, "And I seriously doubt little Miss Prim, and Proper will let anyone dare to look at her virginal flesh."

"Shut up, Josh. I wear bathing suits all the time," I uttered defensively.

He rolled his eyes and looked away.

"Are you coming in, Jessica?" Nikki asked. She and Evan were already sitting comfortably next to Kelly with their legs intertwined and their arms around each other.

I looked up at the clear, cloudless sky and hugged my throbbing shoulders, "Um, I don't know. I want to."

"Well, what's stopping you?" Nikki inquired.

Kelly flapped her fingers, beckoning for me to join them, "Come on, Jess."

I desperately wanted to feel the warmth and gyration of the water, but I was still reluctant for two reasons. "Maybe," I said tentatively.

"I dare you," Josh declared in a dead pan tone, "I *dare* you to strip down to your..." he looked pointedly at Kelly and went on, "*undies* and come in."

Evan cleared his throat and tilted his head towards the volley ball game, "Um...I don't think that's a good idea."

Nikki looked at Evan crossly, "Why not?"

Up until that point, I hadn't realized the other boys were staring in my direction. Their eyes were as wide as saucers, and they wore matching expressions of alarm, fear, and possibly resentment.

"If you come in, I'm getting out," Caleb Flannery said. He rotated his head so he was facing the direction of the volley ball game.

"Why?" I asked, already knowing the answer.

Evan, Caleb, and the other two boys in the hot tub simultaneously pointed towards Jamey,

"Jamey will have a freaking fit if you get in here without clothes on," Tony Luciano, one of the other boys in the whirlpool, announced.

Matt Roarke nodded, "If you get in, we are all getting out," he piped in.

Josh tilted his head, brazenly widened his eyes, and sneered at me, "So, Jessica, are you going to come in and ruin everyone else's good time?"

"Fine," I said, "I won't go in." I felt disappointed because my entire body was in agony, and the solution was sitting right in front of me, but I didn't want to cause a scene or make everyone else unhappy.

"This is ridiculous," Nikki exclaimed.

Jamey was completely oblivious as to what was happening because he was engrossed in the game, but Nikki was about to make him fully aware of the situation. "Jamey! Come here! Jessica needs you," she ordered.

Although the party generated a considerable amount of noise because of all the talking, shouting, laughing, splashing, and so on, Jamey was able to hear Nikki's thunderous command.

He immediately looked in our direction, grinned, and winked at me. He put his left hand over his right, indicating a "time out," and came jogging over.

"What's up?" he asked, plopping down next to me.

We all quietly stared at him. No one was sure how to broach the topic. Jamey initially didn't even notice the tension permeating amongst us. He ignored everyone in the hot tub as he took my chin in his hand, turned my head so I was facing him, and lightly pecked me on the lips. "Hey, beautiful," he greeted, "I didn't even know you were here."

I smiled tightly, cognizant of the fact that Kelly, Erin, Josh, Nikki, Evan, and the other three boys were staring at us in anticipation. Jamey was still completely unaware of why he'd been summoned, but he didn't seem to care. He patted my thigh and tenderly tucked a strand of hair behind my ear, "You look gorgeous, babe. I could literally just eat you up." He started tickling my lower abdomen, and I scooted away.

I need a beer," he suddenly realized, looking around as if he knew someone would appear out of nowhere to produce one.

Sure enough, Aiden Prose, one of the juniors who'd been fortunate enough to get an invite, happened to walk by and overheard Jamey's statement, "Want me to get you one?" he offered.

"Sure. Thanks, man," Jamey said appreciatively.

In the meantime, Jamey took my beer, stole a sip, and handed it back, "Well, what did you need me for?" he inquired in a nonchalant tone.

I swallowed soundly and looked down, nervously tugging on my chin.

Jamey watched me, waiting patiently. I remained silent, refusing to meet his eyes; in my peripheral vision, I noticed his brows furrow with concern. He put his mouth to my ear and whispered, "Is something wrong?"

I shook my head, "No, I mean...I don't know, maybe."

"Talk to me," he pled, "What's the matter?"

When I didn't respond, he looked away from me and ran his eyes across everyone sitting in the whirlpool. "What's going on?" he questioned.

No one spoke for what seemed like minutes, but was probably only a couple of seconds. Jamey threw his hands in the air, "What the hell?" He was getting frustrated because it was obvious something was amiss.

Finally, Josh cleared his throat and raised his hand as if he were electing himself to be the mouthpiece for the group. "Well, Jamey...the problem is that Jessica wants to know...well, not just Jessica. All of us *guys* want to know if you are okay with Jessica stripping down and getting in the hot tub with us?"

When he was done, Josh tilted his head at me and smugly raised his eyebrows. I scowled at him.

"Um, NO," Jamey said with a sarcastic laugh, "I don't think so."

I sighed impatiently and shook my head. I wasn't going to argue. I knew he would get all territorial and over-protective about it- even though there was no difference between me wearing a bikini and he'd never had a problem with situations like that. Nevertheless, I didn't want to attract unwanted attention, so I just rolled my eyes at him and mumbled, "Whatever."

"You aren't her father," Nikki told Jamey with an edge to her voice.

Jamey smiled good-naturedly, "No, I'm not, but I don't want her in there practically naked with these perverts. You don't know how much shit I've heard from them in the locker room."

Josh chuckled, "And you're innocent of that?"

"I never said I was," Jamey retorted, "But that's not the point."

"Just forget it," I said angrily, "I knew you'd make a big deal out of it."

Jamey licked his lips and studied me before putting his arm around me and pulling me towards him, "Is it really that important to you?"

Kelly cleared her throat, "Wellll..." she began, drawing the word out, "Mr. Sexist challenged her, at least that's the way Jessica interpreted it...to climb to the top of the rope in gym class, and, well- she did."

"Another stupid move..."

"Shut it, Josh," Jamey ordered, aggressively pointing his finger at his friend, "I'm getting sick of the way you talk to her."

Josh threw his hands up as if in surrender.

Jamey hugged me tighter, "Listen, babe," he breathed in my ear. He was about to continue, but everyone was still watching us. Jamey mumbled, "What the...," his voice trailed off as he cupped his hands and belligerently released them as if setting a butterfly free.

"Mind your business!" he shouted. And just like that, all nine of our friends averted their gaze.

Once we didn't have an audience, Jamey looked at me imploringly, "If you really want to go in, why don't you let me go in with you?"

"I'm okay with you," he cleared his throat and pursed his full lips, "Um...taking your pants and shirt off, but only if you sit on my lap..."

"What?" I asked, narrowing my eyes.

"I'm not going to try anything, Jeez, Jess. Have I ever...in three years tried to do anything besides kiss you? I mean, seriously..."

"Sorry," I muttered, biting my lip. He was right. I knew I shouldn't accuse him of trying to touch me against my will. He had always been extremely respectful of my boundaries. "It was just an instinct. It just sounded like, you know. Sorry."

He smiled tenderly, "It's okay. I get it. Part of the reason I love you so much is because you're so pure and wholesome. It just turns me on." He got a mischievous glint in his gorgeous eyes, "Especially because I'm going to be the one to deflower you one day, and I can't wait."

"Jamey," I chided, in a singsong voice.

He placed his face inches from mine, "Can I kiss you?"

I nodded, and this time, he wasn't gentle. He forcefully pressed his lips against mine, then slid his warm tongue into my mouth, expertly moving it around. He nibbled on my top and then bottom lip, leaving me panting and breathless. Something stirred in me that I knew I wouldn't be able to keep at bay much longer. I wanted more. I suspected Jamey could read my mind because he had a satisfied grin on his face.

When he pulled away, he stood up and started taking his pants off, "I'm going in, and I want you to come with me," he informed me.

I watched until he was standing in his boxer shorts. I couldn't help admiring his perfect physique. He was all muscle, not an ounce of fat on his toned, bronze body. "Here, I'll stand in front of you so these jack asses can't see you. I don't want them trying to sneak a peek."

"I doubt they even want to," I mumbled, feeling embarrassed.

Jamey ignored me, but I noticed a duplicitous look pass between Matt and Tony when Jamey turned his back to them.

Although I felt safe with Jamey and was in enough pain to get past the awkwardness, I was a modest person and couldn't help but feel somewhat unsettled about disrobing in front of him. Jamey noticed my discomfort and was chivalrous enough to turn around.

"Okay," I whispered when I was standing in my underclothes.

Jamey took my hand, put his arm around my waist, and skillfully carried me in the hot tub with him. We managed to enter without attracting the attention of our peers, or at least they were good enough actors to continue their conversations without looking in our direction.

When Jamey had me firmly in his lap, he placed his sizeable hands on my shoulders and started massaging them in a soothing yet firm way, "How does that feel?" he asked.

"Good," I murmured, "Don't stop, please."

And he didn't. His hands were strong but also gentle. It felt heavenly. He was able to knead the knots out of not only my sore shoulders but also my back and neck.

"I'm not hurting you, am I? It feels good, right?" His voice was a mixture of seduction and concern.

"No. Yes. Yes, it feels so good."

Jamey snickered, "You really messed your back up, babe," he told me, "You are so tight."

"Well, Mr. Rexes is such a jerk. He made me so mad. I just felt like I had…"

"Shhhh…" Jamey commanded, "I get it. You're tensing up. Relax."

I took a deep breath and nodded. He was right, "Okay."

He kissed my cheek, "I'm proud of you," he claimed as he continued to work on my upper body, "You are one strong Chica."

I rested my head on his shoulder as he moved his hands down my arms, "Wow, your arms are in freaking knots. I'm going to work on these."

I was oblivious to our friends around us as I sat on his lap, and he moved his powerful fingers through the muscles in my limbs, alleviating the tension and pain- working his magic. I realized that we fit together like two puzzle pieces. At that moment, my body felt like it was exactly where it was meant to be, and I knew there was no one- no living soul whose frame could match mine so perfectly.

Chapter Twenty-eight: Sleeping and Sports

About a month after the rope climbing incident, in early October, Jamey was planning to have yet another party. It was becoming a weekly occurrence unless his mom was in town, which was rare, or someone else volunteered their home for an evening of waywardness and entertainment. Frankly, I was becoming sick and tired of the party scene. I loved spending time with Jamey and my friends, but the constant parties were becoming tiresome and, to be honest, rather dull. It was the same thing every weekend. It was becoming redundant.

It was raining that evening; therefore, the event would take place inside, and Jamey would put a limitation on the guest list. All of Jamey's gatherings were invitation only, and his friends on the football team basically acted as bouncers if unwanted classmates turned up. Jamey was only willing to host indoor events when he was able to hire a cleaning crew to tidy up after his parties. That way, he didn't have to worry about the aftermath of the shenanigans.

The main reason I was planning on shying out of this event was that I'd been taking college classes in the hopes that I'd have enough credits to start university as a second-trimester freshman. I intended to graduate early by taking online summer classes every year. I wanted to start my graduate degree as soon as possible. My goal was to eventually get my doctorate in psychology.

Jamey and my friends were disappointed I wouldn't be there, but I was determined to finish a paper for my advanced psych class. As I'd explained to Nikki earlier, the problem was that I had writer's block. Apparently, Nikki had "tattled" on me to my Aunt Gina, who felt the need to tell my dad, and that's how I ultimately ended up attending Jamey's latest get-together.

After dinner that night, I excused myself and went to my room. I was surprised to hear a knock on my door a few minutes after I took my psychology book out and opened my laptop, ready to tackle this essay again.

"Jessica, can I talk to you?" It was my dad.

"Sure," I replied, "It's unlocked."

My father walked into my room; he had one hand in his pocket and a glass of bourbon in the other. My parents usually stayed in on Fridays, except First Friday when they got together with Jenna and Nikki's families. Saturday was the day they typically engaged in social activities. My father was usually tired on Fridays after a long work week.

I was concerned about what he wanted to discuss, so I looked up at him with wide eyes and curiosity.

He cleared his throat and nodded at my bed, asking without words if he could sit down.

I nodded back. He took a long sip of his drink as he strode over to my bed. There were throw pillows all over, so he had to move a few out of the way before he took a seat. "I'll never understand why females like pillows so much," he said affably.

I laughed. "Mom bought most of them for me."

"Ah, well, that explains it. Your mom loves these," he said as he placed one in his lap.

"Well," my dad started, drawing out the word, "Aunt Gina called me earlier."

"She did?" I questioned, wondering what this had to do with me. They talked constantly; why would he feel the need to tell me they'd talked?

"Yeah, she said you were going to miss Jamey's party tonight."

I scrunched up my nose and narrowed my eyes, "Why would she tell you that?"

"I guess Nikki is concerned that you've been working too hard on this essay, and she told Gina...well, she wants you to enjoy yourself."

I looked at my father expectantly, waiting for him to continue.

He sighed and took another longer drink this time, "I think she's right, Jessica," he began, "I am so proud of what a hard worker you are. You have achieved an A average while taking higher-level classes every year. You've already accumulated several college credits, and you do deserve to take a break once in a while."

"But I do," I protested, "I go to parties all the time. I just really want to get this paper...."

"When is it due?" my father interrupted.

I looked down and murmured, "Next week."

My dad chuckled, "So you have an entire week to complete it. Go out tonight. Have fun. You'll be in college next year. You don't have to work yourself to death."

"It's just that I can't seem to get a handle on this essay for some reason. I keep trying to start it, but nothing is coming to me."

"Sometimes when you have writer's block, you need to step away from the writing so you can look at it with fresh eyes."

I looked at him for a few seconds without speaking. I realized he was right. I needed to take a break. I wasn't getting anywhere. I also wasn't in the mood to party. I was tired.

My father spread his legs out and put his hands on his knees, "I know it's none of my business, but I am happy to see that things have been progressing with you and Jamey. It's no secret that I've always liked him. I think…well, I have always thought you make a good couple. I'm sure he'd like to see you tonight."

"Okay," I said, sighing. "I'll call Nikki."

My dad smirked, "She's expecting your call."

I was only slightly annoyed with Nikki for convincing her mom to intervene and contact my dad, knowing he would cajole me into attending the party. Nikki always had my best interest at heart, and she was correct in her assumption that I had been working too hard and desperately needed a break. However, by the time we got to Jamey's, I was disappointed. A party was not what I wanted. What I wanted was to go to bed and sleep for twelve hours.

There was nothing out of the ordinary about this particular gathering. It actually felt a little like déjà vu. I'd been to so many parties at Jamey's over the years- and even though the scenery had changed since he'd moved back in with his grandparents- not much else was different. In fact, high school parties were similar, pretty much regardless of where they were held.

Everyone was relegated to the second floor, and Jamey made it clear no one was allowed in any other part of the house. Although only about forty people had been invited, it was a little crammed. Almost all the partygoers were drinking; some were engaging in conversations, others were playing a game of beer pong, and Jamey and some friends were playing a card game. The party was loud and boisterous- like all successful celebrations.

I drank one beer while listening in on conversations. I wasn't even feeling energetic enough to engage. Jamey hadn't even noticed that I was there. I told him I wasn't coming, and he was enjoying what appeared to be a round of poker.

I slipped away from Nikki, Evan, and a few of our other classmates and went to the bathroom, where I made the decision to call an Uber. I'd text Nikki once I left so she wouldn't try to talk me out of it.

I walked to the corner of the room and took out my cell phone. I was about to dial the number for an Uber when I felt myself being lifted in the air, and a big wet kiss landed on my cheek. "Hey, Babe, I thought you weren't coming," Jamey said as he placed me back on the floor.

"I shouldn't have," I said, yawning, "I am really, really tired. I was going to work on my essay, but my dad talked me into coming. He said I needed a break from it. He was right, but I am just not in the mood for a party. I'm so tired. I need to just go home and go to bed."

Jamey vehemently shook his head, "No, no. Don't leave."

I tilted my head and sighed, "I don't want to party, Jamey. I am so worn out. I can't even keep my eyes open."

He leaned in and kissed me; he tasted like beer and potato chips- but kissing Jamey was never unpleasant. "You are so sexy when you're tired," he purred, cupping my chin.

I half-smiled and ran my fingers through my hair, "I am not, and I just want to sleep."

"Well then, go to sleep," Jamey asserted, "Here."

I shook my head, "No, I'll just take an Uber."

"No," Jamey said flatly, "That's not even safe. You can sleep here. In my room."

"I don't feel comfortable...." I said, looking around at all the people having fun.

Jamey suddenly became animated, "Hey, listen. I'll leave Bobby in charge, and we can go upstairs to my room. It's a whole other section of the house. We'll have peace and quiet."

I opened my mouth to protest, but Jamey put a finger over my lips.

"Shhh, let me finish. I promise I won't touch you."

"I know," I said firmly, "I trust you. It's not that. It's just...well, first of all, I have no pajamas or soap. I have special soap I need to wash my face."

Jamey was standing erect, with his hands on his hips, and he was looking at me like I had two heads.

"Jamey, you're having a party. You can't just leave."

"It's my house. I can do whatever I want, and I trust Bobby."

"But I don't want to ruin your good time," I insisted.

Jamey licked his lips and placed his forehead against mine, "There is no place I would rather be than with you. I can do this," he spread his arms out, "anytime. I don't care about this. I want to be with you."

I stared at him, contemplating what to do.

"Please?" he asked so sweetly that I had no choice but to relent.

Jamey placed his hand on the small of my back and led me through the crowd. He was practically pushing me so no one could stop us- our peers were calling out our names as we quickly passed them by, but we ignored their greetings. As we strode towards a darkened crook, I realized I'd never actually been to this part of his new home before. The bend led up curved wooden stairs surrounded by a glass railing.

"My room is on the next floor," he explained, placing himself in front of me as he took my hand, "Careful, these stairs are a little steep."

When we arrived on the third floor, I noticed the walls were painted a bright white and had no photographs or pictures; they were basically just there to hold the house up. It all seemed so bare and in stark contrast to the other part of the house. There were four closed doors and nothing else. It was almost eerie. This entire floor was unadorned, empty. "This is my wing," Jamey explained.

I giggled, "It's kind of creepy."

Jamey playfully nudged me, "Well, you should have seen the way my grandparents had it decorated. The two rooms on that side are still guest rooms," he pointed to the closed doors on the left side of the hall, "They look like old people rooms," Jamey's voice had a shudder.

"Where is your mom's room?" I asked.

Jamey harrumphed, "When she's here, she sleeps on the first floor. She took the master bedroom. That's also where my grandparents stay when they visit, which is hardly ever. Luckily."

Jamey opened the door to what I presumed was his bedroom, "This is my haven," he said smiling, "I picked it because it gives me privacy...well, when my mom or other relatives are here."

"What about the guest rooms?" I asked curiously.

Jamey shrugged, "I guess my cousins or aunts and uncles might use them around the holidays if we have a full house, but they're empty for the most part."

I beamed as my eyes scanned Jamey's bedroom. It was almost a carbon copy of his room at his old house. I looked around, taking it all in. It was Jamey to a T. He had a bookshelf with hardly any books- instead, there were sports trophies, signed footballs and baseballs, stacks of vintage Playboys, and ancient sports magazines that I assumed were worth a lot of money. His walls were painted tan and covered with framed posters of Tom Brady and the Patriots. He had stacks of utilitarian pillows on his bed- nothing like the decorative throw pillows that covered mine, and a fluffy cotton bedspread with nothing on it but an enlarged football.

"Listen, I'll be right back," he said as he practically pushed me inside, "I have to get a few things and talk to Bobby. Make yourself comfortable. Put one of my t-shirts on. It will fit you like a nightgown. There are a ton of extra toiletries in the bathroom- which is right next door. Lucy, the housekeeper, keeps it stacked with all kinds of shit. Okay?"

I nodded as he walked towards the door. "I'll be right back," he said before kissing the top of my head. "Get comfortable."

While he was gone, I went through his dresser until I found a plain white T-shirt and a pair of socks. That was all I really needed to sleep in. The shirt fell to my knees, and the socks practically came up to meet them. When I went to the bathroom, I discovered Jamey was right. His bathroom had plenty of amenities to meet my needs for one night.

I waited for Jamey to come back before getting into his bed. There was a nightstand stacked with his iPad, phone, and laptop. I assumed that was his side of the bed, but I wanted to wait for an invitation before getting in.

When he came back, he was carrying a bottle of vodka. He showed me his mini fridge, which was standing right underneath his nightstand. He said if I needed water, there was a six-pack inside. I watched as he poured himself a glass of vodka and added orange juice from a jar he'd taken from his refrigerator.

He patted the bed next to him and pulled down the covers. I slipped inside. He came over and patted the covers around me, almost like he was tucking me in.

"You comfortable?" he asked.

I nodded and yawned.

He slipped next to me and started scrolling through his iPad, watching sporting events.

"Is this too loud?" he had the volume at a very low setting, and I was so exhausted I knew no amount of noise could keep me from sleep.

"No. It's fine."

He kissed the top of my head and pulled me to him. I rested my head on his strapping chest, and he put his arm around my shoulders. Before I knew it, I was sleeping cozily by his side.

Chapter Twenty-nine: The Point of No Return

Although we spent most holidays with my mom's family, Thanksgiving was the exception. That celebration had always been reserved for my dad's relatives. We rarely saw any of my father's kin except for Nikki's immediate family. This was partially because my dad and Aunt Gina had lost their parents in a car accident right after they graduated from college. They were twins and had always been close, but the death of their parents forged an even stronger bond. My aunt was actually the one who set my parents up when they all attended St. Padre Pio University together- the college I was bound for.

My mother and aunt became instant best friends when they met as roommates their freshman year. When Gina introduced my parents, there was an instant connection, which she had predicted. Gina also met my uncle Phil at college; the four of them had been practically joined at the hip ever since.

Soon after college, our respective parents married and started planning to start their own families. My mom and aunt bought ovulation kits because they wanted to have their firstborn children at the same time. When we were toddlers, our parents also decided to purchase homes in the same newly developed neighborhood. Although, in retrospect, it seems odd that it all worked out the way it did, while I was growing up, it was my "normal."

I didn't find it strange that our lives were entangled and synchronized in so many ways. For instance, both of dads were partners in the law firm started by my and Jenna's grandfathers. Although educated, our moms chose the "stay-at-home mom" route and raised us as sisters. And because the home I presided in was the only home I remembered, our living quarters and time together felt natural. We were extremely close, which was picture-perfect to me because Nikki along with Jenna were my rocks; in some ways, they were like my foundation.

Although we obviously saw Nikki's family regularly, we both only spent time with our paternal cousins in November. My dad's extended family was relatively small. His mother had been an only child, and his father had one brother. He had three cousins, and the oldest one elected herself as the event coordinator of Thanksgiving. It became customary for everyone else to just go along with it. She had very unconventional ideas about how we should spend the holiday. Every year, she would come up with a short vacation, the theme of which had nothing to do with Thanksgiving. This year, we traveled to "The Great Northern Lodge," a hotel, casino, and water park. My Aunt Gina found it hysterical that her cousin's proposals drove my mom crazy. My mom liked and expected things to "make sense," in my aunt's words. Of course, my mother was good-natured and easygoing, so she would grin and bear it. She would make snarky jokes with my aunt but never complained in front of the cousins.

We left for Massachusetts the Wednesday before Thanksgiving and planned to stay until Sunday. We drove up with my aunt's family because they could seat all twelve of us in their luxury van. My mother had a particularly terrible time that year. She hated the noise, the bright lights, the crowds. When Nikki's twin brothers got food poisoning and were forced to leave early, my aunt joked that my mom had somehow contaminated their food, so we'd have to depart the premises of what my mother had deemed the worst Thanksgiving ever.

We arrived home Saturday morning, and as usual, a huge party was planned for that evening. Nikki claimed that *everyone* was talking about it. It was at Halley Hopkins' house; she was in the junior class, and I barely knew her. All of our friends, except Jenna, were going, so Nikki wanted to go too.

"I'm so sick of parties," I complained on the ride home.

Nikki shrugged. "Well, what else is there to do?"

"We could go to the movies, a dance club, play cards or video games."

Nikki laughed, "We can do those things at parties," she interrupted.

"This girl probably doesn't even want us at her house. We don't even know her."

Nikki sneered, "Who cares? We're seniors, and our boyfriends are there. Besides, seriously. No one is going to turn us away from a party."

I sighed. "I don't know. I really don't feel like going."

"Aw, come on," Nikki said, "I heard she lives in an amazing house, and seriously it's going to be so much fun...she's having a DJ. You can dance all you want!"

I lightly shook my head. "I'm tired."

Nikki bit her bottom lip and grinned, "If you come, Jamey will be so happy to see you- just like the last time you surprised him at his party. And...." she stretched out the "d" at the end of the word, "after all the time he spent teaching you to drive- he will be so proud of you if you drive us to the party."

I sucked in air and let out a long breath. I was grateful to Jamey for being the only person patient enough to persist in teaching me to drive. He had taken me out almost every day for a month until I refined my skills.

"If I go, you have to drive back and forth with me," I told Nikki in a resigned tone, "I still can't drive alone without a licensed driver."

Nikki nodded vigorously. "Of course I will," she promised.

I turned my head away from her and looked out the window, "Fine," I muttered.

"Yay! Let's surprise both Evan and Jamey. Evan hates going to parties without me. You know how he is. And Jamey," her voice was a little too chipper, "He will be so excited to see...*his girl*," she said it in an annoying yet semi-cute voice.

I rolled my eyes as she squeezed my shoulder, but I couldn't stop the smile from spreading across my face. I had to admit things had been going so well with Jamey lately.

"Fine," I said again, and she winked at me with something like triumph.

Halley Hopkins' neighborhood was a few blocks away from mine. She lived in a sizeable ranch-style farmhouse in one of the most secluded areas in Rosevalley. Each resident on Tolland Avenue owned a ton of land. Therefore the homes were spread far enough apart to make it the perfect place to have a party. Considering none of her neighbors lived within close vicinity, they wouldn't be able to overhear the noise created by the festivity, and she'd avoid a visit from the police. The police in Rosevalley weren't super busy because there wasn't much crime. Therefore, the cops spent a lot of time breaking up parties on the weekends.

I could see a line of cars parked along the sidewalk outside Halley's house before I even turned onto her road. Nikki had to get out of the car and guide me while I parallel parked- I was still anxious about hitting cars when making that vehicular maneuver. Jamey had convinced me I wasn't bad at it, but it still made me nervous.

When I finally got it just right and stepped out of my car, I was assaulted with a deafening amount of noise. The music was blaring, and although her driveway was long and steep, you could hear people shouting and laughing from the street. I sighed, reluctantly accepting that this was going to be a long, tiring evening. Nikki seemed energized by the scene before us while it was already exhausting me. When did I start becoming so sick of this scene? My boredom with partying seemed to have come out of the blue. For years, I'd enjoyed this. Wasn't I too young to feel that this was immature and monotonous?

About a half hour after we arrived, once we'd made ourselves comfortable inside Halley's comfy, rustic house, I found myself feeling extremely disappointed. For one thing, her house wasn't "amazing," as Nikki had promised- there was nothing wrong with it, but it was pretty basic. Additionally, there was no DJ. I didn't know if Nikki had fabricated that or if she'd heard a rumor. I continued ruminating about the fact that I didn't want to spend the rest of my senior year doing this every weekend. Yet, it was the only thing my friends were interested in except Jenna. But Jenna was always off with her college boyfriend. Besides, things had been going so well with Jamey, and this is what he liked to do. Everyone loved partying. I was beginning to suspect there was something wrong with me. I adored spending time with Jamey and my friends, but I was so tired of this scenario.

I spent about an hour avoiding several people's attempts to give me a drink. There was no way I would drive at night with an ounce of alcohol in my system. I didn't even feel comfortable driving stone-cold sober yet. I made small talk with many of my classmates as I perused Halley's house, taking in the pastoral decor. I watched in dismay as her bucolic house was in the process of being destroyed. Beer was spilled all over an antique coffee table, one of the legs of a countrified entertainment center had been broken, and the couch in her semi-formal dining room had chips and salsa ingrained in the cushions. I actually felt bad for Halley because I knew she was probably drunk and wouldn't realize how much damage her classmates had done to her house until she woke up the next morning. I wondered where her parents were and when they were coming home.

When I'd found most of my close friends engaged in activities I wanted no part of- Nikki and Evan were making out in an armchair, Mickey was doing a keg stand, Kelly was playing strip poker, and Erin was shamelessly flirting with T.J. Robinson, I decided to find Jamey.

The problem was no one seemed to know where he was. I texted him a couple times, but shockingly, he didn't reply. That never happened. He usually wrote back within seconds. I asked several people if they'd seen Jamey, and most said they had run into him earlier but hadn't caught sight of him in a while.

Finally, I found Caleb Flannery, and he told me he thought he'd seen Jamey, Bobby, and Josh headed out to the pool area.

"Why would they do that? It's cold out."

Caleb shrugged, "Who knows? They're wasted. Maybe they decided to take a dip in the pool. You know how crazy they get."

I thought it was strange that they would be outside while everyone else was partying inside, but I decided to go out and look for him.

When I opened the screen door leading out to the pool, I noticed it was dark, but there was a light coming from the pool house. I heard noise coming from behind the closed door. It sounded like people were laughing and possibly cheering. I decided to head over to see what was going on. For some reason, I felt hesitant, but I had no idea why.

As I made my way towards the cabana, my heart began to thump so loudly and forcefully that it sounded and felt like someone was using it to play the drums. Something felt off, although I couldn't contemplate why. My brain was telling me that whatever was going on was jovial- after all, the noises I heard were merry- it was obvious that people were having fun. Yet, my gut sensed that something sinister was happening. At first, I took long strides toward the bright light and clatter from the enclosed area. Still, as I got closer and the sounds became clearer, I almost turned around and strode in the opposite direction. But I didn't. Instead, I began to tiptoe towards the pool house. When I got to the door, an instinct told me that it would be the point of no return if I opened it. I went back and forth in my head for what seemed like hours, but it was really only a couple minutes. Should I open the door? Should I let it be and go back inside Halley's house? I wanted to walk- no *run* away. Yet, I knew I couldn't do that. I had to see what was going on.

It felt like I was checking for heat when I placed my hand on the door - was I walking into a fire? I intuited that I was about to enter into a figurative inferno. I rationally knew I had the option to flee, but emotionally that was no longer a possibility. I listened for a second before cupping my fingers around the door knob. The sounds were loud yet indistinct. There was definitely a lot of laughter. In fact, the only clear-cut sound I could make out was Jamey's chortle. Although I was still hesitant, it was as if an extraordinary force seemed to cajole me into turning the handle and pulling the door open.

When I did, my mouth dropped open, and my head began to spin. I couldn't hear my rapid heartbeat any longer because it felt like it had stopped beating altogether. I had never imagined I would see what stood before me. It was a sight I would never be able to unsee.

Jamey's naked behind was what initially greeted me. He was leaning over a limp body that was strewn across a round aluminum table and belonged to a thin, medium-sized female. The rest of her body was out of view, but I could tell she was not standing erect because her limbs were stilted and didn't reach the vinyl floor.

Josh and Bobby were on either side of Jamey. None of them had seen me enter the room. Josh had his head thrown back, hooting and clapping his hands as he watched Jamey forcefully shoving himself into this girl. He was wearing boxer shorts but was shirtless, "Come on, man, hurry up," Josh commanded.

Bobby's underclothes were around his ankles, and his hardened penis was out, "I'm next," he announced as he stroked himself.

Jamey continued to snicker, "I'm not done yet." He hurriedly rammed himself in and out of the girl, holding onto her hips and grunting as he did so.

The boys were still unaware of my presence. They were too enthralled in what was obviously an orgy or at least that's what I initially thought.

I watched in horror for seconds before I stretched my neck out in order to get a glimpse of the girl Jamey was screwing. Her body was resting on the table, and her arms were swinging flaccidly at her sides. I gasped when I got a good look at the side of her smooshed face and noticed her eyes were closed.

"What the hell are you doing?" I yelled, "Is she asleep?"

All three boys turned to face me with horrified and shocked expressions. Things started to move fast- the very air around me seemed to bend and move in visible waves. Jamey struggled to pull his boxers up. He was panting and flapping his hands in the air as if to wave away what I saw. He pushed me away from the scene as Bobby and Josh rushed to the girl. I couldn't see what was happening. They were crowding her to block my view.

"Jessica, it isn't what…I know it looks bad, but…."

"Are you kidding me?" I shouted at him, "She was asleep. I saw her. Her eyes were closed!"

"No, she wasn't, Jess. She's just drunk." His breathing was rapid, and he started scratching at his head in a panic. He continued to walk towards me, holding up his hands as he might to a cornered animal, but I backed away.

I thrust my hands forward; palms facing out. "Stay away from me. You disgust me. You pig!" I was screaming at the top of my lungs, and I could feel the color draining from my face.

Jamey was anxiously clawing at his neck and shoulders, "This…this is bad, I know. I was just so, so drunk. She propositioned me. I didn't know what I was doing. I'm so sorry. Seeing you- it just instantly sobered me up. You have to believe…."

"Shut up, Jamey," I spat, "I don't believe a word you're saying. Just save your B.S."

He gulped, and his eyes began to blink speedily as I pushed past him.

I felt detached, as if I was watching this nightmare rather than playing a part in it, outraged that they were treating this girl as a non-person, and shocked that I had actually witnessed Jamey and my friends doing and saying such revolting things. I would have thought it impossible if I hadn't witnessed it with my own eyes. This couldn't be happening. It felt surreal. Unimaginable. Impossible. Not only did I walk in on Jamey having sex with another girl- but he was engaged in a foursome. And it appeared as if the girl was too intoxicated to consent.

I wasn't entirely surprised when I shoved my way past Jamey and saw the identity of the girl they were misusing. Kayla O'Neill. Kayla. The girl Jamey had obviously been taking advantage of for years. How could I have missed this? It certainly didn't shock me. It only made me angry and heartbroken on her behalf.

I ignored all the chaos that was ensuing with the guys as I watched Kayla. "Are you okay?" I asked her.

She didn't respond. Her eyes were currently open; slightly. They were like slits; they appeared almost skewed. You could barely see them because her smudged eyeliner and mascara overshadowed them. Her light brown hair was sticking out in all different directions, her shirt was unbuttoned, and her skirt was riding up her thighs. She was in shambles. I couldn't tell if she was completely conscious. She seemed confused, basically like an amnesia victim.

Without thinking, I started shooting questions at her; screeching, "Did you even know what was going on? Were you asleep? Did you consent to this?"

Josh now had his arm around Kayla's shoulders, and she wobbled between him and Bobby. Bobby's hands were at his sides, but he might have been acting as the other side of a wall that was holding Kayla up. I couldn't be certain.

For a few seconds, they were all silent. It definitely seemed as if Kayla was trying to get a sense of what was going on. Bobby couldn't even meet my eyes. He was looking down at the ground.

"Kayla?" I questioned again, "Did you just wake up? Are you...are you okay? Do you even know what was happening?"

"Jessica, stop saying she was asleep." Josh ordered through gritted teeth, "You have no idea what was going on, and you don't know what you saw. You're making shit up based on your own bullshit ideas about sex."

I glared at Josh and shook my head, "Don't try to gaslight me, Josh. I'm not stupid." I became more enraged as I absorbed his words, "You're full of crap. You think putting me down makes what you did okay."

"None of us did anything wrong, Jessica," Josh said my name as if it pained him, "Some girls like doing things like this. Don't accuse us...in fact, *how dare you* accuse us of forcing her. I mean, who the hell do you think you are? She was the one who started this."

Bobby piped in in a gentle tone, "I promise you this was completely consensual, Jess. It might have somehow looked different, but it wasn't. I swear on my life."

Kayla finally gulped and looked around at the boys. Then she adjusted her face and glared at me, "I'm fine. You bitch. I am fine," her words poured out of her mouth like syrup- sticking and slurred. She turned to Josh and then Bobby, widening her eyes as she struggled to focus. Finally, her eyes rested on Jamey. I noticed a pleading expression on his face when he met her eyes. Was he asking her to lie?

"Jessica, look. I didn't think you'd be here. I drank way, way too much," Jamey began.

"It was my fault," Bobby mumbled, "I knew he was drunk, and Kayla was the one who had the idea. Right, Kayla?"

Kayla nodded, "Yeah. It was, Missss Jessica, my idea. Miss frigging *perfect*, Jes-si-ca," she spat, tripping over my name, even as she managed to make it sound like profanity. "I want...wanted to hook up with...with Jamey. We've done it before...not the first time," she laughed without humor and took a deep breath, steadying herself. "But this was the first time Josh..join...joined."

"Jamey was beyond drunk, Jess. Josh overheard us talking," Bobby continued.

"And I asked if I could join in," Josh said, "Kayla was the one who suggested it in the first place. We basically dragged Jamey along."

I stood open-mouthed. I couldn't believe they were all justifying what I had walked in on. I felt like I was in an episode of the Twilight Zone.

Jamey looked at me with an expression of desperation. "I wouldn't have done it if I was sober. I swear."

Kayla laughed again, "Yeah," she muttered, "He only screws me when...when he's drunk. When he's at parties, and then he pretends I don't..ex...ex...ist after."

I walked towards Kayla, unconvinced that this hadn't been a gang bang, "Kayla, are you okay? I mean, even if you started out wanting this. It's not alright for them to continue if you passed out. Are you sure..."

"Please just shut...shut up?!" Kayla yelled, "You are such a phony, stuck-up bitch. This is all YOUR fault. She lunged forward and I thought she might actually push me, but Bobby grabbed and steadied her. This wouldn't have even happened if you knew how to take care of your man. If you did, I wouldn't have to do it for you. You're nothing but a dicktease."

It wasn't Kayla's words that made me feel as if I'd been struck, it was the tone of her voice. She *really* hated me. I'd always pitied her, and I was aware she didn't care for me, but I didn't understand the depth of her wrath until that moment. Being despised to that degree- even in a situation like this was somewhat shocking. It caught me off, guard.

I sucked in a gulp of air and immediately felt the need to flee. I swung open the door to the pool house and started to run. I needed to find my car. I needed to get the hell out of there.

I literally sprinted across the lawn in the direction of the long, winding driveway. It wasn't until I was on the pavement that I heard footsteps behind me. "Wait, Jessica!" Jamey yelled, "Please stop. I need to talk to you. We need to clear this up."

"Leave me alone!" I yelled, refusing to look back and face him.

I'd almost reached my car when I felt his hand on my shoulder. I felt as if his touch had burned my skin. "Get your hands off of me," I ordered through gritted teeth.

I swallowed soundly when I noticed he had tears in his eyes. I didn't think Jamey was even capable of crying.

"I messed up," he whispered pleadingly, "I am so sorry. I can't even tell you how sorry...."

"I can't even look at you." I spat, "Stay away from me. I hate you!"

I ran to my car, swung the door open, and sped away. When I was a block away, I pulled over on an abandoned street. I leaped out of the car while it was still running and vomited. Tears started pouring down my cheeks as I wretched three more times. Once my insides were empty, I returned to my vehicle, took my phone out, and powered it off. Then I turned the car off, placed my head in my hands, and sobbed.

Chapter Thirty: Texts and Emails

<u>Sunday morning</u>- Fortunately, when I got home Saturday night, my parents were sound asleep. They were both exhausted from the trip, and expressed the necessity of getting a good night's sleep. Before I'd left for the party, I heard my mom suggest that they both take one of her rarely used sleeping pills so they'd be rested for church and brunch the next morning. My dad had surprisingly agreed, although he usually shied away from taking medicine. I knew I needed to fall into a dreamless slumber in order to escape the horrible memory of what I'd witnessed. I needed time to process what I'd seen and what I planned to do about it. But, that certainly wasn't going to happen that night or anytime soon. I knew my only reprieve would be to turn my cell off, sneak into my mom's vanity and steal a few of her pills. They would knock me out, and I wouldn't be awakened by phone messages.

The next morning, I faked sick, and after my family left for Mass, I mistakenly powered up my phone. I was assaulted with a barrage of texts and voicemails. I almost felt numb at that point. Despite a full, dreamless night of sleep, I was still drained- depleted. There were no more tears left to cry at that point. For the time being, I was so shocked and disoriented, it was almost as if I was anaesthetized. As I pressed the power button on, and saw the screen light up, I wasn't surprised in the least to see how much I'd missed. I also wasn't surprised by the content of the of texts and voice messages awaiting me.

Josh (voicemail)- Seriously, Jessica. You better not repeat a word about any of this. This is none of your business. You should have knocked before you walked in. You can't be so stupid, thinking that Jamey was faithful to you while you held out on him all these years. He's a normal guy. He has needs. No offense, but you are frigid and I'm not going to let you start spreading lies about me. Just keep your mouth shut.

Nikki (text)- Call me ASAP! What happened? Josh is all pissed off. He's talking crap about you. I told him to shut up, but he ignored me. He actually pushed past me, and Evan was like, *What the hell is the matter with you?* He's like a crazy person- ranting and nobody knows what he's going on about. WTF? And I can't believe you left.

I mean, I'm not mad. Of course not. I'm worried about you. I thought you couldn't drive without me. WHAT HAPPENED??? Did something happen with Jamey? I think that's what Josh is mad about, but what does it have to do with him? He's talking to Kelly and Erin now. I can see him waving his hands around, and they look all sad like they feel sorry for him. Call me. Love you!

 Erin (text)- Wow! Jessica, Josh told us what you walked in on. I'm so sorry that you saw Jamey cheating on you. Or I don't know if it would be considered cheating. Josh doesn't think so. I mean, you never did commit to him. I always suspected that Jamey might be screwing around with other girls, but I never knew for sure. I hope you're okay. Josh said you were yelling at him and Bobby and he doesn't know why. He said the guys were all talking by the pool house, and Kayla came out and hit on Jamey. Apparently, Jamey was drunk and went along with her. She kind of pressured him. Are you mad at Josh and Bobby because they didn't stop Jamey? I can understand that, but you know how guys are. Josh wasn't making all that much sense. Do you think you'll ever forgive Jamey? Anyway- call me! I am worried about you!

 Kelly (text)- Hey, hon. Call me. I am so sorry about what happened. I really never knew Jamey was sleeping with other girls, but I'm not completely surprised. He just has so much, you know testosterone, and when girls are hitting on a guy like him all the time, well... I am NOT saying it's okay, but it was probably just too tempting because you wouldn't- I hope this doesn't offend you. I really don't mean it in a bad way at all. But you wouldn't meet his needs. I still totally think he was in the wrong. You must be so upset. Josh said he and Bobby were standing outside the pool house, while Jamey was inside with Kayla. Then you came outside and stormed in on K and J. Jeez...I know it must have sucked to see that. I get that you're upset, but why are you blaming Josh and Bobby? I'm confused. Well, I guess I kind of understand. I'm here for you when you're ready to talk. Call me.

 Josh (text)- I am so freaking serious Jessica. You better not repeat a word about this. It is not your business, plus you were hysterical, like a lunatic. You weren't making any sense. Making accusations that are complete lies. Kayla was right. This is all your fault. And I cannot believe you had the nerve to say the things you did. Why do you think I never liked you? Always so high and mighty. Always thought you were better than everyone else. And just because you're such a damn prude, doesn't mean everyone else is. Keep your mouth shut!

Bobby (voicemail) – Jess, I am so, so, SO sorry. We were all so drunk. I know it looked bad. It was bad. I am not going to say what we did was okay, but you need to know that she asked- no, I mean begged…she literally begged me to get Jamey so we could do what you saw. She was drunk. Jamey was so drunk. Josh and I drank a lot too. I couldn't see her face. I don't know if it looked like, you know. But, she was the one who wanted it. I know you'll never forgive Jamey. At least, I don't think you will. I don't know what else to say. I really, really care about you, Jess. You are one of my best friends. Please call me so we can talk about this.

Jamey (voicemail)- Jessica, you have to forgive me. I was so drunk. I had no idea what I was doing. She just hits on me constantly. She's so desperate. She begs me to screw her. All the time. You think she was too drunk to consent. Jess, it was the other way around. I had no idea what I was doing. Even Bobby and Josh admitted they all pressured me- including Kayla. I don't even know how I managed to get it up. I can't stand her. She's the one who's a predator. Why do you think I got so mad at her on the bus that time? You know, guys can be victims too. I shouldn't have had so much to drink. I should have had more self-control. But, if I wasn't drunk, I never would have done it. She stalks me at parties when you're not there. I had to block her number from my phone. This is all her fault. Please, please forgive me. I love you so much. I can't stop sobbing, Jess. I never cry. Never. This is how much I love you. Call me. You have to please…you have to forgive me.

Jenna (text)- I seriously cannot believe what just happened. Josh had the nerve to call me and try, TRY is the key word. He TRIED to bad mouth you. I literally just told him that he better shut his mouth or I would kick his ass. We had a huge fight, and I ended up hanging up on him. He was enraged, but I wasn't having any of his crap. I honestly don't even know what he was getting at. He was talking in circles. It was so obvious he was lying because he was so defensive. He mentioned you seeing something you shouldn't have- something with Jamey, and that he and Bobby were there. Jessica, call me. I'm waiting. I'll wait until you're ready. Just know I'm here for you whenever you need me- no matter what time it is- I'll drop everything. I love you.

WTF did those degenerates do?

Josh (voicemail)- I am still so pissed off at you and your ridiculous allegations. How dare you? Why would I or Bobby or Jamey- the most sought after guys in school need to force someone? You really are an idiot when it comes to social situations. You might be book smart, but you have no common sense. I will retaliate if you tell anyone what you THINK you saw. I'm not afraid of your family. My parents have influence too. Just shut up about it. Don't breathe a word to anyone or I seriously don't know what I'll do.

  Me (text)- Josh, I am not, nor will I ever be afraid of you. So, don't you ever threaten me again. If I wasn't so disgusted, I would laugh at your stupidity. Just think of the evidence I have that I could use against you. You have the nerve to insult my intelligence while leaving threatening texts and voicemails on my phone. By the way, you are the moron telling everyone that something happened. Not me. I am going to block your number so I don't have to worry about getting any more messages from you. I've heard enough from you. Now it's my turn. And I'm not making a threat. I'm making a *promise*. Stay away from me. Don't you dare speak my name to our friends or anybody else. If I find out, you are spreading rumors or lies about me, you will regret it. If aren't convinced that I am capable of retaliating against you, try me. I dare you.

  After texting Josh, I threw my phone against the wall, took the third sleeping pill I'd stolen from my mom the night before, and went back to bed.

Chapter Thirty-one: Unknown Caller

I slept through my phone buzzing with text messages and calls until dinner time. When my mom came to my room and checked on me, I told her I thought I had a virus. I feigned a stomachache and nausea. Considering I rarely attempted to avoid family obligations, she believed me without question. I went back to sleep and didn't wake up until it was dark out. Although, I heard lots of noise coming from my cell for hours, I was able to ignore it. That is until precisely 8:52 P.M., when my phone started ringing for the hundredth time that day, yet somehow this time I instinctively knew I had to answer it.

I've been trying to find the nerve to call you all day.
Hi, Kayla.
I think you know why I'm calling.
No, actually I don't.
Listen, Jessica. I'm sorry for what I said last night. I shouldn't have been so nasty. I WAS drunk, never ASLEEP, but yes, I was drunk.
Okay, I accept your apology.
Listen, please don't hang up.
Jessica, are you still there?
Yeah, I'm still here.
I really need you to promise me something. I know I have no right to ask you for anything, but…I would never call you if it wasn't just really, super important.
What is it, Kayla?
I'm waiting. What do you want from me?
I want, no I NEED you to promise me that you won't tell anyone what you saw.
I'm not the one you have to worry about. Josh is the one telling people. I haven't said anything to anyone.
I already talked to Josh. He is afraid you're going to feel obligated to, I don't know lie about what happened.
Lie? Feel obligated to lie? That doesn't make any sense.
Josh said you're jealous about Jamey cheating on you so you might try to twist the story and say Jamey was forcing me.

*Kayla, I've known Josh for a very long time. He is not concerned about Jamey. He's too selfish for that. He's afraid I'll tell people what I saw **him** doing.*

Josh wasn't doing anything. The truth is that Jamey was having sex with me. Nothing happened with Josh and Bobby.

I'm not stupid, Kayla. It looked like a gangbang to me.

Well, it wasn't. It's really none of your business, but I do like kinky sex. A gangbang makes it seem like I didn't consent, but I did. In fact, like we told you last night, I initiated it.

Like I said, Kayla, even if you did ask for it, it doesn't mean it's not rape if you fell asleep in the middle.

RAPE? RAPE? Please do not use that word. That's not what it was. Please don't go around telling people that. You'll ruin my reputation. I will be the one that becomes a pariah. Not them. Me.

Are you covering for them? You don't have to do that. They shouldn't get away with…

They didn't do anything wrong. Will you please stop saying things like that? You don't know what you saw. I close my eyes during sex because I enjoy it. Lots of people close their eyes while they're doing it. Since you're a virgin, you wouldn't know anything about it, so maybe you should stop throwing around opinions and allegations about things you know nothing about.

My sex life is none of your business. Leave me out of this.

Oh please, everyone knows what a tease you are. I'm really trying to be nice here because I know you have the power to ruin my life. And maybe you will. Maybe you're so jealous that you will. You act like you're better than that so I hope in this case, you put your money where your mouth is.

*Jealous? You think I'm **jealous** of you? I feel sorry for you. I pity you because you let boys like Jamey use you. I tried to help you.*

I don't believe you. How could anyone walk in on their boyfriend screwing someone else and not feel jealous?

I wasn't jealous. I was disgusted.

Disgusted, yeah. Well, that's because like Josh says you're such a prude. So holier than thou. I can't stand girls like you.

I'm honestly not trying to be mean, but I could care less about your opinion.

You're not trying to be mean? What are we in grade school? That is so typical of something you would say. Unbelievable!

What is the matter with you? What have I ever done to you? You're the one who's been chasing after my boyfriend for years. I should hold a grudge against you. Not the other way around.

Like I said, if you did your job, I wouldn't have to.

Goodbye, Kayla.

No, No. I'm sorry. This isn't why I called. I shouldn't have said those things.

I'm not going to tell people what I saw. You made it clear that that's not what you want. It is your business. I'm perfectly aware of that. It's not my place to gossip about it. Okay?

I'm not sure if you understand, Jessica. I mean- you can't tell your friends about this. Like if Erin or Kelly knew, they might tell other people. We both know how easy it is to for a couple people to spread something like this around the whole entire school. Everyone would hate me.

*Why do you think everyone would hate **you**?*

Are you serious? Because I'm a nobody. And you're Miss Popular. Everyone thinks you're so perfect, and I slept with your boyfriend. Plus, if people knew I was with three guys at once, they'd judge me just like you did.

I did not judge you.

Whatever. That's not the point. If you breathe a word about this to anyone, my life will be hell. My reputation will be ruined. I'll go from being a nobody to a literal pariah. And maybe you don't care about me, but if you really are such a good person, you wouldn't let this get out.

I have no intention of telling anyone. You don't have to worry about that. Okay?

Thanks.

Okay, then good...

Wait, I also have one more thing to tell you.

What?

I got off track before because...I'm sorry, I really am. But you make me so mad, and I couldn't control myself.

Why is that? I mean, I'm not offended. I won't go back on my word; I just really want to know.

Never mind. What does it matter? Why would you care what a nobody like me thinks? Besides, you just admitted that you didn't care about my opinion of you.

You're asking me a favor. So, in return, I want you to tell me why you can't stand me. It's not that I care *about your opinion. I'm just curious about why I infuriate you. I don't look down on you. I don't look down on anyone. I certainly don't consider you to be a 'nobody.' You're not any less important than I am. I don't think like that. Everyone is equal in my opinion.*

    This is why. **This**. You are like the 'cliqueyest' girl in school. You barely acknowledge anyone besides your small group of friends, who all happen to be cheerleaders and football players- Nikki and Jenna, Erin, Kelly, Bobby, Mickey, Jamey, of course and everyone knows you and Josh are frenemies. Everyone knows because you're like a freaking high school celebrity. You pretend you don't care about how popular you are, but to me, it's obvious that's bullshit. I don't have a problem with people like Jenna. She's gorgeous. She's your stereotypical cheerleader, and everyone adores her, but she's not fake. She doesn't pretend to be so caring and sensitive. She doesn't…

    Okay, Kayla. I got it. I'm fake and phony. I don't need to hear more. What else do you want from me?

    I just wanted you to know that not only was what you saw consensual, but it wasn't Jamey's fault. He was really drunk, and he could hardly walk. We did, all of us did pressure him.

    Even if that's the case, you said this has happened before. What was Jamey intoxicated every time he was with you? How many times do I have to tell you? No matter what you think of me, I'm not stupid. Did Jamey tell you to say that to me? Did Jamey tell you to lie to me?

    No, Bobby asked me to tell you the truth.

    Well, thanks so much for passing that on to me. You can tell Bobby that it doesn't change a thing. I don't want anything to do with him or Jamey. As far as I'm concerned, they can both…never mind.

    Jessica?

    Jessica?

    Are you there?

    Hmmm…I guess she hung up.

    Figures. That self-righteous bitch always has to have the last word.

Chapter Thirty-two: An Unexpected Visitor

Considering I never missed school and, in the past, had even tried to persuade my mom to let me go in when I was genuinely sick, I was able to convince my parents I had a horrible stomach bug for an entire week. They insisted I remain home and asked my teachers to send any missed work home with my sister, Sara. It certainly wasn't difficult to pretend I didn't feel well. Although I hadn't contracted an illness, I was psychologically damaged. My grief triggered physical effects that mirrored an actual virus. Due to my extreme anxiety, I couldn't stop perspiring. I was also legitimately nauseated and sick to my stomach. It was the sorrow that created a sallow, ashen hue to my normally rosy complexion. I had no desire to get out of bed. The only people I was willing to speak to, aside from my family members, were Nikki and Jenna. Nikki assumed I caught Jamey cheating on me because that's what Josh told Evan. She was sympathetic but basically at a loss for how to console me. Jenna was savvy enough to recognize there was more to the situation. She knew I needed space but made me promise to contact her when I was ready to unload. We both knew she would be the one I would eventually lean on- she would be my rock, as always.

I was lying in bed on a Friday afternoon, staring at the ceiling, once again going over the horrific events I'd seen less than a week ago, when my sister, Sara, swung the door to my room open and pranced in.

I looked up, startled, "What are you doing?"

"You have a visitor," she announced with a haughty expression.

"Who?"

"Mickey. He said he's come in peace. He actually gave me a ride home."

I snickered, "What is that supposed to mean?"

Sara sighed, "It means he's not going to try to persuade you to forgive Jamey. He just wants to talk to you."

"What do you know about it?" I asked, perplexed that she had any knowledge of the situation.

Sara sighed for a second time, but it was more drawn out this time, "Jessica, I've heard things. And I know you're not sick. I'm actually worried about you. I was going to try to talk to you, but Mom and Dad said to leave you alone."

"You were worried about me?" I couldn't hide my astonishment at Sara's concern. After all, she'd basically shown nothing but jealousy and irritation toward me our entire lives.

Sara sat on the edge of my bed and looked into my eyes, "Yes, even though we fight, you're still my sister, and I obviously care about you. I think it would be a good idea for you to talk to Mickey."

I shook my head, "No, I'm not going to talk to him. He's just going to try to convince me...."

"No," Sara interrupted, "He's not. He promised."

"Well, I'm still not in the mood. Tell him to go away."

Sara licked her lips, and her face took on a staid, sober expression, "Jessica, if you don't talk to Mickey, I'm going to tell Dad that I'm worried about you."

My mouth dropped open, "You wouldn't?" I whispered, yet I knew she was concerned enough to do it. Although Sara and I had never been close, we always covered for each other. Neither of us would stoop so low as to tattle. Yet, I knew, in this case, that wasn't what Sara would be doing. If she did what she was threatening to do, she would be "telling on me" for my own benefit- not to get me in trouble.

Her green eyes stayed glued on mine; neither of us looked away. It was a battle that I knew I was going to lose. "It's been a week," Sara finally said in a pleading tone, "You need to get out of bed. Mickey came to me. We talked a little. I swear, Jess, he has your best interest at heart. He really does. He's a good guy.." She looked away, "Unlike some of his friends."

I blew air through my nose and rubbed my temples, "Fine," I snapped, "Tell him I'll be there in a minute. I have to get dressed."

After I threw on a pair of yoga pants and a sweatshirt, I walked outside to find Mickey sitting in a wicker chair on my front porch. My mom was constantly redecorating. She had just added a new black and white checkered area rug and a rustic rectangular-shaped "Welcome" sign." I plopped myself down in the wicker chair's twin across from Mickey.

He leaned forward in his chair and clasped his hands, "Hey," he said with a sad smile.

I didn't bother with pleasantries, "Why are you here, Mickey?'

Mickey lightly shook his head, "I'm not entirely sure. I've been thinking of you and wanted to see how you're doing."

I studied him, unconvinced that his primary reason for being here was innocuous.

He laughed nervously and lifted his hands, palms facing out, "I swear, I am not here on Jamey's behalf. In fact, he doesn't even know I came. I actually saw your sister and made a last-minute decision to visit you. She told me your parents wouldn't be around for a while so I decided to just show up."

"O-kay," I replied, "If you're not here on Jamey's behalf, what is it that you want to talk to me about?"

"Listen, Jess," he began earnestly, "I know we're basically part of a group. We've never been super close- just the two of us. We've probably never even had a one-on-one conversation, but we have been friends for years, and I care about you. You're a good person, and I feel bad about all this. I guess I came to tell you I support you."

I looked at him curiously. "Really? What exactly do you mean by that? Jamey and Bobby are your best friends, and Josh too."

Mickey waved his arm dismissively, "Josh is a piece of shit. I never considered him a friend."

"But Jamey and Bobby- you've been friends since you were kids."

Mickey nodded, "Yeah, and we're still friends. I don't have to take sides. They don't want me or anyone else to take sides. They feel terrible. Jamey's a mess."

When I narrowed my gaze, Mickey lifted his head and stared at the sky, "I'm not defending him. I'm just being straight with you." He suddenly guffawed. "Straight, yeah, that's not something people associate with me these days."

I smiled at him, "Anyone who doesn't accept you is ignorant, and their opinion doesn't matter."

"Thank you," Mickey said.

"Don't thank me. I'm just telling the truth."

Mickey nodded once, "Well, I guess I'm thanking you now because I didn't before. You were very vocal when the gossip about me started. You stuck up for me, and it did help."

"Actually, at first, I wanted to say more. I felt like I didn't say enough. But I didn't want to stir the pot."

Mickey tilted his head and looked at me with a knowing grin.

I threw my arms in the air, "What? Why are you looking at me like that?"

"You have always been so hard on yourself. You need to give yourself more credit. You ended up going out of your way to defend me. You didn't have to do that. It honestly meant a lot to me."

"Of course," I said empathetically, "But I wasn't really the persuasive one. I think anyone who was opposed to your sexuality was either intimidated by Jenna or afraid of Jamey and Bobby."

"That's true," Mickey agreed, "They definitely influenced a certain population of people, but there's also the quieter group of kids that listen and follow people like you."

I examined him quizzically before he continued, "The...I guess you could say the judgmental, sanctimonious types. When you spoke out in my defense, they stopped turning their noses up at me. They figured, I guess, that if a good Catholic girl like you is tolerant of me, they should also be. Some people are so impressionable, right?"

"Right, well, I am glad I did help. It's pretty shocking that in this day and age, people are still so mean-spirited and pious about sexuality. I never would have thought your coming out would cause such a stir. I mean, other people have, and no one even noticed, but I guess that's because...."

My voice trailed off, but Mickey continued for me, "No one expects a big strong football player to be gay. It's okay if you're an effeminate choir member or a 'butchy' female basketball player...such bullshit stereotypes."

"That's exactly what they are."

We sat in silence for a while before Mickey spoke again, "You know, I never thought Jamey was good enough for you."

"Why didn't you tell me that three years ago?"

"I should have, but he was...*is* my best friend, but even with that being said, "I saw what was happening, and in retrospect, I can't say that I would do anything differently. It wasn't my business. I witnessed him manipulate you. At times, I guess I thought you were complicit."

It was my turn to cut him off, "I was."

Mickey licked his lips, "Ever since you caught Jamey with Kayla, he's been wrecked...destroyed. I've never seen him like this, and I'm not trying to lay a guilt trip on you."

"Good because it wouldn't work."

"I totally get that, Jess," he said with sincerity, "I only brought it up because I don't feel sorry for him. I watched him cheat on you for years. I knew he was doing it. I was torn, and so was Bobby. Jamey kept saying that you refused to be his girlfriend, but if you would, he'd stop screwing around. I feel bad that I knew and never said anything. I know Bobby feels the same way, but it was such a tricky..."

"I get it," I interrupted, not wanting to discuss Bobby's role in the vile scene I'd witnessed, "I can understand why you couldn't tell me. You don't have to explain. You and I were never super close. I trust Nikki and Jenna. I KNOW they weren't aware of Jamey's 'extracurricular activities.' But Erin and Kelly...the girls- we were all best friends since ninth grade. If Erin and Kelly knew and didn't tell me. I can't get past that."

Mickey shrugged, "I honestly don't think they knew. Jamey wouldn't have risked that."

We sat in comfortable silence for a few minutes, digesting everything we'd discussed. Finally, Mickey leaned forward and tenderly put his hand on my shoulder, "I guess it comes down to one thing- even if I felt like my hands were tied, even though I know that if I could go back in time, I wouldn't betray Jamey. I still...I still want to apologize."

"Are you here to apologize because you feel sorry for me?" I replied as I felt my eyes unexpectedly fill with tears.

Mickey looked stricken, "No...please don't think I pity you. That's not why I'm here." He got to his feet and then knelt before me.

"I know, I know," I said, wiping at my tears, "You're here because you're a nice person who just happens to have a jerk for a best friend."

We both giggled, which broke the tension, and Mickey returned to his seat, "I know all this crap just happened, and it's probably not the right time for me to say this, but you'll meet someone who's more your equal one day. Someone ethical and intellectual and mature, like that guy LaVonn you were dating. I was honestly shocked when you broke up with him for Jamey."

"Yeah," I agreed, shaking my head, "what a stupid move."

Mickey sighed, "Not stupid. It's just that our emotions get in the way of common sense sometimes. It happens to the best of us."

I scrunched my nose and smirked, "Since when did you become so deep? Aren't you supposed to be the class clown?"

Mickey raised his eyebrow and playfully gave me a reproachful look, "Now you're throwing around stereotypes?"

"Sorry," I murmured, "I suppose we all do it sometimes."

"It's human nature," Mickey agreed.

"You know what I keep thinking?" I asked, deciding to seek desperately needed answers now that we were engaged in a heart-to-heart. I trusted Mickey to be honest with me, "How could I not know? I mean, did he do such a good job of hiding it? Was everyone so afraid of speaking out? Now, when I look back at these girls who stared at him or made snide remarks, how could I not know?"

At that point, I couldn't stop the tears from spilling down my cheeks, "I mean, how could all this have been happening, and I was so blind to it? Maybe Josh is right. Maybe I'm book smart, but I have no common sense."

Mickey ran his hands through his hair and gently shook his head, "You didn't want to know, so you convinced yourself it wasn't true. I mean, look at me. How did I not know I was gay for sixteen years? I didn't want to acknowledge the truth, just like you didn't want to follow what I assume were your instincts about Jamey."

Mickey paused before adding, "And don't listen to Josh." His voice had an edge to it, "He's always been jealous of you."

"Why would he be jealous? I don't have any advantages over him. There's absolutely no reason for him to be jealous. People like my mom always say things like that. I don't believe that the only reason someone would dislike me is that they're jealous. Josh always hated me for some reason, and it's not out of jealousy."

Mickey laughed without humor, "Josh is an ass. He's not a good guy. He has no loyalty. He only cares about himself. Do you really care whether he likes you or not?"

"Actually, no. But he's not the only one," I cried, "This is another thing that's been bothering me. Why are there so many people who don't like me? Josh. Kayla. Remember that girl from my English class who wrote a poem about me…I mean, what is it about me? Am I so intolerable? I don't get it?"

Mickey sighed heavily, "I don't think there's anything unlikeable about you. I guess you're right; although some people are jealous, that's not always the reason for animosity. The only thing I can tell you is it's not you. It's not about you. People who have a problem with you have some deficiency within themselves. Some cliches are said often because there's truth to them."

I smiled, "You mean the old, 'it's not you, it's me' cliché?"

Mickey nodded, "Do you know how many girls I used that line on?"

We both doubled over in laughter.

Mickey stood, and I followed suit.

He hugged me, and I easily fell into his embrace. "Thank you for coming by," I said gratefully.

"I'm glad I did," he replied, heading towards his car. As he opened the door to his light blue Prius, he called up to me, "Jessica, one more thing."

I watched him intently, waiting to hear more wise words. I had to admit I was surprised by Mickey's wisdom. I had never seen this side of him before.

"This might not make sense," he began in a sorrowful tone, "But, I think, unfortunately, some people…How do I say this?" He looked up at the sky, contemplating his words, "I think there are kids in school who don't like you because you don't fit into a box. You don't fit the stereotype of what a pretty, popular cheerleader is supposed to be like. You're nice. Genuine. Genuinely nice," he tittered, but then grew serious again. "For some odd reason, there are weird human beings who don't like nice people- especially if they defy their expectations." He shrugged, almost apologetically, before slowly and steadily getting into his vehicle.

I stood outside leaning against the steel gate encircling our front porch, pondered Mickey's words as I watched him drive away. I stood like that for so long that I lost track of time. Trying to analyze such a complicated and confusing situation can do that to a person. I must have stood out there for over an hour before my mom pulled into our driveway and roused me from my reverie. Regrettably, after all that contemplation, I was still just as perplexed and clueless about what I should do next as I'd been before Mickey's arrival.

Chapter Thirty-three: Coffee Corner

When I woke up on Saturday, I was feeling a little stronger, less grief-stricken, and shocked. I wasn't sure how I was planning to move forward. I was still clueless as to how to make my life work. How could I face Jamey every day? And Kayla? And Bobby? As sickened and angry as I was by Jamey and Bobby, Josh made my stomach turn because he had no remorse and had actually managed to turn his guilt into rage directed at me. My head was spinning, but I knew I had to devise a plan or at least find a way to move on. I still had six months of school to get through.

I decided it was time to get out of bed and face what my world had become. The first thing I did was call Jenna. She advised me to erase all the texts and messages I'd missed during the week and start fresh. She said people were gossiping, but everyone had concluded that Jamey had cheated on me, I'd caught him, and I was devastated by his infidelity. She claimed that our peers' attention had turned elsewhere by Friday- apparently, newer "scandals" had developed.

When I hung up with Jenna, I received a call from Kelly, begging me to come with the girls to Coffee Corner, a café we frequented quite often. Somehow, it had become a place that only the female members of our crew visited over the years. It was sort of "our" place, like the coffee shop in the television show "Friends." I reluctantly agreed because I knew I had to start living my life again. I couldn't hide away forever. Although I'd never felt so distraught and heartbroken, I was resilient and determined to deal with this in a mature and dignified manner. I agreed, mainly because Kelly was so sweet and persistent. She promised that everything would be okay and I'd feel much better after spending time with my best friends.

Jenna insisted on driving me to the café because she said it was about time I told her what had happened the night of the infamous "event" involving Jamey and Kayla. I agreed but expressed my desire to wait until after we met with our friends. I knew I'd crumble while recalling the horrific scene I'd witnessed. I obviously wanted to remain intact while visiting with the others.

When Jenna and I walked into the trendy, chic coffee shop we often attended, our other friends were already seated at a high wooden table in the corner of the room. I was familiar with the voguish atmosphere of Coffee Corner. I immediately felt at ease because it had been a place where Jenna, Nikki, Kelly, Erin, and I spent many jovial, comfortable hours over the years.

Jenna and I both ordered flavored lattes; I added an extra shot of expresso. Even though I'd been in bed for a week, I hadn't gotten any peaceful sleep and was still lethargic. As we brought our drinks to the table where our friends were sitting, Kelly and Erin began waving empathically. They had huge smiles plastered on their faces. Kelly was beaming, and her cornflower blue eyes were enlarged. Erin appeared to be mimicking Kelly's enthusiasm- they acted as if it had been months rather than a week since I'd seen them.

After their initial overly animated greeting, we fell into a somewhat awkward silence. Yet, once we were all settled in, Kelly began yapping about everything I'd missed at school the previous week and the upcoming parties our peers were planning. I was taken aback by her need to talk incessantly as if she thought something terrible would happen if there was a break in the conversation.

"Jeez, Kel," Jenna said, interrupting her overzealous, non-stop chatter, "You're acting like you're on speed. How much caffeine have you had?"

Kelly laughed a little too boisterously; it was clear that she was anxious for some unknown reason. "Sorry, it's just been such a strange week without Jessica. I mean, I don't think you've ever skipped a day of school in almost four years." She turned her attention towards me, "We all missed you."

I took a sip of my latte and forced myself to grin. I was feeling somewhat edgy because they were coming on so strong. Plus, I didn't enjoy being the center of attention.

Erin sucked in a long gulp of air before asking, "Are you coming back next week?" She was also trying unsuccessfully to mask her uneasiness.

I nodded. "I guess I have no choice."

Kelly and Erin exchanged a look of relief. "That's great," Kelly began cheerfully, "I'm so glad to hear that."

"Me too!" Erin piped in, placing her hand over her heart.

"You know we've been thinking of you all week," Kelly said as she lifted her finger in the air and swung it back and forth between her and Erin. They were sitting on one side of the booth, and Nikki, Jenna, and I were on the other.

I wasn't sure how to respond, so I remained quiet, which only encouraged Kelly and Erin to continue gabbing.

"Jamey is really sorry, Jess. None of us know exactly what happened. I mean, Josh gave us some of the details. He's angry; at least he was. Who knows how he feels now?" Erin hesitated before carrying on, "Bobby feels bad; he won't say why. But Jamey has just been so upset. I mean, SO upset. We've never seen him like this...."

"Blah, blah, blah...." Jenna interjected before placing her finger in her mouth as if she was about to wretch.

Erin ignored her. "I just think that Jessica should know how sorry Jamey is. It's important for her to take that into consideration. I mean, Jess, I do understand how you feel. It's a shock. I get that. You don't have to talk about it if...."

"Of course, she doesn't!" Nikki exclaimed.

"I know. I know," Erin went on, "I'm not saying she has to. I'm not saying that at all. I'm just confused. I mean, we are all friends, and it's a very touchy topic, but it has been hard for Kelly and me to understand it all. I mean, even though Jamey is sorry, we get why Jessica is mad at him. But we don't understand how the other guys got dragged into it."

Kelly looked at Erin and sighed, "I sort of get it. They probably got dragged in because they were outside the pool house and knew what was going on."

Erin bobbed her head up and down but looked unconvinced. "Jess, you never...you never told us why you were so mad at Bobby and Josh," Her statement was actually more of a question.

Jenna cleared her throat with unmistakable irritation, "First of all, Jessica never said she was mad at Bobby and Josh. Josh said that. Jessica hasn't said anything about any of this."

Kelly and Erin flinched at the anger in Jenna's tone; they both seemed surprised that Erin's inquiry had aggravated her. They began to mutter indecipherably before Nikki suggested we change the subject.

Kelly looked up at the glossy taupe ceiling before she spoke, "The thing is...we can't. We have to talk about this. We can't pretend none of this happened. It's just not...it's not possible."

I placed my hands around my coffee mug and looked down at the brown liquid. I was unable to find my voice because I didn't know what to say.

"Why?" Jenna questioned, through gritted teeth, "Why do we have to talk about it? In my opinion, it's none of your business."

"We have to talk about it because it will affect everything!" Kelly proclaimed, "In fact, it already has. It's all anyone is talking about."

"That's not true," Jenna disputed, turning towards me with a look of concern, "People have already started to move on."

We were all mute for an incredibly long time, doing all the things people do when they are uncomfortable- hair fidgeting, finger tapping, drawn-out sighs. The tension was so thick you would have literally needed a machete to cut through it.

Erin finally exhaled, "O-kay," she began, "Change of subject then." She sucked on the paper straw protruding from her cold brew before muttering, "I guess it really doesn't matter why or if you were mad at all of them."

"Like I said, "Jenna began, "Josh is the one who is going around spreading those rumors. It's hearsay, and Jessica shouldn't have to answer for it...especially when it's coming from someone like Josh, who we all know has always been antagonistic towards her."

"Yeah," Nikki agreed, "So please, change the subject."

"Okay," Erin perked up, "There are two amazing parties happening tonight. I think we should all go to both! The guys are going to Garrett Butler's, so I do want to eventually make our way there. But I think we should start the night at Danielle Bouvier's. She is having male strippers. Do you believe that? She claims they will perform lap dances. So cool! That would be so much fun!"

"Are you serious right now?" Jenna threw her arms up in the air in exasperation.

"Why wouldn't she be?" Kelly asked with a knowing glare, "This is the stuff we always talk about. You said we should change the subject, so why not talk about our plans? I mean, Nikki probably wants to spend time with Evan tonight, right?"

"Don't bring me into this." Nikki ordered, "I am having a hard time following this bizarre conversation. I think it's pretty obvious you invited us all here for more than a friendly cup of joe, which is how you presented it. So, to be honest, I think that was pretty crappy on your part, Kelly."

"Fine. You're right. I didn't mean to be deceitful. That was not my intention, and I'm sorry. Yet, since we are all here, I think we need to…" She placed her fingers on the bridge of her nose and tilted her chin so far down it almost met the whipped cream sitting atop her hot chocolate. When she looked up, a pained expression coated her face.

Erin patted her back. "Go on," she encouraged.

Kelly swallowed soundly, "We have to address the elephant in the room," she stated, "I mean, come on, Jenna and Nikki- you've been at school all week. You know how odd things have been. What's going to happen when Jessica comes back? If we all hang out tonight at Garrett's, it will totally ease the tension. Obviously, Jessica and Jamey are done for now, but we could put this whole mess behind us if we all spent time together. Jessica doesn't have to forgive Jamey or even talk to him, but it would stop the rumors and awkwardness if we were at least seen together."

"He'd do anything to undo what he did with Kayla," Erin once again jumped in where Kelly left off, "He was super drunk, and he wouldn't have done it if he was sober. He knows you won't forgive him right away, like that," Erin snapped her fingers, "But he's hoping over time that you will."

"No," I stated firmly, "I will never forgive him. I want nothing to do with him."

Kelly arched her neck and nervously started to scratch at it, "Yeah, well, obviously, that's why there's a problem," she sounded frazzled as if my response had triggered her.

"Why is that, Kelly?" Jenna spat. "Why does their relationship create a problem for *you?*"

Kelly's demeanor seemed to instantly transform as a sympathetic smile spread across her face, "Listen, Jess. I am so sorry about what happened. I feel so badly for you. I do. I really do," she took my hand in hers as she continued, "But I also have been listening to Jamey this past week because he's…well, he's been answering my calls. You weren't, and I have to admit, I feel sorry for him too."

"You really are a piece of work, Kelly," Jenna bellowed. "You beg Jessica to come here and then bombard her with all of this."

"Yes! This has to be said," Kelly asserted with a heightened level of confidence, "We have all been friends since before freshman year. We've been hanging out since the summer we met at cheerleading practice. Erin and I have known Jamey since...geez, since kindergarten. But that summer, we all become like one, and it's been that way for three and a half years."

"Kelly and I need to know what happens now," Erin maintained, "Also, what about Nikki? I know you don't want to get involved," Erin laid a palm out in Nikki's direction, "but seriously, Evan is your boyfriend, AND he is also one of Jamey's best friends. Where does that leave you?"

"Wow!" Jenna began, "you two are being so insensitive right now. And, YOU..." Jenna aggressively pointed at Kelly, "*Miss Sweeter, than Sweet*, are blowing my mind with your selfishness. It's been a week, Kelly. How can you do this to Jessica? I know...WE ALL know how long you've been friends with Jamey, but Jessica has been your *girl*friend for all this time. Isn't there any sense of loyalty? Any at all?"

"Of course!" Kelly said, loud enough for heads to start turning, "I love Jessica. I'd do anything for her."

Jenna rolled her eyes and took a long gulp of her drink.

"Okay, I am really trying to be sensitive," Kelly stated in a controlled tone, "I completely understand that you don't want anything further to do with Jamey romantically, but I guess what Erin and I are concerned about is your willingness for all of us to hang out together...you know, like we've always done."

"I personally couldn't care less about hanging out with Jamey," Jenna muttered with disgust.

"We know that," Kelly continued with the same measured voice. "You've moved on. Jenna, you've made it pretty obvious you'd rather spend time with your *college* boyfriend than with us. That's fine. But in school, we all sit together, and the rest of us hang out on weekends."

"If Jessica doesn't want to go to parties, that's well, it's not a problem," Erin chimed in, "But, what's going to happen at school? I mean, at lunch? Do you think you can...you know, sit with Jamey- at the same table, I mean?"

"I haven't even thought about that," I mumbled. "I feel like you're both interrogating me...." My voice trailed off as unwelcome tears filled my eyes. I had certainly not expected this when Kelly invited me to get coffee.

Jenna slammed her palms down on the table. Once again, people sitting at neighboring tables turned to face us, "Is this necessary? Isn't this a little too soon? I mean, why is this so important to you two? Why are you doing this to her?"

"I'm so sorry, Jessica," Kelly said sincerely. "We didn't mean to upset you. It's just that it has been a whole week, and…."

Erin and Kelly continued to tag team me; it was once again Erin's turn to complete Kelly's sentiments, "Don't you see how this is already dividing us? I mean, Jenna and Nikki are getting mad at Kelly and me. We never used to fight like this."

"Well, nothing like this has ever happened before." Nikki hissed, "I mean, Jamey just cheated on her a week ago!"

Kelly cleared her throat, and a meaningful look passed between her and Erin; Erin nodded, and Kelly continued, "Technically, he didn't *cheat* on Jessica. All this time, all these years, there's never been a commitment. I mean, Jamey tried, but…."

"What's your point?" Nikki questioned.

Erin looked and sounded exasperated, "My point is, well, I mean, what's going on with Evan? What does he say about all of this? It has to be affecting your relationship."

Nikki vehemently shook her head. "No, it's not. It hasn't affected anything at all."

Jenna looked pointedly at Erin and then at Kelly, "This is a disaster! I honestly can't believe the two of you. Did Jamey put you up to this? Why are you doing this?"

Nikki's phone buzzed. She turned it over and shook her head, "That's Evan; he's here to pick me up. He finished running errands," she turned towards me with a solicitous look on her face, "Want me to tell him to come back later?"

"We're fine," Jenna answered for me. "Nikki, you can go."

Nikki stood up and took a wide sidestep so she was directly behind me. She placed her arms around me and rested her head on my shoulder. "Call me later, Jess. I love you."

"Okay," I murmured, "Love you too."

We all sat in very uncomfortable silence when Nikki left. My head was spinning. I honestly believed Kelly intended to comfort me- not bamboozle me into thinking this was a friendly get-together. Even Jenna was now at a loss for words.

"I need to go," I asserted, looking desperately in Jenna's direction, "I don't feel good."

Jenna started to stand, but Kelly stood first, "No. We need to finish this conversation."

"No, we don't, Kelly!" Jenna snapped, "you've damaged her enough this morning."

"Jessica isn't some fragile creature who needs your protection," Kelly went on in a voice I'd never heard come out of her mouth in all the years I'd known her. She sounded self-possessed and rather bold, "She is perfectly capable of speaking for herself."

"Well, she just did! She said she wants to leave."

Kelly's words had the desired effect- she wanted me to stay and finish this discussion. She felt it needed some sort of resolution, and she obviously had more to say. She knew me well enough to poke at my pride by suggesting that if I left now, I was weak and incapable of defending myself.

"Fine," I stated, meeting Kelly's eyes. "Let's finish this. Go on, Kelly. You have more to say. Just say it."

Jenna sat back down with an enraged expression; she began to drum her fingers on the table as she glared at Kelly, almost daring her to insult me.

"I do not want to be inconsiderate or unkind. I think you both know me well enough to realize that isn't my intention," Kelly began gently, "After all the years we've been friends, I feel like you at least owe me," she stopped and turned towards Erin, who was now sitting as still as a mannequin. She appeared unsettled as if she'd seen a ghost, "you both owe me and Erin the benefit of the doubt."

Jenna started to say something, but I placed my hand over hers, indicating that I wanted us both to allow Kelly to continue.

"You have the floor, Kelly," I said, matter-of-factly, knowing in my heart that I wasn't going to enjoy hearing what she had to say, but there was no turning back at this point.

Kelly looked up, took a deep breath, and released it before clasping her hands together. She then took a sip from her cocoa, tucked her auburn hair behind her ears, and began, "Look, Jessica. I love you. Erin and I love you. You're one of our best friends. You always will be; at least, we hope you will. The thing is, we've watched this... *relationship* you've had with Jamey for years now, literally over three years. He's not innocent. He can be a jerk- he was a bit of a bully when we were younger. At first, we could see why you were hesitant to commit to him, but then it just became confusing. I know he spanked you, and you were pissed off about that. But you forgave him. You made out with him in the hallway. Everyone saw you. What stopped you from committing? It just never made sense. I personally don't think it made sense to anybody. You obviously had feelings for him. After LaVonn, there was never anybody else. It just is very, very weird. He wanted to be your boyfriend, but you wouldn't let him. I mean, maybe you think it's none of my business...."

Jenna harrumphed and arched her eyebrows, "Obviously, *you* think it is."

Kelly licked her lips and looked at me, waiting for permission to continue.

"Go on," I said.

"Well, it *is* my business because we all are part of a friend group. You are part of that, and so is Jamey. We all were involved in your relationship. No one can deny that. I just think that if you had made it simpler, just gave in and dated him- committed to him, let him call you his girlfriend, and vice versa. I mean, you were obviously in love...."

"In love?" I questioned, feeling startled, not angry. I had just never considered that.

"Well, he was in love with you, Jess," Erin alleged, "He desperately loved...*loves* you. And did you ever think about how he felt when you kept rejecting him? It was sort of like the reverse of how most relationships work. He was chasing you- begging you to be monogamous, and you kept making him wait. I mean, in a way, sorry to say, but maybe your constant rebuffs, you know, forced him to look elsewhere."

"And," it was now Kelly's turn again, "I think that maybe you are commitment-phobic or something. There's no reason why you would sort of string him along all this time if not."

When Kelly finished, I looked over at Jenna, who was puckering her lips and rubbing her temples. I knew it pained her to listen to all of this without speaking up in my defense.

I nodded my head at Erin and Kelly and stood up, taking my purse, "Okay," I replied, "Thank you for being honest. I appreciate that. I understand how you feel. You have a right to form your own opinions, and I can see why you may have come to those conclusions. It will take me some time to process all of that."

"We really, really hope you're not angry," Kelly said earnestly.

"Or hurt or offended," Erin inserted.

I shook my head, "No, no. I'm not- like I said, it's just a lot to process."

"You promise you're not mad?" Erin asked, pleadingly.

I looked down at the terra cotta floor tiles and nodded. The tears were forming, and I needed to get out of Coffee Corner before they started to flow like a freaking waterfall.

Jenna was already standing. The minute she looked into my eyes she knew. She knew I was about to fall apart, and I couldn't do it in front of them- partially because there was truth in their words.

"We're leaving," Jenna informed Kelly and Erin.

"Well, bye," Kelly chirped, as she stood in an attempt to properly see us off, "Love you, Jess."

"Love you both," Erin added. She had also hoisted herself up and was holding her arms out.

Before either of them could offer physical affection or utter another word, Jenna grabbed my arm and started tugging on it. Neither of us looked back or responded as she literally dragged me out of the café.

Chapter Thirty-four: A Lightbulb

As we exited the café, Jenna and I switched positions because I was in such a hurry to evacuate the premises. Jenna trailed behind me as I rushed to her cobalt blue Lexus in flight mode like I was trying to escape a serial killer. Kelly and Erin's ignorant yet hurtful comments had triggered panic in me, and Jenna, fortunately, discerned my need to flee. She was able to intuit my desire to be securely inside the confines of anything other than the café. I yearned for my racing heart to decelerate, my body to stop trembling, and to regain the ability to breathe. I NEEDED safety. At that moment, safe meant a place that included Jenna and nobody else.

Once we were inside her vehicle, Jenna sped away from the café. In fact, I don't think her door was shut completely before she raced out of the parking lot. The dam immediately broke when I felt comfortable enough to release the tears I'd been frantically attempting to keep at bay. I toppled forward in my seat, placed my head in my hands, and sobbed uncontrollably.

Ironically, Jenna hauled her car into the same side street where I had parked the night after I witnessed Jamey screwing Kayla. It was always deserted; therefore, it was highly unlikely, we'd be met with unwelcome intruders. We were almost guaranteed privacy, which I desperately required at that time.

Once she parked the car, Jenna sighed audibly and enfolded me in her arms. She patted my back and made soothing noises as I bawled; my shoulders were shaking, and I couldn't stop myself from howling as the tears flowed down my face. I have no idea how long we stayed that way, but I finally felt safe enough to share my grief with the one person I felt I could trust more than anyone else in the world.

When I finally calmed down, and there were no more tears left to cry, I let out a long breath and swiveled in my seat. I pressed the nape of my neck against the cushioned headrest and tilted my chin up so I was staring at the tan vinyl roof of the car. I had run out of adrenaline. Consequently, my anxiety dissipated. I was left feeling exhausted and drained.

Jenna was quiet for a few seconds, allowing me to collect my thoughts. She stared at me, waiting. She knew me well enough to understand that I would begin talking once I was capable.

Finally, I turned to meet her violet eyes- the uniquely beautiful eyes of my best friend. If her face was any indication of the sadness I was feeling, and I assumed it did mimic my grief, I knew I must have looked forlorn and dejected.

"Tell me what happened," Jenna ordered, but her voice was tender and sympathetic.

Although I trusted Jenna, I needed assurance that she would never repeat what I was about to tell her. Therefore, I made sure my tone was stern. "I can't keep this inside any longer. I have to tell someone what I saw, but you have to promise that you will never tell another soul."

Jenna nodded once. That was all I needed. My faith in my closest friend was so fervent that a nod from her was comparable to a guarantee or an oath.

"Not even Nikki," I continued, "It would be too much for her. If she knew, she would feel, I don't know. It would just be awkward."

"I get it," Jenna replied as she ran her fingers through her white-blond hair.

I placed my hand on my forehead and rubbed at my temples, feeling a dull ache spreading across my scalp, "I don't even know where to begin. It was just so awful."

"Well, just tell me what you saw," Jenna encouraged, "I know from the way Josh acted and how upset you've been that it's *bad*."

"It was all three of them, Jen," I began woefully, "I saw Jamey pushing, *shoving* into her from behind in a really aggressive way, and Bobby and Josh were waiting. They were watching and laughing and cheering."

"Oh shit," Jenna interjected. "Shit! Shit! Shit! Disgusting, and Bobby," her voice took on a somber tone, "*Bobby*. That sucks. I thought he was halfway decent."

"He had his you know- *thing*- in his hand and was rubbing it while he watched Jamey screw Kayla," I didn't feel comfortable describing profane things. Yet, there was really no other way to describe it. Vulgarity was necessary when recounting this particular situation.

Jenna closed her eyes and pinched the bridge of her nose. "That's revolting."

"Yeah, and the worst part is that it looked like Kayla was asleep?"

"Seriously?" Jenna sounded incredulous.

"Yes. Her eyes were closed, and she was like just lying there- limp," I paused. "It was horrible. The worse thing I've ever seen."

"I can imagine!" Jenna looked like she wanted to vomit; she was obviously disgusted, "I gather that Kayla denied being asleep."

"Yes, she insisted that she was awake. She acted like I was a lunatic and said the worst things to me afterward. I started freaking out because I didn't know if they were assaulting her," I swallowed soundly and shook my head. "The next thing I knew- she was awake, even though she didn't appear lucid. I don't even remember what B.S. the guys were spewing, but I tried to help Kayla. She basically told me that she hated me and if I took care of Jamey, she wouldn't have to."

Jenna snorted, "She's a bitch, but geez…that poor, pathetic girl."

I sighed, "Yeah, and then she called me on my cell. At first, she changed her tune. She tried to be nice, but it was apparently too hard for her. She hates me that much. But she begged me not to tell anyone, that is, in between berating me. She basically said I was fake and…."

"You know what, Jess? Who cares? Who gives a crap what she thinks of you? I'm sorry, but she is obviously lashing out because she's messed up."

"I get that. I just feel so torn," I took a deep breath and slowly exhaled, "I know I can't say anything. It's her story to tell. Not mine. I promised her I wouldn't. And I don't really know what I saw. Were they assaulting her? I don't know. Is it date rape if someone consents and then falls asleep? I don't know. I just keep going back and forth."

"Listen to me," Jenna said firmly, placing her hands on my shoulders, "Like you said, this isn't your story to tell. It's hers. It's not your job to figure out what happened. Kayla doesn't want you to get involved. This weight that you've placed on your shoulders," She squeezed the top of my upper limbs as she said this, "it's not your weight. You saw something…something sickening. You tried to help. That's all you can do. You have to understand that. If you took this any further, you'd only be violating Kayla- the way they might have been."

"That's true," I uttered, feeling slightly relieved. "There really isn't anything else I can do, right?"

Jenna forcefully bobbed her head up and down. "Right. It's out of your hands. There is nothing else- NOTHING you can do, honey."

I sucked on my finger as I digested her words. "You're right. I just can't stop playing it over again in my head."

Jenna took hold of my chin and pointed at me as if I were a child, "Jess, this is not your problem to fix. You have got to stop obsessing about this. Like you said, Kayla doesn't want you to say anything."

"She literally *begged* me not to. I couldn't do that to her."

"It is *her story*- your words. It is *her* life," Jenna paused and smiled sadly, "I know you are heartbroken and sickened by all this. You have a right to feel that way. But you're concentrating on the wrong things. You should be focusing on dealing with your feelings for Jamey."

"I hate him," I spat.

"I know. I don't blame you."

"I seriously will never forgive him."

Jenna harrumphed, "Well, I certainly hope not. He's a pig."

"Never," I sniffed.

"Listen, Jess," Jenna started, sounding earnest, "THIS is what you need to focus on. Not the other crap. You've really got to forget about the shit with Kayla. Seriously. What you need to deal with is YOU. Your future. Your feelings. Let the rest go. The only thing you need to worry about is how YOU are going to move forward."

I puffed out my cheeks and nodded several times. Jenna was right, and thankfully, her words were helping to alleviate my feelings of guilt and anxiety.

We sat in comfortable silence for a few moments while I digested all we'd discussed. I was beginning to feel just a tiny bit better, but then I recalled the confrontation with my friends at Coffee Corner and a feeling of desperation overtook me, "Jenna, how can I go back? How am I supposed to pretend like none of this happened? I don't think I can face any of them. I didn't realize how awkward things were going to be until today. I mean, you heard all the stuff Kelly and Erin were saying. I am just going to make *everyone* uncomfortable. I can't go back. I just can't."

Jenna arched her perfectly shaped eyebrows and shrugged, "Then don't."

As I processed Jenna's words, I realized that all the hard work I'd put into my education over the years, especially taking on numerous college courses, could potentially pay off in a much more significant way than I had predicted.

Suddenly, a lightbulb went off in my head, and I knew what I had to do.

Chapter Thirty-five: Purgatory

After meeting with my girlfriends and listening to Kelly and Erin express their concerns about our clique's future, I concluded that if I wanted to stay sane, I couldn't return to school. The thought of it made me nauseated and, to be honest, terrified. I couldn't bear the inevitable anxiety attacks that would result from Jamey's attempts to apologize, Josh's wrath, and everyone else's discomfort. Jenna and Nikki would feel the need to defend me. Kelly and Erin would try to stay neutral, although they had already made it clear that they expected me to forgive, forget and move on. I couldn't do that. I could not pretend as if nothing had happened.

Jenna and I had talked at length about my options. I'd worked extremely hard for years, and consequently, I had one semester of college under my belt. I could technically begin at a university during the second half of the year. However, there would be a few mild kinks to work out. I had actually wanted to earn more college credits during my senior year. Still, both my parents insisted that I take fun, undemanding courses. They wanted me to enjoy my final year as a higher schooler without all the pressure I'd previously put on myself. Therefore, it wasn't mandatory for me to complete any of the fluff I was enrolled in. Plus, I had already been offered early admission at both The University of Los Angeles and St. Padre Pio. In light of the fact that Jamey was planning to go to St. Padre Pio, and it was in the vicinity of Rosevalley, I had ruled out attending that institution. At this point, I knew I wanted to take my grandmother up on her offer, move in with her and attend the school she so desperately had been pressuring me to join.

My plan had only one obstacle- my father. I was uncertain about his reaction to my proposal. I wasn't sure I'd be able to convince him it was practical to make a last-minute, seemingly impulsive decision such as this. I didn't want to have to recount the awful scene I had walked in on. I was hoping it wouldn't come down to that, but after my discussion with Jenna, I was prepared to do so if necessary. Confronting my parents with my desires would be one of the most difficult things I'd ever had to do, but it was a necessity.

Once I did it, if I was successful and they were willing to help me, I would be set free.

I approached my mom when Jenna dropped me off. I explained that I had something enormously important that I needed to discuss with her and my dad as soon as possible. She appeared concerned and attempted to gather more information from me, but I insisted I wanted to wait until later when both of my parents were present. She reluctantly agreed and promised we could meet in my dad's study later that evening after dinner.

It was obvious that my parents were not only curious but also nervous about my desire to meet with them. My dad was silent during dinner, while my mom made uncomfortable small talk. My sisters didn't even seem to notice the uneasiness. They were lost in their own thoughts. When supper was finished and we all helped clean up, my mom sent my sisters to their rooms and instructed them to shower, study and then go to bed. She was vague about why she and my dad needed some private time with me, and neither of them questioned her about it.

It was unusual for anyone in my family, aside from my father, to spend time in what we all jokingly referred to as "his mancave." It was a place he usually went to for work-related activities, alone time, or occasionally to drink bourbon and smoke cigars with friends and colleagues at dinner parties. I wasn't sure why my mom suggested that we all meet in that particular room. I assumed it was because of the seriousness of my request. The rest of my house, except for my sisters' and my bedrooms, had been decorated by my mom with an artistic homey touch. The only room my father had any interest in designing was his study. He wanted a vintage-themed office, reminiscent of "The Godfather."

My parents and I were silent as we made our way to my dad's den. He pulled the door open and waved us inside, closing it behind him once we were securely inside. I surveyed my surroundings as I thought of a way to explain my predicament. I couldn't remember the last time I'd been inside my dad's study. It was dimly lit, which added to the somber, formidable ambiance. The bookcase, which stood against the back wall, was filled with colorful classic novels that I would bet my father hadn't read for years, if ever. They were meant to be decorative, just like the old-fashioned typewriter, tuber radio, and rotary phone, which sat atop his mahogany rolltop desk. My mom sat on one of two leather couches, which were facing one another, while my dad strolled over to his retro home bar and fetched two glasses from the cabinet- a wine glass for my mom and a tumbler for himself. I watched as he poured himself a tall glass of bourbon and my mom a white wine.

"Would you like anything, Jessica?" He asked as he handed my mother, her Pinot Grigio.

I shook my head, "No, thank you."

"Why don't you sit down, Jessica?" My mom swept her arm in the air, indicating that I should place myself on the couch opposite her.

I obeyed without speaking.

I licked my lips nervously and looked down at the wooden floor as my dad positioned himself next to my mother. They silently stared at me for a few seconds before I looked up to meet their matching, distressed expressions.

Finally, my mom met my gaze and smiled encouragingly, "Jessica, honey, what is it you wanted to talk to us about?"

I gulped and fiddled with my fingers which I'd been tightly clutching to the sides of the couch, "I don't know where to begin," I whispered.

"Did something happen?" my father questioned sternly. His jaw was tightly clenched, and his green eyes had clouded over, making them appear dark and murky.

I nodded. "Yes. Yes, it did," I responded. My eyes started to fill up with tears as I continued, "I don't want to talk about it. It's too…it's just too terrible."

My father put his head in his hands and leaned over so his chest met his legs. My mom jumped off the couch, came over, knelt, and put her hands on my legs. "What is it, honey? You can tell us. You can tell us anything."

I shook my head. "No, please. I don't want to. I really don't want to."

My mother turned towards my dad, who was sitting in an unnaturally rigid position; he looked as if he'd seen a ghost. He was staring blankly ahead, not meeting her eyes.

She shifted so she was once again facing me, "Please, Jessica. You can trust us."

"I can't…please don't make me describe it…"

My father stood up and started pacing. His mouth was set in a grim line, and he had his hands in his pockets. He didn't stop walking as he spoke. "Jessica, did something happen to you? Did someone hurt you?"

"No," I stated in a small voice.

He stopped and started running his hands through his hair, "Jessica, I don't know if I believe you. Tell me now," he ordered through gritted teeth, "did someone hurt you?"

"No," I repeated, "No one hurt me."

My father's fists were clenched at his sides, and his previously nervous expression had morphed into anger. "Are you sure? Are you positive that no one harmed you?"

I shook my head; I had never seen my father so unraveled before, and it was disturbing. He was usually so stoic and composed.

"Answer me!" he demanded.

My mouth dropped open, and the tears started spilling down my face. I couldn't figure out why my dad was interrogating me in such a heated way.

"Anthony," my mother chided in a harsh voice she rarely used. "You are upsetting her. You need to calm down and stop."

My father shut his eyes and breathed in and out a few times before he spoke again. "Please...please tell me, us the truth. Please tell us if someone did something to you."

"No, Dad," I whimpered, "I promise. No one hurt me."

My father slowly exhaled, closed his eyes, and placed his hands together as if in prayer, "Thank God," he said as if the weight of the world had been lifted from his shoulders, "I couldn't bear the thought of something..." he shook his head and regained his composure.

My mom and I were both staring at him; I could see that she was just as shocked by his atypical reaction as I was. Neither of us had ever seen him lose control before.

"I'm sorry," he mumbled, sinking into the chair behind his desk. "I didn't mean to upset you. I was just so afraid that someone had hurt you."

Everyone was silent for a few minutes as we contemplated where and how to continue this discussion. I finally spoke up, "Nothing happened to me. I saw something. I saw something awful."

"What did you see?" my mother inquired.

"I...I really don't want to talk about it."

"But Jessica?" My mom started, "Is it something you need to report?"

"No," I said firmly. "It's nothing like that, Mom. It involves Jamey and another...." I stopped talking because I couldn't stop the tears; I was suddenly sobbing.

My mom came over and threw her arms around me. "It's okay. It will be fine, honey. We will do anything. We can help you. What is it you want to do?"

"I can't go back," I cried, "I just can't. I changed my mind about school. If I had known then what I know now. I've been afraid to ask. I thought Dad would think I was being irresponsible. I made the wrong decision, and now I don't want to wait to go away."

My father was standing over my mom and me now with a look of realization. "Do you want to go to Los Angeles? Is that what you're trying to say?"

"Yes."

My parents exchanged a look I couldn't decipher. I placed my hands in my lap and leaned forward, eagerly waiting for one of them to say something. If they agreed to let me go, I would never have to face Jamey, Josh, Bobby, or Kayla again. I could start over across the country. I would probably never get past this. I was positive I'd never trust or be interested in another boy again, but I could handle that. I couldn't handle having to go back to Lomonoco Creek and deal with the fallout of what I had witnessed. The image made me want to vomit whenever it appeared in my head, which happened too often. I'd have to banish it and force myself to think about anything else. It felt like an eternity before my father finally spoke up, and he changed my fate with one word.

"Okay," he replied, shrugging.

My mom smiled brightly, "Yes, Jessica. We can make that happen."

I had never felt so relieved in my life.

My mother was the one who did most of the talking after that. My father seemed to still be in somewhat of a trance. I felt a little guilty for the way I'd handled this situation. I had definitely scared him into thinking that someone had hurt me. In a way, I was using that misunderstanding to my advantage. He was so grateful and relieved that that hadn't been the case; consequently, he was willing to go along with the plan my mom had rapidly concocted. It certainly wasn't unheard of for a student to transfer in the middle of the year. I did have the grades, SAT scores, a list of impressive extracurricular activities, and connections to be able to do it. I probably would've been able to get into an Ivy League school without my famous familial relations. Yet I knew that my great-grandmother's influence would clinch the deal, at least when it came to attending The University of Los Angeles. As far as I could tell, that particular school was not only looking to recruit students with excellent grades and notable college applications but was also interested in enlisting kids with influential and prominent backgrounds.

My mom was well aware of her grandmother's power. She had hidden from fame, but she grew up watching the positive and negative effects of celebrity. After years and years of experience, she was savvy enough to immediately formulate a solution to my problem. She informed me that the first thing that had to be done was for Nona Jessica to make a call to the school.

"I'm certain that ULA will be ecstatic," my mother promised. "There's no problem there."

"What about all the classes I was taking at Lomonoco Creek?" I asked nervously. I didn't ever want to set foot in that building again. I was praying that I wouldn't have to.

My mom snuck a questioning look in my dad's direction. He raised his eyebrows and put his hands out in a "V" shape as if to convey that he was okay with whatever scheme my mother was in the process of machinating.

My mother grinned, obviously feeling satisfied and reassured, with the understanding that my father was on board. "I'll take care of all that," she promised.

I furrowed my eyebrows quizzically. "But...are you sure, Mom? What do I have to do? Will I have to possibly take the end-of-the-quarter exams?" I gulped. "I can't go there. I can't bring myself to chance seeing..."

"Jessica," my mother said sharply, cutting me off. "I will take care of it."

I looked back and forth from my mom to my dad. Could it be this easy? I'd anticipated that it would be more difficult than this.

"You've worked extremely hard for years," my dad piped in. "If something is bothering you this much that it's creating such an extreme reaction, there's no reason why we can't solve this. You deserve it after all the extra effort you've put in."

I must have still looked doubtful because my dad snickered. "Have you ever known your mom to fail at anything?" he asked.

I shook my head.

"Have either of us ever let you down or made a promise we didn't keep?"

I shook my head again.

My father licked his lips and looked admiringly at my mother, "I think we both know that when your mom says she can make something happen, she will damn well make it happen."

My mother shrugged and plastered a humble expression on her beautiful face.

Tears came to my eyes again, but these were tears of extreme relief. "Thank you, Mom. Thank you, both," I exclaimed.

Before I left the room, my mom threw her arms around me and enveloped me in a bear hug, "It feels good for you to need me sometimes," she whispered. "You have always been so independent." She kissed my cheek and took my hand in hers, "If you want to talk to me or both of us, you know we're here for you."

My dad came over and put his hand on my shoulder, "We love you, Jessica. We're proud of you," And in a moment of affection that was rare for my father, he hugged me just as hard as my mom did.

When I left the study, I felt lighter. My muscles started to relax, and the tension began to melt away. I slept well that night. I certainly didn't feel happy or even content, but I was still naïve enough to believe the worst was over. Unfortunately, that was not at all the case.

Chapter Thirty-six: Cold as Ice

My mom was true to her word. She worked her magic, and everything fell into place by January- right before I was to start my first trimester of college in Los Angeles at ULA. My grandmother was ecstatic. I was grateful for her excitement. It meant a lot to me, although my feelings and emotions were so jumbled and confusing. I felt disconnected most of the time, and I was perpetually sad. I had moments- a minuscule amount when I forgot to feel despondent, but they were few and far between.

Nikki and Jenna were the only friends I'd had any contact with over the weeks after Coffee Corner. My mom and Jenna made sure I kept busy. They wouldn't let me do what I wanted to do- which was lay on my bed and stare at the ceiling. My sisters were also there for me, which surprised me because I could tell that their concern was genuine. My mother kept me on a routine, ensuring I ate breakfast, lunch, and dinner. My friends and siblings were in school, and my dad was at work. During the day, my mom would plan activities to keep me entertained- such as massages and pedicures, which I was too lethargic and gloomy to enjoy. Jenna and Nikki called me every day. I stopped answering Kelly and Erin's calls and texts because I was too exhausted and hurt to correspond with either of them. When I expressed guilt about this, Jenna assured me that it was okay to concentrate on my well-being. She also insisted that I stop worrying about Kayla; she kept reminding me that there was nothing I could do about what I'd seen.

The one positive that came out of my time in what felt like purgatory was the shift in my relationship with my sister, Sara. Megan was a lot younger than me and carefree. We'd never had a strained relationship like mine and Sara's. She basically did her thing, and I did mine. During this time, Sara made an effort to form a better connection with me. She would come into my room every night after dinner, and we would lay on my bed together. She never asked me what had upset me. She'd only informed me once, right after the incident, that if I wanted to talk, she'd be there for me. She never mentioned Jamey again, which I was extremely grateful for. In other circumstances, Sara's approach to "bonding" might have seemed self-centered. However, I didn't perceive it that way because I knew she had good intentions. She rambled on about her problems in an effort to take my mind off my own troubles. And it worked. I realized that she needed to talk about her various grievances in order to process her thoughts and feelings. In the past, I'd always seen her as a self-made "victim," but I realized during that time that she was insecure, and seeking reassurance boosted her self-esteem. I also began to appreciate her sense of humor and perceptions about the people in her life.

Ultimately, the weeks before college went by in a blur. I was in survival mode. Basically, swimming through feelings of extreme melancholy and desperately trying to keep my head above water. A few days before I was set to depart, my mom and Jenna asked to speak with me. I was a little taken aback when there was a knock on my door the Friday night before I was scheduled to leave and greeted by both Jenna and my mother. They looked somber and morose.

"Can we talk to you?" My mom asked.

"Sure," I stated without bothering to make an attempt at cheerfulness. "You're scaring me. What's this about?"

"There's one last thing you need to deal with before you leave," my mom informed me, exchanging a distressful glance with Jenna.

"O-kay…"

They basically burst into my room and made themselves comfortable; my mom sat at my desk chair, and Jenna on my bed.

I reluctantly sat down next to Jenna and looked from her to my mother, waiting for one of them to explain what all this was about.

"Jamey," Jenna said in a steady, grave tone.

"What about him?" I inquired.

My mother licked her lips and hesitated before speaking, "Jessica, before you leave, you must tie up loose ends."

I threw my hands in the air, exasperated, "Why? I never want to see him again! What does that even mean?"

"It means that you have to confront him," Jenna alleged, "If you don't, you will never be able to have a fresh start."

I sighed and closed my eyes, feeling dread spread throughout my entire body. "I can't."

My mother crossed her legs and started to tap her manicured nails together, "I know it seems like you can't, but you can. We can't fix this for you because if we step in, he might listen at first, but eventually, he will try to contact you."

"Maybe he won't," I argued. "He might let it go. Maybe he's already moved on."

Jenna put her hand on my knee, "No. We haven't wanted to upset you, but he's obsessed, and unless you let him know that there's isn't a possibility of reconciliation, there's no guarantee, he won't try to get in touch."

"Jessica," my mother stated, "You need a fresh start at a new school like Jenna said. You have to leave all this behind. You have to settle things with Jamey. You have to let him know in no uncertain terms that this relationship is over."

"I thought he already knew," I whined.

Jenna shook her head with a sad smile, "It has to come from you," she paused before adding, "Sorry, Jess."

If this was coming from anyone else, I would have had doubts, but Jenna and my mother had done everything in their power to protect me. I was absolutely certain that they would fix this for me if they could. Although the idea of meeting with Jamey felt like a manifestation of hell on earth, I knew I had to do it.

"Fine," I replied, 'I'll do it."

Jenna, my mom, and I discussed precisely the hows, whats, and ifs; we covered everything I needed to say, all possible scenarios at length. When they left, later on, when I was lying in bed, I realized what it really came to was one thing; when dealing with Jamey, I needed to be as cold as ice.

The first part of our plan was for me to text Jamey and invite him to reunite at a fast-food restaurant located in mid-Rosevalley. That way, I wouldn't have to be concerned about wait staff, and I could scurry out of there without worrying about the bill. I could make a quick exit. I had Jenna text Jamey to make arrangements because I didn't want to unblock him as a contact. Jamey immediately accepted my request to meet at "Happy Burger" that afternoon. My mom, Jenna, and I agreed it was best to get it over with. That way, I didn't have to obsess over the details and what I needed to say. I was extremely uneasy about seeing him again. In fact, I paced my room for the entire two hours before it was time for me to leave, mulling over the plans I'd made with my mom and Jenna. I agreed this was necessary, although I desperately wished it wasn't. The idea of seeing him made my stomach churn. My heart was beating wildly, but I knew I had to focus. I had one goal- to convince Jamey that it was over between us and there was no way for him to reverse what he'd done.

I arrived at the restaurant a half hour early and sat in the very back in a corner seat where there were hardly any tables surrounding the booth I'd chosen. I hadn't been in this or any fast food joint in years. I wasn't a fan of greasy, fried food. I had to admit that it was contemporary, clean, and up-to-date. It did resemble your stereotypical idea of what a fast food diner would contain- a fountain soda machine, a play area for kids with a huge burger placed on top of a sliding board, aluminum trays to carry food, and tables made of perforated sheet metal. I ordered an iced tea because I knew I wouldn't be able to stomach food- especially the type of food they served there.

I almost, but not quite, felt sorry for Jamey when he sauntered in. He had a massive smile on his face. He appeared overly enthusiastic. He looked at me, winked, held his hands out, and pointed to the registers, asking without words if I wanted anything to eat. He nodded after I held my drink up and walked to the counter. While he was ordering, my stomach continued to do flip-flops, and although it wasn't hot, beads of sweat started to form on my forehead. I kept nervously running my hands through my hair, tucking it behind my ears.

After he'd received a tray of food, Jamey came and sat across from me, still beaming. He placed his platter down and slid into the booth. "I can't tell you how…" he looked up at the ceiling, trying to find the right word, "relieved, grateful…just, I don't know. I've never been so happy in my entire life. When I got Jenna's text, I just felt like I got my life back."

I stared at him blankly, waiting for him to continue. He took a bite of one of his French fries, "You're not eating?" he asked. "I know that's not soda," he chucked, "What is it, iced tea?"

I nodded.

"Like I said, I was never so happy in my life when my phone buzzed, and I read Jenna's text. I mean, I knew you'd eventually come around."

I raised my eyebrows as Jamey rattled on, but I don't think he noticed. He was acting as if he was on a caffeine high. For a second, I wondered if it was adrenaline or speed. I had never witnessed him acting as strange as he was at that moment. I sat in complete silence as he rambled between taking bites of his burger and sipping his large soda.

"You are the only one I will ever love. I made the biggest, BIGGEST mistake. Ask anyone, I was just so drunk, and Kayla, I mean seriously. You want to talk about sexual harassment. She has been coming on to me for years."

I tuned out, but I noticed the dark circles under his chestnut eyes; his typical bronze skin was pale, and his hair was too long and a little greasy. Jamey had always taken care of himself. This was the first time I'd ever seen him look so disheveled.

He cleared his throat and guzzled a huge gulp of his drink. He looked at me for a split second and then continued talking. I wondered if he was worried about what I would say if he gave me the opportunity to talk.

"I know," Jamey continued, "I mean, I'm not stupid. I know it will take me a long, really long time to win back your trust. I am so stupid." He smacked himself on the forehead and sighed, "We were getting somewhere...finally. Our relationship was so good. You can't deny that."

He stopped and looked into my eyes, trying to gauge my reaction, but I gave him nothing.

He swallowed soundly and carried on, "I get it. You're punishing me." I wanted to guffaw, but I stopped myself because I knew he needed to say everything that was on his mind. If I stopped him, he might try to contact me in the future with more promises, denials, proclamations...I had to allow him to get it all out so there'd be nothing left for him to say.

"I just made a really big mistake. I am not going to try to make any more excuses. The only thing I will say, and this isn't an excuse, but I think a part of me was hurt that you wouldn't commit, so that kind of, well, it contributed to me having a super weak moment," He seemed to be thinking as he stalled for time by taking a bite of his burger and chewing on it at a much slower pace than was typical. He took a swig of his drink before he continued, "Even though I know it will take you a while to forgive me, I think...." At this point, he was actually avoiding eye contact, "I think we really need to make a serious commitment and take our relationship to the next step. That doesn't mean you'd immediately become my girlfriend. It would just...well, I'm sure if we basically," He lifted his hands and made air quotes, "Put it in writing," he laughed, "You know, make a commitment. Then, I would never be tempted and have a weak moment again. And let's face it, we are meant for each other, you know that, right? Isn't that why we're here?"

He stopped prattling on and finally regarded me, surveying my expression. He'd spoken his peace, and now it was my turn.

I looked Jamey square in the eyes while he waited for my response. I recognized that this was one of the most significant moments in my life. If I didn't succeed, if I wasn't strong or brave enough, it could have detrimental effects. I had to speak my peace without hesitation or mercy, without letting Jamey interrupt under any circumstances.

"I need you to listen to me, Jamey," I stated in a stern tone. "Do you understand? I really need you to listen, just like I heard you out. I want you to promise me you will do the same."

He nodded subtly. "Okay," his voice still had a chipper tone that irked me, but I managed to keep a flat, neutral expression on my face.

I tapped my fingers on the table and sighed, "I need you to pay very close attention to what I have to say, and I'm going to get right to the point. To be honest, I don't have all that much to say, but what I do have to say is," I paused for emphasis, "very important."

He looked hopeful yet slightly fearful, which gave me a sense of empowerment. He puckered his lips and jutted back and forth, waiting for me to continue.

"Jamey, unfortunately, you are under the wrong impression," I began with as little affect as possible. I needed him to recognize the fact that I was not overreacting. I was not behaving irrationally based on heightened emotions. Basically, it was necessary for me to be composed, stern, and unyielding. There was no room for error if I was to be successful in ridding my life of him. I needed a fresh start. He'd taken up too much of...*me*, and that had to end now.

"I want nothing to do with you," I watched as his entire demeanor shifted, but I continued before he could even attempt to interrupt me, "I am done with you. Not just for now. Forever," I said the word again, drawing out the syllables, "FOR-EV-ER.

"You disgust me. I am literally repulsed by you. I am sickened that I wasted so much time thinking you were an actual decent human being. I feel so upset with myself for believing there was any possibility we could have a relationship because there's not. None. Not now, not ever."

Jamey's hooded eyes filled with tears, and they immediately started spilling down his face. "You can't do this to me. How can you do this?" He placed his face in his hands and started sobbing. I turned in my seat and noticed that he had attracted the attention of patrons sitting a few seats back from us.

He removed his hands and smacked them on the table, not noticing or caring about the prying eyes. "Please, Jess...I am begging you. You have to reconsider; you have to at least...."

"No," I growled, through gritted teeth, "No. I will not."

"Listen to me, Jamey." He refused to look up; he kept his face buried in his palms, incessantly rubbing at his eyes. I went on, "If you try to contact me, I will get a restraining order. I will make sure your football scholarship is revoked. I will tell my father what you did."

"No," Jamey gasped, pulling his fingers away from his red-rimmed pupils. "Please, Jess, don't do that."

I nodded, "I will."

"Why? Why are you being so cruel?" He had a perplexed, genuinely shocked expression, yet the vulnerability was easing out of him. I never thought I would witness Jamey Russo in such a state. He was broken, wrecked...*desperate*. I was so flabbergasted that it, unfortunately, started to take the wind out of my sails.

I felt a flutter in my chest, and my own eyes started to tear up as I examined the boy that I loved. I hadn't processed the enormity of my feelings for him until he was sitting across from me, weeping; I realized at that moment that although I'd refused to admit it for all these years, I truly loved him. I felt frozen in time as I continued to gaze into the eyes of the gorgeous, cocky boy who'd wink at me every day on the football field while I was trying to practice my cheerleading moves. I remembered the grin he'd had on his face the night we played "Never Have I Ever" and I was forced to acknowledge that I had engaged in self-exploration, our first kiss-how his lips were smooth and soft during a game of "Spin the Bottle." I recalled the day we worked on a project together, and he listed all the things he liked about me; none of which were superficial...the way he threw himself on the ground in front of our entire tenth-grade class and announced that he loved me...finding the flowers he'd bought after he'd spanked me, his sincere apology, and genuine acknowledgment that he had been wrong. I'd fit so perfectly in his lap while we were in his hot tub- like he was the missing portion of a puzzle piece we both belonged to, and the gentle touch of his lips on my head before I drifted to sleep when he chose so stay with me, while all his friends were partying- he left the party to be with me. He loved me. He didn't care about Kayla. He was using her. I was the one he loved. Why had I strung him along? Why hadn't I committed to him? Was it my fault? Was there something wrong with me? Was I commitment-phobic? Would this have happened if I'd agreed to be his girlfriend?

"I'm so sorry, Jess," Jamey tried to take my hands in his, but I instinctively snatched them away before he could.

His words immediately flipped a switch, and I subsequently snapped back to reality. I came to my senses. His apology evoked memories of all the moments he'd said those same words over the years- all the many occasions he'd screwed up. But this time was different. This was the point of no return.

"This is it, Jamey. This..." I pointed to him and then to me, "is over. Don't ever try to contact me again, or I will take legal action. And believe me, if you don't leave me alone, I will do everything I can to destroy you."

"But, your dad. He's always liked me. He wants us to be together."

I snickered. "Don't be naïve, Jamey. How do you think he would react if I told him what you did?"

"You wouldn't, Jess," he said pleadingly, "You wouldn't do that to me."

I tilted my head and widened my eyes sarcastically. "Oh no, you really think I have reason to protect you."

I stared at the half-eaten burger on his tray, took a piece in my hand, and threw it at his chest. He gasped as I continued, "Why don't you chew on this?"

I stood up and placed my hands on my hips. "You must realize the extent of your revolting behavior if you are that upset at the idea of my father finding out. Why would I ever want anything to do with you if you can't stomach the idea of my dad knowing what kind of person you are? I know now that you are a pig."

Jamey's mouth dropped open, and he reflexively moved back in his chair as if I'd punched him.

"Don't ever contact me again."

"But…"

"There are no 'buts.' These are not threats, Jamey. I don't threaten people. I'm not a bully like you. This is more like a warning, and I will follow through on it. I want you out of my life. No contact. Don't come near me, and don't try to get in touch with me. If you do, all I can say is, I promise you- you will regret it."

Jamey placed both hands over his face, moved his tray out of the way, and laid his face down on the table; his body was convulsing as he once again began bawling.

I watched him for a millisecond and then looked around the room, taking in the fact that we were alone. There were a few people scattered about in other areas of the restaurant, but we must have scared away patrons who had contemplated sitting anywhere near us. I felt relieved that I could slip away without having to pass by anyone who would be a witness to what I was leaving behind. I didn't look back at Jamey's collapsed figure as I grabbed my purse and marched out of Happy Burger.

Part V.
College

Chapter Thirty-seven: A Time to Grieve

6 months later

My first semester of college was over, although I'd earned enough credits while still in high school to be considered a sophomore. My parents, sisters, Jenna, and Nikki- the only people I'd stayed in touch with over the course of half a year understood when I said I didn't want to come home for the summer. It was actually May, still spring, when I completed my finals and received perfect scores in all my classes. My father was so proud of me. It was the first time in my life when his praise didn't elevate my spirits. I felt nothing when he said, "Jessica, I have never been prouder of you. You've accomplished so much in your life, but getting straight A's your first semester at a university like ULA is unimaginable and beyond impressive, even for a diligent, hard-working student like you." Of course, I thanked him and claimed to be excited about my success...but I wasn't.

    I thought life would improve when I moved to Los Angeles- I truly believed I could leave it all behind, escape and start over. In theory, that was what I did. I left- I never had to see the people, specifically Jamey, who I found it necessary to avoid. Yet, I learned that you can't run away from your own thoughts. The moment I stepped off the plane and moved into my Nona Jessica's beautiful mansion, I became my own worst enemy.

    I can't begin to describe my rapid ascension into misery. At the time, I didn't have the vocabulary to describe what I was feeling. Initially, I felt sad. I could handle that. It made sense. Everyone periodically experiences melancholy; it's a typical reaction to what I'd endured. My whole life had crumbled apart in one night. The guy I thought I'd spend the rest of my life with had betrayed me. However, confusion and guilt soon ebbed their way in, adding an extra layer of despondency. I kept thinking that it was my fault. So many people had pointed out that I was the one who refused to commit. The unwelcome memory of what Jamey had done would creep into my head, initially eliciting anger and disgust. Then I'd be reminded of Kayla's mean-spiritedness about the incident- actually, it went beyond that- she truly loathed and blamed me for what the guys had done.

What's more, is that she wasn't the only one who insinuated I was to blame. The words of Kelly, Erin, Josh, and even Jamey would play out in my already muddled head, and I'd soon begin to feel a sense of culpability. My brain felt like it was caught in a cyclone; contradictory thoughts were swirling through it at an exceeding pace.

These were the kinds of conversations I'd have with myself every day:

"It is definitely not my fault. Jamey has complete control over his actions."

"But, this never would have happened if you had just agreed to be his girlfriend."

"I wasn't ready to be his girlfriend. I had every right to take my time."

"Why would you lead him on like that? What made you do that?"

"I didn't lead him on. I was upfront about my feelings."

"Everyone was judging you, IS judging you because they think you're a tease."

"I'm not a tease. I never lied, I never...."

"Yes, you did. You acted like a girlfriend but wouldn't even let him get past first base."

"It's my body. I didn't feel comfortable."

"That's not the point. If you had committed, he wouldn't have been with other girls."

"Maybe that's not even true. He might have been."

"You'll never know because you chose to keep him at bay. You could have at least tried out a relationship. What's wrong with you? You're not normal. How could you not have realized how weird you are? Jamey wouldn't have been able to hurt girls like Kayla if you had agreed to be his girlfriend. You admitted that he loved you. So, why did you hold out?"

It would go on and on, and even if I wanted to, which I didn't, I wouldn't have known how to explain what I was going through to anyone. No one would understand. Nona Jessica tried to get me to open up to her, but I sunk into myself. I spoke to everyone on a superficial level. It's difficult to recall everything I experienced during those six months because I felt like a volcano had erupted in my mind. I was constantly fighting to rid myself of negative, troubling fixations.

I was existing, but I was just as broken as Jamey had been at Happy Burger.

Before I left, I'd heard whispers that Jamey was using alcohol to self-medicate. Fortunately, I had more productive ways to deal with my pain. I studied constantly. Studying was the only way I could make the voices go away. I knew the voices weren't real- I wasn't having hallucinations or delusions. Up until that point, I'd only taken low-level psychology classes and wasn't particularly knowledgeable about mental illness. Aside from feeling guilty and grief-stricken, I didn't think anything was wrong with me. It wasn't until later that I learned about the nuances of depressive and anxiety disorders.

Additionally, I hadn't realized until my great-grandmother pointed it out that I'd developed an unhealthy aversion and distrust of males. Nona Jessica took me out to dinner one evening, and our waiter started to flirt with me in a sweet, harmless way. I don't recall the exchange because my level of distress was overwhelming during that entire time period. My only recollection of the evening was Nona Jessica interrogating me about when and if I'd been sexually harassed or assaulted. When I vehemently denied that anything like that had occurred, she swallowed soundly and muttered, "I'm sorry, darling, it's just that your reaction to innocent coquetry is similar to how a survivor would respond."

She didn't press the issue, and I was quiet after that, reflecting on her words. Afterward, I began to notice my response to boys at school- when they looked at me for more than a millisecond, I found myself flinching. I also recognized that since I started at university, I'd unwittingly been dressing in looser clothes, pulling my hair back in tight buns, and refusing to wear any makeup. Once this realization sunk in, my irrational thoughts took on a life of their own. I began berating myself for "pretending" to be a victim when I'd suffered no abuse. In fact, I had the benefit of being fortunate enough to escape an uncomfortable situation. It wasn't fair that I had that advantage when others didn't. Life wasn't fair. Subsequently, I became fixated on all the inequities in the world. I rebuked myself for being self-centered and entitled by taking my privileges for granted. Then a slew of new, abstruse, and disturbing thoughts commenced, which were even more toxic. My mind would race sporadically throughout the day whenever I wasn't listening to a lecture or studying. The obsessions became nonsensical; contradictory thoughts cycled in an extremely toxic and scary way. It was like someone had tossed a match on gasoline- my brain felt as if it were on fire the majority of the time.

As I previously stated, my education was the only thing that saved me from myself. I was able to listen during lectures, participate in group activities, and study without the obsessions creeping in. I had no idea why academics was the only reprieve I allowed myself.

After telling my family and friends I was staying in L.A. for the summer, I told Nona Jessica. I was surprised that she wasn't happy about my news. In fact, she looked crestfallen. At first, I was mortified. I thought I'd overstayed my welcome. I apologized and interrogated her, begging her to divulge whether she wanted privacy. Did she need a break from having me as her house guest? She assured me in no uncertain terms that that wasn't the case.

"What's wrong then?" I inquired, "Why do you look so forlorn at the idea of me staying?"

She sighed, a long, drawn-out, distressing sigh.

It was then that she said the words that changed my life. She saved me, although, at the time, I wasn't ready to acknowledge the severity of my *issues*, for lack of a better word.

"Jessica, my dear, you are severely depressed, and I'm sorry, love, but it has to be said. You desperately need help."

My mouth dropped open; I thought her assertion was a major exaggeration, yet I knew in my heart that there was some truth in her words.

I looked down at the floor as she stared at me, awaiting a response.

I silently nodded, acquiescing.

And so it began...my time to grieve was about to turn into my time to heal.

Chapter Thirty-eight: A Time to Heal

6 months after that

I'd been in therapy for six months before realizing I was starting to heal. Unfortunately, things got worse before they got better, which I've learned is often the case. I agreed to see Dr. O'Hara, who my great-grandmother informed me was one of the best psychiatrists in L.A. She came highly recommended. I didn't want my parents to know; I was afraid my father would see it as a sign of weakness. My Nona tsked at that and muttered something under her breath. It was the first time she'd expressed disapproval of my dad. However, I knew they had very different opinions about certain things.

Dr. O'Hara was in her thirties; she was attractive and warm. She was professional but not at all what I expected in a psychiatrist. I had old-fashioned ideas about the profession because my knowledge was solely based on what I'd seen in movies or television shows. I expected to lie on a couch next to a serious, humorless woman holding a notepad and writing down everything I said. I did not anticipate the judgment-free, safe environment created by someone who was extremely good at her job. I couldn't help but like Dr. O'Hara, and I could tell that she genuinely cared about her patients. She didn't push me; she allowed me to reveal and divulge at my own pace.

It took me about a month of weekly visits before I really began to open up. At the start, I was afraid to because I didn't want to admit I had a problem- a very serious one and I had reservations about being diagnosed. I sidestepped questions without elaborating. The first visit ironically triggered an anxiety attack. Dr. O'Hara immediately detected my distress. She prescribed a low dose of Xanax and suggested breathing exercises and meditation. I admittedly began to trust her because although the meds helped take the edge off, her therapeutic counsel had a huge impact on soothing my trembling, palpitations, nausea, and chest pain.

Around my fourth visit, I felt comfortable enough to open up to her about what led me to L.A. and how those experiences were causing me to feel. The way she communicated inspired me to be more forthcoming, and the most surprising thing to me was that none of what I said shocked her; she would nod and encourage me to continue. She not only guided me in recognizing that Jamey's actions were not my fault, but she also helped me see that I was not responsible for how other people, including Kayla, responded to the situation. We ended up discussing my perfectionism and drive to succeed, which she slowly and delicately implied could potentially have something to do with my father. It took a while for us to delve into some of the negative parenting methods employed by both my parents. I was a little resentful at first and confided in my great-grandmother.

"Dr. O'Hara doesn't know enough about Mom and Dad to make assertions like that," I'd said, somewhat angrily.

Nona smiled and tilted her head, "No one is perfect, Jessica. Not me, not you, and not your mother and father. Everyone's parents manage to screw them up a little." We both laughed because she didn't ordinarily use expressions like that.

"I don't think it's my father's fault that I want to succeed…."

"Wanting to succeed is different from desperately seeking approval."

I was quiet for a minute, reflecting on her words, "How is that his fault? He was always complimenting me and using me as an example for my sisters."

She gave me a pointed look, "What do you mean by that?"

"Nona," I began with a chuckle, "you sound like Dr. O'Hara; maybe you missed your calling."

"You didn't answer my question," she stated in a serious tone.

"Well, he would chastise them when they didn't get all A's and…" my voice trailed off as the truth in Dr. O'Hara and Nona Jessica's words sunk in.

"And what did your mom say about all this?" Nona asked, feigning innocence.

"Nothing."

"Right, she let your dad be the disciplinarian."

I sighed and scratched my head. "Well, yeah. I guess."

Nona threw her hands up in the air. "Jessica, I love both of your parents. They're wonderful people, but this is about you, honey. When you're young and inexperienced, it's sometimes difficult to admit your parents are less than perfect. It doesn't mean they didn't do their best. We're all human."

Dr. O'Hara diagnosed me with situational depression, panic disorder, and obsessive-compulsive disorder. I was very bothered by the labels until I truly took in my psychiatrist's words and the meaning behind them. She explained that my emotional problems were **pieces** of a pie- they didn't make up the **whole** pie; they were only part of my overall persona. She didn't tell me I *was* depressed and anxious. Instead, she said I was an intelligent, strong, caring teenage girl who *had* depression and anxiety. She said those fractions of my psyche did not define me.

The first three times she mentioned antidepressants, I was taken aback and, to be frank, terrified. I initially refused to even consider the idea. However, after talking to Nona Jessica and doing some research on my own, I realized how common it was for people to be prescribed Serotonin Reuptake Inhibitors- like Prozac or Zoloft. I eventually caved because although talk therapy was helping, the obsessive thoughts were still debilitating. She kept assuring me that taking them might be a short-term thing- I didn't necessarily have to stay on them for a long period of time, but it might help me to recover. I reluctantly agreed, and after about a month, I began to notice that I wasn't perseverating as much. I started to feel a little bit better.

My road to recovery was long, and the healing was slow and steady. I learned so much in therapy, and I definitely began to understand myself better as a result of my interactions with Dr. O'Hara. She acted as a facilitator and a guide- her questions and statements led me to identify how my familial relationships affected my feelings and decisions. For instance, my dad's constant praise for Jamey and the similarities between the two of them. Of course, there were also many differences, which is why it was hard for me not to notice at the outset and throughout the years he spent courting me. Besides, the comparisons were nuanced- they were both alpha males, although they presented their masculinity in different ways. My father had a cool, calm, and collected way of demonstrating dominance, while Jamey was more passionate and impulsive.

My emotions took on a life of their own during those months; I was sometimes angry with my dad and blamed him for encouraging me to date Jamey. I also felt ashamed of my mom for allowing my father to discipline my sisters and me in such an authoritative way. As I began to heal, I eventually digested the fact that they were human, as Nona Jessica had pointed out, and flawed like everyone else. It wasn't simplistic enough to say I forgave them and accepted what I came to refer to as their shortcomings. I couldn't completely shake off feelings of bitterness and resentment. Still, Dr. O'Hara told me those were normal sentiments that would take years to fully comprehend, and over time, the negativity and blame would slowly dissipate.

No one does a three hundred and sixty degree rotation overnight; I didn't wake up one morning and realize I was cured. Anyone in crisis knows that isn't the way it works. Although, I do remember walking along campus one afternoon in November and smiling as I looked up into the clear blue California sky and felt the warmth of the sun on my face. I remember thinking, "Wow, there literally isn't a cloud in sight. It's such a beautiful day." At that precise moment, I contemplated that I must have experienced so many similar days. Because of my depression, I didn't notice or appreciate the beauty and warmth of my surroundings. I suddenly felt a sense of gratitude and contentment.

In the following days, I also began to notice my interest in reading and watching movies had returned. When I discussed this with my therapist, she pointed out that as depression lifts, people begin to enjoy the things in life they'd ceased to appreciate while being overcome with despondency.

And…

Although I didn't recognize it until almost the end of the semester…

For the first time in my life…

I realized…

That finally…

After all this time…

I was attracted to someone other than Jamey!

Chapter Thirty-nine: The Reunion

Around the time I started to feel as if I was healing, I realized that I hadn't spoken to Erin or Kelly in a year. It seemed difficult to believe when the recognition sunk in. After all, for almost four years, they had played nearly as significant a part in my life as Jamey. During the six months I spent grieving and the following six that I devoted to recovery, I hadn't even thought about how our friendship dissolved in one afternoon. They had tried reaching out for weeks following our trip to Coffee Corner, but I ignored their texts and calls. After I left to move to L.A., they stopped trying. The only constants in my life from Connecticut for the past twelve months had been my immediate family, Nikki and Jenna. I'd needed a fresh start, and looking back, I acknowledged that I definitely had been granted one.

After roughly three hundred and sixty five days, I finally decided that I was ready to go home, and Thanksgiving break would be the ideal time. Although Nona Jessica wouldn't be accompanying me, she was ecstatic and saw it as a major triumph. She clapped when I told her and boasted that she had been right. "I told you, a good therapist was just what you needed!"

"Well," I murmured, feeling a little scared at the prospect of returning to Connecticut, "I'm not completely *better*. I do have anxiety and...."

"Of course you do," Nona cut me off, "Therapy isn't like magic. We are not meant to feel blissful all the time. That's just not how human nature works. I've always strived to be...."

This time, it was my turn to cut her off. "Content."

She nodded vigorously, "Perfect word, dear."

Although I wanted to reunite with Kelly and Erin, I wasn't sure how they'd feel. Were they mad that I had ghosted them? I hoped they would understand my fragility was the catalyst for many of my previous choices. I'd been hurt by my perception of their priorities; it appeared as if their devotion towards Jamey and determination to preserve the dynamics of our clique outweighed their concern for my grief over Jamey's infidelity.

Since I spoke to Nikki quite frequently, she was the one I confided in about my wish to reconcile with the female members of our high school clan. Jenna and Nikki never mentioned any of our old friends when I spoke to them. They knew I was trying to recuperate, and discussing what I left behind would have hindered my growth. Therefore, I had no idea how Kelly and Erin would respond to my request to visit with them over November break. I also wasn't even aware if they would be in Rosevalley for the holiday.

Nikki assured me that everyone would be around. She claimed she had recently received a text from Kelly stating that she and Erin would be visiting over Thanksgiving. Although Nikki and Jenna were currently attending St. Padre Pio, the other girls were at separate universities. Before she even ran it by them, Nikki insisted that she was certain Kelly and Erin would be thrilled to see me. She promised to arrange everything. I agreed, but I told her my only request was that we meet up once again at Coffee Corner. I thought it would be nostalgic. Nikki was initially afraid meeting that might conjure up the negative memory of our last visit. Still, I managed to convince her that our reunion would be reminiscent of all the pleasant memories we'd shared there over the years and possibly negate the one unpleasant encounter.

I planned to meet all of my friends at Coffee Corner after visiting with my family and unpacking. Jenna and Nikki had both offered to pick me up, but I assured them I would be fine on my own. I needed to start asserting my independence; I'd recently begun exploring the "whys and hows" of my almost lifelong reliance on them in therapy. Another issue to dissect.

From what I could recollect, Coffee Corner had not changed much in the past year. The café was still just as stylish and contemporary as I remembered, with its glossy taupe ceiling, Terra Cotta floors, and high wooden tables. I arrived a few minutes earlier than my friends so I could take everything in, do some breathing exercises, and contemplate what it would feel like to see them all in person after such a long time. I was alone for barely ten minutes before they began to arrive. Just as I finished ordering a green tea, I heard Jenna and Nikki's voices calling out my name. As I turned to face them, they rushed up and hugged me on opposite sides. We were soon entwined in a group embrace. As Jenna ordered, I noticed she'd added a few purple and green highlights to her frosted blonde hair. Nikki had let her black hair grow even longer, and she'd added some layers. I self-consciously pulled my hair behind my ears, realizing I hadn't even been to the hairdresser since moving to L.A. For as long as I could remember, I'd gone every two months while living in Connecticut.

Jenna suggested we sit on one of the three sofas strewn throughout the café. We typically sat at a table, but Nikki and I agreed. The change would be nice. We didn't have long to wait before Kelly and Erin strolled in together. They both had huge smiles on their faces when they saw us. We all stood up, but Kelly and Erin eagerly greeted me before they acknowledged Jenna and Nikki. They must have felt as if they wanted to make amends, or maybe it was just because I was the only one of us that they hadn't seen in a year.

Erin stood directly behind Kelly as she drew me in and held me for seconds, her hands wrapped snuggly around my shoulders before letting go. She was so close I could smell the familiar floral perfume she always wore. When she pulled away, she had tears in her eyes, "I've missed you," she exclaimed.

Erin playfully pushed Kelly away and put her hands tightly on both my forearms, "And so have I," she announced, "You look great!"

I smiled sheepishly, unsure if she was being nice or honest. "Thank you, I've missed you all too," I fibbed. I actually hadn't even thought about the two of them while I focused on recovery.

Once everyone had ordered and we were sitting comfortably in a semi-circle on the sectional sofa, we began to make small talk.

"Remember the summer we all met?" Erin asked enthusiastically, "Geez, that seems like such a long time ago."

We all agreed, nodding and commenting on how much everything had changed over the past five years.

"We were barely fourteen that summer!" Kelly pronounced, "Just babies."

"Well, unfortunately, although we are so much more mature than we were then, we're still technically teenagers," Jenna piped in, sounding cynical. "I hate being underage. I can't wait to be legal."

"Eighteen used to be the legal drinking age. I mean, we can vote; we should be able to drink, right?" Nikki threw her arms in the air in frustration.

Kelly giggled and snuck a glance at Erin. "Well, it's not like the law ever stopped us. And I don't know about you guys, but we have fake I.D.s, and there are parties at our school every night."

Jenna and Nikki nodded. "Yeah, we have I.D.s, too," Nikki said.

"And the law isn't stopping us either," Jenna admitted as they all snickered conspiratorially.

"What about you, Jess?" Kelly inquired, "It must be so fun in L.A. I can't even imagine all the cute guys, the parties. You must be having the time of your…"

"Does anyone want anything else?" Jenna cut her off, sitting upright. There was a protective edge to her voice- it was familiar, but when I met her eyes, I nodded once. I was okay. I could handle this.

"Well," I drew the word out before I continued speaking. Jenna and Nikki knew all about what I'd gone through since moving in with Nona Jessica. I hadn't been sure if I wanted to share that with Kelly and Erin, but at that moment, I decided that I would own my story…my struggles. I had grieved, and I wasn't ashamed.

"I've actually had a difficult time this past year," I stated in an even tone.

Kelly's face fell, and Erin reddened, "I'm sorry!" they blurted in unison.

"We never should have ambushed you," Kelly's eyes filled up, "We've regretted it."

Erin was bobbing her head up and down. "That was awful of us. We were so selfish."

I shook my head. "No, no, please, it's okay. It is not your fault," I replied vehemently. "It's just that I…I didn't realize…it sounds so ridiculous, but I didn't *know* I was in love with Jamey. Isn't that so stupid?"

My friends all looked at me with sympathy; it wasn't pity. I wouldn't have been able to handle pity. They were genuinely sorry for all that happened.

I sighed. "Anyway, I went through a lot; I've been dealing with anxiety and depression. To be honest, I've been spending all my time in therapy or studying." I guffawed, "I guess I haven't had time for partying."

Everyone was quiet and still, watching me; there were a few seconds of uncomfortable silence before I went on. "But, I am doing MUCH better. I am really starting to heal."

Erin gulped, "I'm so glad you're feeling better, Jess. And Kelly and I were so incredibly happy when we heard you wanted to see us."

Kelly tilted her head towards Erin, indicating agreement. "Yes, definitely. I couldn't even sleep last night. I was so relieved," she put her hand over her heart, "And ecstatic that you...."

"Forgave us?" Erin finished for her; it was more of a question than a statement.

"Yes, yes, of course!"

Kelly cleared her throat, "The ironic part of all this is that we were trying so desperately to protect our crew. Obviously, that's why we acted the way we did."

Erin shrugged, "And when you left, our crew immediately broke apart. It fell to pieces."

I furrowed my brows and glanced from Nikki to Jenna to gauge their reactions. They hadn't mentioned a thing about tension among our friends. They both had neutral expressions on their faces. I supposed that this was old news to them. I also realized that every time I'd spoken to either of them the past year, we'd discussed our own individual lives- our "small worlds" and nothing outside of that.

"Really?" I asked with intense curiosity, drawing the word out, "Are you serious? I had no idea…what, what happened?" I was genuinely shocked and very interested in what had occurred after I left.

"You don't know?" Kelly questioned, sounding somewhat surprised. She quickly scanned Jenna and Nikki. Apparently, she was also trying to assess their thoughts about the past and possibly grasp what they had (and hadn't) told me.

Nikki casually shrugged.

"It never came up," Jenna replied dryly.

Although they both exuded nonchalance, I noticed an amused glance pass between Nikki and Jenna. I think they were entertained by the fact that I obviously found this tidbit of information rather compelling.

"Anyway," Kelly began with uncertainty, "Yeah, like I said, we basically stopped hanging out after you left."

"But why?" I was intrigued; the idea that the group *split* had never occurred to me.

Everyone was quiet for a few seconds. I sat forward in my chair, feeling extremely inquisitive. They were all looking at one another, apparently trying to figure out where to begin.

"I think it started with Bobby," Kelly finally said, pulling on her bottom lip. "He basically ditched us. He avoided Jamey at first. It was like Jamey was desperate to talk to him. Jamey was calling all of us, begging us to convince Bobby to return his calls. There were even scenes in the hallways."

"What kind of scenes? What do you mean?"

"They had fights," Erin said, sighing, "Not fist fights, just Jamey chasing after Bobby and Bobby refusing to give him the time of day. After a while, Jamey stopped trying."

"Well, that was after the principal and guidance counselor got involved," Jenna added, "And Bobby quit sports. He started hanging out with different people all of a sudden."

Nikki was nodding, "He wouldn't even talk to Evan. The only thing he said was that he needed a change. The coaches were upset, but what could they do?"

"Wow!" I widened my eyes in disbelief. "Wow," I repeated, processing what I would have thought was an impossibility, "So, was it just Bobby? You said the whole group broke up?" In a way, I felt like I was sliding down a rabbit hole, but I couldn't help it. Admittedly, my curiosity got the best of me.

Kelly cleared her throat and shook her head with a look of pity. "Josh. Josh kind of…ruined his reputation. I guess you could say he…."

Jenna finished her sentence, "Made a fool out of himself." She was smirking as she said this, and I was the only one who truly knew why.

"What did he do?" I placed my hand over my mouth when I realized I had shouted my question.

Nikki fiddled with the layers in her hair as she answered in a semi-uninterested manner, "He tried to get Kayla to hook up with him. We were all at a party."

Jenna yawned, "I wasn't there."

Nikki raised her eyebrows and playfully threw a pillow at Jenna, "Miss-I-Only-Date-College-Boys" was absent that night," she replied in a faux haughty tone, and we all laughed.

"Actually, Bobby wasn't there either. He'd already started to ghost us at that point," Erin piped in, "But Jamey was there."

"Well, what happened?" I was desperate to find out what Josh had done. "Go on!" I ordered.

Erin cleared her throat and continued, "He...well, he was like grabbing her. She was drunk, of course, and chasing after Jamey. Jamey apparently didn't want to hook up with her THAT night. She was crying, I think."

Kelly nodded, "Yes, she was hysterical; she was like pleading with Jamey. She even made comments about...."

She looked like a deer stuck in the headlights for a millisecond. I immediately guessed the reason why and did a quick shake of my head, "It's okay."

"She was saying that you were gone and you weren't coming back, and he should get over you. He kept pushing her away. He was really pissed off. I think he finally left. Then Josh hit on her, and she must have turned him down. He started saying all kinds of things to her. He was calling her a slut, and he was basically bullying her. I mean, it was like sexual harassment. At first, no one said anything because it was...Josh. *Josh Kowalski-* the freaking quarterback. But finally, some football players, Josh's 'friends,' had to step in. They were gentle at first, but he got really aggressive, and it turned physical."

My mouth had dropped open. "You're kidding me!"

Kelly shook her head, "No. There were all kinds of rumors afterward. Everyone- *everyone* was talking about it."

I glanced in Jenna's direction, and she elevated one eyebrow. "It was awesome," she snorted smugly.

Kelly and Erin looked confused but chose to ignore her comment.

"People kind of lost respect for him after that," Nikki stated, "I mean, even Evan confided in me that he was embarrassed to hang out with him- he became so just angry and hostile all the time."

"And Jamey never got over you," Kelly alleged, "He was...*is* a mess- drinking, drugs."

"Drugs?" I repeated, "No way."

"Let's change the subject," Jenna chimed in, "Jessica has moved on. She doesn't need to hear about Jamey. He made his bed."

Although my curiosity was piqued, I knew Jenna was right. I couldn't afford to feel sorry for Jamey. I'd learned in therapy that I was not responsible for other people's actions or reactions. I had to take care of myself, and my relationship with Jamey was over forever. His mental state was not my problem; I didn't need to know.

At that point, we all realized we'd exhausted the topic of our broken clique, so we went on to discuss a variety of other topics, such as new boyfriends, gossip about old classmates, career aspirations, and interesting classes we'd be taking or wanted to take. Hours passed in the blink of an eye. It was starting to get dark by the time we decided it was time to leave so we could respectively go home to be with our families.

We stood around the parking lot for a few minutes, saying our goodbyes. We all hugged and promised to keep in touch. While driving to my parent's house, I smiled with contentment. I felt like I'd come full circle after meeting with my friends. This meeting had obviously gone so much differently than our previous one the year before. It felt good to reunite with my best friends from high school. Regardless of what happened, our shared memories would always be a significant part of my life. I was relieved that I was now ready to let Kelly and Erin back in. It was another step in the healing process. The funny thing was, I hadn't even realized how much I missed them until our reunion.

I now had one more thing left to do before I could officially move on with my life and say definitively that I was "over" Jamey Russo and all that had happened between us.

Chapter Forty: "Contentedly" Ever After

About a month after the reunion with my friends, I realized it was the first day of winter. The start of a new season...I had been planning to do something for about two months now, but I hadn't had the nerve. I was entering into new territory, and taking risks had never been my strong point. I wasn't impulsive; I was not a risk-taker. That morning, when I looked at the calendar and saw the date, I finally felt compelled to take the initiative and step out of my comfort zone...gamble...roll the dice, so to speak.

I was taking an advanced Abnormal Psychology class that was about to conclude. Actually, the final would be given the next day. Today was the last day of classes before exams and the beginning of winter break. In retrospect, I think it wasn't only the fact that we were entering into the next phase of the year, which was literally broken up into quarters when you lived in New England. My resolve to act on my feelings was also due to the reality that time was running out.

On the first day of Abnormal Psych, approximately four months before, I felt something stir in me that was initially perplexing and inexplicable. When I sauntered into the small lecture hall, I noticed a boy- a boy with wavy, longish raven hair and huge, round eyes that were as dark as obsidian. My heart began to flutter when we exchanged glances, and he smiled at me. I was *attracted* to him- magnetized by how good-looking he was, and he had the best smile. I was astonished at first because I hadn't ever felt this way about anyone other than Jamey. Of course, I was still in recovery mode at that time and had no intention of acting on my emotions. I was not in the right frame of mind.

Over the course of the semester, I grew more and more mesmerized by "Guzman," our teacher always referred to the outgoing students by their last names. I learned his first name was Alex only because I was walking by his desk and noticed it written on his laptop. Although I had never had a conversation with Alex Guzman, I felt as if I knew him on a personal level. He participated frequently in class. Ironically, I didn't contribute much during discussions. I was still feeling fragile and withdrawn. In fact, my grade was an A- although I'd aced all my tests because the participation portion was only average. In therapy, Dr. O'Hara convinced me to celebrate my ability to accept a less-than-perfect score. I was learning to work on my "perfectionism," which my therapist attributed to my father's parenting techniques.

Anyway, even though Alex was very extroverted and opinionated, he never attempted to dominate conversations. He also didn't listen to respond, which was something I realized I had been guilty of in the past. When he was involved in a debate, he was attentive. His facial expressions indicated he was concentrating and analyzing the other person's point of view. I respected and admired those qualities. I also tended to almost always agree with him. He was very sensitive about psychological disorders, and it was obvious he knew a lot about the topic. I concurred that this potentially could mean a lot of things- which ranged from personal experience with mental illness to decent study habits. There was no way for me to identify how or why he was so knowledgeable about the subject matter.

The only person I confided in about my attraction to Alex was my doctor. I told her he appeared to quite possibly be one of the most caring and sympathetic males I'd ever known or encountered. Needless to say, our session that day led me to ruminate about the male role models life had provided me and their influence on the boys I'd chosen to hang around with. Consequently, I realized I was ready to get to know men who were different from Jamey and my father. Young men like Alex Guzman.

There was definitely a flirtation between Alex and me during, before and after class. We'd never had a conversation, but there were lots of once-overs, batting of eyelashes, winks, smiles, and even reciprocated yawns. I couldn't be certain, but I thought that just maybe he found me attractive. Possibly, he'd be interested in going on a date. My only concern was that he'd had four months to ask me out, and he never had.

I attempted to discuss and dissect the reasons why Alex had never approached me with my therapist, but she didn't have it- she said she would not participate in an "OCD party" with me. She claimed that in this day and age, there was no reason why a young woman couldn't be the pursuer. She insisted that the only way I would find out whether Alex wanted to go out with me was for me to approach him.

In all honesty, this was an odd concept for me- I'd always been on the receiving end. In high school, I would never have dreamed of making the first move. Dr. O'Hara's response to that was, "Well, that's the way you were raised. It's time to take control. Write your own plot twist."

I grinned, feeling empowered. My life definitely was going in a direction I wouldn't have foreseen even a year ago. I never would have thought I would ask a guy out. But here I was- on the first day of winter...the start of a new season. I was about to do something really big, and I hadn't consulted any of my friends or even Nona Jessica about it. I was independent. I was strong. I was prepared to do one of the most significant things I'd ever do, and I hadn't asked anyone's advice on how to do it.

I didn't even have a plan- but I knew that no matter what, I'd be content. There were so many reasons why Alex might turn me down- he might have a girlfriend, he might have a boyfriend, he might like blondes or redheads or taller girls or curvier girls. However, I was still going to take the chance that he might say yes.

When class was dismissed, Alex lingered behind as I slipped out of the room. I waited for him to have a quick discussion with the professor. When he walked out the door, I was leaning against the brick building. "Hey, Alex!" I called in a singsong voice.

He had a shocked grin on his face when he turned to face me. He pointed at his chest, "Are you talking to me?" he asked.

I nodded, and he strolled over. I couldn't tell if his countenance was one of joy or dread. I was too nervous to make sense of it. Would he be happy and accept my request, or would he turn me down? At that moment, I had no idea. No matter what happened, I wouldn't be surprised. However, I was determined to be brave and follow through. For the first time, I was going to take charge when it came to my love life. I was diving head-first into the cold water. Obviously, being rejected was not on my bucket list, but if it happened, Que sera, sera...

I knew life would go on.
No matter what.
If he said, "no," I would survive.
I wouldn't take it personally.
Life isn't about happily ever afters or miserably ever afters.
One rebuff wouldn't break me. I would bounce back.

The important thing is that I was now content no matter what, and I was prepared for change. With one simple action, one phase would end, and another would begin. I was entering a new stage in my life. Change is scary but necessary. Life changes. People change. Change can be really good. Change is what makes life so difficult and terrifying and sad and fun and beautiful. Our stories don't end. They are constantly in a state of:

TO BE CONTINUED

Because the seasons are always changing.

Epilogue

He said, "Yes!"

Gratitude

This book would not have been possible without the help of my best friend, Lauren McNeill, and my sister, Kim Kulenych. You started out as my fervent cheerleaders and then became my brilliant editors. I am forever grateful to you for guiding me through this exciting yet sometimes excruciatingly painful journey. I know in my heart that these characters would not have come to fruition without your wisdom, influence, and constant reassurance.

I am also tremendously grateful to my parents for your constant support throughout my life, and especially during the editing of this novel. Your encouragement meant so much, especially considering that you are avid readers. Thank you for talking to me about Jessica and Jamey like they were real people. Your honest opinions and praise helped bring my creation to life.

Writing a book while teaching full-time and becoming an Integrative Health Coach isn't easy, and I would never have been able to do it without the constant love and support of my husband and daughter. You are my rocks. You keep me sane and grounded.

Also- a huge shout out to all my friends who rooted for me along the way. I can't even express how much it meant to me to hear, "I can't wait to read your book!" I am forever grateful for every single one of you who uttered those words.

Much love to all of you. This book would not have been possible without you!

About the Author

Natalie Gould spent her entire adult life teaching elementary students. Being an educator was one of her greatest passions. She recently stepped away from her full-time job as a third-grade teacher to pursue writing and health coaching. She recently became an Integrative Health Coach.

Natalie lives in Connecticut with her beloved husband, daughter, dog, and cat.

Made in the USA
Middletown, DE
06 January 2024

47344033R00229